By Zoe Whittall

FICTION

The Best Kind of People

The Middle Ground

Holding Still for as Long as Possible

Bottle Rocket Hearts

POETRY

Precordial Thump

The Emily Valentine Poems

The Best Ten Minutes of Your Life

THE BEST KIND OF PEOPLE

THE
BEST KIND
OF
PEOPLE

A Novel

ZOE WHITTALL

BALLANTINE BOOKS | NEW YORK

Published in the United States by Ballantine Books, an imprint of Random House, a division of Penguin Random House LLC, New York.

BALLANTINE and the HOUSE colophon are registered trademarks of Penguin Random House LLC.

Originally published in Canada by House of Anansi Press Inc., Toronto, in 2016.

Grateful acknowledgment is made to W. W. Norton & Company, Inc., for permission to reprint seventeen lines from "The End and the Beginning" by Wisława Szymborska, translated by Joanna Trzeciak, copyright © 2001 by Joanna Trzeciak. Reprinted by permission of W. W. Norton & Company, Inc.

Hardback ISBN 978-0-399-18221-1
Ebook ISBN 978-0-399-18222-8

Printed in the United States of America on acid-free paper

randomhousebooks.com

2 4 6 8 9 7 5 3 1

First U.S. Edition

Book design by Susan Turner

For Jake Pyne

After every war
someone has to clean up.
Things won't
straighten themselves up, after all.

Someone has to push the rubble
to the side of the road,
so the corpse-filled wagons
can pass.

Someone has to get mired
in scum and ashes,
sofa springs,
splintered glass,
and bloody rags.

Someone has to drag in a girder
to prop up a wall.
Someone has to glaze a window,
rehang a door.

—WISŁAWA SZYMBORSKA,
"The End and the Beginning"

[Rape culture's] most devilish trick is to make the average, non-criminal person identify with the person accused, instead of the person reporting the crime . . .

—KATE HARDING, *Asking for It*

THE BEST KIND OF PEOPLE

PROLOGUE

ALMOST A DECADE EARLIER, A MAN WITH A .45-70 Marlin hunting rifle walked through the front doors of Avalon Hills prep school. He didn't know that he was about to become a living symbol of the age of white men shooting into crowds. He hadn't slept in four days. He was the kind of angry that only made sense outside of language. He had walked three miles from his new studio apartment above Harry's Cottage Times Bait Shop, oblivious to the downpour, the thin rip along the seam of his right leather boot. Soaked. Unaware. He walked, a head without a body. A head with one single thought, looped and distorted.

Students attending all twelve grades were amassed in classrooms, a blur of uniform plaid, settling in after the first bell. Except for Sadie Woodbury. She was standing in front of an open locker, retrieving her lucky koala bear eraser and straightening her thick brown bangs in a heart-shaped magnetized mirror. The sparkling unicorn sticker at the apex of the heart was beginning to peel away from the plastic glass. It was class speech day in the fifth grade. She had five yellow index cards in her kilt pocket with point-form notes In Praise of Democracy in America. She tongued a mass of orange peach gum to the top of her mouth, flavorless, unwilling to discard it just yet. Her parents didn't allow chewing gum. Amanda had pressed the white paper strip into her palm on the playground before the first morning bell.

She saw him behind her in the mirror's reflection. He was a smudge of indecipherable movement.

THE GIRL WAS NOT part of the plan. He'd drawn a map using a feathered red marker on the back of a pizza box. There was no girl in the diagram. It used to be a ceremonial drug. It was called *crystal*. A jewel. Like all party drugs, it had purpose. It wasn't like they make it seem now, on the commercials, like your life is over. They all had jobs and near-completed graduate degrees and they went to Burning Man and electronic music festivals and then back to work on Monday. He did it once or twice a year with friends and the point was to dance, dance, dance. Large groups of regular people. But friends who had jobs and babies now averted their eyes on the street. It didn't used to be a big deal.

Except no one else did it anymore, and he had skin like punctured and torn fabric.

He stood still, staring at her, the gun hanging from a leather strap around his right shoulder. His grandfather used to hunt with that gun. Hounds at their heels. He had a daughter at this school. He'd forgotten about her too. He didn't think it was possible, that a son could be disinherited, disowned, as an adult. That he would go "too far." He never left this town. He didn't go anywhere. He came to Sunday dinners when he remembered it was Sunday. He was *struggling*. But every addict is a liar. When he said that, he wanted to be excused from anything he did or said. He just needed to stop being punished by everyone.

SADIE CLOSED HER LOCKER. The sound startled him. He blinked in a way that meant to wish her away from sight. He was not a killer of children, he knew, despite all evidence to the contrary. Even he had his standards, for fuck's sake.

Who have I become? Am I a killer of anyone? These questions broke through the concentrated wall of destructive will, and then dissolved. He hadn't thought this through. Hailstones pelted the arched front windows as it dawned on him. The black-and-white floor tile was messy with slush and the imprint of over six hundred children's boots. He noted the weather and its impact on his body. He thought about turning back; but his focus returned. Nothing had been fair since his first black eye. He took the rifle off his shoulder. He cradled it in his arms as though it were a parcel to be delivered.

Even this he couldn't do right. What kind of man can't hold a gun?

If his dealer hadn't gone to sleep finally, he wouldn't have to be here.

Everyone is against him.

Especially her.

It's always someone else's fault, have you ever noticed that?

Every story you tell, it's always about someone who has done you wrong. But you're the common denominator. She'd said this as she was pulling on a pair of beige cotton tights at the edge of her bed, getting ready for work, her hands shaking. Her big toe poked through a hole in the right foot. He had been apologizing, begging her forgiveness for banging on her door in the middle of the night. When she'd let him in, he'd crawled on top of her and she'd had to push him off. But she wasn't as strong as he was, and eventually she just lay still, clenching her jaw and willing him to die.

When will you ever take responsibility for your own life? When will you grow up? He didn't have any money to give her for a morning-after pill. She'd grabbed a roll of twenties from the emergency cookie tin on top of the fridge. It was a bright red tin his mother had filled with Valentine cupcakes, before she had stopped talking to him and after she'd all but adopted his ex, whom she described as having "the patience of a saint." *You're pathetic,* she'd said. He'd crumpled in the corner, agreeing with her. That only made it worse. *Your self-pity is disgusting.*

The rage spiked.

His grip around the rifle tightened. The pad of his index finger, slippery with sweat, touched the trigger. He remembered what the gun was for. But the girl looked to him so much like his own daughter, the one he'd last seen by accident, through a window at the community center where she was practicing gymnastics dance, twirling a long pink and green ribbon through the air.

· · ·

SADIE STARED AT HIM for a beat, blowing a half-assed bubble that popped before fully forming. She wasn't certain, from this distance, what she was seeing, but her heart had accelerated involuntarily. It took only a few seconds more to understand *danger*. The man lowered the rifle, pointing it at her, then put it back on his shoulder. She brought into focus some motion behind him.

THE MAN THOUGHT, *Fuck it. I can turn it around. I can turn it around. This doesn't have to be the way it ends for me. I can change.* I CAN CHANGE! All at once he was euphoric, coming back into his own body.

SADIE'S FATHER, GEORGE WOODBURY, was a science teacher with a free period that morning. As the man stared at Sadie with a trancelike smile on his face, George yelled a string of astounded gibberish before tackling him. Sadie gripped the eraser, imprinting half moons in the gummy texture as it gave way to the pressure. A trickle of urine ran down her left leg, soaking her green cotton kneesocks.

In the midst of their graceless pas de deux of grappling, the gun discharged an aimless bullet. It hit the window-pane behind them with a crack; a fireworks display of shards rained down on both men, shocking them into momentary submission. The janitor emerged from around the corner and wielded his mop to help secure the gunman to the ground. George's chest was heaving, his sweater vest stuck with chunks of glass. It looked as though the man had fallen during a game of Limbo. He was pinned. He yowled, rabid, face in a bloom of madness.

Sadie stood stationary as chaos began to reign around her. The emergency task force. The volunteer firemen. The organized rows of oblivious children marching past her with their hands on their heads, heading towards the parking lot where they were counted and then released to their parents. Her father cradled her in his arms as though she were still a toddler. "It's all okay now, Sadie. Everything is fine. You're safe," he'd said as she saw a blur go by, her chin tucked into his corduroy shoulder. The smell of electric-blue dandruff shampoo. Ivory soap. She hadn't been lifted up by anyone in years.

The story came out later that the gunman, the recently disinherited son of a wealthy business owner, was the school secretary's boyfriend. He had come to kill her, and then himself. The front page of the newspaper declared George Woodbury a hero for ambushing the armed man. "It was just instinct," he'd said. "I saw my daughter. I saw the man with the gun. I knew it was better that he get me than her, than the other children. I did what anyone would have done."

Most people, when they read that line from the front page of the *Avalon Hills Gleaner* or the back of the news section of *The New York Times,* asked themselves, *Could I have done that? Who am I in this world if not someone who would do just that?*

After the incident, Sadie spent an hour every Wednesday with Eleanor Rockbrand, a child psychologist with an office above the stationery store on Peabody Street. She would doodle intricate butterflies in the margins of her feelings journal, and talk about the banal details of her days at school. She didn't tell her that she had kept the koala bear eraser, and carried it with her everywhere. If she didn't, she would be overcome by heart palpitations. Even now, at sixteen, if she forgot it at home, she would go back to retrieve it. It didn't smell pleasant anymore, and the koala's eyes had rubbed into a stoner blur. She sewed a special pocket for it on the inside lining of her uniform skirt. After that, Mr. Woodbury won Teacher of the Year every year without exception, until the second incident, the one that split the town in half.

No one in the Woodbury family had a particularly memorable face. George could be recognized by his trademark brown tweed jackets with the corduroy elbow pads, and his perpetual armload of books and papers. Everybody knew him, from school or from the many boards and committees he sat on. He was a fixture in town. He remained the *man from Woodbury Lake who'd saved the children.* The older people knew him as the son of George Woodbury Senior, at one time the sole general practitioner in town, turned real estate tycoon and land developer.

But even after George's face was splayed bare across page-one newsprint for the second time in a decade, it was hard to conjure the precise shape of his nose, the angle of his chin. He was a type of every older white man who could be a politician or a dentist, someone advertising a credit card on television. His wife, Joan Woodbury, under five foot two with the practical haircut of every nurse on the trauma ward, also blended into the faceless mass of small-town life. There were four Woodburys before their son Andrew grew up and moved away. They motored around together in the Volvo through all kinds of weather, to track meets and debates, school plays and speech nights. When Joan thought about her family, they appeared in her mind as a foursome around the table every night at six o'clock sharp, or driving down route 32, stopping for ice cream at the Lakeside Super!Soft!Serve! Their faces paled in winter, reddened in summer. No one stood out as particularly attractive, until daughter Sadie was midway through her sixteenth year and morphed into a striking young woman. There was a practical sort of utility to their bodies, draped in corduroy with sturdy hemlines, shirts of strong cotton blends. Say the words *wealthy* and *Protestant* and picture a family. That's them, or close enough.

No one saw it coming.

PART ONE

The First Week

SUNDAY NIGHT

1

SADIE TURNED SEVENTEEN YEARS OLD ON TOP OF HER boyfriend, Jimmy, in the Woodbury family boathouse. It was a white wooden structure with turquoise trim, both colors frayed and chipped around the edges, on the shore of Woodbury Lake in rural Connecticut. Jimmy had a small tattoo of her name in an Old English gangster-style font cupping his right pectoral muscle, a secret hovering underneath his crisp school uniform shirt and blazer. She had gripped his sweaty hand in the tattoo shop in Boston when they'd stolen away for an hour on class trip day. He'd peeled back the bloody gauze on the bus afterwards, kids crowding around in quiet awe. A lot of students in their class had tattoos—including a girl whose entire back was covered in a passage from a Father John Misty song—but no one had proclaimed his devotion to a girlfriend so permanently before. Sadie thought that she'd get his initials tattooed sometime, maybe inside a tiny illustrated heart. "I can't handle the pain," she'd say, but it was the permanence that felt dizzying.

His watch beeped midnight as she pressed his wrists to the tarp that separated their bodies from the splintery floorboards. Her long brown hair formed a tent around his face, which smelled of sixty-proof sunscreen, an organic brand redolent of almonds. Sometimes she rubbed it on her hands to smell during the day when he wasn't around. She made a birthday wish for continued academic success while pressing both thumbs to his radial arteries. She knew that if he had a wish, it would be to stay with Sadie forever, to suspend time so that there would be only her and him. She was a Virgo, and therefore infinitely more practical.

She curled her toes, pulled away, her lips bruised and pillowed from kissing.

"Wanna?" He wrestled his arms away from her grasp and cupped both hands around her ass and squeezed, pulling her even closer.

"Swim first," she said, sitting up but still straddling him. "The lake is so still right now, it's the best time."

Outside, the September air aped mid-July heat.

Jimmy pulled her in for a pre-swim kiss and sang "Happy Birthday" into her mouth. They could hear the slight waves under the boathouse, occasionally a dog barking across the lake. Sex was a relatively new thing. An amazing thing. The primary reason for hanging out in the otherwise damp and spider-filled world of the Woodbury family boathouse.

A raccoon they'd nicknamed Conan O'Brien wobbled across the roof and pushed his face against the screened-in skylight, pawing at a rip in the seam. He had a distinct patch of reddish fur above his eyes. Sadie turned towards the noise to lie beside her boyfriend, pinning her shoulder blades to the floor. The boathouse ceiling peaked in an A-frame and was jammed with Woodbury family detritus going back to the 1970s. Between the rafters: yellowed life jackets, canoe paddles, a rusty-handled tricycle, deflated water toys, and decaying file boxes labeled with words like *1997 Taxes*.

"He wants to celebrate your birthday," Jimmy said.

"He just loves an audience."

They'd been back at school for one week. Their senior year in high school at Avalon prep had begun with aplomb. They were both in the accelerated stream, their sights set on prestigious universities, afternoons filled with student government meetings, sporting events, community volunteer hours, making out between the rows of woody ancient texts in the school library. The week had been busy and thus ordinary. This was the last weekend that anything would feel normal until they were halfway through college.

Conan sat by the ancient weather vane atop the boathouse, watching as the couple peeled off their simple tanks and cutoff shorts. They ran naked out onto the dock, launching knees to chests in cannonballs, breaking up the swarms of night insects circling the lake in a uniform frenzy.

Sadie thought about how her body would pop up with a force equal to the weight of the water that was displaced, something her father taught her as a child that she found hard to grasp while it was happening. Her body cooled instantly. She launched forward into the darkness, a swim of pure muscle memory, with Jimmy in pursuit.

They reached the floating dock near the middle of the lake, clambering up the ladder slick with wet moss. They sat with their knees touching under the full moon, Sadie twisting the lake water from her hair and then retying it with the elastic band around her wrist. She crossed her arms over her breasts. Jimmy reached under her elbow to touch her right nipple.

"Did you know that dog bites are twice as common on a night when there's a full moon?" she asked, pulling him towards her.

"Is that a fact?"

"Anecdotally," she said. Their lips were almost touching. She ran her hand along his jaw, feeling the faint stubble. "My mom noticed it at the hospital. Every full moon, a few dog bites. Then she found a study that confirmed it."

Jimmy lifted her breast to his mouth. Could they have sex on the floating dock without being seen or heard? She moaned, cupping one hand around his head. A dog barked again across the lake. Doubtful. They pulled apart.

"Mr. Eglington," Sadie said, giggling. He was always on his deck with the binoculars. Jimmy nodded, thankful for the darkness.

Sadie picked at the scab on her knee that had dried in the shape of Florida. A chunk of Key West broke free under her nail.

. . .

THE WOODBURY HOUSE WAS dark except for two glowing squares of kitchen light. A quarter of the way around the lake, at Sadie's best friend Amanda's house, Carter the family dog continued to bark ceaselessly as a police car pulled into the driveway. The red and blue lights blinkered in a lazy swirl. Sadie and Jimmy stared as though they would be able to tell just by looking why the cops were there.

"That's weird," Jimmy said. "Should we swim over?" He dipped a toe into the still water.

"Nah, it's late. Let's just call her when we get back."

Jimmy curled up into a ball and somersaulted back into the lake. Sadie watched him tread water for a moment and then followed. When they reached the shore, they pulled on their clothes on the strip of rocky beach. Conan gripped the bark of the largest oak tree, shimmying upwards, teeth tearing a sheaf of moldy paper from *1997 Taxes,* green eyes aglow.

JOAN WAS DRYING THE last dinner plate, about to go wrap Sadie's birthday presents, but her husband, George, took the dishtowel from her hand and replaced it with a glass of red wine. She took a sip, turned back to the expansive bay window, trying to make sure Jimmy and Sadie were not in any trouble. She hated when they swam at night. She would get flashbacks of a teenaged girl she'd worked on at the hospital who had drowned and come back to life but remained essentially brain-dead. The image would be of the girl's cold arm hanging off the gurney as she was wheeled down the hall at the trauma center.

George kissed her cheek. "Come sit down, the kids are fine. Remember those nine hundred years of swimming lessons? Those ceremonies with the badges?"

"Maybe I should go check on them anyway," she said.

George gave her an affectionate squeeze. "The water is so calm right now. They're okay."

She joined him at the table, placing an open Tupperware of lemon squares between them. She looked at the wine, tilted her glass in his direction in a gesture of *what's up?*

Marriage is so much about embedded routines. That night they'd had grilled salmon and rice noodles, sautéed greens. The same as every Sunday night. Usually George was watching the news by now, head leaned back and mouth agape with a slow, murmuring snore. Joan glanced towards the window again, unable to stop herself from getting up and leaning over the sink on her tiptoes, pressing her forehead against the glass. All she was able to see in the moonlight was a dark blur of water beyond the edge of the hill, and the tip of the long wooden dock. George made a whirring sound and a helicopter motion with his hand, gently mocking her overprotective nature.

Joan surrendered with a laugh and sat back down. George raised his glass in a cheers, and pulled at the side of his lips before speaking. "Honey, for weeks I've been receiving these cryptic messages in my office mailbox," he said, handing her two scraps of torn loose-leaf paper, both folded in half, that he'd pulled from his blazer pocket. One read *People Are Watching You,* and the other *Be Careful.*

"Teenaged nonsense." She sipped her wine, swirled it around, and set it back on the table. She was excited to see Sadie open her presents in the morning at breakfast.

"Or so I thought, but today Dorothy told me to call a lawyer. She knows everything, working in the front office all day long, of course. She said there's a rumor *you're being set up.* It was all so Hollywood movie–sounding that I laughed at her. But she looked deadly serious. She wouldn't tell me anything else. Dorothy was acting strange— stranger than normal, anyway."

"She's such a nutbar, Dorothy. Set up for what? Did you believe her?"

Dorothy McKnight was the secretary, and she irritated both of them, especially at parties, always wanting to talk about conspiracy theories and how Barack Obama was a Muslim.

"So I called Bennie during my free period this afternoon—he's the eldest son of my father's lawyer. You know, they're always at our Christmas parties?"

"Isn't he a kid?" asked Joan.

"No, he's forty, if you can believe it," he said. "I called him again tonight. I'm on edge, Joan. I just wanted to tell you this. I don't know what's happening." He took another generous sip of wine.

"A practical joke? It's so strange."

George shook his head. "I really don't know." This was a phrase George—learned, stoic, opinionated—rarely used. He prided himself on knowing the things that mattered.

SADIE AND JIMMY JOGGED up the dirt path, wet bare feet on the stones between the bramble that curled into the sloping backyard. They were breathless when they reached the plateau, pausing where a row of kale and lettuces grew, waiting to be culled on her mother's gardening day the following weekend. The rectangular in-ground pool that bordered their back deck made its usual hum of white noise. A circular hot tub, currently on the fritz, faced out onto the lake, edging out over the sharp lip of the hill. Ornate gardens sculpted carefully to appear wild surrounded the pool. Sadie leaned down and rubbed some lavender between her palms, cupping her hands around her face to inhale the warm scent on her way to the side entrance.

They snuck up the back stairs, rubbing their wet heads on the threadbare sunburst swim towels hanging from the coat hooks by the door to the basement. Jimmy traced a finger along Sadie's spine, causing her to pause, shiver, and bat his hand away before she stepped over Payton, the fat sleeping tomcat on his designated fourth-step nap space. She headed for the kitchen barefoot, in search of iced tea. The plan to sneak up to Sadie's room and finish what they had started was immediately thwarted by the unusual presence of her parents, seated at either end of the kitchen table.

The Woodbury parents were the academic sort, floating brains in denial of the body. Sadie reasoned that it was better not to talk about sex with them, to ensure that both she and her parents retained the privacy they both needed. It was less denial, she reasoned, more maturity. The same way that they all went to church on Sundays but never talked about God. Some things were meant to stay inside our own heads. When Jimmy stayed over, she was never sure if they knew or not. She did know that neither party was eager to discuss it.

When they entered the kitchen, the adults reacted with a sudden and uncharacteristic silence. Her mother's brownish-gray bob was pushed back behind her ears with the help of her glasses. Joan usually had two facial expressions—tired from work or happy to have a day off. Her face betrayed a sense of resigned incredulity. She never drank after dinner.

"What's up with you guys? You're not usually up this late."

"Nothing," Joan said, in a way that sounded the opposite. She picked up the container of lemon squares and held them out to Jimmy, who put a whole one in his mouth and grabbed a second, grinning appreciatively while he chewed.

"It's past midnight . . ." Sadie sing-songed expectantly. Joan stared at her daughter for a few moments before realizing what she meant.

"Oh, happy birthday, darling!" Joan said, half present.

"Yes, happy birthday, beautiful daughter," said George, standing up to give her a hug.

Sadie felt a brief moment of birthday excitement, and then the house seemed to shake with a pounding on the front door, followed by an insistent baritone call: "We're looking for George Alistair Woodbury!"

"What's going on?" Sadie said, peering through the kitchen entrance and down the hall to the foyer. Red and blue flashed through the open windows, a light show for the symphony of cicadas. She approached the door tentatively. George sat back down at the table, staring into his glass of wine.

"Sadie, don't. I'll get it," Joan said as she approached the door, peering through the peephole cautiously. She opened it slowly to find two plainclothes detectives and several uniformed officers.

"Hello, ma'am, is your husband home?"

They made it only a few feet down the front hall before spotting him through the living room, still at the kitchen table. He stood, knocking over his glass. It pooled, then slowly dripped onto the kitchen floor.

For months Joan would replay this moment, trying to decipher the look on her husband's face. Was it guilt? Confusion? Indignation? Stoicism? Acting? But nothing, not even a revolving camera of omniscience, a floating momentary opportunity to narrate, would allow anyone to truly understand the truth about George. He became a hard statue, an obstacle, a symbol.

The father and the husband, from that moment, had been transformed.

EARLY MONDAY

2

JOAN WATCHED AS GEORGE WAS CUFFED IN THE FOYER OF
their home. *Sexual misconduct with four minors, attempted
rape of a minor.* The words didn't make sense. The police
were gentle with him, and he did nothing to resist but
offer up a face blooming in perplexity. Joan was baffled by
her own reaction. Politeness. WASP accommodation. She
just let them take him away, standing there as detectives
filled the house like a swarm of unwanted bacteria. She
didn't know what to do. She did nothing. The shock and
shame consumed her. She noted a blush creeping over
George's stubbled neck and face as he tried to maintain
some semblance of authority. He was still wearing a blazer,
his collar loosened, his tie draped over the back of his chair
at the head of the kitchen table. It felt as if she were being
forced to watch someone attack him and she felt a violent
urge to protect him at all costs. But she stood still, watching.

"We'll get this mistake sorted," he said. "You've noth-

ing to worry about, Joan. Tell the kids it's just an error."
He leaned over and kissed her. His tone was assured, commanding, but Joan noticed that his right eye twitched in an insistent triple staccato, as it did when he was getting a stress headache.

A search warrant was placed in Joan's hand, which she gripped out of instinct but did not read. She was overcome with dizziness, and leaned into the coatrack, watching as the police car drove away through the front stone gate.

"Ma'am," said a nameless officer, "can you show us to your husband's computer?"

"Certainly," she said. Certainly? Who speaks like that? What the fuck are you looking for? How would you like to hand your computer over to a stranger wielding infinite power? *Certainly* echoed in her head, mockingly, as she walked up the stairs, a stranger's steps mimicking her own.

She was in crisis mode. To remain calm was to her advantage. Politeness gets you further than outrage. Joan had been an emergency room nurse for almost twenty-five years. Hysteria helps no one. Triage is second nature. But this time she had no idea what to do first, let alone what to do next, and so she followed the most identifiable chain of command. There was a ringing in her right ear that got louder as she watched while the heavyset cop with one wonky eye unplugged the computer and lifted it, trailing the cord behind him as he walked back into the hallway, then turned to survey her briefly before continuing down the stairs into the living room, the kitchen, pulsating with sweat. She gripped the banister. She stopped herself from kicking him in the back.

She picked up the phone and called her sister Clara in

the city. "I need you to come here. George has been arrested. Please call Andrew too. I can't explain right now, the house is full of cops." Clara's alarmed voice came through the receiver, but Joan couldn't accommodate her questions. She was being approached by a man in an expensive suit who had appeared at the door, which was now propped open with one of the decorative garden stones from the front yard. A ladybug. He was red-faced with hypertension, and sought her out from the crowd.

"Joan! I am your husband's lawyer, Bennie." He reached out his hand to shake hers, and then took her arm and led her into the living room.

"How did you know to come?"

"George called me earlier this evening, said it was urgent."

"But it's so late." His grip was solid, paternal, and it made Joan want to fight him off. Something felt off, his arrival out of the blue. He motioned towards the couch, directing her to sit, before sitting himself on the edge of the coffee table across from her like a child.

"What's best right now is if you just let the police do their job and cooperate. We're going to get everything sorted."

She watched as police continued to carry everything of value into their trucks, or throw it about the room like robbers in a cartoon. She slowly blinked the room back into focus.

"Do you want to post bail?"

"Of course," she said. *If your loved one is trapped somewhere, you do what you can to get them out.* It was primal.

"There has been a mistake," she said.

Bennie didn't agree, he just stared at her briefly and looked down at his iPhone.

"You should be at the station with my husband," Joan said to Bennie.

"My associate is there on my behalf. We have the whole firm working on this."

"This is a big deal? Why the fuss? This is a misunderstanding," she said.

"This is going to be very high-profile, Mrs. Woodbury. I need you to brace yourself."

As GEORGE WAS BEING processed at the police station, it seemed to Joan that everyone in the town knew immediately. She was not certain how it happened, because she sure didn't tell anyone, but everyone knew almost as soon as she did. They talked. It must have felt nearly involuntary—it was simply too beyond the realm of possibility to *not* talk about. Humans crave connection, after all, even when it's about another's misfortune. Perhaps especially then.

3

JIMMY AND SADIE SAT ON THE LOVESEAT, THEIR HEADS still wet with lake water. Jimmy held on to Sadie's hand the way he had on the Cyclone in the summer. A female police officer in uniform sat across from them on the La-Z-Boy, right leg propped on her left knee like a table, and opened up a spiral-bound notebook. Sadie dug her nails into her bare legs, and then twisted her drying ponytail around her fist.

"Was your father ever inappropriate with you?"

"No."

"Did he ever talk about sex too frequently, or in an odd way?"

"No."

"Did he walk in while you were changing?"

"No."

"Did your friends ever mention feeling uncomfortable around him?"

"No. This is totally insane."

"I get that this is confusing to you, but we have to follow procedure."

"It's not confusing. You're making it pretty clear what kind of person you think my father is, and you are wrong. There are real criminals in the world. My father is not one of them."

Sadie tried to stay alert, sit up straight, answer honestly, anything to get them out of the house, but this was too much. She twisted her ponytail around her fist for the twentieth time.

The police officer didn't offer any words of comfort or contradiction after her outburst, she just kept asking questions as though she were conducting a survey.

"Have your father's moods changed lately? Has he been irritable?"

"No. My father is . . . honest, kind. He never even looks at women," she said. "He's a nerd. He knows what's right and wrong. God, he gave me *this*." Sadie pulled out the red plastic whistle she always wore around her neck. She'd tied the leather string with a double knot and just never took it off. "It's a *rape* whistle," she said, a frustration building in her chest. She blew it sharply. Everyone in the room was silenced, looked in her direction. She spat the whistle out, the taste of stale plastic and trapped lake water lingering on her tongue as everyone went back to destroying their home. She felt as though she were having one of those dreams where she was screaming but no one could hear her.

"It's my birthday," Sadie said. "I'm seventeen. We have plans to celebrate. This can't be happening."

The cop showed no emotion. She transcribed whatever Sadie said. When she leaned over to write, a tattoo of a swallow was visible underneath her clavicle. Her ponytail ended in a web of split ends touching the collar of her uniform shirt. Her gun lay so casually on her hip. *There are guns in our house,* Sadie thought. *Our anti-gun house is full of steel and bullets.* They had an old rifle in the basement, but it was ornamental, historic, passed down for generations. Sadie couldn't even look at it; that's how much guns scared her. She flashed to the man with the gun at school. The rain on the black-and-white floor tiles.

"I think that's enough," Bennie said, sitting down beside Sadie and Jimmy, shutting down the conversation. "All other questions should go through me."

Joan, who had been following the detectives around, walked into the room holding a dripping mop, which was oozing soapy water into the carpeting.

"Can I go pay bail now? This is ridiculous," she said, looking at her watch as if she were in a waiting room and the doctor was hours late.

"He'll be arraigned Tuesday morning, and bail will be set then," Bennie explained.

"He has to sleep . . . in *jail,* for two nights?"

"It's late, and the paperwork takes a bit of time."

THE DETECTIVE LOOKED AT her. It was the same look she gave people at the hospital when they were being entitled and clueless, acting as though the emergency room was an extension of their living room. Joan noted the scar on his left cheekbone, spreading out like a tree limb towards his ear.

"Burst appendix, last spring. Your wife's name is Josie. You've got twin boys."

The detective took a step back and cocked his head to the left in a question.

"I was the head trauma nurse on duty when you came in."

He had been stoic at first, and then a classic baby, like most men when they get sick, especially cops and other authoritative types. He was wailing and afraid. His wife left the twins, six years old at the most, to wander through the waiting room. Groups of other cops showed up, demanding and dramatic, and caused problems.

The detective blushed a little. "Yes, that sure, uh, was painful." He laughed as though they were engaged in casual small talk. She knew then that he'd mistaken her for some Woodbury Lake society wife, someone he could delight in bringing down. His body language changed after that. He softened, convinced the group to gather and head out the door quickly, with a nod and a motion of his hand.

Joan paced the house cleaning up, talking to her sister Clara and son Andrew on the speakerphone as they drove towards Avalon Hills. The drive normally took over three hours, but she knew they'd be speeding, and there wouldn't be much traffic in the middle of the night. In his early thirties now, her first-born returned home infrequently for short weekend visits. He was often too busy for anything beyond Christmas and Thanksgiving. His agreement to drop everything and drive in the middle of the night surprised Joan, though she felt relief that she'd soon be joined by other adults. She could not fall apart with only Jimmy and Sadie around to watch. Not that falling apart was really in her character. But she knew that the dissociative state she was currently functioning in had a time limit.

Joan stood at the window waiting for Clara's head-lights, while Jimmy and Sadie slept curled up on the couch. She watched as Clara clicked the gate open with the extra remote she had clipped to the rearview mirror of her mini Smart car and pulled up beside Joan's Volvo. She got out of the car and ran up the stone steps. Andrew got out more slowly, stretching his long legs and cracking his neck in the moonlight.

Clara, her angular face smudged with raccooned eye-liner, her salt-and-pepper bob slightly askew, pulled her older sister into a hug. An editor at a beauty and lifestyle magazine in the city, Clara described herself as "lucky to be a satisfied spinster" and liked to use the house as a refuge. She had her own suite on the second floor that served as a vacation property of sorts, with its own small kitchen and bathroom. Clara's perfume filled the room before she did, a spicy floral scent hovering. She draped a long black coat over the living room couch and it slid to the floor like liquid.

Clara pulled away from Joan's embrace, both women's faces streaked with tears. Sadie, woken by the commotion, picked up the coat and hung it on the wooden rack by the entrance. Clara spoke dramatically, as though addressing a crowd. "I've taken a week's leave from work, and I can take care of things while we figure this out," she said, turning to Sadie and embracing her again. Andrew took his mom in his arms and hugged her.

"How was the drive?" she asked, as though it were any other visit. She didn't know what else to say, how else to speak.

"My knees touch my chin in that car, and we drove like someone was chasing us with guns, but we're here," he said, pulling away from her embrace. "This will be over before it begins. They can't have enough to hold him, and there has obviously been a mistake. Let's just stay as calm as possible, okay?"

Clara nodded, sat in the reading chair—George's ancient recliner he insisted on reupholstering in lieu of throwing out—and went to work unlacing her tall leather boots. Andrew was gaping at the curving wall by the front staircase—and that's when Joan first noticed it too. The family photographs had all been taken, leaving light white squares of lack against the ivory walls that had darkened with age. He walked up three wooden steps on the carpeted liner and pressed his palm inside a square of white. "They're fucking overreacting, aren't they? What could they need with my graduation photo? Do they think it's lined with heroin?"

He turned to survey the room. Sadie and Jimmy on the lounger and ottoman, eyes open again, like drowsy, cornered rabbits. Despite Joan's best efforts, the mess was still everywhere.

"They do this to destabilize the family, to show they're serious. It's not as though they think they'll find anything in our Kodak moments," he said, returning to the living room, sitting cross-legged in front of the long antique coffee table. He pulled a laptop from his shoulder bag. "I've done some research on his charges. Is his lawyer still available by phone? We should talk to him right away."

"He just left. Here's his card. He'll be back tomorrow morning," said Sadie.

"Sadie, I think you should go to bed," Andrew said.

Joan nodded, grateful someone else could take charge in that moment.

"I'm not twelve anymore. I want to know what's happening."

"I just think it's best. You need to sleep," Andrew said, more softly.

Sadie scoffed. "Mom, my room has been torn apart. I think it makes more sense if I just go crash at Jimmy's house tonight."

A detective had emptied Sadie's dresser drawers on the floor, fingering her bras and panties with what seemed like excess enthusiasm. Sadie had folded her arms across her chest and stepped aside as he nodded at her then descended the steep ladder staircase to the second floor. She'd gathered up the mess in her arms and then thrown it all down on the bed and left.

"No," Joan said, "everyone has to stay together."

"Mom, my room is a disaster. I just want to go to sleep. C'mon, it's still my birthday, right?"

"Sure, sure. Let me just call his mother," Joan said, getting up and heading towards the phone, hands shaking.

"She's asleep," Jimmy said. "But don't worry, it will be fine. Sadie can sleep on the couch."

Joan absorbed this lie easily, kissing Sadie on the forehead. "Everything will be figured out tomorrow, Sadie. This is all a strange misunderstanding. I'm so sorry to have ruined your birthday. We'll fix this."

"Of course it is. Of course it's a mistake," said Sadie.

· · ·

JOAN GOT UP TO put on a pot of coffee. She pulled the bag of grounds from the freezer and pressed it against her face. Joan turned on the radio and heard the early morning broadcast.

"A high school teacher at Avalon Hills preparatory school, George Woodbury III, has been accused of alleged sexual misconduct with three female students, ranging in age from thirteen to seventeen, and the attempted rape of a fourth. All incidents are alleged to have taken place on a school ski trip this past February. The accusations have rocked the small town of Avalon Hills. Woodbury is the youngest son of the founder of the exclusive Woodbury Lake community, and a well-respected philanthropist, member of the town council, and leader at the Avalon Hills United Church. He is best known for having stopped a school shooting at the academy, garnering him an American Citizen Award for Bravery. The principal of the school could not be reached for comment but News Talk 1010 has learned that Woodbury was temporarily relieved of his duties yesterday and is currently being held until his bail hearing later. Stay tuned for more details on the official charges as the story develops."

Joan left the radio blaring the early morning traffic, allowing it to sink in that George had lied to her; he'd come home knowing he'd lost his job, however temporarily, and didn't say anything. He'd sat and eaten dinner and talked about Sadie's birthday and their winter vacation plans as though nothing had happened.

. . .

When Sadie looked at her phone in the car, she had nine missed calls, all from Amanda. Two texts. The first one read *Happy Birthday, my best girl*. The second: *I'm sorry*. Sorry for what? Sadie texted back. Amanda didn't answer.

"She texted me too," Jimmy said, reading, " 'Tell Sadie I'm sorry.' "

Jimmy shifted into reverse, edging the car back towards the gate, and pressed the remote control clipped to the visor that slid the iron gate to the side. There was a closet-sized booth where a security guard used to sit when Sadie's great-grandfather had built the house. She used to love to play pretend games in it when she was a child. As soon as they were through the gate, as Jimmy was preparing to do a three-point turn into the road, a man appeared in front of the car, startling them. Strangers were rare on Lakeside Drive, especially at night. Jimmy auto-locked the doors, while Sadie gripped the koala in her right pocket. The man pulled out a camera and snapped their photo.

"He must be a reporter," said Jimmy. She exhaled loudly and reached over and laid on the horn to get him to move, her fingers on the steering wheel vibrating involuntarily. Her phone, synced to the car stereo system, began to play automatically, and at a high volume, a Wu-Tang Clan classic that shook the windows. The reporter kept clicking, yelling out questions, mouth in motion, but they couldn't hear him.

"We'll drive to Amanda's house," Jimmy suggested, but the reporter blocked their way, in the middle of Lakeside Drive, peering down at his camera, scrolling through his photos.

"Get out of the way!" Jimmy yelled to the reporter. Sadie laid on the horn again and he moved.

"If there's one reporter here in the middle of the night, there's going to be a million tomorrow," he said as he turned on the high beams, illuminating the tree-lined winding road, only recently paved, that bordered Woodbury Lake. Sadie's great-grandfather, a reclusive but wealthy man, had originally owned the lake and all the property that bordered it. Her grandfather had developed it all when he inherited it, selling to twelve families in the 1970s, who all built their dream lakefront homes. Originally a rural area far from the town, it was now the most prestigious address in the township, the suburban sprawl reached its borders, and it was almost walkable from town. Woodbury Lake was quiet and scandal-free, and Sadie knew this was going to be big news for that reason alone.

When she drove, Sadie habitually watched for bright-eyed bunnies and deer poking their noses out into the road, beeping the horn before turning around the blind corners to warn any oncoming traffic. When she was young enough to still be in a car seat, her father hit a deer. They were alone in the car. Though he'd told her to keep her eyes shut tight until Daddy got back in the car, she'd been unable to stop herself from staring as he dragged the deer through the triangles of the car's high beams, hauling it by its hind legs into the ditch. When he got back into the car, he reached back and grabbed her hand and squeezed it, saying, "It's okay, honey. The deer needs to take a long sleep." His hands were slippery and wet, and he was crying while he spoke, and for weeks she asked him, "Is the deer still asleep? Can we go wake up the deer?" Her father was always a cautious, friendly driver, and she had inherited these traits.

Within minutes they were on the winding dirt driveway leading to Amanda's house. It had originally been a log cabin, meant as vacation property for Amanda's grandparents. When her parents inherited it, they'd moved in and renovated, adding several incongruous-looking wings to the house, all in a boxy modern style, with clean lines and tall, symmetrical gray surfaces. The blend of old and new was dizzying. Joan called it a "pretentious eyesore," even though *Dwell* magazine had recently come to take photos of it. Sadie thought it looked as though it belonged to a group of committed off-the-grid activists preparing for the end of the world. Amanda's father was an architect and her mother a painter. All of her mother's paintings were of the same human-sized rabbits that looked like they were haunting the viewer. They had sold very well in New York in the 1990s, but now she couldn't really do anything new. Amanda had told Sadie never to talk about it in front of her mother.

Jimmy parked the car beside one of Amanda's father's many oversized status vehicles. They got out wordlessly, shutting the car doors slowly to make as little noise as possible, and crept towards Amanda's window at the side of the house. A fox darted across the lawn in the soft light of the full moon. Startled, Sadie grabbed Jimmy's hand as they watched him retreat behind the smooth block of cedar hedges.

Amanda sat in her window seat, as though she was expecting them. Her thick brown hair was up in a messy high ponytail; she wore sweatpants and an old basketball T-shirt from their junior high team. She slid open her window and climbed outside.

"My mom cannot see you here, Sadie. She'll fucking shoot you," she said.

"What did *I* do?"

"Your father, apparently, came on to my sister on that ski trip last winter. It's all coming out now. Apparently, four girls have filed charges."

"It's a lie. You know my dad. You've known him since you were a *baby*."

"I know," she said. "Maybe she's lying. God knows she lies about everything to get her way."

"Why would she do this, though? I don't understand. Amanda, they came and took my dad *away. He's in jail. This isn't a joke.*"

"Sadie, I don't know what to say to you. I'm not even allowed to talk to you. Apparently the cops said that."

"Um, you're my *best friend*. The cops can't tell you what to do."

"I think that if anyone can, it's the police."

"Who are the other girls?"

"I don't know all of them, but apparently Miranda Warner is like the ringleader. She convinced everyone to call the police about the ski trip. My sister says she has the most convincing story, compared to everyone else."

"Miranda Warner is such a mean girl," Jimmy said, "no one will believe her."

"Or everyone will," said Sadie.

Above their heads, the lights in the long rectangular window of the living room flicked on. Amanda grabbed Sadie's hand. "Get out of here, guys, or my mom will legit go crazy."

They ran towards the car, then watched in the rear-view mirror as Amanda's mother stood on the front porch, arms crossed, in her long red housecoat, the same one she had been wearing when she hugged Sadie's young face to hers the first night she'd slept over, when she was seven years old, and Sadie was too scared to stay the entire night.

AT 4 A.M., SADIE sat curled on Jimmy's couch with her laptop and typed in: *prison sentences for attempted rape* and *average prison sentences for attempted rape of minors.* She googled the definition of *sexual misconduct,* which could be just about anything, all of it varying degrees of horrifying. She scanned the list of potential articles without opening any of them. Then she typed in *why men rape,* before clicking her laptop shut. She volleyed between wanting to know everything and wanting to clip her own brain stem in order to remain unaware. She'd never thought about *why* before. It was just something girls were told to watch out for; she never thought of rapists as actual people she could meet or know in real life.

She re-opened her laptop, clicked on an essay, and read the first paragraph. Rape wasn't about sex, it was about power. She rolled that around in her mind. Objectively, her father had more power than most people. He was re-spected, he was on several corporate boards, he had generations of family wealth and prestige. He flew first class, for pete's sake. He didn't really even *need* to work, but it was a passion. He won Teacher of the Year *every* year.

She felt blank.

It reminded her of a project she'd done on eating disorders. The disease is about control, not about being thin. This seemed too simple to her. After all, weren't they willing to die to avoid being fat? It had to be a factor. How could forcing someone to have sex not be about sex?

Sex was so new to Sadie that she'd only told one person that she was no longer a virgin. She'd texted Amanda: *Dude, the deed is done.* Amanda had sent back laughter emojis, and then asked for the highlights. She wrote back: *Uncomfortable. Sorta good. Over quick.* She finally felt on equal ground with Amanda when they talked about boys; previously, Amanda had always had the upper hand.

Jimmy was upstairs sleeping. She didn't want to wake anyone by walking around, even though sitting still felt like a prison, so she compulsively chewed at her thumb to keep herself from moving. In her own house it was possible to walk around at night and not disturb anyone, or be detected at all. It was double the size of Jimmy's house, and she could slip down the east stairs from the attic, avoid the squeaky steps, tiptoe past the second floor where her parents slept, past the first floor, and into the basement playroom with the pool table and the giant TV—the only room in the house that looked modern. Every other room still looked the way it had when the first generation of Woodbury parents lived there. Whenever she put an electronic device down, it would look incongruous next to the gold-framed painting from the 1800s or the Turkish rugs or the rows of first editions of classic works of literature. George never cared if the children left a ring of hot chocolate on top of the blue cloth fabric of a first printing of *Oliver Twist*. "I like that the house looks lived in," he'd say. There was always a pile of papers or magazines, odd collections of antique sculptures. It just looked old. And to Sadie, old was comfortable. Other people's houses always looked sterile, like doctors' waiting rooms. Too much glaring white and plastic.

Jimmy's house was built after Jimmy was born and looked like every other house on the street, mirrors of each other: pink bricks and cylindrical front yards. The walls were painted various shades of white and beige, the carpets a thick gray or ivory, the pale color of dust and absence. The artwork on the walls was mostly generic photography prints. His mother was obsessed with sunflowers, so there were a lot of them around. Things were always breaking and being replaced. To Sadie, it felt less like *their* home and more like *anyone's* home, which she used to find weird, but this night she found it comforting.

90% of rapists assault people they already know.

She clicked around, looked at Facebook, which was already filled up with status updates that were variations of "WTF, I can't believe it, he was such a nice teacher!" Penelope Braydon wrote: "Don't believe everything you hear. Innocent until proven guilty, right?" Others weren't so democratic: "Bitches lie."

Sadie padded upstairs to Jimmy's room, which was right across from his mother's, walking softly on the carpet and trying not to breathe. She saw TV light flickering under her door but heard some gentle snoring. Jimmy's room smelled of sweat and cum and she involuntarily wrinkled her nose, shutting his door quietly, and shoved some sweatshirts against the crack between the door and the carpeting. She opened his window slightly to air out the room and turned to look at him. He was lying with his head back.

"Babe. Baby."

He didn't move.

She didn't really want to have a conversation with him, but she didn't want to be alone either. She sat on the edge of his bed and placed her hand on his leg, feeling comforted by the warmth. For a moment her mind relaxed enough that she felt normal, drifting off. Her head fell forward, and she curled up beside him. Then she remembered with a start, and sat up again, dangling her legs over the edge of the bed. She shivered, uncomfortable, unsure what to do with herself. There was no way she could sleep, feeling like a hundred sparkling wires. How do people calm down? She'd never had to think about it before; calm was her default state. Then her body had an idea. Throwing one leg overtop of Jimmy, her knees sinking into his duvet on either side of him, she inched her hand up under the blanket and slipped it inside his boxers. He moaned, and then startled awake. She had never started anything before, not like this.

"What are you doing?" he whispered, his eyes popping open. She smiled, leaned in to kiss him. "Is this a dream?" She didn't answer, just kept at it. He was making all the sounds he normally made, only usually she was also feeling turned on, so she didn't hear him this clearly, or stare at him so closely. She was fascinated, watching him become someone else, undone by a simple movement of her hand. He was trying to be quiet but eventually couldn't be, letting forth a series of indecipherable sounds when he finished. His eyes went from blurred slits to wide again, embarrassed. He pulled her close to him in a hug. She leaned her ear against his chest to hear his heart racing. He drew back and looked at her curiously. "That was kind of weird," he said. "Are you okay?"

"Weird how?" she asked, but she knew exactly what he meant.

"Come here," he said. She curled around him. "I love you, Sadie. You should try to get some sleep. Do you want me to, you know?"

"No, it's okay." He'd only done that once, and she mostly just felt embarrassed and eventually made him stop. He went back to snoring. She listened to him breathing for a while then felt the surge of restlessness return, so she left him there and went back downstairs to her computer.

AN EMAIL HAD COME in from her brother. "The arraignment hearing is Tuesday at 3. If you're not home, text me your location and I'll pick you up. We need to support Dad as a family. Stay calm, I'm confident this is going to blow over. Stay home from school to get some sleep and remember to eat, ok? I'm so sorry your birthday is ruined. Let's have a do-over, ok? Big cake!"

Andrew had always been a calm and rational person, a considerate person. His opinion almost slowed Sadie's heartbeat enough for her to fall asleep, face pressed into the corduroy couch cushions. But after a few moments of rest she considered this: if even a portion of the allegations against him were true, then what would her support mean? She was hit with a powerful surge of guilt. When your family needs you, you should be there. He was a man capable of throwing his body between her and a murderous madman, he was a generous mentor, he was the role model of the freaking century.

But what if he wasn't? Or what if he was a bunch of different things, a mix of good and bad? Of course, real people aren't the way they are in action movies or Disney films. We all have the capacity to behave in moral ways and to make mistakes, right? But still, these allegations went beyond that, would cancel out the good things. Even though Sadie had recently begun the transition from agnostic to atheist, there was no ignoring the impact that going to church every Sunday for her entire life had made on her psyche. Those things you learn at the age of five come right back to you in times of crisis. Do unto others; honor thy father and thy mother. *If I was in prison and I believed I had done nothing wrong, would I want my father to abandon me?* She sat with these thoughts. There were no answers.

She kept replaying the memory of watching a cop grab their family photo albums and carry them outside to a waiting truck. All of their memories, clutched in a bear hug.

JUST BEFORE SIX IN the morning, she drifted into a shallow sleep, waking half an hour later when she heard a noise. She leaned over the top of the couch, pulling the blankets close around her, and saw Jimmy's mother's boyfriend, Kevin, sitting at the kitchen table eating a giant bowl of cereal, a stack of papers in front of him.

Kevin had moved in when Jimmy was six. He was a novelist who was always home, locked away in a second-floor office that was so dusty and filled with crap that Jimmy said he half expected to have to go in and find his body there someday. He was generally quiet and uninterested in them. Whenever he did leave the house, Jimmy went into the office and stole pot from the film canisters in the bottom of his filing cabinet, and borrowed porn magazines he had filed in a folder called "Civil War Research 1998–2000."

"The life of a writer, huh?" Sadie said now, waking Kevin from his daze, chin resting on the back of the couch.

"Hello, little girlfriend-of-Jim."

Girlfriend-of-Jim was what he liked to call Sadie because, she suspected, he rarely remembered her name.

"What are you doing up so early?"

"I have to go to the city today, meet my agent."

"Oh."

When Kevin's first novel came out, he had been compared to Jonathan Franzen in *The New York Times*. He had the review laminated on the wall of his study. Kevin had been trying to live up to that review ever since, and Jimmy's mother, Elaine, was fond of remarking that it was ruining his creative spirit and he should take it down for a while.

Kevin loved Elaine. It was clear to anyone around them, from the way he looked at her—with quiet awe—

and the way he'd leave her love notes almost every morning, on Post-it Notes on top of the coffee maker. He bought her presents every time he went anywhere, and this extended to picking up red licorice and an Almond Joy every time he went to the grocery store or to buy gas. But he never wanted children, so he wasn't involved in any parenting decisions. He actually wasn't involved in many decisions at all. Jimmy suspected he didn't contribute financially to their house, except for the occasional evening when he'd make pasta or homemade pizzas to give Elaine the night off. Jimmy said he didn't mind, that he liked to have the extra company and the occasional male perspective on things.

"He's a man-whore, essentially," Sadie had joked, as they leafed through the pages of Kevin's *Barely Legal*. They'd both seen their share of online porn, easily bypassing the blockers their parents had set up, but the magazines felt like real pornography somehow. Online porn to Sadie was like watching surgery: too much to see, too much sound. Jimmy felt differently, but rarely shared his opinion on the subject. Kevin's mags, all of the fake-teen variety, made them laugh and roll their eyes, and then made them horny like dogs. Sadie would put the pages down and imitate the ridiculous poses, which looked really funny when you were wearing sweatpants. She was always kind of embarrassed later when she thought about it, but a few days would go by and they'd both want to look at the pictures again. Sometimes when she looked at Kevin she'd think of the magazines and would feel sick and nervous and make an excuse to leave the room.

"How's your book going, the one about . . . the mountain climbers?"

"Good, good. Lots of interesting research, you know." Sadie thought of Kevin's research file and blushed.

"It's my birthday today," she said. "I'm seventeen."

"That's a big-deal birthday," he said, eyebrows raised.

She nodded, and then felt foolish. As if she'd just said "I'm this many" and held out her fingers. "Anyway, see ya," she said, and ducked down the carpeted basement stairs to the bathroom, where she dressed quickly, and left Jimmy's house in the predawn light through the back door.

She didn't have the keys to Jimmy's car, so she borrowed Elaine's bicycle, intending to practice her sprints at the track outside the school. The bike was heavier than the one she was used to, and it took her two blocks to feel like she wasn't about to fall at the slightest provocation. She stood up and pumped as fast as she could. The streets of the subdivision were empty, only a few lights on in the uniform front windows.

Outside the Circle K convenience store she paused at a stoplight, jarred by the row of newspaper boxes, two of them with her father's face weighing down the front page. She felt as though the early morning commuters and the guy filling up his SUV all knew who she was, all saw her shame. She darted as soon as the light changed, biking so fast that when she leaned the steel frame against the bleachers by the track her chest was heaving and her sweatshirt glued to her back.

She walked right to the starting line, trying to slow her breathing and focus. Running always made sense to her, but even more so now. She knew where to go and she got there. After a few laps, she collapsed on the grass still dotted with dew, breathing in the earthy smell and staring at the sky as it changed from pinky orange to blue.

She lay still while her breath evened out. Hearing footsteps approach, she didn't turn; she knew it would be Jimmy, lumbering towards her, pillow lines across his cheeks, his hooded sweatshirt pulled tight around his head.

"I figured you'd be here," he said, loosening the strings, pulling off the hood to free his matted hair. "Make good time?"

Sadie shrugged and pulled him down onto the grass beside her. "Didn't clock it."

When Sadie was growing up, until she was about thirteen and learned to stream anything she wanted, her parents only allowed her to watch PBS, and that for only one hour every week. There were no video games systems, because Joan thought they contributed to societal violence and antisocial behavior. George would sit reading *Harper's* while she ran track meets. "So, they just run back and forth and jump over that bar?" she remembered her father asking her, watching the athletics field filled with ecstatic children, a mix of bewilderment and boredom on his face. "Well, *good* for you, champ!" he'd said, reaching out to touch her first-place ribbon. But he was never more proud than if she won the science fair or a speech contest. Fair enough. What's going to serve you better in life, she'd thought—to be able to run back and forth really fast, or to possess critical thinking skills and the ability to innovate?

Still, nothing made her feel more present and alive

than running back and forth idiotically between lines on the ground and beating her best time. She liked the literal quality of the action. Jimmy put his hand on her shin and squeezed, and that one sweet motion prompted sharp shots of tears. He rolled on top of her, propped himself up on his elbows, and kissed her nose. His breath smelled of cereal. She ran her hand under his shirt, grabbed him on each side, and kissed his mouth. They broke apart and lay back against the grass.

He handed her a small box. She popped it open, and inside was a gold antique locket with a large heart that she opened up with her thumbnail. Inside was a small scrap of paper. "What's this?" she asked.

"I went to the hospital and asked your mom if I could have an ECG test, and then I cut a scrap of it. It's my heartbeat!"

"Wow, wow. That's so cool," she said, and kissed him. "So romantic." She was having a hard time faking enthusiasm; she knew this was supposed to be such a special moment, one he'd planned for weeks. She dangled the necklace, pretended to admire it, then handed it to him to clasp around her neck.

They were silent for a few minutes, both thinking about her father. "It's so weird. Of all the people to be accused of something like this, your father would be *last* on the list," Jimmy said, taking off his ball cap and replacing it twice—a nervous habit. He reached out and straightened the locket on her chest.

"I would never have suspected him of even cheating on my mother. He has always been an example of one of the 'good guys,' like"—she started counting things off on her fingers—"one, he's pro-choice; two, he donates to the local women's shelter every single year; three, he's been giving me the 'girls can be whatever they want to be' speech since first grade!" She was sitting up now, shouting and using her hands for emphasis. "He taught me how to defend myself against an attacker! He read the Gloria Steinem biography!"

"I've always been a little bit jealous that you have such a good father."

"I mean, besides his inability to notice dirty dishes and bring them into the kitchen to be washed, he is pretty much, like, a perfect man. Other women have always wondered how my mom ended up with such a great guy. I've noticed that my whole life."

She knew that feeling, the one that would spread across her chest when she realized an adult was flagrantly ignoring the social codes that dictated when kids were kids and not sexual objects. She'd had coaches with the propensity to stare too long; a camp counselor who liked to tell dirty jokes and take Missy Lederman on long walks to discuss what Jesus thought about her virginity. She could see it. She had a keen sense of people. Her dad treated her like an equal; he was interested in her opinions. He never seemed to care about whether or not she had made her bed; those kinds of life lessons were reserved for her mother.

She knew that Jimmy trusted his mom. Elaine was like a rock of stability. Boring, boring stability, he joked, but it comforted him. From her thick brown horn-rimmed glasses to her wraparound wool sweater from the L.L. Bean catalogue of the mid-nineties that was neither brown nor gray but a color so basic and earthy it didn't even need a name—everything about her was consistent.

"I don't think we have to go to school today," he said. "At least, you don't. Cheryl can run the meeting."

Cheryl was student council vice president. Sadie was president, Jimmy treasurer. Cheryl was odd, obsessed with animated Disney movies and playing the trombone. Sadie was nice to her, because she was nice to everyone, but she felt an uncontrollable sense of both pity and disdain whenever she watched her brushing her hair and gazing at the collection of Mickey Mouse postcards she had taped to her locker.

The kids at Avalon prep school had everything that most children in America lacked. Not just money, food, and shelter, but the vast majority also had attentive parents who wanted them to achieve. Parent–teacher nights scared the crap out of the teachers, because almost all of the parents seemed to care, wanting to know what was going on and keeping their own scorecards on each teacher. Some of them even brought their lawyers along. The town seemed ripe for parody, with its perfect greenery, cafés boasting fair-trade coffee and chocolate, a yoga studio on every block, and its low high school dropout rate. Sadie was the kind of kid other parents used as an example. But now she was going to be the kind of kid who would be talked about for at least a decade: the daughter of Mr. Woodbury, the man who had once stopped a gunman from killing all the children, the school's most popular teacher, arrested for being a predator. Sadie stared up at the sky while Jimmy talked, but she couldn't hear him.

. . .

GEORGE WOODBURY HAD NEARLY completed his PhD in physics in his mid-twenties. He did everything besides defend his thesis, which he'd been constantly updating ever since, during the summer months. Joan was studying journalism when they met—which was baffling to Sadie now, that her mother ever had such aspirations. She switched to nursing when she got pregnant and was living in Boston, where George was studying. Andrew lived in that city for the first few years of his life—something he still clung to, defining himself as *not* being from *this* town—and in his last year before defending his thesis George decided to quit and move back to Avalon Hills to be a teacher. "Happiness can be a lot more simple than you think, bug," he used to say to Sadie, explaining how he gave up this dream. "I wasn't cut out for the competition. I want to nurture the basics and watch kids' eyes light up when they first understand something about classical mechanics. That's where pure joy is. And I wanted to raise a family somewhere stable, so your mother would be happy. She wasn't happy in the city. She's a small-town girl."

Joan always used to say, when she told this story, "I don't know why he gave it all up for me," and she'd smile. George would say, "Oh Joan, you know how special you are."

JIMMY DREW AN ENERGY bar from his sweatshirt pocket, unwrapped it, and pulled it into two chewy pieces. "You shouldn't have to go to the hearing if you don't want to. You're the kid, not the parent. You don't have to accept everything they do."

"I hadn't thought of it that way," Sadie said, pushing her thumb into the protein bar, making a thin fingerprint.

Jimmy didn't have a father. Elaine used an anonymous sperm donor to get pregnant when she was tired of waiting around for a good man to marry. This made sense to Sadie; a woman has more chance of contracting the plague than of marrying after the age of forty. In this town, however, a DIY pregnancy made her a bit suspect. She was older than most mothers in the town, although a year younger than Joan. Sadie hadn't been planned, she'd realized only recently. "A beautiful surprise," her mother had said.

"But his blood is *in* mine," Sadie said. "What if he *is* guilty? What would that make me?" She balled up her portion of the bar and threw it onto the grass.

Jimmy rolled his eyes. "Come on, you *know* you're a good person."

A flash of the man with the rifle came to mind, as it often did in times of stress. Like a blink went off in her head, and it was a clear image floating behind her lids. She wondered, what made him do it? What makes someone do something so insane, as though they have nothing to lose?

"How does anyone *know* they're good? Isn't goodness a lifelong process?"

"You think too much," Jimmy said. "Some things just *are*."

A mere month previously, she'd read an article about the genetics of a criminal disposition. She'd been horrified and entranced by every family story of criminal birthing criminal, even when the child was adopted and raised by ordinary, law-abiding citizens.

"Well, our frontal lobes are still developing. According to science, I don't even have the maturity to understand the consequences of my actions," she said.

"Science isn't always right. Scientists used to believe skull size was the key to our intelligence. Plus, as soon as you start blaming genes for criminal behavior, then you open up this whole world where everyone is blameless. It's not credible."

"I'm worried. You know, they rarely arrest people without enough proof. You know—white, powerful men, they get given every benefit of the doubt, right? It makes me nervous. What if he is guilty?"

"People, and systems, make mistakes all the time. You can't start thinking he's guilty," Jimmy said, though he didn't sound at all convinced.

"Right, right. He's not guilty," she said.

Jimmy's phone rang the dog-bark ring tone he had programmed for his mother. Sadie knew he would ignore it; he usually did.

"Sixty-eight percent of American teens say they would rather lose a limb than have to go without their cell-phones," Sadie said. Statistical non sequiturs was a game they played.

But Jimmy didn't want to play. "I know you told the cops that he didn't, but seriously, he didn't touch you, did he?" Jimmy asked, cutting the coolness of his normal face with one that expressed concern, rolling back onto the grass beside her.

"Fuck no, *no. Gross.*"

"Yeah, your mom would not let that happen. She's like one of those moms who could lift an entire car off a child if she had to. I want her around when the apocalypse hits."

Jimmy and Sadie stayed curled up together on the grass until they heard the first bell from across the field. Jimmy jumped up and looked towards the school.

"Oh shit, Sadie."

"What?"

"Amanda."

Amanda was walking towards them, barreling actually, like she was looking for a fight. But when she reached them, she smiled a normal Amanda smile, brief and all teeth as though for a camera.

"Dudes," she said, catching her breath. "I'm sorry I couldn't tell you or explain much last night. The cops freaked me out so much. Are you okay?"

"Not really. I mean, I guess."

"Yeah, of course, that was a stupid question."

"How . . . *exactly* . . . is your sister involved?"

"Apparently your dad . . . you know, asked her inappropriate stuff, on that ski trip?"

Amanda's sister had just turned fourteen; Sadie could remember her when she was seven. She ripped out handfuls of grass, depositing nervous little hills around her body.

"What stuff?"

Amanda twirled her hair with a finger and scowled. "I'm not supposed to talk about it."

"Right."

"She was drunk, apparently. But she took off and nothing happened, you know. He just said strange things, was acting totes weird."

Sadie pressed the grass in her palms so tight her fingers hurt.

"I just wanted to come over and make sure *we* were all . . . okay . . . you know. This doesn't change anything with us . . ."

"Of course not."

Amanda leaned over and gave Sadie a limp hug. She smelled like the rosemary and mint shampoo her mom bought in giant pump bottles.

"Do you think your sister is telling the truth?" Sadie yelled after her as she walked away.

She turned back and squinted, cocked her hip to one side. "Of fucking course she is. She's a kid, Sadie. What kind of question is that?"

Sadie shrugged. "Last night you said that she lies about stuff."

Amanda walked back and bent over so that she was eye to eye with both of them. She spoke a little softer. "I know that I said that, because it's true, she's a little shit sometimes. But I dunno. This morning she started crying at breakfast, like real crying, not for-attention crying." She stood up again, and paused before she continued. "You better not spread any lies about her, just because it's your dad. She's been through enough."

"We can't know, though, Amanda, what's real. You have to admit this is weird. You *know* my dad."

"I know. It *is* weird. I have no idea who to fucking believe."

They watched her walk away, not speaking until she

was inside. Sadie's mouth felt sour and dry at the same time, as though something was blocking her from breathing. She took a deep breath in and exhaled, hearing that she was indeed breathing, but it didn't feel like it. She placed her hand on her neck, the spot where she felt her throat was closing.

"I'm going to go home to check in with my mother."

Jimmy nodded. He grabbed her hand and they headed towards Jimmy's car. Sadie put Elaine's bike in the trunk, one tire sticking out, and they drove in silence, away from the school on the edge of town, curving around the lake until she was down the block from her house. They watched the media trucks as they idled, journalists sipping on coffee from the Hut—shorthand for the exhaustively named Country Cottage Fair Trade Ethical Coffee Hut, a few blocks away by the public beach, a place mostly known to residents. The owners, Pat and Alex, kept a spiral note book with locals' tabs scrawled in ballpoint so you could come and get a coffee if you didn't feel like carrying your wallet on your morning jog. Pat and Alex loved her dad. Pat gave him free coffee all the time and every year Alex made him a cherry pie for his birthday.

Jimmy drummed his fingers on the dash until Sadie placed her hand on his to soothe him. They watched the neighbors out pretending to get their mail, or re-oiling the gates at the ends of their winding driveways. It made Sadie want to change the plan. She didn't want to check in with her mom. They pulled up to the gate, which was blocked by a line of journalists who didn't even react to their car's presence because they were so entranced by the house in front of them.

. . .

Sᴀᴅɪᴇ ᴀɴᴅ Jɪᴍᴍʏ ᴜsᴜᴀʟʟʏ chose to hang out at the Wood-bury house because its size and splendor allowed them to imagine they were alone most of the time. Sometimes they would sneak into Clara's guest suite and pretend it was their own apartment. At that moment, as she looked at the house, with the journalists at the gate, she knew her family would be gathered in the kitchen. The house seemed to shrink before her eyes.

Jimmy beeped the horn, then laid on it. The reporters turned, flashbulbs popping. The neighborhood had trans-formed from familiar haven to movie set, the same way the school had transformed on the day the man with the rifle walked through the door. Sadie had returned to being a spectacle again. She remembered standing on the front steps of the house when the reporters came after the school incident. She'd worn her favorite red terry cloth dress with the white plastic belt, and the perfect white Keds that all the girls wore that year. She'd gripped the eraser in her hand the whole time. Her mother had wrapped her arm around her while they huddled together before they took the photographs, and she remembered being surprised that her mother was nervous. Joan smelled like she did on hol-idays, as if she'd worn perfume for the occasion, even though you wouldn't be able to smell her in a photograph. Later, Joan said, "A whole lot of fuss. That was a whole lot of fuss, right?" She'd laughed nervously while preparing supper, a flush in her cheeks. George had thrived in the spotlight. "Your mother is a bit shy about these things," he'd explained to Sadie, pouring Joan a glass of wine. "I'm just not meant for the spotlight," she'd agreed. "But you're a natural," she'd teased, and kissed him on the cheek.

"What should we do?" Jimmy's voice brought Sadie back to the moment.

She looked at the reporters, and realized she'd rather have the house be engulfed in flames than have to go through the scrum of strangers. A skinny guy with a goatee emerged from a purple pup tent in the ditch and started fiddling with his camera.

Jimmy leaned his head out the window.

"MOVE!"

He laid on the horn again and Sadie hunched down in her seat, lifting her arm to press the remote that allowed the gate to open. She half expected the reporters to run in with the car, but they didn't. She saw her mother's face peek through the living room curtains and felt relieved at the familiar sight, at knowing Joan was there to protect her, as she had throughout her life.

4

ANDREW SAT, HEAD IN HANDS, ON HIS CHILDHOOD
bed in the late morning. He pressed his fingers
into his cheekbones, massaging the points where
he could feel a sinus headache about to bloom. His whole
system felt off. He was very tired but couldn't imagine ever
sleeping again. Andrew Woodbury the teenager would
have relished the opportunity to lounge in bed, but adult
Andrew was a regimented machine. His work, exercise,
and even social schedule were precise and unwavering. He
woke at 5:30 A.M., an hour before his partner Jared, and
was at Cyclefit by 6:00. He went to bed by 11:00 P.M. on
weekdays. Tuesdays usually began with a breakfast meeting with Olivia, one of the senior partners. He'd sent a
hurried late-night text to explain his absence, then stayed
up most of the night researching his father's charges and
checking on his mother, whom he'd given a Xanax before
bed. When he'd gone to check on her, she was sitting up
in bed, arms clutching a pillow to her chest, staring at

nothing. He handed her the pill and she'd sighed before putting it into her mouth for a dry swallow and a *sotto* thanks.

He made the bed, pulling the antique farmer's quilt tight over his pillows, making sure each corner was even and symmetrical. Several of the quilted squares had faded so much that they were ripping along the seams. He selected several safety pins from the night table drawer and placed them around in all the spots that were starting to unravel. He pulled on a pair of boxers and grabbed his old drama club T-shirt from the closet. It was from a senior year production of *Fiddler on the Roof*. His mother had replaced his adolescent posters with framed antique oil paintings, portraits of British Woodburys through the ages that Joan found ugly and wished to hide away in a room largely unseen by guests. The room smelled of dust. Everything needed a wipe-down, a shake-out. He punched down the throw pillows then opened the window, propping it up with a leather-bound Bible.

He unpacked his luggage and tried to smooth out a plain white button-down shirt that he could wear to the arraignment hearing the next day. His mother had kept some of his old clothes, relics of another moment in fashion that was almost back in style, hanging in the closet. He lit a clove candle on the dresser top out of habit, running a finger over the film of dust coating the top of the wax, trying to clear the room of its musty, unused smell. He found a gram of pot in the bedside drawer that he'd left almost a year ago, at Thanksgiving. It was stale but would do the trick. He rolled a joint on the cover of an outdated issue of *InStyle* magazine, crumbling it on top of Drew

Barrymore's face. The candle made the room smell like a pie baking in an aura of neglect. He lit the joint from the candle and then blew it out.

It had been a long time since he'd woken up and felt a heavy presence on his chest. He used to go back to sleep for fear of having to deal with the day. It happened a lot in Avalon Hills, even when nothing out of the ordinary was going on, a sadness that rendered him semi-useless and un-productive. When he woke up in New York, it was as though the city was inside him like a coiled spring when he lifted back the covers, singing to himself, talking back to the radio, stretching up and out. His hometown made him lethargic. His father used to make him get up and go canoeing first thing in the morning when he'd visit on breaks from university. They'd pull their paddles up and float, watching the pinkish-orange glow as the sun barely crested the trees, mostly in silence until his dad told a corny joke. Something like: Why doesn't a lobster give to char-ity? Why? Because he's shellfish! Groan.

Andrew didn't question why he reacted so strongly and immediately in his father's defense. It was primarily a feel-ing of complete and utter implausibility. His father was a man very detached from his body. George also seemed rel-atively unconcerned with power; he was afforded the care-lessness of not having to think about it because he had a lot of it.

Andrew took a second hit from the joint and coughed. He rarely smoked anymore because he was too busy at work. Plus, it seemed like a childish habit, best reserved for the holidays. He'd rolled this one too tightly and could barely get anything from it. He associated getting high with Avalon Hills, with getting through the grind of family visits. He wondered if Jared would like his vintage collection of Hardy Boys books. He took a photo with his phone and messaged him, *Do you want these?*

Jared responded immediately. *Are u ok? I've been waiting to hear from u. I'm going crazy.*

Jared was a one-man master class in the art of being self-aware, and did not indulge in WASP denial. He tired Andrew sometimes, as much as he knew that being in touch with one's emotions was a better way to be in the world. Andrew operated in a kind of cut-off and highly functional fog, rarely knowing how to answer the question "How are you?" with any kind of certainty.

ANDREW HAD BEEN IN the middle of watching *The Great British Bake Off* with Jared when he got the call from his aunt Clara. "You have to go home. Your father has been arrested."

"Arrested?! For what?" He jumped up from the couch and muted the TV.

"I'm coming to get you right now," she said.

"What do you mean? What on earth for?"

"One count of attempted rape, sexual misconduct with several minors."

"Are you serious?!"

Are you serious? might be the dumbest thing people say, as a way to buy time to let very serious things sink in.

Jared got up and helped Andrew pack. He'd texted Andrew several times throughout the night and early morning.

I'm here for you, Andrew. Anything you want to talk about. I'm here. You want to take a vacation this weekend? I'll arrange it.

Jared thought a vacation would cure any and all stress, even though Andrew often found the process of vacationing to be stressful in itself—the planning, the potential chaos of airports and delays, then all that insistence that you relax after months of constant mental and physical activity. He felt the same way about holidays—like they were a kind of work with associated stress.

Jared and Andrew had recently begun to be more *intentional* about their relationship. Jared had been taking mindfulness classes on his lunch hour and was full of ideas on how to reconnect with the world, and with each other. He'd been teaching Andrew about a type of tapping therapy, where you tap on certain spots of your body and repeat positive sentences about whatever is stressing you out. Andrew would watch him in the living room, tapping at his forehead and saying, "Even though I want that cream cheese muffin, I will make a healthy choice not to eat it." He tried not to laugh. Jared's hopefulness and his desire to be a better person were actually among the things he loved most intensely about him.

When they'd met, they were both recently single and heartbroken. Neither was eager to jump right into something new. But the physical attraction was undeniable, and no amount of pretending they didn't also like each other and want to spend time together could change it. They'd recently celebrated their three-year anniversary, the longest consistent relationship for Andrew. Most of the time he felt solid with Jared, as though they shared a home base and a core connection too strong to be broken. Occasionally things came up that made him wonder if he was actually settling for less than he wanted. Did all relationships feel that way after a while? He had no real point of comparison. His parents were one of the few couples he knew who had actually stayed together. He often held them up as the ideal, espousing to others that gay men gave up on each other too quickly, that commitment was a lost art.

His parents were very affectionate, but Andrew would never say they were outwardly sexual. As a teenager he was aware of the way most men stared at women, because it seemed to be an automatic impulse that God had not granted him. It gave him some comfort to note that his father also seemed to lack this impulse. He eventually learned that gay men are granted a free pass, in certain geographical areas and using certain coded behaviors, to be overtly sexual amongst themselves without having to know one another. Once Andrew emerged from closeted suburbia, and had access to the ways in which sexuality was communicated through quick looks, gestures, and open admiration, he noticed when it wasn't present. When you first discover sex and falling in love, for a while it's all you can see. Coming home from college after months of cruising and gay bars, and burning through the syllabus of his Queer Literature course, he felt as though he saw the subtleties of sex everywhere.

His father was a stark reminder of an old school puritanism, yes, but he also seemed too nerdy and book-bound to be a person with an acknowledged body, let alone a sexual person. He was often described as a floating head or absentminded professor, never caring much about anything beyond the brain.

. . .

ANDREW TAPPED AT HIS forehead the way Jared had suggested he do in moments of crisis. *This is a stressful moment, but I can get through it if I remember to breathe and be in my body,* he thought. When Jared told him about the forehead-tapping theory, Andrew had made fun of him, but he felt desperate for any strategy at this point, staring at the old dusty computer monitor that his mother had covered in a ridiculous cotton doily for when guests stayed over. It would probably feel better to take the computer outside and bash it with a bat, just like the printer in his favorite scene in the movie *Office Space.*

He stubbed out the joint in the ashtray he'd made twenty years ago in shop class. He remembered trying to make it look shitty so that his classmates wouldn't think he was artistic.

My father is in a *jail cell* right now. He grappled with that thought. He clutched at his chest, his fingers coated in sweat. The joint wasn't helping. He didn't feel stoned really, just more sad, helpless, as if a film were covering his skin.

He opened the drawer beside his bed and pulled out a cigar box. Inside was a hollowed-out Bible filled with envelopes. Letters from Stuart, Andrew's first boyfriend, who was also his coach in high school. His aunt Clara was the only one who knew about Stuart, and she hadn't really approved because he was older, and because he chose to live in Avalon Hills and was therefore either dumb or "self-loathing," a term Andrew didn't understand at the time.

But she understood that he wasn't being harmed, and that their feelings for each other were real.

Andrew hadn't spoken to Stuart since his second year of college, when their phone conversations included a lot of long pauses while Andrew tried to think of excuses to hang up. Andrew had been surprised to realize that once he left Avalon Hills, and ceased to be the only gay guy he knew, he and Stuart actually had very different interests, and weren't very compatible at all. Andrew broke up with him over the telephone one night in his dorm room after he drank too many beers with his best friend, Lindy, who convinced him to let her give him a blow job that he felt guilty about the next day when she wouldn't speak to him.

Stuart showed up at his dorm room two days later, drunk and begging him to reconcile. Andrew had reacted with cruelty, although cruelty when you're that young and newly free from your parents feels like your right. Andrew opened the door and handed him the sweater Stuart had given him as a going-away present. He shook his head and said, "Please go home, Stuart." He shut the door, whispering another unconvincing "Sorry," and waited until he heard security escorting him out. They hadn't spoken since.

Months later he felt terrible about that moment, though he knew it had been the right decision.

Andrew hadn't thought about Stuart for years, and really only mentioned him when anyone asked him for his "coming out" story, which rarely happened anymore. Younger guys didn't seem to have that ritual of exchanging stories of revelation, denial, acceptance, estrangement.

These days they seemed to say, "What? I've always been gay. Here I am in day care in my *Glad to Be Gay!* onesie. What are you harping about, old guy?"

He'd never run into Stuart on visits to his parents over the years, probably because he rarely left Woodbury Lake when he came home. He preferred to lounge on the dock, sequestered in silence.

Andrew put on a pair of his old jeans. They were too loose for him now. He wrote *buy a belt* on his phone's notepad. He left his room and peered down the hallway towards the master bedroom. He heard his mother's shower running. Downstairs he discovered a pot of coffee, still warm, and poured himself a cup. He looked out the back window and saw Sadie and her boyfriend running down to the lake wrapped in old swim towels. How could they act as though nothing was happening? He felt a twinge of annoyance that Sadie wasn't helping take care of their mother. He took a sip and knew where he had to go.

When he drove past the Coffee Hut by the beach, Pat was outside watering the petunias. The newspaper box had a photo of his father on the front. He lifted one hand from the wheel in a partial wave, and Pat offered a tepid nod in return.

He continued to drive too fast, the way he had as a teenager, through the bucolic Avalon Hills Main Street with its carefully tended foliage, passing every store where he could potentially buy a belt. He turned right at the public library, going up the Mason Street hill, feeling both repelled by and drawn to the nostalgia he felt when he approached the school, which was set back from the road in a shroud of trees. He pulled in by a side lane, into the staff parking lot, and was waved through by a security guard who noted the staff parking sticker on his parents' Volvo. He watched a student leave through a side door, loosening his school tie and throwing off his blazer, jumping on a bike he'd stashed by the cedar bushes that encircled the janitor's house.

Media trucks lined the parking lot, antennas popped. Reporters checked their hair in the reflection of their phones and held microphones at their sides while camera crews took shots of the school. Police cars blocked the main road's entrance. Andrew walked behind the building towards the athletic field, trying to be inconspicuous. A group of girls were playing lacrosse on the field closest to the school. The grounds looked smaller, shabbier than he remembered them. He was now walking where he used to scurry, hoping not to be noticed, wishing he could disappear. It was comical, the way the land looked so anonymous and nonthreatening as an adult.

The north field, beyond a line of trees, was where Stuart and Andrew had had a meeting spot at a certain boulder. You could be seen, but not always. The shrubs in the area had grown thicker. He passed through the thicket on the dirt path, well worn by sneakered kids over the decades. The track looked exactly the same.

Stuart was standing in the middle of the field holding a clipboard while students ran around him. Andrew sat in the bleachers and watched, astounded that while he had gone to university then law school, while he had had dozens of relationships and finally found someone he could be with long-term, Stuart had been in the same spot, running the same circles around the same field. Yelling the same shouts of encouragement, ogling the same broad-shouldered closet cases year after year. It was both sad and comforting.

Stuart looked towards the bleachers and Andrew waved at him. Stuart looked in his direction again, puzzled, and waved in a way that indicated he wasn't sure who Andrew was from that distance. Eventually he sent the class indoors, and as he approached, his eyes widened. His hair had receded, and the beer he loved to drink to excess on the weekends at the gay club in Woodbridge had certainly done a number on his midsection. He looked tired, significantly older, and he blushed when he saw Andrew.

"Holy shit, Andy Woodbury."

No one called him that anymore, not in years. They hugged. Stuart smelled the same, like a spicy drugstore cologne. In his final year of high school Andrew used to spray it all over his sweater before leaving Stuart's apartment in the middle of the night to bike home, just so he would be able to breathe in his scent, his head swirling with love.

"I had no idea about your father, Andy. We're all in shock."

"Worried they'll come after you next?" he joked.

Stuart didn't laugh. He looked mortified. "That's not funny, Andy. You were seventeen—that's not really the same thing."

"I know, I know."

"And I held off for a long time . . . You were the one who chased me. I didn't do a thing until you came to the bar that night and shocked the hell out of me. I figured if you were going to go home with some old guy, may as well be someone who cared for your well-being," he said.

"You weren't old. You were twenty-five, for god's sake. I'm older than that now. I was just kidding . . ."

"I know, I know." He looked over at the school, as though expecting someone to come out and catch them, even though they were just two grown men chatting.

"Do you know the girls?"

"Some of them, yeah. I know a few of them. I don't know, Andy. It's a tough position to be in, a male teacher away on a trip with a bunch of drunk girls. It's always easy to judge . . . You know, we all want to stick up for your dad. He's always been such a solid guy."

"Well, I know that. But the girls? They're still kids, right? I mean, that's what they're going to say, the people who believe them."

"Right, right," Stuart said. "Kids are so different now, Andy. They scare me a bit with how much they know."

"I dunno. We knew a lot. Doesn't every generation think the next is so scandalous?"

"No, I'm telling you. These kids have no innocence anymore."

Andrew didn't want to debate Stuart on this myth he was clinging to, so he just nodded, saying nothing.

"Plus, everyone remembers how your dad took that gunman down."

"Of course."

"Shit, I still can't believe I'm looking at you, Andy. You broke my heart, you know that?"

"Whatever!"

"That's the truth. I was really fucked up about it for a good year or so. No one was good enough after you broke up with me."

There's always a power shift, Andrew thought as Stuart scratched the sides of his face. The initial pursuer usually ends up being the one with less to lose. He wondered what the balance would be with him and Jared.

"So, do you have a boyfriend now?"

"Nah, nah. I don't do relationships anymore. I've got Katie, you know, we still live together. We have the baseball team, and we've got the dogs." He opened his wallet to show Andrew a photo of two golden doodles. Katie was Stuart's roommate, a woman who made angel statue crafts out of wire and papier-mâché and worked at the library. Andrew had always assumed she was gay, but she never had any girlfriends. Most people, including his parents, thought they were a couple.

A car came barrelling down the side road and stopped. Only staff usually used that road, and kids skipping class. Andrew felt the same fear and anxiety he had in high school—that they would be caught—and then he laughed. Stuart looked uncomfortable. "I better go, I'm late for my next class. Don't be a stranger, Andy. Call me if you want to have a drink and catch up."

Andrew watched him walk through the open field towards the school, the same limp in his right knee from the college football injury that had crushed his athletic dreams. He didn't seem like an older man anymore, just old.

When Andrew got back to his car, he turned the key in the ignition and the radio played a song from his high school days, a ballad from one of those awful post-punk bands the girls used to cry over. It started to rain slightly as he pulled out of his parking space, but it was still sunny in the distance above the mountains. The crescendo of the song sparked something in his chest, and Andrew started to cry. What the fuck was happening? What was he going to do about his father? At work he felt confident in his ability to argue his clients free. Now he felt like a doctor with a family member who was sick and whom he couldn't care for. He was powerless.

He got to the exit gate, but it was blocked by police cars. A cop made the universal hand gesture for him to roll down his window, which he did, slowly and only halfway. The joint in his back pocket started to feel as if it was burning him, though he knew this was his imagination. He wiped away the remaining tears clinging to his stubble.

"Hello, sir. Are you a teacher at this school?"

"No, no. My sister goes here. She forgot her lunch, so I was dropping it off," he said.

The cop took off his sunglasses and leaned closer to the window, placing one hand on the top of the car. "Can I see your ID, please?"

Andrew sighed. "You actually don't have a right to do that unless I'm suspected of a crime. Am I suspected of a crime? I'm a lawyer, you see." He would never say such a thing in the city. But he wasn't going to let some redneck townie push him around in Avalon Hills.

The cop squinted at him, unimpressed, with the pained look of anyone forced to work harder than they want to.

"Andy?"

Andrew looked at his face. Despite the lines, the sagging skin under his eyes, and the salt-and-pepper beard, it was definitely Alan Chambers, a former jock from the public school down the road. Andrew had tutored him after school at the learning center, a job he took because it would look good on college applications.

"Alan?"

A wave of nauseous recognition passed between them.

"It's been a long time," Alan said coolly.

"Yes, it has."

Alan continued to stare at him, blank, and then grinned. "You're the reason I graduated, remember? Goddamn fractions!" He laughed, slapping his hand on the top of the car for emphasis. Andrew's pulse sped up, but he knew immediately how the interaction would play out.

"How you been? Got any kids?" It was the standard thing to say. Andrew wished he could just press the gas pedal, speed away. He imagined reaching through the passenger window and punching him in the face, his tobacco-stained teeth reduced to rubble against his fist. Once he was on the ground, he'd grab for his gun and press it against his temple and wait for him to cry.

"Yup, three girls. Beautiful angels." He took off his cap and showed him a laminated photo of three kids under a Christmas tree pinned to the underside of the hat's brim.

"Yes, angels," Andrew deadpanned. "That's great."

"Yes, the best thing I ever did in my whole life, you know. The best thing," he repeated, as though saying it twice made it more true, while putting his hat back on his head.

Andrew was never asked the same question in return. "Anyway, it was nice to see you again," he said, carefully turning to look ahead. The thickness of their dishonesty seemed to contribute to the front window fogging up. Ahead, two cops leaned against a cruiser, sipping coffees and watching them.

"Andrew, look, your father is in a lot of trouble, and they've upped security here, of course. I don't want to see you back here, okay?"

Andrew nodded but couldn't hide a sneer. "It's ironic, isn't it, Alan? You telling me that I'm a potential danger?"

Alan looked away. "I dunno know what you mean, Andy."

It bothered Andrew that Alan still didn't pronounce words separately. *I dunnowhatchomeanAndy.* He still spoke as though trying to outrun his childhood stutter.

"Yes, you do. *I'm* not the threatening one, am I?"

Alan picked up his radio and said something coded into it before turning back to Andrew, who was tapping the wheel, rage surging in his chest.

"That was a long time ago, man. High school, kids' stuff. You're not still upset, are ya?" Andrew could hear the whispered slur Alan might as well have said after that, and his laugh, the same as in high school, after he'd said *fucking pansy ass faggot* under his breath when he walked by him on the street.

Andrew didn't respond, just stared at him, willing Alan's heart to stop.

"Look, look, sorry about that. You know, I was a shit. I've changed now, right? People should be free to be anything they want to be, right?"

Andrew eyed the gun on Alan's holster. *Which people, asshole?*

"Right," he said, "very astute, Alan."

"Anyway," Alan said, looking at the row of cars gathered up behind them, "please don't come back round here until they get this thing settled, okay?"

Andrew sped off without answering, shaking with an electrified anger he hadn't felt in years. It was like the time he was in California during an earthquake, one the locals thought was insignificant but he interpreted as the end of the world, the way everything solid around him became fragile and movable. Everything outside the car wasn't real, and his body was aflame, hot and awful.

At the light, a group of Avalon Hills girls stood at a bus stop. The uniform was the same timeless kilt and white blouse, and were it not for their hairstyles, cellphones, and array of designer handbags, it could have been the late 1990s. He remembered how the kids wore toques over their flattened, messy hair when he was in high school, plaid shirts that clashed with their kilts tied around their waists. The girls used to carry canvas army bags that cost five dollars at the surplus store in Woodbridge. At the stop, a girl with long blond hair was looking through her purse, a Louis Vuitton that must have cost more than his monthly rent in New York. She wore very high heels, also designer. She didn't look like she was actually a kid until she pulled a plastic bag of jujubes out of her purse and threw one at her friend, then emptied the whole bag into her mouth and puffed out her cheeks like a squirrel. The light changed and he pressed on, following the familiar yellow lines that curved through downtown and then around the lake.

He pulled into the Coffee Hut and looked at his phone, surprised to see that his hands were still shaking. Four texts from Jared. *I want to know you're ok. Will u just text me back a simple ok? I know it's hard.* He texted back an okay. He read the texts over and felt a bit calmer. Jared really did ground him. He followed it with an *I Love You.* He perused the screen of emoticon options and decided on a simple pink heart.

He'd been feeling guilty lately for leaving Jared hanging, and for being a bad boyfriend, even before this happened. He'd been taking him for granted. No more. He was lucky to have found Jared, and he shouldn't forget that.

5

JOAN STOOD IN THE EN SUITE SHOWER STALL FOR SEVERAL minutes, watching patchy scenes from a nightmare trapped in a looped refrain in her mind. Water on the edge of painfully hot pulsated between her shoulder blades. She opened her eyes to thwart the dream memories, staring instead at the stone bench along the perimeter that had seemed ostentatious when the designer had suggested it. The master-bathroom renovation had been a fiftieth-birthday gift from her husband. The room had originally been designed to suit George's mother in the 1970s, complete with hideous floral wallpaper, sink the color of Yardley rose soap.

The claw-footed tub was the only thing that remained of his parents' era in the house, and Joan rarely used it. Relaxing in a bath for too long made her feel she was waiting for a late train and couldn't quite settle.

The new shower stall could comfortably fit five people, had three types of shower heads, a sauna function, and all sorts of bells and whistles. She made the water even hotter, aiming it at her neck, and hung her head like a broken tree limb. Images of a panther jumping into the lake to eat her children played over and over in her head. In her dream they were twin toddlers despite their age difference in real life. She could only stand on the beach, helpless. Such an obvious metaphor, for god's sake. A single sob, and then nothing. Empty. Her neck raw. A halfhearted shampoo. Squeezing the conditioner bottle hard but coming up empty, chucking it to the ground and watching it roll. *This shower is too large,* she thought. *Who would need such a thing?* It was a sign that her values had been distorted somewhere along the way.

GEORGE LOVED TO MAKE breakfast. But when Joan got out of the shower this morning, she wouldn't smell coffee brewing downstairs, or hear the spoon clank against the side of a pot of steel-cut oats. George often made fresh bread in the bread-making machine the night before, got up early to go for a walk, and by the time Joan roused from sleep he would be toasting almonds for their hot cereal, or chopping fresh mint into bowls of mixed fresh berries.

What would she do without him? What if this wasn't temporary?

Getting out of the shower, she felt a surge of betrayal so forceful that she had no time to towel off before leaning over the toilet to throw up. She flushed, knelt, and gripped her fingers to the edges of the seat. For the first time she missed the softness of the ugly dusty-rose toilet seat cover from the pre-reno years.

Eventually, when she couldn't feel anything in the lower half of her legs, she stood and wrapped herself in the white plush robe hanging from the back of the door. She knotted a towel around her head and dotted serum under each eye. Her mind felt sticky, like it was stuck on one note in a melody, and she remembered the pill Andrew had given her with a glass of water before bed.

Coming down the stairs, she smelled coffee and was momentarily hopeful it had all been a dream, but of course that only happens on TV. In the kitchen, faced with its stale air from the unwanted parade of bodies the night before, she unwrapped the towel, hung it limply on a stool, and shook out her hair while it slipped to the floor. She didn't retrieve it before pouring herself a cup of coffee. She stared at the towel, tasted the coffee, and winced. Someone had been up earlier and left it for her, but it was stronger than she liked. A white mold was beginning to blanket the raspberries on the counter. She tore open a packet of sweetener and threw it in the garbage without using it.

If George was guilty, and she was far from convinced, then he could be sick. She took a sip of black coffee and contemplated this. She understood sick. Everyone is generally pleased to reduce a complicated situation to the notion of *evil*. Or *a typical sleazeball man. He's just evil.*

Evil is a word that's lost its meaning recently, like *bully*. Overused, and weakened.

She dissolved an antacid tablet in a glass of water. If it's a sickness, it would not be his fault. There could be an undiagnosed tumor in his orbitofrontal lobe, causing him to have no control over his impulses. She grabbed a pen from the cup beside the phone and drew a sketch of a brain on a scrap of paper. She should call Bennie and suggest an MRI. She could choose to have compassion. *Maybe this is a lesson from god, to see how much compassion I can have!* She stood up at this revelation and drank the fizzing water down. Then she sat down again on one of the tall bar stools at the kitchen island. Every time she was sitting, it seemed impossible to imagine standing. She wrote *Sick???* next to the brain doodle. She'd ask Clara what she thought of this possibility when she woke up.

Joan was staring down the hall at the front door when she was startled by the click of the back door opening. Sadie and Jimmy emerged wet from a swim, much like other mornings, only they weren't joking around or smiling. Joan's eyes flooded with tears when she saw them.

"Oh, shit, Mom. You look so awful," Sadie said as Joan embraced her and pulled away to look at her. Joan brushed a strand of hair away from her daughter's face and placed it behind her ear. "There are still reporters out there . . ."

"I know, don't talk to them."

"I didn't."

"I'll make you guys breakfast," Joan said, taking a deep breath and turning to busy herself in the fridge. The date walnut muffins George had baked the day before sat on a plate wrapped in saran. Sadie leaned against the island, playing with her phone, while Jimmy ducked upstairs to change.

"It's okay, Mom. I went for an early run, and just felt like . . . jumping in the lake. It feels weird to be here."

Joan hadn't even realized that school had started and that that was where her daughter should be.

"I cleaned up your room," Joan said. "I stayed up late

last night organizing everything again. There are a lot of things the police still have." Joan remembered the man in an ugly green shirt pulling the portraits off the wall and throwing them in a plastic tub.

"Thanks," Sadie said, leaning over to fill her water bottle from the sink.

"You should eat."

"I'm not hungry."

"You need some protein after exercising," she said, grabbing a small container of cottage cheese from the fridge door and peeling back the foil. Mothering, like nursing, can be performed methodically, a habitual ability to put one's own needs last, and that erasure of herself was a balm to Joan in this moment. If she could get her daughter to eat, that would soothe Joan.

"I saw Amanda this morning. Apparently her sister is one of the girls . . ." Sadie paused to eat a spoonful of cottage cheese.

Joan froze in front of the toaster, holding two floppy pieces of multigrain bread. She bowed her head. Then she put the bread into the toaster as though she hadn't heard correctly.

"That can't be possible. She is, what, twelve years old? For god's sake, Sadie. This just *can't be true.*"

"She just turned fourteen. But if this *is* true, if it's true what those girls are saying . . . what the hell can we do?"

"Honey, we don't know anything for sure yet. And who are you going to trust? Strangers, or your own father? We have to wait and see what Bennie says. Someone is lying and out to get him."

"That sounds crazy."

"This situation *is* crazy!"

"I know, I know it is," agreed Sadie. "I want to go see him and talk to him myself. It just doesn't make *sense*."

Joan wasn't sure what made her say this, but she felt a sudden surge of protectiveness for her husband. "We need to stick by your father," she said. "We don't know the real story."

"But if it *is* true . . ."

"Sadie, don't say that."

"Come on, we can't *not* think about that possibility."

"Everyone is innocent until proven guilty, and who knows your father better than us? He is a friendly guy. Perhaps some girls, who are told by everyone not to go near men because they're all evil monsters, maybe they misinterpreted his kindness and interest in their lives."

When someone is your husband or father, that's simply who they are. You don't stop to question much about them, unless you're given reason to, and they'd never been given reason to.

"Well, keep an open mind until we know more. Until we can see him. You are coming with me to the hearing tomorrow, right? We'll figure out bail and he'll be home again and we can put this behind us and let the lawyers do the work."

"Mom. What if we're just in denial? What if it's true, what they're saying?"

Something cracked against the front window. Joan ran into the living room, expecting to see the smear of a bird carcass across the grass, but when she moved the blinds aside, she saw remnants of eggshell and the smear of yolk, and saw the blur of teenagers running and jumping over the Hendersons' side hedges.

"Maybe you should stay inside today, honey."

"Okay, Mom," Sadie said as she headed upstairs. She paused at the landing and turned around. "We have to face the facts of what is happening."

"We need not to jump to conclusions. This is a shock, but we're not going to help anything by being hysterical and convincing ourselves that your father is some sort of ax murderer."

"Two-thirds of all sexual assaults are committed by someone who knows the victim. Someone who the victim trusts."

"So? Most murderers murder people they know, but that doesn't mean if you know someone, you'll murder someone."

"No one is charging anyone with murder. You're obscuring the point. We have to look at what's really happened here."

"We need to stay calm and focused on helping Dad beat these ridiculous, baseless charges. He'll be home soon, and we'll figure this out."

"I think we just, like, need to make sure we know that they are baseless."

Joan stopped buttering the toast and stared at her daughter.

"I mean, it might be a misunderstanding or something," Sadie mumbled.

They were silent for a moment before Sadie went upstairs.

Joan stirred her coffee slowly, the carton of skim milk sweating on the table in front of her, anchoring the morning newspaper. Joan ignored her toast. Above the fold was a headline about George, screaming out in thick, bold lettering. She watched as the liquid in her cup cooled, the text blurring behind it. Outside, the leaves appeared to have reddened overnight, going mad alongside her.

Whatever the police had tried to find wasn't discoverable, but they dug and sifted anyway, with no regard for personal history, for the meaning humans attach to objects, for the symbols of a family's life. They took the family albums, the diaries, the telephone bill printouts.

The phone rang. Joan answered, and heard her husband's voice on the other end of the line, sounding far away. "I am being set up," he said. "I only have a few seconds, but I wanted you to know that. Watch your back. Who knows what these people are capable of."

He didn't sound like himself. Joan took the approach she took with emotionally disturbed patients at work: clear questions, empathy, calm.

"Have you been having headaches? Blurred vision?" she asked. "George?" She said his name a few more times, couldn't quite believe that he'd already hung up.

Joan turned on the small TV that lived on the wall above the microwave. Normally it was only on when the housekeeper was over, or when something big was happening on the news during dinner prep. She clicked from channel to channel, past layers of footage of her husband being walked in handcuffs from the police car into the station.

She heard the beeping of the intercom from the front

gate, something so rare that it confused her for a moment. She muted the TV and pressed Talk, trying to adjust the video screen so she could see who was at the gate. She saw a close-up of a middle-aged man, just one eye at first, then he pulled his face back. Probably a journalist.

"I'm not talking to journalists," she said, pressing Talk again. "You're trespassing."

He held up his hands, spreading his fingers. He spoke too loudly into the intercom, as though he was yelling across the front yard. "I'm not the enemy, don't worry. I'm here in support," he said, as though she should applaud him. "See? Look at my T-shirt," he said, stepping back for the camera.

She peered a little closer. His T-shirt read, *Justice for Men and Boys.*

"I'm not going to open the gate," she said loudly.

"I understand, you think every man is a predator. But it's the feminists who are going to ruin your husband's life, you know," he said.

"What?"

"No one in the media ever wants to discuss the very real fact that women lie to get attention, to excuse behavior they regret. It's way more common than anyone wants to admit."

She didn't know what to say, so she just stared at him on the screen. Then she pulled back the living room curtains and pressed one finger to the glass, as though pointing at him.

He reached into his bag and pulled out a stack of papers. She saw him waving them in the air. He looked like one of those unkempt socialist newspaper sellers.

"I'll put these under the gate," he shouted. "We just want to help your husband."

Joan watched him walk away. She waited twenty minutes before she walked up the laneway and grabbed the flyers he'd slipped under the gate. Some were starting to blow away in the wind, others had stayed beneath the rock he'd placed on top. On the front of the flyer was a photo of George. Above, the headline read:

RAMPANT MISANDRY TAKES A HERO DOWN IN WOOD-BURY LAKE.

Oh, brother.

JOAN'S AFFABLE HUSBAND, WHO would have called the man at the gate a crazy misogynist, was being defended by him. Had she woken up in an opposite world?

Back in the kitchen, starting over again with another two pieces of toast, she scanned the headlines on Sadie's iPad and noted that George's likability turned out to work against him in the press. She kept the news station on, and read each article. Most of them said the exact same thing, but some editorialized. The local newspaper, as well as all the big-city affiliates, were really keen on exploiting George's status as a man of distinction in a town they said was "corrupt with old money" and "entrenched in the antiquated ways of archetypal New England WASPs." The reality—that Joan worked as a nurse, that George collected a teacher's salary, that the house was paid off when George was still in diapers—the complexity of that reality didn't fit into column inches. Joan knew, from her one and a half years in journalism school, that once there was a simple narrative to attach to a story, that was the one they ran with. Nuance is too complicated for the daily news. One station replayed the archival footage from when George stopped the gunman. "It was instinct," he said to the camera, beaming. Played out of context, it was monstrous and humiliating.

A MONTH BEFORE THE arrest, Joan had been the recipient of a gold-plated brooch in the shape of an angel, an annual municipal award presented to someone in the community who demonstrated compassion or heroics. The accompanying plaque was engraved with *Joan Woodbury—true compassionate care.* On an outdoor platform behind City Hall the mayor recounted a story about a child Joan had saved before presenting her with the plaque and pin. He'd used the word *heroine.* At first she'd considered the whole ceremony a lot of fuss over nothing; she was doing her job and shouldn't be rewarded for it. She'd remarked to co-workers that it was likely a hogwash public relations exercise meant to make City Hall appear as though it cared about workers. In fact, she knew the mayor personally—something she didn't really brag about at work—and knew the gesture was likely genuine. This feeling was bolstered as she stood there, wearing a new bright green cotton dress, and she choked up. The emotion was so unexpected that her face grew flushed and she produced an abrupt sob. George and Sadie were in the front row taking photographs. Joan smiled as wide as she had at the piano recitals of her children and felt something she hadn't felt in a long while, which she only later identified as *valued.* She did feel valued at home, but at work she'd long felt exhausted and cynical. The award was motivating. Photos appeared in the Life & Arts section of the Saturday paper, which she'd clipped and pinned to the bulletin board at work. A second copy went on the fridge, beside Andrew's graduation photos from law school and the article about Sadie's county track and field win.

CLARA CAME DOWNSTAIRS JUST as the news broadcast the story again, on high volume. She towered over Joan, her lips a slash of red lipstick, expertly applied. She took off her glasses and cleaned them with her silky coral scarf, then went over to the radio and pressed Off.

After every broadcast, the phone rang, with people who were hearing the news for the first time. Joan stopped picking up after George called, because she did not know what to say. Clara silenced the phone.

"I'm here, Joannie. We're going to get you through this." Clara was suddenly red and sweaty, pulling off the scarf and dotting her forehead with it. "Fucking hot-flash bullshit," she said.

The answering machine picked up. It was Bennie. "Bail might be set astronomically high. I think that someone is trying to make some sort of political point with this arrest. I will come pick up the family in a Town Car tomorrow at ten. The more family members who show up . . . the better it looks."

JOAN POURED CLARA a cup of green tea and handed it to her.

"How high could they possibly set it?"

"You'll be able to handle it. He wouldn't leave such an important detail on a voice mail if it was something we couldn't handle."

"I've been thinking," Joan started carefully, knowing Clara was not an easy one to convince of anything.

"Yeah?" Clara sipped her tea, then made a sour face. "This tastes like mowed grass." She reached for the antique sugar bowl on the counter.

"No one knows better than someone with my job that everyone on earth is a variation of crazy . . . right? Everyone's got a loose screw. Nobody stays the same their whole life!"

"So?"

"I'm just saying that we shift around on a seesaw moral continuum for our whole lives. *Nobody* stays the same! I'm not saying that he did it, but what if he is sick? What if he has a tumor?"

"You're feeling ashamed, but you shouldn't. This is not your fault."

"I am not ashamed," Joan spat at her. The truth was that the shame Joan felt was so expansive and so forceful that it couldn't be something described by as few as five letters, something so commonplace. This was something else entirely. "A word doesn't even exist for what I'm feeling," Joan mumbled.

Clara pushed her hair behind her ears and looked out the back window at the lake. "I really don't have any idea what the fuck to say to you, Joan. I feel like I usually have at least one answer to a problem, but I'm dumbfounded."

Joan sat down again at the kitchen island, rested her head in her hands, and started to cry.

Clara squeezed both of her shoulders. "I'm surprised you aren't angry."

Joan's voice was muffled against her arms. "I *am* angry. I feel like someone has attacked my family!"

"You're very concerned for him," Clara said carefully.

"Of course I am. You don't stop loving someone in an instant because somebody accuses them of something despicable. Nothing is that black-and-white."

"Of course not," Clara mumbled. "I just think that *I* might feel a little more . . . betrayed."

"Well, we are not the same person, are we?"

"No, no, we're not." Clara sipped her tea.

"Plus, he's obviously innocent," she said.

"You're right, there is that possibility." Clara didn't look convinced.

"It's so easy to make assumptions," Joan said. "I see it all the time. Doctors think they know everything before they actually get tests done, or bother to really listen to a patient. Not everything is as it seems."

"Of course, Joannie, of course. Where is Sadie?"

"Upstairs, I think. And for the record: if it *is* true, I didn't know," she said to Clara, who nodded in a way that said she believed her sister. "I knew Andrew was gay by the time he was seven. I knew Sadie had a higher than average intelligence before the special tests came in and pronounced her a mini genius. I can spot a fake seizure from across a crowded emergency room. I know how much pain even the most stoic man is in by the way he walks!" Joan was circling the kitchen island now, arms in the air for emphasis. "I knew Dad was having an affair when I was only fourteen!"

"Mom did used to say that you were unusually intuitive," Clara agreed. "But you know the cliché—love is blind, et cetera."

"Clara, I would have sooner guessed that he had another whole family in another state, or an online gambling addiction, or a sudden religious conversion. There were *no* signs. He never uttered an inappropriate word, or watched anyone in a disturbing manner, or made any attempts to role-play anything even vaguely inappropriate in the bedroom."

"What is your sex life like?" Clara looked down at the table, uncomfortable.

"Normal."

"Come on. No one is normal. Normal sex doesn't exist."

"Of course it does. I have girlfriends. I know what's normal."

"Girlfriends?" Clara cocked a brow.

Perhaps *girlfriends,* plural, denoting some kind of group that went out together, confessed secrets, had a certain kind of intimacy, was a bit of an exaggeration. Joan and George tended to be one of those couples that had a community, but not friendships, really. They had each other, and Joan had Clara.

"I have friends! I have co-workers. I read articles. Stop looking at me like I'm an Amish housewife or something."

"C'mon. Every guy has a kink or two. I once had a guy who wanted me to play Robin to his Batman."

"Fuck off, Clara. He didn't act like a pervert. He did not ask me to wear a fucking schoolgirl kilt or put my hair in pigtails. It was good sex, okay? It was the best I ever had."

Joan felt that the humiliation of this conversation was possibly going to kill her.

"I think," Clara said, weighing her words, "that everyone has a secret they keep from their partner, no matter how healthy they appear from the outside, how communicative they are. You and George really did appear to be the pinnacle of normalcy, but nothing is ever as it appears to be."

"That's cynical."

"I dunno. I always thought of you as the perfect example of a successful marriage. It never occurred to me to think that in itself is a bit curious, maybe a red flag. You've never had an affair, you never expressed boredom or uncertainty. That is odd, and a bit improbable or something."

Joan had stopped listening to her sister, stuck on her and George's sex life, replaying every intimacy. What was intimacy when you really thought about it? Joan couldn't understand it when she focused on it. She was a private person, believed privacy wasn't valued enough these days. She was always trying to impress upon Sadie the importance of keeping some things sacred and personal. Those were the euphemisms she used. Sadie always looked at her as though she were trying to teach her the alphabet again.

"What if the sex was just good for me, and so-so for him, Clara? God, that is so heartbreaking to contemplate."

Clara was silent.

"What does it mean, if it was the most fulfilling relationship I've ever had, and it was a lie?"

"I don't know, honey. It's probably not about sex."

"That's depressing. You always think you know every-thing."

"I've written some articles about men who are sex of-fenders, and they tend to fall into certain categories. You know, some are emotionally arrested at the age of their victims, from a past trauma, and they act out as though they are peers experimenting with bodies, and some are your garden-variety sadists and psychopaths, and some are, well, I don't know, sick in some way?"

"Well, they're not accusing him of going after young children," Joan said, and then caught herself.

Joan and Clara stayed in the kitchen for the next hour or so, Clara making lists of things that needed to be done while Joan re-dusted the rubber plant by the window overlooking the backyard.

The silence was interrupted by the answering machine—Dorothy, the school secretary, calling to leave a message. Joan sipped her cold coffee while Clara sat with the laptop looking up legal information about George's charges. Joan let the secretary's awkward nasal voice fill the room. *It's Dorothy. Sadie is not in class, Mrs. Woodbury. I just wanted you to know. We are all very concerned about her well-being.*

Joan played the message twice over the speaker before pressing Delete. Mrs. Woodbury. That was new. Messages used to be: *Hey Joan! Hey doll! Hot as heck out there today, huh?* Dorothy used to sound friendly in voice mail. Now she sounded like the automatic voice you get when you call the phone company. Emotionless.

The phone rang again. Clara and Joan watched as the

machine picked it up and George's voice greeted the caller with a formal flourish. *The Woodburys are unavailable right now, kindly leave your number after the beep.*

"Why do you still have an ancient machine?"

"I didn't want to pay the phone company more money than we had to. Plus, we all have cellphones."

"You live in an effing mansion. I can't believe how cheap you are."

A sound of wind or breathing came on the line. "I hope you burn in hell. You and your whole family." The voice was elderly.

Joan took down the time and details on a pad of paper. She felt that if anyone did break down the door, she'd just lie down in the middle of the room and let them kick her. That was how little fight was left in her.

The gate buzzer rang again. She looked out and saw a UPS truck. Clara offered to go greet the driver, and she came back a few minutes later with a basket of fruit and a card.

"Do you think it'll blow up?" Clara asked, handing it to her sister.

The card read, *I hope you're hanging in there,* and it was signed by all the nurses at work. Accompanying it were a pamphlet for victims' services, one for a support group for women survivors of violence, and another for a group for women with loved ones in prison.

" 'Call if you need to' . . . Yeah, that means please don't, I'm just trying to be polite."

"Joan!"

"I know WASP sincerity when I see it . . . it's so rare."

No one else, none of the neighbors who claimed to *love*

George, had called or dropped by. The day after George stopped the school shooter, there had been a lineup of cars to come visit and offer congratulations. If Joan hadn't had Clara, she felt as though she would have walked into the lake with her pockets full of pennies.

Joan disappeared downstairs to check the laundry and brought up the old dusty hunting rifle that George's father kept on a rack above the pool table in the basement. It was a .22. She didn't know how to shoot it. She wasn't sure it had bullets; they probably didn't even make them anymore. But it was symbolic. It was too heavy to hold on her shoulder. She'd have to cradle it in her arms around her stomach, knocking objects behind her on the floor as she tried to walk around.

"I'm not exactly intimidating, but its existence is comforting," Joan said to Clara, who winced when she looked up from her seat and saw her sister with the rifle.

"Put that thing away," she said.

"I don't know why the cops didn't take it," Joan wondered out loud.

"You have permits?"

"Yes, I suppose. I don't even think it has bullets."

"That's why."

"Why do guns freak you out so much? Daddy had about a million."

"The city changes you," Clara said. "I used to see guns and think of dead deer. Now I see them and think about going to the bodega for a carton of milk and getting caught in the crossfire."

Joan picked up the phone and called her boss, requesting to cash in her backlogged sick time and take four weeks off. When she hung up, she felt an immediate sense of relief. Saying something as simple, as elementary, as "*I didn't do anything*" seemed entirely beside the point.

Clara turned on the radio. "Castrate him!" said an elderly voice. The DJ laughed uncomfortably. All the callers to the talk show uttered variations on *men will be boys, boys behave badly, young girls dress too sexy these days, Mr. Woodbury's family practically created this town and we owe him the respect of innocent until proven guilty, every man is tempted.* The latter opinion was something that would've provoked Joan to rant a couple of days ago, condoning the lack of responsibility men assume for their behavior. *We sexualize youth, every young actress and pop singer, and we have no right to then act puritanical when a red-blooded man has a natural reaction to this display. You can't put Britney Spears in a thong everywhere and expect men not to want her just because she's sixteen Men are animals, after all.*

"Britney Spears?" Clara laughed. "She's thirty!"

Joan turned the radio off and looked out the window and when she squinted, she could see that Andrew was lying on the dock, curled up like a toddler.

BENNIE CALLED AND JOAN picked up the phone. He read the victims' statements over the speakerphone. Joan placed her head down on the table, and Clara took notes on her phone as he read. "He approached Victim A after she had consumed alcohol at the ski lodge. He told her he would walk her back to the girls' cabin because she felt ill. He asked if she considered him a friend and she said yes, that she did. He then proceeded to tell her that he would inform her parents about the drinking, about her giving lap dances to boys in their rooms, unless she obliged . . ."

Joan gripped the arms of the chair and whimpered. Even if they turned out to be lies, those stories were there, obstacles between them, things she couldn't un-hear or un-imagine. Someone had taken Joan's only confidant, the one person who actually knew her completely, and her best friend, and replaced him with a monster. The person she knew and trusted was gone.

Joan and Clara decided to go to the Woodbridge Super-Save grocery store since they were unlikely to run into anyone they knew there. Bennie's recitation of the victims' statements was still ringing in their ears. Joan filled a basket with corn, avocados, and bundles of fresh herbs in clear plastic bags. She ran her hands under the sprinklers that were keeping the heirloom carrots fresh, mesmerized, until her fingers turned red and she recognized that they were cold. In this moment of disembodiment she didn't see Clara approach, pushing a cart filled with frozen foods, whole grain waffles, Lean Cuisines, pizza, and frozen yogurt, food for a working mother of toddlers, or for stocking a bomb shelter.

"I don't buy that stuff anymore," Joan said, picking up a package of frozen breakfast burritos. "Too many preservatives."

"You do not want to have to shop or go out, just trust me," Clara said, grabbing several bottles of wine and thrusting them at her chest. "You're going to need these."

"I'll just break out the expensive wine in the cellar!" Joan laughed, a sudden inappropriate blurt. Phil Collins was singing on the in-store speakers. Something in the air tonight.

"That's the spirit," Clara said.

It started in the lineup. A woman in an orange and white maxi skirt ahead of them held open the local paper and said to her friend, "I feel sorry for the wife, you know."

It was then that Joan realized the paper had reused the photograph of her from the awards ceremony. Underneath the photo the cutline read, WOODBURY'S WIFE TOLD POLICE SHE HAD NO IDEA.

The other lady, in green plastic gardening shoes Joan could see as she stared down with her head bowed, replied, "She had to know. To know and to have not said anything, that's worse than anything he's done."

Clara grabbed her hand and whispered, "Go to the car, I'll pay."

Joan wanted to kick the women. Her foot actually involuntarily fell forward. But she did as Clara instructed, pushing by them and breaking into a run after she got through the sliding doors.

They were mostly silent on the drive home, until Joan drew a heart on the passenger-side window and said, "Imagine the person you love and trust becoming a different person overnight. What would you do?"

"I'd want a bottle of Percocet, and a gun to go shoot him with."

"I thought you didn't like guns."

"That's why—I'm afraid if I had one, I'd use it."

"You've never been married," Joan said.

Clara frowned. "I've been in love," she said. "I understand devotion."

"Marriage is different."

"That's archaic."

"Someone could be setting him up," she said.

Clara pursed her lips, checking her blind spot before changing lanes. "Yes," she said.

"George is essentially a very good person," Joan said. "But that is one of those meaningless sentences. What is a *good* person? Under the worst of circumstances, who can say what we would do? For all we know, we might be the worst people on earth."

"You're not, Joan. You know that."

Joan remembered what the woman in the grocery store said.

Joan was no longer a mother and a nurse and a person with her own history. She symbolized evil, and for that, people were not kind. That the front windows of her house were streaked with egg yolk said it just as plainly.

Monday Afternoon

6

SADIE WENT TO SCHOOL AT THE END OF THE DAY, UN-
sure what to do with herself otherwise. Her mother
and Clara went to visit her father at the police station
and she didn't want to go. The house felt empty and imposing, and she was afraid of the journalists buzzing around
outside. Going on as usual might actually be comforting,
even though she had to show her student ID to a police
officer to get in through the front gate of her school, and
the security guard was extra-thorough going through her
knapsack.

She walked with sneakers squeaking out her presence
on the polished hardwood towards the principal's office,
where the rules of high school dictated she acquire a note
to explain her absence. Her right toe poked through her
green cotton school socks. Everything felt askew. She'd
never been to school this disheveled, but like a lot of things
that had mattered before, she had ceased to care about her
appearance. The sixth-period bell rang as she neared the

principal's office. The hallway succumbed to bodies in plaid and green and white, suffocating with chatter and screams. The sea of uniforms shocked her as she minnowed her way towards the office, forcing her shoulder blades to kiss in an approximation of confidence. Eat or be eaten.

She said hello to Susan Taylor, who was standing at her locker applying hot-pink gloss in a tiny square of mirror. Susan, who normally greeted Sadie with a warm hug and a slug of gossip, half waved and scurried away as Sadie passed by. Mr. Solomon also ignored her, offering a mumbled hello but clearly reticent to look her in the eye. This was an enormous shift. She had known most of the teachers since she was a child. She also had the highest grade point average in school, with Jimmy behind her by a fraction of a percentage point. She had always been greeted with enthusiasm and respect. Simply put, Sadie was not treated the way other adolescents were treated. *I'm one of them now?* she wondered. *The regular young. Or maybe worse.*

SADIE WAS IN THE accelerated academic program, a group of well-regarded students who, barring a stint in the eating disorder wing or a trip to rehab for Adderall addiction, were all heading to prestigious universities. They operated as a separate microcosm within the school's structure, mostly taking classes in their own wing on the west side of the building. They ate lunch in the student government lounge, because naturally they were the student government. There was an adjoining library, funded by her grandparents and now several corporate donors, with gold-rimmed antiquarian books and a long oak table. There was a small room with a rich red velvet couch and imposing desk, a room of un-known purpose when the school was built in the 1800s as a private college. This was their quiet contemplation room that they could book with Dorothy in order to have com-plete privacy while writing essays. Most of the time, though, they used it as the make-out room. No one knew this be-cause it was assumed that the nerdish spent their time preoc-cupied only with cerebral issues. It was possible, while on the third floor of the west wing, to be in complete ignorance of the activities occurring throughout the rest of the school, and out of the watchful disciplinary eyes of authority.

Most of the accelerated students in the upper grades were students of George Woodbury. He taught applied physics, chemistry levels one and two, and one ninth grade science class in the regular stream. Sadie was able to take an independent study for physics, because it would have been too peculiar to be his student.

She nodded as Dorothy, who was peeling back a con-tainer of yogurt, pointed Sadie towards the open door of the principal's office. Sadie poked her head inside.

"Hi, I need a note to get back to class and I was told I had to come see you?"

"Have a seat, Sadie," he said, and motioned towards the blue leather chair where students sat when they were getting disciplined or told bad news about a dead relative.

He had wispy graying-blond hair that fell below his ears and a face with subtle acne scars along his jaw. He was thin in a way that one assumed was his genetic destiny but still made his bones appear out of place. It occurred to Sadie that she had never really looked at him in the face for very long before. They regarded one another for a few seconds. He had several empty coffee cups on his otherwise empty desk.

"I'm worried about the stress you're under, because of what has happened," he said.

"I'm fine."

"And how is your mother getting along?"

She shrugged.

"I think you should see Mrs. Caribou," he said, reaching for a permission slip that he tore from a pink stack on his desk. Mrs. Caribou was the flaky guidance counselor, whom her father once referred to as a Jungian hack. Students always made fun of her matching cotton-knit sweater sets. If you got out of line in any way, the solution was to see the counselor, just as celebrities go to rehab any time they misbehave. Sadie had never had to see her. Everyone she knew who had experienced the pleasure essentially described it as a digging session to ensure you had no plans to shoot up the school.

"That won't be necessary."

"I'm requiring it," he said, writing out her slip and handing it across the desk. When she didn't take it, he thrust it impatiently in the air with a stabbing motion and she grabbed it.

"Dan," Sadie said. He bristled at his first name. "I've known almost every teacher at this school since I was in diapers. I've been to your summer cottages. I've seen you and coach Johnson drunk on tequila and singing 'Hotel California.' Don't pretend I'm just some regular student with a criminal father."

Dan paled. "Sadie, you really don't sound like yourself right now. I don't appreciate the tone that . . ."

Sadie folded the piece of paper in half and then quarters and slipped it into her blazer pocket.

Dorothy appeared in the doorway. "Sadie, darling," she said, "your father isn't a criminal. We have all loved your dad for a long time, and we will continue to support him through this." She dipped a spoon into her yogurt, holding it aloft while waiting for Sadie's reaction. Sadie stared awkwardly until Dorothy finally put the spoon in her mouth.

"Dot, we can't say that," said Dan in a stage whisper. "Don't put ideas in her head. This is a complicated legal situation."

Dorothy scraped her spoon along the bottom of the container and smiled wide, the kind of creepy clown smile you got from dental hygienists when you were a scared toddler. A Valium smile, Joan would have called it. "Your father has done so much for us at this school, and in this community. There is such a thing as innocent until proven guilty in this country, and I for one will not just stand by and watch someone we love get assassinated by the perverts in the media." Dorothy stormed out and went back to her adjoining office. When Obama was re-elected, Dorothy had cried for most of the day.

Dan looked down at his desk in a defeated fashion. "You can go, Sadie. I'm sorry you had to witness such unprofessional behavior."

"Again, 'Hotel California,' Dan."

"This is hard on all of us, and we want to support you and your family until the courts determine what to do."

It sounded like a line, and like he couldn't wait to get her out of the office. She could see that he wanted her whole family to move away so he could stop thinking about it.

"Anyway, you should start attending your advanced physics class with your father's replacement. Overseeing an independent study is not something we can ask of the new teacher, so you should be in room 306, okay?"

She nodded and exited the office, standing in the deserted main hallway.

"We'll be in court tomorrow," Dorothy called out when Sadie passed her door. "I'm organizing a large group of supporters."

Sadie didn't know what to say about this. Dorothy reached into her pocket and pulled out a postcard and handed it to her. It read *Men's Rights Under Attack* on one side and *Just Because You Regret It Doesn't Mean It's Rape.* There was a website at the bottom. Sadie made a face and handed it back.

Dorothy furrowed her brow. "Keep it. What's happening to your father is a symptom of what is wrong with young women today. Men are victimized, and no one cares. Does that sound right to you?"

"I guess not," Sadie mumbled. She curled the card up in her hand and shoved it in her kilt pocket before making her exit. She was expected in room 306, a class of about fifteen gifted students. She was second-last to arrive, making it just before Alison the pothead who smoked between every class, claiming it was for her ADHD. The teachers knew and didn't say anything. Sadie sat in the front, pulled out her peppermint lip balm, and applied it carefully in her pocket mirror, mostly for something to do. She and Amanda had made the lip balm together one afternoon in the winter, using essential oils and shea butter melted in the microwave. She saw others watching her in the mirror's reflection while she pursed her tingling lips, trying to look unbothered. It's any other day. Act like it's any other day.

George's replacement arrived, a dotty-looking bald man in a bad brown suit. He wrote *Mr. Taylor* in serial-killer script on the blackboard and moved the portable table with the laptop on it to the side of the room with a flourish, as though pushing aside the idea of interactive technology. He removed his suit jacket, which only served to confirm the pit stains Sadie knew would be there. She turned to look at her classmates, and they were almost all leaning forward like a pack of leopards getting ready to circle and attack from all angles.

In the middle of the teacher's mumbling introduction, Jonathan Moore stood up abruptly and cleared his throat. Jonathan was understood to be a kind of genius, socially isolated but seemingly uninterested in high school in that way anyway. If he'd had any proficiency in art, drama, or English, he would've matched Sadie's grade point average. George thought him exceptional, which was saying a lot considering he never spoke that way about his students. In public he would claim, "You can do anything you want to do!" and the students would smile bright, beaming tooth-filled symbols of their inner confidence. He considered it part of his job description to instill the anchors of self-esteem. At home he was more disparaging, admitting most kids weren't bound for greatness but conceding there was a kind of greatness in choosing to be ordinary as well.

George and Jonathan would often have lunch together

on the courtyard grass. Jonathan, who normally skirted the edges of the halls, lit up around her father. It was well known that he was a scholarship student who lived in an apartment above the Mac's Milk Mart with a disabled, housebound mother and a father who liked to sit on the back balcony and shoot at any pigeon or squirrel that dared to approach his Ford Explorer.

"This is bullshit. Mr. Woodbury was the best teacher in this whole mediocre school full of privileged assholes, and now we have to deal with you? Mr. Woodbury has been slaughtered by some gossip perpetrated by some fucking cheerleading sluts. This is not fair! You cannot even compare!"

The sub slammed his hand on the desk. "I won't tolerate that kind of language in my class. I understand the situation with Mr. Woodbury has been very stressful, and no doubt you are all feeling . . . so much . . . right now," he stammered, his brow growing sweaty. "But I will not tolerate this language in my class," he repeated, as if it were the language that was the problem.

"Punitive tactics will not work with this group. We are not ordinary students," Jonathan muttered.

Madeleine Stewart, who normally never spoke in class, stood up and turned towards Jonathan, arms crossed. "Jonathan, you don't, like, know the situation. I know you're grieving the loss of your mentor, but you have to consider how many students got hurt. This isn't some trivial debate about cheating on a test. This is a lawsuit, and it took a lot of guts for those girls to stand up after what happened and try to make it right. That took *guts*." Sadie wondered if it took the kind of guts Madeleine wished she'd had. This made her stomach turn.

"America is the most ridiculously litigious country. We sue someone for breathing on us. It is not meaningful!" Jonathan's voice was robotic, monotone, but forceful.

Sadie's hands began to tingle. A brief swirl of vertigo overtook her. She felt as though she was an ambassador from some appalling country, forced into the job and now having to defend where she came from. As Jonathan started in again, Sadie got up and walked out. As she walked, the room got quiet. She couldn't stand to hear another person debate whether or not her father had done any of the things he was rumored to have done. She didn't want to hear him defended. She didn't want to hear him torn up either.

If only she could have the privilege of believing him entirely. What kind of person, what kind of ungrateful daughter, doesn't believe her own father? She had never doubted him before. She never thought he was anything but moral and civilized. She wasn't even sure what those words meant. But if someone puts the possibility of something terrible in your head—and people around you believe it—you can't go back to thinking it completely inconceivable. The possibility is there whether or not you choose to believe it, and you can't go back to not knowing that the possibility exists.

IN THE THIRD-FLOOR GIRLS' bathroom, Sadie sat on the wooden window ledge holding a copy of *The Crying of Lot 49,* open to the same page she'd read eleven times. Of all the students in the building, it had to be Amanda who walked in. Amanda had been in accelerated classes but had dropped down to regular stream last year after a series of emotional breakdowns from the stress. She still came upstairs to skip class, especially when Sadie had her independent study, because she knew the area wasn't monitored.

"Sadie, fuck man, you've been avoiding me," she said, one hand on her hip, the other pulling a pack of Marlboros out of her uniform skirt. "I know your dad's a fucking perv and all, but you don't have to act like I'm dead."

Sadie laughed. "He's not! I don't know." She curled her book in her palm, looking at Amanda through the cylinder. "God, I just feel so terrible about . . . your sister."

"The bitch has never been so popular. Mom is letting her stay home for like the next week or two if she wants, and she can eat whatever she wants and we're like not allowed to get mad at her ever, and we all have to go to therapy."

"But is she okay?"

Amanda shrugged, lighting her cigarette. Sadie opened the bathroom window wide, propped it open with her math textbook, and stepped away so Amanda could blow the smoke outside. She hated secondhand smoke.

"I was reading some statistics?" Amanda started, her voice going up at the end of her sentences. "It is very rare that people lie about stuff like this. People just want to think they do, but why would they? Why bring all that scrutiny on yourself? It's not as though victims get justice most of the time."

A girl walked in, glaring at Amanda for smoking. They held eyes for a few seconds.

"Problem?"

The girl rolled her eyes and entered a stall, coughing dramatically.

Sadie stayed silent, rolling and unrolling the paperback.

"Of course, I already fucking know that, right?" Amanda continued, ignoring the girl but pushing the end of her cigarette into the green chipped paint beside the sink and running it under water. "Anton Chevalier raped me at that party last year, and everyone knows it. The whole party knew it—half the party fucking witnessed it. But do I get to stay home from school? No. Did I have to see him in gym class every Wednesday? Yeah. Does he have to go to jail? No. You can't throw a fucking rock around here without hitting some kind of rapist. It's like you have to be fifty years old in order for it to really matter."

"You could've gone to the police," Sadie offered, as she had the day after the party. Sadie had even sent an anonymous note to the police department on Amanda's behalf. No one did anything. It had been the first time in Sadie's life that what was good and true and fair didn't seem to matter.

"Right. 'So, how many wine coolers did you drink, Miss Mitchell? And we have several boys willing to share how many blow jobs you gave in the senior girls' bathroom in the ninth grade.' And then Dr. Chevalier would talk about Anton's exemplary grades. My life would have been over in even more ways than it already was. Not fucking worth it."

"Still," Sadie said gently, "we should be sticking up for each other, right?"

"Girls fuck each other over on the daily, Sadie."

"Yeah. You never told your mom, did you?"

"No, and now I can't ever. Can you imagine? It would kill her."

Sadie leaned into the mirror and was surprised to see she hadn't even attempted to put on any makeup this morning.

"Anyway, I'm sorry you're a social pariah right now."

"It seems selfish to worry about my own concerns, considering all that's going on. I just can't wait to get out of here. Be an adult and never come back."

"Amen, sister."

They linked arms and pushed their way through the girls' bathroom door, heading towards the lockers at the end of the hall. Melissa Greer and Teresa Brock paused in the process of putting up a poster for a school dance, stopped talking, and stared at them. As they passed, they heard the whispers. *Sick. Her own father. Trash.*

"Mind your own business, you cunty bitches!" yelled Amanda.

The poster seesawed through the air to the ground.

SADIE LEFT THROUGH THE front entrance, but paused on the landing when she noticed Dorothy with a group of parents and teachers at the front steps that led to the school's exit, blocking her way out. They were all wearing T-shirts that said *True Love Waits,* from the Abstinence Club. The fabric was stretched over their frumpy blouses and dresses, making the message hard to read. She bumped into a woman she surmised was a reporter at the top of the front steps with a photographer.

"We're trying to teach our girls to value their virtue," Dorothy was saying to the bewildered-looking reporter.

Sadie stood behind the reporter, hiding for a moment. She wore bright red tights and had thick black bangs, and she rolled her eyes to a fey photographer trying to take their photo. "This is just so tacky for a private school," she mumbled to him while writing a Tweet on her phone. "Is there a new breed of wealthy redneck now?" Sadie was squished in so close behind her she could smell her strawberry perfume and read everything she typed. She didn't want to make a noise and be noticed, but she couldn't turn around and go back inside.

The photographer snapped some photos, Sadie ducking her head down before he stopped to scroll. "Let's just file this and jet. I need a decent coffee."

The reporter looked up and locked eyes with Sadie as she snuck by them, trying not to draw attention to herself.

"Hey," she started softly, nudging the photographer with her hip to get his attention. "Are you by any chance the daughter?"

Sadie pushed her way down the stone steps and through the crowd of Dorothy's minions who'd begun their ascent.

"Can I just ask you one question? No photos, just one question!"

Sadie started running and jumped on her bike as if the school had just exploded.

7

ANDREW DECIDED TO TAKE A TWO-WEEK LEAVE FROM work. He called the office from where he lay on the dock after seeing Stuart. They were under-standing—he knew they would be—but he still felt guilty. Now what? What was logical? What was right? A dock spider popped up between two of the planks of wood. He stared at it as though daring it to move close to him, and it did. It touched his leg before he was rattled enough to pull off his sandal and snuff out its life.

He dipped his sandal in the water and scrolled to Jar-ed's name in his contact list, where he was listed under ICE for *In Case of Emergency—Partner.* He paused, pressed Details and scrolled through all the photos they'd sent each other over the last few months, then pocketed his phone again. If he invited Jared to come to Woodbury Lake, he would close up shop and be there in a matter of hours, selflessly preparing healthy meals, doling out hugs, taking care of everyone. His presence would make the calamity real and feel more than temporary.

The lake was choppy, no boats making their rounds. He pulled out the phone again and sent Jared a text. *I miss you.* It was both sincere and meant to keep him at bay for a few more hours.

It didn't feel like the right time to start integrating Jared into life in Avalon Hills, not when everyone was still in crisis mode. The house, however large, felt full of people and pressed tight with anxious energy. Sometimes it is easier to be alone in these situations. Having Jared there would mean Andrew would have to answer the question "How are you holding up?" truthfully.

He went back inside when he knew his mother and aunt would be gone for at least an hour. He made a strong pot of coffee, unable to get the picture of Alan Chambers bragging about his children out of his head. In New York you could be in your thirties, living an exciting life, and not be seen as a failure for not having a family. In Avalon Hills having children was just what you did if you stayed in town. Most of his graduating class hadn't stayed, of course. They'd gone on to be lawyers, policy-makers, congressmen, researchers, journalists, and doctors. A few of his theater buddies had had small parts in television shows or films. The handful who remained were mostly from the public school.

ANDREW WATCHED SADIE AS she ambled down the stone path and kicked off her flip-flops when she reached the dock. She handed him a mug.

"Your hair is a nightmare," Andrew said, taking a sip.

"Well, surprisingly, my conditioning regime hasn't exactly been my first priority today."

"I didn't get a chance to ask you, are you still queen of the jocky student council cabal? Spitting on the minions?"

"We're not like that," she said, turning to look at him. "Nobody bullies anymore. I'm serious! We have assemblies about bullying. Poster campaigns. We turn our frustration inward now. How's the loving and morally upstanding world of corporate law?"

"I've switched over, actually. I've been hired on at a civil firm."

"How I manage to excel in your shadow is really quite stunning of me."

"Agreed," he said.

They sipped their coffee, dipping their feet in the water.

"What the fuck is happening, Andrew? I don't know what to do."

"We can't do much right now except wait. But we're going to get through this as a family."

"I haven't spoken to him," Sadie said, looking ahead again. She wanted to, but something stopped her. "I told Mom I'd go with her to visit him if he wasn't released right after the hearing. But I'm nervous about seeing him."

"It's normal to feel nervous, but it's just discomfort, and you can ride out discomfort. This is the first big trauma you've ever had to endure, really. Well, besides that whole guy-with-a-gun thing. But you didn't really know what was happening then, right?"

"Right. I guess. But what if he's guilty, Andrew? What

if he did those things?" She said it really fast, as if trying to race through the possibility of it being true.

Andrew zipped up his hooded sweatshirt. It snagged. "That is not the right attitude to have. First of all, you don't really know. It could be some sort of conspiracy born of small-town idiocy and girls wanting to blame their daddy issues and the fact that they aren't getting straight As on someone, so they take it out on a friendly, harmless man, someone who has always been encouraging and openhearted, and they figure they can crush him." He finally freed the fabric from the metal pull and zipped up. "Maybe he had an affair with one of the older girls. It is not the first time something like that has happened."

"An adult cannot have a consensual affair with a student. It is a factual, moral, fucking *legal* impossibility. You should know the law."

"I'm not talking legal. I'm saying that younger and older people can both be willing partners. How else do you explain that my first boyfriend was twenty-five when I was seventeen?"

"Who was your first boyfriend? You didn't come out until college!"

"Coach Johnson."

"No way! He is gross. Don't even joke."

"He was hot back then. There was only eight years' difference between us—that's less than Mom and Dad. Happens all the time."

"You know that's not what we are talking about. This is different."

"Because it's girls?"

"Because the age difference is much greater, and because someone—many someones—are *saying* there was a crime. You are blaming the victims here."

"I think that is very simplistic and moralistic."

"Sexism. Perhaps you've heard of it?"

"I'm not some right-wing monster, but there's a lot of sexual puritanism and denial around these parts. I should know."

"And maybe it was different because you were boys. It's not like the town is crawling with gay men."

"You would be surprised how many 'straight men' are lurking around in the parks, still wearing their wedding rings. I chose Stuart and pursued him because he was hot. I wore *him* down. Teenagers have sexual lives, Sadie. I know the Church and politicians—pretty much the same camps—around here think they can legislate it away, but teenagers will always have sex, because they can and because they want to."

"You can be as sexually liberated as you want to be, but the point is people have to *both* want to be doing it—otherwise it's a crime. Sex is sex. Crime is crime."

"I'm just saying not every situation is black and white."

"I think men always think that."

"When did you become such a feminist?"

Sadie swirled the coffee in her cup, took a sip. "I've always been a feminist. I just don't use the word much because people lose all their rational thinking skills when I do."

"The point is, this is our father you're talking about."

"I know, it's different. It doesn't make sense."

"You owe him your loyalty. When something like this

happens, you circle the wagons around your family. It's just what you do."

"Now who is sounding archaic?"

"That's just the way it is."

"I don't know. I feel bad for him. I feel huge guilt even contemplating that he's not innocent. But this shouldn't be about loyalty—it should be about the truth and honesty."

Andrew snorted. "If you really think our legal system is about honesty, you've got a lot to learn, little brain."

"That makes me very sad for you," Sadie said. "I thought you became a lawyer to do good in this world."

"This thing will be over soon. I read some statistics last night and the majority of these types of cases are thrown out for lack of reliable evidence, especially when the accused is a good citizen like Dad. It's all 'he said versus she said,' no hard evidence. It looks suspicious. We'll go back to the way things were, and you'll be out of this town soon, and Mom and Dad will go on their trip to Europe, and next year it will just be something we never talk about."

"As much as that sounds lovely, Andrew, I have to say that I completely disagree with you. Dad is fucked. We're fucked. Hasn't it totally shattered your image of him?"

He shook his head.

"I agree with you that he'll probably get off—only six percent of rapists actually ever spend a day in jail in the United States, and he's only accused of impropriety and attempted rape—but that doesn't mean things aren't totally, irrevocably changed."

"When did you become so Rain Man about statistics?"

"It turns out my memory is excellent. Mom got me tested."

He reached out and squeezed her shoulder. "Fuck that school," he said in his teenaged voice. "Take a break for a while. Catch your breath."

Sadie reached into her kilt pocket and pulled out the weird postcard Dorothy had given her from the men's rights group. Andrew read it, sneered.

"This is some end-of-the-world shit," Andrew said. "They look like wing-nuts, but I'm betting they're more powerful than we know. 'Save George Woodbury,'" he read. "This isn't good. We need to make sure people know that our father is a reasonable man, who loves and supports women and their autonomy, and isn't some crazy woman-hater like these insane people."

"But you kind of sound like them, a bit. Automatically assuming the girls are lying."

"No, I don't. I'm not denying women are harassed and assaulted. I'm just saying that Dad deserves fairness and the benefit of the doubt, and that it is possible that there is some sort of framing angle, that's all. I'm not making some pronouncement about gender," he said, getting up and throwing the rest of his coffee in the lake.

8

KEVIN ARRIVED HALF AN HOUR EARLY TO MEET HIS agent at Café Mogador in the East Village. He ordered a soda water with a wedge of lime from a tall, busty waitress in a blue A-line dress, a bird print circling the hem. It was technically lunchtime, but he couldn't eat. He sat on the slim patio that edged onto the sidewalk of St. Mark's, watching some children file out of a private school that looked like all the other tenement buildings on the block save for a small sign with the academy's name. He was too nervous. His usual waitress here had been a fan. Angela with the baby bangs and the bob haircut always scrawled a heart on the bottom of his receipts with her phone number. He really wanted to see her today, because her delight in him buoyed his spirits. The busty waitress hardly glanced at him at all.

Everyone walking down the street was alone, walking dogs and talking on phones, carrying yoga mats. A man in a linen suit leaned against a car, yammering to the air.

Twenty-something NYU students sat on benches outside the pudding shop, gesturing with their plastic spoons. Why were there suddenly restaurants that only served one thing? This neighborhood had been cool and a bit dangerous when he was a teenager. He'd lived in Alphabet City for a year after his first book came out and he'd had a residency in the city. It still thrilled him to be here, and part of him wished he could have stuck it out. At the time it had been too expensive to contemplate living here, which was laughable, looking back, considering how much more expensive it was now. He appreciated how individualistic Manhattan was, that you could eat in a restaurant here by yourself and no one would bat an eye. The suburbs looked upon solitude with suspicion. People sat in groups even when they had nothing interesting to say to each other.

It had been a year since he'd met up with his agent, who'd canceled their last two meetings. He was ten minutes late, no doubt a symbol of the recent shift in their power dynamics. In Kevin's plaid canvas messenger bag were 287 pages of a new manuscript that Kevin knew didn't "shine" the way it was supposed to. It was a contemplative novel written in a lyrical style, mostly about the meaning of death and consumer culture, that he had grown bored with writing nearly three months ago. He wrote and rewrote the sex scene between the professor and his intern, but that was all he could do. Those were the three pages he'd offer as "sneak peaks" at reading events, and they'd been published in an issue of *Tin House,* which generated a lot of interest. But that was three years ago now, and no one was offering anymore. For the last two weeks Kevin had been spending his afternoons watching DVDs of television box sets, staying up late at night, staring at the manuscript, unable to see how it might be improved.

Elaine's career as a professor, a job Kevin used to think of as the worst kind of prison, began to look like a comfort. He'd done a few stints as an adjunct professor teaching creative writing, but he mostly hated it. Every terrible-student story felt like an insult, and their unwillingness to edit, or read challenging books, and their desperation to publish—it was too much to take. He'd turned down most offers when they came in. He hated to admit, even to himself, that he was sniffing around for contracts again. When he confessed he was open to teaching jobs, that he needed some stability, Elaine had joked dryly, "Welcome to adulthood. We've been expecting you for twenty years." He had one thousand dollars left from his last book advance. The new manuscript was two years overdue for delivery.

"You've got to get back to the essential Kevin that characterized the first few books," his agent had written in his last email. "*Reread them.* Then go for a long hike, connect with people, get out of that suburban house that seems to be ruining your creativity. Have an affair! Just shake it up, somehow. You're not that twenty-six-year-old genius-to-watch anymore. You've got to write a serious novel worthy of attention."

The trouble was, Kevin was battling a feeling that was much more serious than the question of whether geographical banality might be ruining his creativity. He was feeling as though perhaps it was true, that he only had one great book in him and it had been published a decade ago. Every sentence he wrote felt leaden and embarrassing. New novels were coming out every month that were innovative and fresh and written by twenty-three-year-old graduates of MFA programs whose only publishing credits were in *The New Yorker*. They made the same lists that he had made ten years ago, those dreadful "Hot Under-40" lists that were both meaningless and career-defining.

A patch of eczema on his foot itched—it flared up only when he was stressed out—and he longed to be able to scratch it. Instead, he banged his foot against the table leg and sighed, spearing the lime wedge with his straw. He watched the waitress lean over an older male customer and touch his shoulder. He remembered this tactic from when he was a bartender; light touching meant higher tips. She stayed leaning. He could see the top of a black push-up bra. He tried to remember the last time he had had sex with Elaine. They'd become like siblings; lately, she bristled when he touched her. He'd been falling asleep on the couch a lot. "We'll get back on track," she had said. "All relationships go through ups and downs." He knew this, but he still felt helpless to change it.

Kevin scanned his Twitter feed on his phone. He'd been semi-flirting with a young novelist from LA via article retweets and quips on events of the day. He was scanning her feed when one news headline caught his eye: AVALON HILLS TEACHER ARRESTED FOR SEXUAL INDECENCY CHARGES. He clicked on it lazily as he sipped the last of his drink and looked over at the clock, reasoning a crime story in Avalon Hills was a rarity to say the least. When he saw George Woodbury's name in the lead, he choked on the last of his soda water.

He texted Elaine, chewing on the straw. *Did you hear about George W.?*

Kevin sat with the shock of it while waiting to hear back. She was in class, she taught back to back until eight at night, so he couldn't just call.

The waitress approached to pick up his glass. "Another?" She brushed against his shoulder. It worked, he reasoned. He felt a connection that he knew wasn't actually there.

"I'll have a pint of whatever you have that's light, actually. And the hummus with pita."

When she handed it to him, lightly touching his index finger as though by accident, he took a sip of the froth and a feeling came over him he hadn't felt in a very long time. He took a small notebook out of his bag, the kind of notebook he insisted all of his writing students keep with them every day, and which he hadn't written in for six months. He'd filled two pages with a passionate, impulsive scrawl by the time Elaine responded to his text. *I'm hearing about it now. Jimmy asked if Sadie could move in for a while. I said yes. I hope you don't mind.*

TEN MINUTES LATER, HIS agent arrived, apologized too many times to be sincere, and ordered a Turkish coffee while locking eyes with the waitress a little longer than was necessary. She snapped her gum and made sure he was the first one to break the stare before she turned away. His agent laughed and turned his attention back to Kevin.

"You look well, Kevin," he said. "A young intern was very excited that I was meeting with you today. Seems your first book *changed her life* in high school," he said.

Kevin marveled, as usual, at his agent's silver hair,

every strand shining in a puffy pompadour, a visible manifestation of his personality. Was it possible that Kevin used to like this man? Respect him?

"I never get tired of hearing that," Kevin joked, running his hands through his own hair nervously, pulling some strands forward to hide what he thought was a receding hairline. Lately these compliments only served to cement his feelings of emerging obscurity. He had gone from "most promising" to "over the hill" without stopping on success mountain. He had no other skills, he fretted. What on earth could he do for work? Kevin finished the last sip of his pint. Why didn't he learn a trade? Could he go to carpentry school now, or was his back too injured? He couldn't risk losing his fingers in case he ever had a good idea again.

Good ideas seemed as far away as good, nonmarital sex.

"So, did you bring the manuscript?"

"I didn't," Kevin said.

His agent frowned, looked out at St. Mark's Place as though scanning for a cab.

"Because I have a new idea," Kevin said, shaking his hands around like he was on a game show. The waitress placed the coffee in front of his agent with a little too much force.

Kevin pulled out his notebook and flattened the lined pages down on the table. His agent picked up the copper carafe, poured the coffee into his cup, and swirled it around, annoyed. A girl walked by in bright green booty shorts, holding hands with a flustered-looking man in horn-rimmed glasses. They were walking a giant bulldog.

"Like I said, you're a very smart girl," he was saying to her. She looked at her phone and then off into the distance as the man kept talking. Kevin and his agent both stared as they made their way down the street.

"So, hit me," his agent said.

Kevin looked down at the notes, barely decipherable. His anxiety about his career had tipped over into *fuck it* territory. It could not possibly get worse, so who cares? Kevin ran his fingers along the paper and heard himself outline the project that hadn't existed before he ordered his first drink, making it up as he went along. His agent nodded, first warily, then curiously, then emphatically.

"Kevin, you little shithead, I could sell that on the idea alone! It's topical, it's based on real life, it's a fucking genius idea."

Kevin nodded, flushed with the energy coursing through his body. He curled the notebook up, holding it in his fist. The schoolchildren cheered across the street.

"I think this may call for some champagne, no?" he said, laughing.

The waitress obliged with a bottle served on ice and two tall glasses. Kevin gulped the first glass down, shocked that he had somehow saved himself. By his second glass he felt the balm of his arrogance returning, like a sly old lover slipping him a hotel key card.

Kevin left the meeting with a slight buzz and instructions to write a two-page synopsis that would go out to publishers the following week. He walked north on First Avenue feeling drunk and high on his own ambition. He bought a copy of a Lorrie Moore book from the guy selling them on the sidewalk at East Tenth. He felt as though he could run away from his life in Avalon Hills and make up for the years of banal drudgery and failure. If his next book was successful, maybe he could move back to the city.

He wrote the pitch on his iPad on the train back to Avalon Hills. The ride, normally three hours, passed in a flash. He sent the proposal, arriving home with a few hours to spare before the family would return.

The house was empty. He poured himself another drink. He wished he had someone to high-five.

9

JOAN, CLARA, AND BENNIE SAT IN A CUBICLE AT THE First National Bank, on plush ergonomic office chairs upholstered in uniform beige that reminded Joan of the hospital. Across the desk was a pretty South Asian woman named Mary, wearing a blinding red blouse that was giving Joan a headache. Mary was smiling at her in a pained, pitying way as she clicked on her keyboard and stared at the computer screen. She could be surfing Facebook for all Joan knew.

Bennie sat beside them, clicking on his iPhone, rubbing his left foot with his right. Joan had a motherly urge to tap his leg and insist that he stop fidgeting. Above Mary's head were posters of happy bank customers, living various dreams of financial security. One couple stood on a beach, another in front of their first home.

Like many of the tasks required of Joan since the arrest, this one involved what seemed like an endless amount of waiting and personal discomfort.

Mary turned the computer on its swivel stand and tapped her pen at a number.

"This is the balance of George's account," she said.

The number was so far below what she'd assumed that her voice made a sound she'd never heard before; it was the sound of trying to speak and nothing coming out. Not even a whisper. Mary looked oblivious. After all, this could be a tidy sum to Joan.

"Where has his money gone?" she wondered aloud. "Are you certain?"

Mary turned the screen back and tapped away at the keyboard. She paused. "Yes. His other accounts are frozen. The family trust money cannot be accessed until it comes to term, so that should be reassuring. This is the money that is available to you, as his wife."

"Perhaps this is just the tip of the iceberg," Clara said gently. "Maybe there are other things that you don't know."

Mary looked at them helplessly, aware now of what was happening. Joan picked up the container of hand sanitizer on the desk and pumped it once into her palm. She felt the beginnings of what could best be called catastrophic humiliation and bewilderment as she rubbed her hands together, wriggling her fingers as the alcohol dried, the smell making her nauseated.

"Can you double-check the balance of my account?" she asked, even though she knew what it was, and Sadie had just taught her how to check her balance at home online. She was second-guessing everything. She rubbed at her eyes wearily, the sanitizer causing them to sting. "And our joint checking account, the trust account for my daughter, Sadie, that her grandparents left for her."

Joan always thought that her savings were modest in comparison with Woodbury money, but she felt secure with it. The joint checking account was also relatively modest, as every month money was transferred from George's savings account with the excellent interest rate, so that they could maximize savings.

Or so she had thought.

"If I can't pay his bail tomorrow, what do I do?"

"You'll get a bail bond if you have to," Bennie said.

Joan made a face. Mary looked embarrassed to be overhearing this conversation, twirling a gold wedding ring around in circles.

"People will probably think you're being strong if you don't," said Clara. "Or cruel. It definitely appears as though you're rolling in it."

"I'm not mortgaging the house, and I'm not cashing in Sadie's college money or her trust fund. My retirement is off limits. I don't want to do anything rash because, come on"—she looked at both of them—"this is going to be over soon. For god's sake, this is just a weird roadblock. They won't find him guilty. George isn't a monster."

Joan was aware of airing her laundry in a public place, in front of a stranger, in a room full of people who had read the morning's paper. She stared up at the photo of the couple on the beach. The gray-haired woman was barefoot, smugly sunk into the sand with triumph. Joan stood up and excused herself, walking through the near-empty bank and out to the street. She held back her tears until her hand pressed against the automatic door, and she was sobbing by the time she held the door awkwardly for an elderly woman coming in, balancing on a cane. The woman had a face like her late mother, and when she smiled, Joan sobbed more.

Joan's mother had always taught her to be practical and save a percentage of every paycheck, but the money that allowed her to feel as though nothing was ever impossible— that was the Woodbury money, the money she assumed would be there forever. Joan cursed herself for not paying more attention, for thinking that everything would always be fine.

Clara and Bennie joined her on the street, led her to Bennie's Lexus in the parking lot. He drove silently on to the small municipal jail where George was being held until the hearing. When he pulled into a spot, Joan put her hand out and touched his arm.

"Did you know, Bennie, about the money?"

"No, no, I didn't."

"Where could it have gone? I know how much we had when we got married, I've checked it over the years. It's practically gone."

"Thirty years ago a lot of money was quite a different amount, and our memories, you know, don't stay the same. Plus all the trust funds are still there, for the kids at twenty-five, thirty-five, and yours. You'll still get more when you retire, of course. If you, uh, stay together."

Clara snorted in the backseat, opening her door. "I think you need to remember, Joan: Bennie is George's lawyer, not yours."

Bennie ignored Clara's comment and led them to the front door, holding it open for them. The Avalon Hills police station looked a lot like the post office that neighbored it—standard bureaucratic decor, unchanged in generations. Joan had been here once, for what she couldn't remember. They talked to the front desk clerk, who signed them in. "The mayor is in with him now. It will be a few minutes," the clerk said.

"The *mayor*?" Clara said.

"They're old friends," explained Joan. "Their families go way back, generations, in fact." After a few more stale minutes she began to resent the mayor, taking up George's time when his family was waiting. When the mayor came out, his voice boomed her name across the room, and he held his arms outstretched for a hug.

"This is just awful, Joannie, just awful. We'll get it sorted."

She pulled back and looked at him, his face red from a drink or two at lunch, his hair a uniform silver, stiff with product. "Thanks so much," she said, unsure if she really felt appreciative.

Clara was bug-eyed at this, incredulous. "It's not a traffic ticket," she muttered under her breath as the mayor walked away. She grabbed Joan's hand as they waited. They were going in first, and then Bennie would meet with him privately.

When she finally got into the meeting room, Joan was surprised to see that it was nothing like on TV—no glass partition, no shackles. It was a simple room with a table and three chairs, with a uniformed policeman at the door. George wore the same clothes.

"Oh, Joan, I have never been so happy to see you in all of my life," he said, embracing her in a hug. When they pulled back, he looked to Joan's sister. "Thanks so much for being here for us, Clara. It means a lot."

"We have a lot of questions for you, George," Clara said evenly, as she sat down across from him.

"I didn't do it. It's all lies. All of it. Someone is out to get me. You know me. You know I'm not like that."

"Why would anyone want to do this to you?" Joan fought to keep her voice steady.

"I haven't a clue, Joan. I haven't a clue. I've never hurt anyone in my life, you know that, right? I'm not a *pervert*."

Joan nodded, didn't say anything out loud.

"The bail, has Bennie spoken to you about that?"

"We're about to talk about it. Your personal assets have been seized. I still have my accounts, and a portion of our shared money. I'm not sure how I'm going to do it, unless I take a mortgage out on the house, and I couldn't do that."

"There's the children's trusts."

"George . . ." She took a deep breath. "Legally, the trusts can't be touched. And you are innocent and this will all be undone shortly. We can't go broke in the meantime." She wasn't sure she believed her own words but knew that they would help the situation. In her mind all that she had access to was their shared emergency money, their money to use in retirement when her nurses' pension paid out something comparable to welfare. She didn't tell him what she had found out. Yet something clicked in her gut that said *something isn't right*. But that's all she could decipher. Not *what* wasn't right, but that something wasn't adding up. For the first time in almost thirty years of marriage she questioned how well she knew the man she'd shared a bed with since she was practically a girl.

"I need to know . . ." she began, hesitating. "I need to know why those girls said what they did. All of them.

Some of them don't even *know* each other, George. Why would they all be lying? *Why?*" Her voice came out like a strangle. She didn't want to bring up what had happened at the bank. The possibility of what it meant kept her from mentioning it just then.

"I haven't the foggiest, Joan. I really don't know. I feel like I'm in a nightmare, a conspiracy, that everyone is suddenly against me."

"Tell her the fucking truth, George," Clara insisted.

"Clara . . ." Joan said. "Let him talk." She was surprised by the desperation in her voice, the only time she'd heard it like that outside the hospital, where it came in handy when motivating a patient to calm down.

"I've been framed, Joan."

Joan wanted to believe him. There were so many details, specific details, compelling details. But who was she to trust? The man who had never let her down, not even once, in their entire marriage? The one who promised to love her, grow old with her? Or faceless police and children she didn't raise?

They were silent for nearly a minute before she blurted out, "Why is there so much money missing from our bank account?"

George withdrew his hand and rubbed it along his jawline. "What do you mean?"

"I just came from the bank. There is significantly less than I expected."

"That's because I moved some money into investments, trying to maximize what we had. I didn't tell Bennie. I'll let him know."

"What investments?"

"Honey, you're asking a lot of me to remember all these details right now. I'm in *jail*. We'll figure out your money questions when I'm out, okay? We'll be fine. We always are. Money isn't an issue."

The guard at the door motioned to them that their time was up.

"What is the mayor going to do for you?" Joan asked as she stood.

"I don't know," George said, "but he'll do what he can. He's promised. He trusts me."

Joan reached out and grabbed his hand. Clara was already outside, waiting by the locked exit door. Joan squeezed his hand and his eyes lined with tears.

"I love you, my Joannie."

She turned and left, chest heavy, axis off-kilter. One eye seemed more open than the other, and she felt as though she were on a boat, the floor moving uncontrollably.

Joan loved to be in control. She could orchestrate and delegate and be a leader. This was the first time in years she wished someone could just tell her what to do, what was right. She wasn't able to understand and then organize her thoughts and make a plan. She got back into Bennie's car. He drove fast. *Why does everyone think they're in a race? It's so aggravating, nauseating.* She gripped the edge of her seat when he turned the corners too quickly. The heat was on so high she thought she might throw up.

"Can you let me out, please?" Her voice came out in a squeak. Bennie was startled and pulled over to the gravel shoulder.

"Are you sure, Joan? It's still quite a ways."

"I'll come with you," Clara said, unbuckling her seat belt.

"No, I need to be alone," she said, exiting the car, taking deep inhales of fresh air. Maybe she'd go into the woods and burrow there. Maybe that's what she needed. Her head was a thick ball of yarn. She walked down into the ditch and up the other side, pressing her fingers into the tiny rocks to help herself up. She was a few rows of trees in when she was startled by a red fox that darted past. She held on to the trunk of a teenaged maple and caught her breath. She pulled away some bark, dug a heel into the dirt, gently and then forcefully making a hole.

JOAN GOT HOME AN hour later. To avoid reporters, she'd gone to the public dock behind the Coffee Hut and taken one of the tourist rowboats. John, who manned the dock, waved from his chair inside the little hut where he spent most of his days in the off-season. She yelled that she'd return it, and he nodded. She rowed slowly around the curve of the lake, close to shore, before tying off at her own dock. She walked barefoot up the hill, startling Andrew, who was looking out the kitchen window. She put her shoes back on and let the cat inside the back door.

Andrew was sitting in the kitchen with Clara.

"Where the hell have you been?"

"I took the rowboat home," she said, noticing that Clara was fixating on his laptop. She walked over to read the headline on a blog: PERVERSION RUNS IN THE FAMILY.

"You can't just take off right now, Mom. We were getting worried."

"What are you reading?"

Andrew turned the laptop away. "Don't bother."

"No, I need to know everything."

He turned the screen to face her.

Infamous high school teacher George Woodbury's son attended Avalon Hills preparatory school and started a gay-straight alliance club while protesting the school's reluctance to allow him to bring a male companion to the prom. Former school secretary Milicent Yardrow told the press it was believed Andrew's opinions were tolerated because of the Woodburys' long-standing financial support of the school. He has since graduated from NYU law school, with a thesis exploring legal issues surrounding the decriminalization of prostitution in America. "I think leftist kooks like this family can hide in all of their money," said the president of the Values Council.

"Values Council? How did these types of organizations gain credibility?"

Clara nodded her head. "Totally. Thank god you got out of this town, Andrew."

A megaphone outside yelled, "Can we speak to the son? Is Andrew Woodbury there? Just a few questions and we'll leave you alone."

"No, they won't," said Clara, continuing to tear up a head of slightly wilting lettuce. "Don't speak to the press at all. They will spin you all to hell, as evidence." She held up the paper and read, " 'Wife Joan Woodbury is a nurse at the Avalon Hills trauma center and is a respected member of the community. But how could a wife of over twenty years not know her husband's predilections?'"

"Stop reading, Clara," Joan said.

"I think the only way to deal with this is to look at it as a problem we need to solve," Andrew said.

"It's not like we're capable of being objective," said Clara.

"But you can hear the facts, or what appear to be the facts, and have an instinct. And I understand that all human beings are capable of exercising bad judgment, of behaving immorally. Dad is not exempt from that reality, but I'm too astonished by this. It's *too* odd."

Joan leaned against the kitchen cabinets, her chest filling with what felt like sparks of hope. If Andrew, someone with a complicated understanding of criminology and the law, in addition to loving and knowing his father, could feel this, then maybe she wasn't deluded. His stance fueled her intense leanings towards denial, already ripe for expansion. She and Andrew would fight this.

"What did the bank say?" Andrew asked.

"He'll have to stay in jail until the trial. We're broke," she said. "Basically, we're fucking broke, and I have no idea why."

Andrew ran his hand under his chin for a moment. "I have the money. I'll get him out. I just have to call my broker."

Joan shook her head. "No, Andrew. That money is for your future, and I won't allow it."

"He could be in for a long time. I can't let him stay there."

"How long could it be? He's innocent."

Clara, holding a glass of red wine, went outside. Andrew joined her and they watched the sun sink behind the mountains across the lake. Joan sat at the kitchen table making lists of things to get done, anchored by tasks, her jaw clenching and toes tapping against the floor.

MONDAY EVENING

10

ANDREW HALF-HEARTEDLY SCOOPED THE WINGED IN-
sects and various detritus floating atop the pool
with a long net, banging the metal pole against the
grass to empty it. Clara watched, holding a glass of wine,
taken from a bottle in the off-limits cellar in the basement.

"I don't know how to help your mom, kid," Clara said
to Andrew, who paused mid-skim to look at her and then
kept at it. "Joan is usually the one conspiring to help *me*
out." She laughed. "I'm not sure what anyone can do for
her that will make any difference."

"When Jared's dad died, he said the most appreciated
thing was when friends would offer to do things like laundry or cooking, things that you lose the ability to care
about in the face of grief," Andrew said, putting the skimming tool on the grass and joining her at the edge of the
pool. He took off his shoes and socks, and dipped both
feet in.

"I can't imagine Joan letting anyone else do the laundry." Clara laughed. "She'd re-fold everything."

Andrew laughed.

They could hear the slow lap of the waves against the shoreline below them. They watched in silence as a fat raccoon climbed the oak tree and sat chewing on a stalk of broccoli retrieved from the Henshaws' trash next door.

"What are you planning to do about work?" Clara asked.

"I took a few weeks' leave. You can't really be there half-time. I took a medical leave, actually. Stress."

"No kidding. Will Jared be joining you?"

"He wants to come down this weekend to help out."

The raccoon climbed down the tree and ambled towards them on the grass, climbing up the steps of the patio.

"Hey, little fella . . ." Clara called, raising her glass in a cheers. She turned back to Andrew. "You've got balls. Might be nice to have someone around who isn't losing their shit all the time."

Andrew shrugged.

Clara's BlackBerry rang, and she answered an email before setting it down on the end table between them. "You know what I think we need to do, Andrew?"

"What?"

"Dance it off!" She sat up straight and stretched out her arms. "I usually go to yoga every morning, and I haven't moved a muscle since we got here." She got up and twirled around like a little girl, scaring the raccoon back onto the grass at the base of the tree. He turned and looked at them again, got up on his haunches.

Andrew laughed. "Are you serious?"

"Why not?"

"Might be better to go for a hike or something. We're in *Avalon Hills*. The only thing around here are square dance classes—could be kind of kitschy?"

"I seem to remember you were a secret regular at that club in Woodbridge, no? A little house mix of Gloria Gaynor? Come on!"

LATER THAT EVENING, THEY parked Joan's car in the dimly lit lot outside Icons! bar, where Andrew hadn't been in over a decade. Icons! was a purple cement block on the edge of a strip mall on Highway 2, just outside Woodbridge, and was the least iconic place Andrew could imagine. No sign or advertisements announced it was a gay bar, or any kind of bar at all. Inside it smelled just as he remembered: beer, settled-in sweat, and cologne. It sounded the same too: low, pulsing house music, ten years outdated, on a tinny system. There was a bar along one side of the cavernous main room; the walls, floor, and ceiling were painted black, except for one length of floor-to-ceiling mirrors. Tacky all-season Christmas lights were strung under the bar and around a small DJ booth. There was a disco ball that had seen better days, but it continued to move in an endless optimistic twirl.

BEING AT A GAY bar with Clara was nostalgic in and of itself. When Andrew was young, Clara was his stepping-stone to the gay world. She was a staple on the 1990s New York City party scene. She used to joke that she hardly knew any straight men, a scandalous thing to say in front of Andrew's grandparents at Thanksgiving dinner. She would breeze into family gatherings hours late wearing bright purplish lipstick and gaudy, shining scarves, and she never wore practical footwear. Even as a toddler he was drawn to her every movement. Joan used to joke that he learned to walk one day when Clara was visiting, for the express purpose of following her around the house. She would sit on the dock in heeled sandals with an oversized sun hat while everyone else was in flip-flops and cutoff shorts. "I don't need my own kid, you'll be my little minion forever, won't you, Andrew?" she'd say, happy to sit at one of his many tea parties, taking tiny sips of water from his carefully presented cups.

WHEN ANDREW WAS TWELVE or thirteen, Clara started giving him mixed tapes and CDs of music that his parents would never have introduced him to—the Bronski Beat, Depeche Mode, the Pet Shop Boys—coded musical messages he was still too young to recognize. Then she began bringing soundtracks to Broadway musicals and old-school punk music, with little messages on the covers like "Listen to the lyrics—there's some revolution in there!" with a luminescent lipstick kiss and "Love, your old auntie!" scrawled at the bottom of the track listing. In a town that loved the Spin Doctors and whatever happened to be on the radio, Clara was Andrew's window to culture beyond the borders of Avalon Hills.

While George and Joan were nonchalant about his sexual orientation, vaguely uninterested almost, Clara actively encouraged him to "let the freak flag fly"—her words—as soon as he was old enough to come to the city by himself. She would take him to edgy art gallery openings, plays, and restaurants, dressing him all in black and putting gel in his hair. They'd eat ice cream in the park and watch boys and she'd introduce him to her friends, who seemed to always be elegant gay men, and their female best friends. The men would fawn over him like he was a bunny, and that admiration made him able to go back to Avalon Hills for another few months and survive it all. By the time he was sixteen, she was sneaking him into clubs with her and they would dance until dawn, something they didn't confide to Joan.

One of Andrew's most cherished memories was of the summer he was fifteen years old. It was a particularly difficult year, and Clara insisted that he come to visit one day earlier than his family for their annual New York City trip. When he arrived at the train station, she was waiting with an ugly plastic rainbow necklace that she insisted on putting around his neck despite his protestations, and they got on the subway and then emerged out onto the street, where she screamed, "Surprise! It's your first Pride parade!" He still had defensive bruises on his hands from fighting off Kenny and Bruce Shea in the latest locker room incident, and when Clara spun him around to look at the crowd of people celebrating what those guys had beat him up for, he actually started to cry like a confused, feral child. "Oh, baby," Clara said, giving him a hug. "This weekend, I'm going to make you forget that terrible little town you live in."

He met a group of boys his age in the parade and Clara handed him her apartment key and a clump of bills, and made him write "I will not take any pills and I will always use a condom" on a piece of paper and sign it before she let him go. He laughed because the idea of needing a condom seemed insane to him. He ended up dancing outside until the sun came up, and making out with another shy, geeky kid named Brian from Long Island, who came back and slept on Clara's couch. It remained one of his most tender memories of adolescence, alongside the times he spent with Stuart.

Until he told his sister, Clara was the only one he'd ever told about Stuart.

ANDREW RECOGNIZED THE BARTENDER, slicing up limes on the counter, as the New Wave guy who used to work the door when he was young. The room was pretty empty except for two tables of regulars and one lone, elderly leather daddy showing off his moves in the middle of the small dance floor. The only thing that had changed was that the bulletin board in the hallway near the bathrooms didn't just advertise the health clinic and leather ball anymore, but had brightly colored posters publicizing a fundraiser for the local college's LGBT club, a gay men's running club, a drag ball, and a dance-a-thon.

"Well, I forgot what small-town bars are like," Clara said, looking around at the half-empty room but still having to shout over the music. They clinked their beer glasses and decided they probably wouldn't stay long.

They danced to a Blondie song, finished their drinks, and had just decided to leave when Stuart and his ball team arrived, a jovial group of men in their thirties and forties wearing red-and-blue team shirts. They pulled several tables together and were served metal buckets of bottle beers on ice.

"*That's* Stuart," he said, grabbing Clara's arm before nodding in his direction. "I can't believe there's an actual gay baseball team. That would have been inconceivable when I lived here!"

"It gets better," Clara said sarcastically, mocking Dan Savage's recent anti-homophobia campaign as she eyed the sad, lone dancer and the table of drunk jocks.

Stuart looked up and caught Andrew's eye. His face didn't light up the way it used to. Still, Andrew felt obligated to walk over and say hello.

"Hey guys!" Andrew said, to everyone at the table, and then touched Stuart's shoulder. "Hey, Stu."

Clara hovered behind, trying to get reception on her cellphone. A few of the older guys smirked at each other when they saw Andrew. Stu pulled a cigarette out of his pack and tapped it on the table, then put it behind his right ear.

"Hey, Andrew," Stuart said, "I'm surprised to see you here again."

"I'm here with my aunt Clara. Remember I used to talk about her?" he said, nodding towards Clara, who stood shaking her hips back and forth a few seconds off the beat of "Dancing Queen." She met Stu's eye and nodded hello. Stuart didn't offer them a seat, just pushed his chair back and stood up, tapping his smoke as explanation.

"Can I chat with you outside?"

"Sure," Andrew said.

They went outside and stood awkwardly around the old Heinz ketchup can where smokers deposited their cigarettes, looking across the parking lot to the highway.

Stuart lit his cigarette and offered Andrew a drag. He declined.

"I know, I should quit. I can barely jog around the track anymore," Stuart said, shaking his head in shame. Andrew noticed a yellow tinge to the skin under his eyes.

"Listen, I spoke to one of the girls involved in the case, and I think it's legit, what she's saying," Stuart said, looking around in a paranoid way. A car pulled into the parking lot and Stuart walked behind the building, under an awning where they wouldn't be seen.

Andrew had managed to forget about their predicament for almost an hour, losing himself in nostalgia. He kicked at the gravel. "What did she say?"

"She's a real nice kid, and fuck, she's young. She said he paid lots of attention to her, too much, really. Asking her if she had a boyfriend all the time."

"So? He took an interest in her life . . ."

Stuart looked at Andrew. "Whatever. I just thought you should be warned."

"Thanks," Andrew said, watching Stuart take another paranoid scan. "I'm sorry for snapping. It's happened really quickly, and I've been buried in legal documents and I don't really have perspective, you know. My dad and I, we were starting to get close again. It's just so fuckin' weird."

"Yeah . . ."

Andrew started back towards the door. Stuart called after him.

"I just want you to know that you really were my true love . . ."

Andrew turned. Stuart was standing close to him now. He could smell hours of beer on his breath and was slightly revolted, yet at the same time he felt a familiar wave of nostalgic attraction. Stuart leaned in to kiss Andrew, holding his hands at the waist like they were kids at a school dance. The kiss was gentle, and Andrew pulled back before it got sloppy, or before he tried to draw him into a hug. The smell of Stuart's cologne and cigarettes was enough to make Andrew feel as though he could fall over from the associated emotions.

Andrew went in to retrieve Clara, who was energetically dancing to the B-52s' "Love Shack" on the dance floor, while the leather daddy stabbed a wooden cane in the air for the *bang bang bang* parts. Andrew waved at the table of Stuart's teammates as they left. Stuart, standing by the bar, pretended not to see him go. Andrew noticed a young man beside him, probably a teenager, who looked totally enraptured.

"He's still got that charm," Andrew said to Clara, nodding towards the young kid.

Clara rolled her eyes. "He should be more careful."

TUESDAY

11

BENNIE PICKED UP THE FAMILY IN A TOWN CAR FOR the hearing. Clara, Joan, and Andrew were all standing in front of the gate at the end of the driveway when he pulled up. Joan had spent twenty minutes looking for Sadie before she noticed a scrawled note on a napkin by the coffee machine reading "I couldn't sleep, went for a run and to Jimmy's."

Joan had found her at 2 A.M. listening to three threats and several hang-ups on the answering machine in the living room. She had been crying and Joan had walked her back to bed, barely concealing her own shaking limbs.

The car smelled of stale booze and cigars, and the driver wore a surfeit of peppery cologne that competed with the cherry-scented air freshener hanging from the rearview mirror.

Once everyone was seated, Bennie turned around from the passenger seat to address them. "This is the arraignment hearing, and it is likely they'll set bail at some exorbitant amount because they know how wealthy he is," he explained, though they already knew.

"So, they'll use it as an excuse to re-pave the parking lot or to put another Starbucks in the courthouse complex," said Clara.

"Yup," Andrew said, sipping from a travel mug of coffee.

Before long they were curving through the subdivisions on the hill that hadn't existed when Andrew was young. They pulled up in front of Jimmy's house.

Elaine showed Joan to the breakfast nook where Sadie, still in her running clothes, was eating a bowl of cereal.

"It's time to go, honey."

Sadie looked down at the bowl, circling the spoon around the remaining Cheerios. "I'm not going."

Sadie looked up to briefly meet her mother's eyes and then returned her gaze to the cereal bowl. Elaine went into the kitchen and rinsed out the coffee maker.

Joan gripped the back of Elaine's kitchen chair, poking her fingers through the lattice wicker. She tried her most patient voice. "I understand this is hard, but we have to stick together right now. We need each other. I know you are hurting, and believe me, we all are."

"I'm sorry, I can't go." Sadie dismissed Joan with a wave of her hand, scraping her cereal bowl with her spoon.

"This is a very complicated situation, Sadie. Love just doesn't dissolve when something terrible happens."

"See? It's even in the language you choose. Something terrible didn't just *happen*. There was no tornado or act of God. Dad may have *committed a crime* using his own free will."

"*May* have," Joan said, and then corrected herself. "*Didn't*. And maybe if you weren't seventeen you'd be a little more forgiving of the fact that not everything is black and white."

"I understand the dangers of binary thinking, I just don't think that in this situation there are many shades of gray," Sadie said, standing up and walking towards the kitchen sink with her cereal bowl.

"You don't know everything, honey. No one can. That's not how the legal process works."

"You know what I *do* know, Mom? I know that the weekend Dad chaperoned that ski trip, you went to work and helped a dozen people live through the night. Those are acts that are commendable, Mom. Why do *you* have to be the one to suffer?"

Joan pulled her jacket tightly around her waist. "Sadie, I'm trying to be patient and supportive. And neither you nor I know exactly what happened. There is innocent until proven—"

"Do you think that maybe you need to be feeling less empathy and more rage, Mom? Do you think the situation might call for that at this point?" She turned on the faucet, scrubbing at her bowl and then rinsing it again. Elaine left the kitchen, walking up the carpeted stairs.

When you're a teenager, it seems that the time for rage is always. Joan tried to think of things to say that might change Sadie's mind. "You have the right to feel however you feel. Your feelings are valid."

"I *know*," she said, as if Joan were the stupidest woman in the world, saying the most obvious things. "Mom, sometimes you forget I am no longer twelve."

"Believe me, I know how old you are. I would appreciate your support, is all that I'm saying." She said this so quietly, and it pained her to admit it. She wanted her there; she wanted them all there in a group, together.

"Mom, it's not just that I'm mad. It's that I'm mad and I'm worried that if I see him, my heart will just break. I just don't know what I'm supposed to do with this information, with all these rumors. I can't organize it all in my head. It's like Dad has just disappeared. It's too devastating. I just have to stay away." She said this while she looked out the window at the Town Car idling on the street.

"Okay, honey." Joan started towards Sadie to embrace her, but Sadie stuck her hand out in protest. She turned and noticed Jimmy's stepfather, Kevin, standing in the doorway, holding a bowl of cereal. ·

Outside, Clara called Joan's name.

"Mom, just go," Sadie said.

Joan felt as though she didn't have any choice, so she left, hands curled in fists at her sides.

THE SCENE OUTSIDE THE courtroom was actually fairly benign, as if they'd all shown up to pay parking tickets, except for the ever-present media team. The building was on the edge of town, next to the golf course. It looked like a community center. Joan had never really absorbed the fact that it was the courthouse. A group of teachers were there to support George. They had buttons and signs reading things like *We Support Mr. Woodbury! Still Teacher of the Year Every Year!* A group of angry parents were also present, a small crowd of their supporters shouting outside. In the adjacent municipal park there was a picnic, some sort of community gathering for children, unrelated to the court date.

Joan wasn't prepared to see the girls. In her head, she'd imagined them the way teenagers look on television when they're played by twenty-five-year-old actresses and dressed in skimpy designer jeans. Instead, they looked the way Clara had looked in junior high, with braces and legs that hadn't grown at the same rate as their arms. They looked the age Joan had been when she'd daydreamed at night about her first kiss. Joan's face burned when she looked their way, tears formed when she saw the pained looks on the faces of their parents standing behind the prosecutor. She immediately thought of someone hurting Sadie, which produced a sudden thrum of nausea, and pain in pricks all over her body.

She was even less prepared emotionally to see George.

After they were seated, two guards led him into the room. They'd given him prison attire, which was very jarring, and he looked so pale and frightened, different from yesterday. He was so disheveled, holding up his pants because they'd taken his belt. She'd never seen such a previously confident and commanding man so vulnerable. She was immediately thankful that Sadie wasn't here to witness him like this. Even Andrew, who was used to trials, who had displayed the stoicism of his grandfather through the journey up to this point, began to shake, and had to turn his head away.

Joan saw that George was scanning the crowd, looking for her. When they locked eyes, she broke down. After that, he kept his head bowed.

The judge greeted the crowd and read a summary of

the charges, including a new charge Joan wasn't aware of, and announced that his trial was set for eight months from now. He would be incarcerated until then, with no chance of bail, due to his being a considerable flight risk.

Joan felt as though she couldn't hear; or rather, sound receded into the distance and was replaced by a persistent ringing, a swell of voices. She could make out Bennie's voice, in the distance, as he announced his intention to appeal the no-bail decision. The gavel struck the bench.

The judge basically said, in legalese, go ahead, but fat chance.

When they led him away, a slip of himself in hand-cuffs, Joan watched herself as she fell to the floor, hands on the cold tiles breaking her fall. Mom, she heard. Mom. She was on her knees, palms down, fetal. Take a deep breath. Joan, Joan, her sister's voice. Andrew grabbed Joan's hand and helped her up and encouraged her to sit down, then held onto her firmly. The judge banged his gavel again. The room quieted and Joan regained her senses.

A man in a plaid sports jacket yelled, "Send him away for life!" George's shoulders shook with sobbing as he walked away.

"Innocent until proven guilty!" shouted Dorothy in a hysterical tone.

"This is a conspiracy!" a voice rose from the crowd.

Andrew grabbed Joan's hand and helped her up. The judge banged his gavel.

"George saved my life!" shouted the former Avalon Hills secretary, the woman whose boyfriend had tried to kill her a decade earlier. Joan hadn't seen her in years; rumor had it she'd been on long-term disability for PTSD after the incident. "He's got a good heart! He's being framed!"

"Order," the judge shouted. "Please clear the room," he said, annoyed at the spectacle.

"Why didn't you see this coming?" Joan asked Bennie in the car. He offered a run of apologies before admitting that he was basically stunned. Had he angered that particular judge? It made no sense to him.

There was an awkward silence as everyone absorbed the reality that George wasn't simply coming home as they'd all expected.

After a few moments, Clara read aloud from an editorial published in that morning's paper, written by a group calling itself Citizens in Defense of George Woodbury. "'While we can't know for certain, we can speculate, based on witnessed past behavior on the part of Avalon girls while on school trips, that there is often contraband alcohol consumption and subsequent bad behavior. According to one teacher chaperoning the senior trip in question, single-sex dorms were deemed coed once the chaperones had gone to bed. Many girls confessed to waking up ashamed of their behavior, and one can easily speculate that some sought out a way to abdicate responsibility for their actions, many of which they have little to no memory of, except for what is caught on camera phones. Let us all remember that six students were suspended and three expelled when video footage of the trip was anonymously posted online, and none of the footage contained anything involving Mr. Woodbury. It is clear to us that Mr. Woodbury, who has never before been anything but a well-respected role model, going back to the day he literally saved the school from an armed gunman, is being framed by a group of girls unwilling to look at the role their own decisions had in a weekend trip gone awry. We have led our girls astray in our pornofied culture, and we should go back to the days of propriety and self-respect, something our young women so sorely need.'" Clara's voice was thick with sarcasm. "I can't believe the paper actually printed this disgusting, archaic, victim-blaming letter!"

Joan would normally have vehemently agreed with her sister on this, but she could only place her hand against her tender heart and weep for the confusion she felt.

12

ANDREW DROPPED BY TO SEE HIS SISTER AFTER THE hearing. She was sitting on Jimmy's back deck with her schoolbooks and laptop.

"They held him without bail," Andrew said, trying to sound as gentle as he could, despite the rage he felt at his father's incarceration.

"Oh my god," she said quietly. "Holy shit. I don't understand."

"Neither do I," said Andrew. They sat awkwardly for a few minutes, sipping iced tea and watching Kevin weed the garden.

"No school today? Are the kids being terrible?"

"Someone threw a can of Coke at my head from a Town Car when I left the track this morning."

"Good to know chauffeured kids are still the worst."

Sadie nodded. "So, *why* isn't Dad out of jail? He was going to be home today. I thought that was just, you know, a fact. How things work." Sadie gulped her tea, chewing on a shard of ice. The afternoon clouds broke apart for a brief bit of sun.

Andrew shook his head. "No, it's a bit complicated. They've held him without bail on a technicality that Bennie is appealing. Something is going on with the family trust money, though. Mom was surprised she didn't really know how much money they had, and it was less than she'd assumed."

"I can't believe that Mom didn't know how much money Dad had. That's weird. She's such a control freak."

"I also found that odd," Andrew admitted. "But the wealth that Grandpa had, you know, it doesn't last forever unless it's properly invested, right, and Dad was never good at that stuff. Perhaps that's what happened, you know. They have a nest egg, but it's not limitless, the way we've always assumed."

"Do you think she's abandoned him?"

Andrew shook his head. "I don't know. I don't think it's that straightforward. I think she really does think that this will all magically blow over."

"Do you think so?"

"Not after seeing those girls today in court. I'm not sure at all."

He opened up his iPad and showed Sadie an article. The headline read TOWN DIVIDED OVER POPULAR TEACHER. A photo of Dorothy holding up a sign of support accompanied the story.

"Teachers are going batshit. Most of them think it's a witch hunt," Sadie said. "Oddly, mostly it's the female teachers. They can't say it outright, but they don't believe the girls."

"This town is fucked-up, Sadie. I've always told you that. Not that I can know exactly what occurred," he said carefully.

"I don't know. I've always felt so safe here, but . . ." She handed him her phone and opened it to her text messages. The first one read *pervy bitch, go kill yourself.* They got worse the further down he scrolled.

"Bullying is out of style now, you say?"

"I guess I was wrong."

"How are they treating the girls who accused him?"

"Most haven't been back to school, I don't think."

"Change your number," he said. "I can do it for you. You shouldn't have to read this. Nothing is your fault."

"I feel weird at home. I don't feel safe. It feels safer here," she said.

Andrew nodded, though he was a bit taken aback that he couldn't protect her from feeling this way at home. They watched as Kevin put the lawn mower into the shed. He stopped and pulled something out of his jeans.

"What's this guy's deal? Uncle?"

"Stepdad. Sort of."

"He's a bit . . . young, or just looks it?"

"A bit of both," Sadie said as Kevin approached them and put a joint to his lips and sparked it.

He held it out to Andrew. "Do you smoke?"

"No, not usually," he lied, "but all right, seems as good a time as any."

Andrew took the joint and inhaled. Then he looked at Sadie. "Shit, are you okay with this?" He pointed to the joint and then turned to exhale a long stream of smoke behind him.

"Totally," she said.

"I'm having a hard time understanding you're not twelve, and then I do something like smoke drugs in front of you."

"It's not a big deal."

Sadie smiled and reached up to grab the joint. "Oh no, honey. You're far too smart for this buzz, believe me," Andrew said, handing it back to Kevin. "Don't be sharing with her."

Kevin nodded in agreement and stubbed out the joint in an ashtray.

When no one was looking, Sadie took the roach and slipped it in her pocket for later.

WEDNESDAY

13

ON WEDNESDAY, CLARA AND ANDREW WENT BACK to the city for the night, promising to return the following day. Joan and Sadie were alone in the house, and did what they hardly ever did on a weekday night: they put on sweatpants and ordered a pizza with pineapple and double cheese from Gino's. Sadie had been scarce, and it seemed every time she was home there were threatening phone calls, reporters, or local teenagers harassing them from the road. There'd even been a rowboat of photographers at the dock before Clara ran at them with her own camera and a few choice words. Sadie had had to shut down all her social media accounts.

Gino's was the Woodburys' usual pizza place.

"What's your address, ma'am?"

"It's Joan, you know, at 235 Lakeside." She pulled a credit card out of her pocketbook and tapped it against the living room end table.

"I'm new here, ma'am. Credit card number and name as it appears on the card?"

She did as requested, spelling out her name.

There was a long pause on the line. She waited almost a minute. There was no goodbye, just some ambient kitchen noise, a muffled receiver, and the sound of an older man's voice. "Just hang up the fucking phone, Jake." A shaky sound of a receiver and then a click. No pizza.

She thought about calling back, about yelling into the receiver that she wasn't a criminal, she was a loyal customer who always tipped handsomely. One time she had even given CPR to a man having a heart attack in their restaurant, and he'd lived, thanks to her. They had a clipping about it from the newspaper up on their wall. Still, she couldn't have a pizza? Ungrateful! She unplugged the landline phone and sat on the couch, hugging a throw pillow to her chest.

The house was pretty empty and quiet save for the purring of Payton, curled up on George's pillow where he always slept whenever George was away. Sadie was upstairs studying. She'd told Joan earlier that she needed some alone time.

She contemplated asking the neighbors if she could order a pizza from their house, but she hadn't talked to them since George's arrest. Instead, she made a pot of spaghetti with some pesto and brought up a bowl to Sadie, who was sitting on her bed in front of her laptop, chewing on her hair. She took the bowl of pasta and sat it down on top of a textbook.

"Mom, come look at this," she said, going over to the

peaked attic window that looked out onto Lakeshore Drive.

The reporters were still there. One sat on a lawn chair, hunched over a laptop. Sadie handed Joan the binoculars George used to use for birding.

"Okay, now look," she demanded.

Joan peered through and saw a car speeding up to the gate. The reporters turned and took some photos. The car sped forward a bit and then stopped on the other side of the hedge on the far eastern side of their property. A bunch of teenagers got out and started climbing the fence.

"Call the police, honey," Joan said.

"No, I know who it is. It will make things worse."

Once over the hedge, the kids hurled objects at the house, laughing drunkenly before ambling back over. Joan ran downstairs and saw that it was paper bags of dog poop and some broken beer bottles. Reporters clicked away as she picked up the mess, unable to stop herself from crying.

When she came back in, Sadie was standing by the door fully dressed, a duffel bag over her shoulder.

"I'm going to stay with Jimmy, Mom. I can't handle it here. I'm worried. Maybe you should go to Clara's?"

"Honey, you need to be with family right now. We're going to see your dad Friday afternoon."

"Mom, we're not going to visit him at work. We're going to *prison*."

"I am well aware of that, honey."

"Jimmy's mom said I could crash there for as long as I want to."

"Did she? Without even talking to me first?"

"She asked if she could, but I said you were probably going through enough."

"I'm still your parent. I'm still here for you. Nothing will change that."

"I know, I know." Sadie shifted her weight impatiently, checking an incoming text message. "Jimmy is parked at the Coffee Hut and I'm going to row the boat over to the beach and return it. Is that okay?"

"Of course that's not okay. I'll drive you to the Coffee Hut, for god's sake."

"Mom, there are too many people out there. It's too stressful."

"This is our house. We haven't done anything wrong. Those people out there can just *go to hell*."

Joan's cell rang and she picked it up without thinking. "I hope your husband gets the shit kicked out of him in jail. You had to have known. What kind of fucking idiot slut couldn't have known?"

"How did you get this number?" Joan demanded, but the person hung up.

Joan grabbed her keys and they walked out to the Volvo. Sadie ran behind her, shielding her face with her hands as cameras clicked. Joan pressed down on the horn and turned on her bright lights as she drove up to the gate, clicking it open and leaving reporters to scramble to the side as she sped through. Sadie crouched down in the passenger seat.

In the Coffee Hut parking lot, Joan turned off the ignition and touched her daughter's shoulder.

Joan wanted to explain that Sadie was too damn young to stay over with a boyfriend. That it was not acceptable.

What would people say? "You're so young, Sadie. You have a whole lifetime ahead of living with boys. People will talk . . ."

"I think I'm the least controversial member of the family these days, Mom. Plus, I'm not living with him. It will be temporary." Sadie opened the passenger door and got out, opening the back door of Jimmy's car and throwing her duffel bag in before turning to wave.

Joan waited until they were out of sight to cry.

THURSDAY

14

THE NEXT MORNING, JOAN SHOWED UP AT JIMMY'S house. Her hair was flattened on one side. She was wearing the old tattered University of Boston sweatshirt she normally reserved for Sunday mornings after church when she cleaned the house. She tried to fix her hair and gave up, ringing Jimmy's doorbell half hoping his mother wouldn't be home.

Elaine welcomed her into the house, offered her a cup of coffee.

"Did you really say that my daughter could stay here? I'm not a huge fan of the idea," Joan said, "but Sadie is very convinced it's what she wants to do."

"I said she could, but only if you were okay with it."

"I don't want her to be a burden," Joan said, looking out the window. It was quieter in this neighborhood, no reporters or vandals. It might be a good idea after all. "I could give you money for groceries and for the bills," she said, feeling herself giving in.

"She's not a burden at all. I hardly notice her, and when I do, it's nice to have another girl around, you know? You don't have to worry about money, Joan. Really."

Joan raised her eyebrows. "She will have her own room?"

"We've set her up in the guest room," Elaine said, and then paused before leading Joan upstairs. Joan was relieved to see Sadie's clothes there, folded on the lilac bureau, her track shoes lined up against the baseboards, her hair products fanned out on the top of the dresser, alongside some novels and schoolbooks.

"And you will watch, to make sure, uh, they aren't alone together at night?"

Joan was one of those people who thinks sex only happens at night in bedrooms and clings to this rule.

Elaine said, "Well, they're seventeen. You know I can't watch them constantly, right? We just have to make sure they both know . . . what they need to know."

SADIE STOOD OUTSIDE THE guest room, eavesdropping on Elaine and her mother. What Joan didn't know was that Elaine bought condoms in bulk at Costco and kept them underneath the sink in the bathroom. One time when Sadie was visiting, Elaine showed her around the house and opened up the cabinet to say there were tampons there and she could use them anytime. The condoms were beside the tampons. "You can help yourself to absolutely everything," she said, in case Sadie wasn't getting the picture. "I don't count . . . anything," she said, picking up the box of Trojans and pretending to adjust them neatly.

Elaine was the kind of mother who, if she'd had a

daughter, would've offered her the pill as an option at fourteen after giving a speech over dinner about the struggle for women's reproductive freedoms in the 1960s. Her own mother hadn't spoken to Sadie about sex since she'd given her an illustrated copy of *How Babies Are Made* at the age of eight.

"I'm against this. You know, I want her at home. She belongs at home. I miss her."

Sadie was stunned by her mother opening up like this, so vulnerable, so unlike herself.

"I know," said Elaine. "But I have the feeling that if I tell her she can't come here, that would be worse, you know? Who knows where she would go."

"Well, you don't know her like I do. Sadie is not stupid or impulsive," Joan said.

"I agree. I don't know her. I'm not trying to be her mother. I'm just trying to give her some options, in a difficult situation."

Sadie couldn't believe this didn't provoke a Joan-style rant about permissive and unconventional parenting styles that are damaging, and how children need rules and respond to systems of order imposed on them so that they feel safe in a world full of chaos. "Children need boundaries!" she would normally have shouted, while demanding Sadie get into the Volvo "this instant!"

Instead, she heard her mother clear her throat. "When did it switch, you know, from when we made the decisions to when we just gave up and let them do it? When did we stop being in control?"

Sadie felt confused; she'd never heard her mother express doubt before. She always knew what to do.

"Well, parental control is always somewhat illusory, right?"

"I don't like this, but I understand how hard it must be for Sadie to be at home. But I want her to know that she is welcome to move home at any time of the day or night, and that I will never stop being her mother."

"Have you told her this?"

"Of course. Many times. Anyway, let her know I'm expecting her tomorrow at one, like we talked about," she said.

Sadie felt so guilty, hearing her mother sound so unsure.

"I will."

FRIDAY

15

THE GATE BUZZED AS JOAN WAS PACKING UP AN OR-
ange plastic cooler for the ride to the prison. The
cooler was from the 1990s, and had *Woodbury*
scrawled in black marker on the white top from when the
kids used to play team sports. Inside she'd placed ice packs,
a bag of green grapes, two small yogurts, hard-boiled eggs,
a bottle of water, and a tub of coleslaw left over from Clara's
last takeout order. She rolled up utensils in thick cloth nap-
kins and had just clicked it shut when the gate's buzzer
rang.

She peered through the window and pressed the intercom. "It's Nancy, from work," a voice called. Joan buzzed
the gate open and watched as Nancy, wearing her pink
work scrubs and bright purple raincoat, pulled an oversized warming dish out of the trunk of her red compact
car. She blew at the long blond strip of bangs that were
falling across her eyes. Joan was both happy to see her and

embarrassed to have to remember work niceties that felt so irrelevant in the face of what was happening.

"Oh, uh, hi Joan. I'm just, I was just. I was feeling badly, you know, and wanted to know you were okay, so I brought you a tuna casserole." She held it out to her.

"Thanks. That's very kind of you. Come on in." Joan took the dish in her hands and took a step back so that Nancy could come inside.

Nancy smiled awkwardly, cocking her head to one side. "Oh no, I can't. I'm on my way in, you know, I'm on tens this week, right? But I just wanted to check in. You know, a lot of us have been concerned."

Right. There had been no phone calls to Joan, nobody checking in, beyond the card and flowers sent right after the arrest. Probably half of them were hoping to be promoted to Joan's position if she left for good. Joan had no idea if these thoughts were incorrect or if she was experiencing a paranoid cognitive impairment of some kind, thinking everyone had terrible intentions. Normally she didn't think ill of her co-workers. They weren't a bad lot, for the most part.

"Thanks so much. You know, I only really have my sister, since this all . . . happened."

Nancy's face dropped into a concerned frown, and she pushed her hair behind her ears, a useless gesture, before the strand fell forward again. "You know, Joan, I lost my husband last year."

Of course, Joan knew this already. Nancy's husband John had hung himself in the window of the flower shop he owned on Main Street. Nobody knew why. He didn't leave a note. Nancy used to be a laugh; now she startled easily, took more overtime than anyone else just to avoid going home and being alone. The other nurses all used to pity her and started a weekly girls' night just to make sure she wasn't alone every night of the week. Some of the younger ones took her out to a pub and did karaoke after work sometimes.

"My husband . . . had secrets too," she said, "so I feel for you, Joan."

Joan nodded, looked down at her feet, and noticed that teardrops were falling.

"Thanks," Joan said, letting more tears fall onto the top of the casserole dish. When she looked up, Nancy was halfway to her little red Honda Civic already, waving. She reversed back up the driveway. Joan buzzed the gate open again and watched her disappear behind the trees.

Joan walked the casserole into the kitchen, opened the fridge, and nudged aside two heads of wilting iceberg lettuce. "My husband had secrets too." *George doesn't have fucking secrets. He's being set up!* She wished she had yelled that. But she didn't really know. Not knowing felt worse than knowing something for sure, even something terrible.

She tried to pull herself together, placing the cooler by the front door, catching her reflection in the mirror. What does one wear to a prison? Suddenly Joan's plan to look clean and presentable seemed ridiculous. It's not like she was going to park the car and waltz into a prison like she was ducking into a Best Buy. She didn't even really know what a prison looked like. She had printed out directions from Google, highlighted all the major interstate exits. She drew a pink square around the building.

She eventually dressed in the outfit she normally reserved for student–teacher nights, a sort of plain caramel
pantsuit with a scarf, a getup that comfortably blended her
age and status in life. Sadie called it her ugly old lady suit.
In the mirror the outfit made her almost disappear, except
for the red streaks across her face from crying, the deep
circles under each eye. She looked old.

She was about to get in the car to go pick up Sadie
when her daughter appeared at the door, wearing the same
sweatshirt she'd been in for days.

"Give me a minute, I need to change," she said, briefly
stopping to squeeze her mom's arm.

"Okay. Bennie told us that you're only allowed to
bring your ID and nothing else. Also, you have to wear
baggy clothing, and no reds or yellows, and no jewelry."

"Why?"

"I have no idea."

"I don't think I really own any baggy clothing except
sweatpants."

"Those will do."

Joan paced the first-floor hall for a few minutes before
announcing that she would be waiting in the car. She
found it covered in eggs, and went around to the side of
the house to open the hose and spray it down, which was
her new morning ritual. She didn't bother with soap, just
adjusted the nozzle to the hardest pressure, not wanting
Sadie to see the viscous evidence of their new status in life.
She gathered the eggshells in her hands and threw them in
the outdoor garbage by the side of the house. Inside the
trash bin was Sadie's red canvas school bag, which she ex-
tracted angrily. It was a good-quality bag, with leather

straps and detailing, and had been purchased only recently. Then she saw the scrawled black letters across it. WHORE. Joan pushed it back into the trash, punching it down, and covered it with the eggshells as a sharp, hot feeling rose in the back of her throat.

When Sadie came out, she was carrying one of Andrew's old backpacks, which she tossed into the car.

"The nineties are back again," she said, shrugging.

Joan wanted to say something but couldn't, so she switched on the radio and reversed a little too frantically, toppling the trash bin.

16

S ADIE WAS NOT PREPARED FOR THE DIRE GRAYNESS OF
the institution that now housed her father. Any prior
knowledge of prison architecture had been gleaned
entirely from television, but in real life the prison looked
even more frightening than she'd imagined. They pulled
into a parking lot where a Greyhound bus was unloading
visitors, who all joined a line by the front door.

"There's a down-on-their-luck bunch if I've ever seen
one," Joan said, making Sadie shudder a bit.

When Joan turned the car off, she unclipped her seat
belt and turned to Sadie. "This is going to be very weird,"
she said.

"Duh."

"Some things might shock you," Joan said, "but I'm
here for you, and soon your father won't be here anymore
and we'll be back to normal."

Sadie nodded, wishing she could be as hopeful as her
mother, and opened the passenger-side door. They headed

towards the lineup, which had only grown longer since they'd arrived. They took their spot and Sadie stared at the patterns on the cement, the lace-up sneakers and shiny high heels in bright blue and soft pink, and one particularly vibrant pair of red knee-high boots. They stood quietly in the line for close to an hour, Joan rocking back and forth from foot to foot. They didn't even try to make small talk with each other, just withstood the discomfort in silence. Children ran around, their mothers periodically scolding them, but they were doing what everyone wished they could do, running off the energy and nerves that raged inside them. Sadie curled her toes and then uncurled them, over and over, until she could barely feel them.

Eventually the line moved. One male guard who looked as though he was cast from a 1980s prison exploitation film waved them through to a stern, blasé female guard with a red mullet and raccoon eyeliner. She gave both women a pat-down. Sadie tried to open her eyes naively, betray a hapless uncertainty. The guard looked right through her, touched her roughly, and exhaled a sour smell through her mouth as though she had a cold. Sadie grimaced, feeling so anonymous but guilty at the same time, with every prod and pat of the woman's hands, as though they would find something that could keep her out or, worse, force her inside.

After the security and ID check, they walked through two sets of electrified gates made of razored wire, past the gun tower, and across a courtyard. Their ultimate destination looked a lot like a grammar school cafeteria. They sat in rows and waited on hard-backed chairs.

It was announced outwardly—by their clothing, their

straight white teeth—and inwardly in an uncomfortable, involuntary monologue—*I do not belong here*—that Joan and Sadie Woodbury were outsiders in the penitentiary waiting room. Sadie, as she realized this, felt ashamed of her feelings of superiority.

"Thirty-five percent of people of color are imprisoned in America for bogus reasons. We have more people in prison here than any other industrialized nation," she whispered to her mother.

Joan looked at her when she spoke but did not respond. Eventually she said, "You might want to keep your voice down," and looked around anxiously, as if talking about race in this context was implicitly racist and they were, as they both wanted to scream, *good, civil people,* and *not racists.* Their discomfort said otherwise.

All of the other visitors seemed to know how to *be* in this environment. Their postures betrayed the kind of re-laxed waiting stance one adopts at the dentist's office. Joan picked at her nails, her clothes, and could simply not be still.

When Sadie had watched her mother work in the hospital—something that had happened only a few times, when she was a child—she admired the assured way she could command a chaotic situation. Amanda's mom was always deferring to other adults, especially Amanda's fa-ther. It never seemed as though she knew how to make a decision for herself. She was afraid of what Joan might do if she knew they'd watched a scary movie or eaten some ice cream. "Does your mother allow sugar?" she'd ask be-fore scooping into a brick of Heavenly Hash. And Sadie would nod, even though desserts were a rarity. Watching her mother now, after the humiliation of their entrance, and now having to meet her husband in this environment, was almost as destabilizing as the whole ordeal itself.

When they called Joan's name, she and Sadie were led into an adjacent room and given some rules. They were told that they were allowed one hug when they met and one at the end of the half hour, but no contact in between. They had to keep their hands on the table and in sight at all times.

Sadie didn't have her lucky eraser to squeeze, because she wasn't allowed to have anything. She'd left it sitting on the front seat of the car, where she hoped its proximity would still help her through this. If she got up and ran out, as she was beginning to feel that she wanted to do, she was sure she would be breaking some jail regulation and be arrested. She felt the need to get close to the floor, as they tell you to do if a building is on fire.

George walked into the room in handcuffs, in the same orange jumpsuit he'd worn at the hearing. He looked like an actor playing a criminal. Some white-collar crime.

Joan hugged him and then stifled several sobs.

Sadie gave him a hug, as though he were a stranger at first, patting his shoulder, until the comfortable memory of thousands of hugs brought her closer, feeling safe, and then she remembered where they were. When she pulled back, at the urging "Okay, enough" from a prison guard, her body was an earthquake. She could not look at him and feel anger. When he spoke, her facade broke.

"This is just a mistake," he said. "Someone is out to get me and I know that sounds crazy, but that is what has happened."

"Okay," Sadie whispered to him, sitting down again. In that moment, no matter what had happened, she wanted him to be okay. She wanted him not to be beaten in prison by the people inside who truly *were* evil. She wanted him not to be despondent. She wanted him to get out of there. The flood of empathy she felt for him was unstoppable.

"You can feel more than one thing," Clara had said the night before over the phone. "This is a complex situation, and you can have an open heart."

Sadie watched and listened as her mother and father talked nonstop about the hearing, about his health and safety, and about *Bennie said this, Bennie advised that, Andrew said this.* There was no talk of media reports, or the things girls whispered to each other at school, or the death threats on the voice mail. It was all about how they were going to get him out. Pragmatic and pointed, fake calm. This was all Joan. She was deeply practical and results-oriented. George didn't break until the end, when a single tear formed in his eye. "I miss my girls," he said.

Later, Sadie wouldn't remember leaving; all of a sudden they were in the parking lot again, gulping for air.

Joan sat in the driver's seat and sobbed so hard that the car shook. Sadie placed her hand on her arm, squeezed it, and then gently prodded her to change places so that she could drive them home.

"You're in no condition," she offered.

"Neither are you, Sadie. Just let me get some air and I'll be fine."

"A hundred thousand crashes per year in America are a result of driver fatigue," Sadie said as Joan clicked open the driver's-side door and began to pace the parking lot, clutching her arms around herself. Sadie got out and circled the car, hoping her mother's pacing wouldn't concern the men in the high tower with the sniper rifles.

She got into the passenger seat without protestations, and Sadie drove all the way home. Having something to do and things she had to pay attention to allowed the trauma of what had just happened to recede into what was, at that point, a bubbling and full reserve of pain she would rather avoid thinking about.

I can keep it together. I can just be stoic. Just like Grandma used to say before she went senile. "Don't let anyone see you break," she'd said when Sadie was upset over a girl who'd stolen her favorite pony toy and then smashed it to pieces. "You are better than her, and it's just a stupid toy. Just pretend it doesn't bother you, and eventually it won't. You'll see."

And even though Joan had the child and her mother over and they sat in the living room talking about their feelings, and the child feebly apologized and they all had a good laugh about children and the crazy things they do, Sadie kept her grandma's words in mind.

When they stopped at the roadside for gas, Sadie checked her phone. There were five texts from Jimmy, all asking if she was okay. *Do you have reception? Are you ok?*

Just say it is and it will eventually be so, she thought.

She slipped her mother's credit card into the slot to pay for the gas, and then washed the front window. Her mother slept in the front seat unaware.

"It will be almost a year before the trial," her father had

said, resigned. "And that's being optimistic. So, hold tight. I'm going to try to finish that old thesis of mine, so maybe there's a bright side."

"But that's doubtful," Joan had replied. "I mean, doubtful that that is really a bright side, right?"

"Yes, yes, it is doubtful. I'm trying . . . to create something of worth out of this whole . . . mess."

Sadie got back in the car and turned on the radio again. Joan stirred, adjusted her head to lean against her rolled-up sweater. Sadie texted Jimmy back. *I'm totally fine. It was weird. I want to watch movies and forget about it. Go steal some pot from Kevin so we can just relax.*

The phone blinked again and she put on her headset to answer. It was Andrew, wanting details about the visit. He'd been to visit George earlier and had to return to the city. "I don't know what to tell you. Wasn't it so sad, how tired and old he looked?"

"I know," he said. "I'm sorry you had to experience that."

Sadie drove in silence for a while with Andrew breathing on the other end of the line.

"Get home safely," he said gently. "We'll get through this."

SADIE WAS BECOMING ACCUSTOMED to waking in a manner that made it seem as though she had never been asleep in the first place, usually at four in the morning. REM sleep was a rapidly fading memory, a privilege that no longer belonged to her. She did not feel tired. It was not even a possibility. She felt absent.

She stared at Jimmy sleeping curled around his pillow, clutching its blue and green plaid pattern. Across the room, the blinking blue cursor on his laptop bloomed and receded, lighting up the poster of Noam Chomsky above his desk. There was a line of light underneath the door, as though someone was awake. She sat up and wrapped one of Jimmy's hoodies around her. It reached below the hem of the boxer shorts she'd taken to sleeping in. There was nowhere to step that involved actual foot-to-carpet contact. Where there wasn't strewn clothes, there were magazines, discarded art projects, statues of cups and plates. She'd cleaned it up once, and the change had not been welcomed. So she came in to sleep and kept her belongings in the guest room.

She walked downstairs into the kitchen and turned on the kettle to make some Sleepytime tea. Her phone on the table blinked with a voice mail. It was from her father.

"I just want to know how you are doing with school." He sounded oddly formal, as though they hadn't just spoken that day, and as though he was inside a cave. "I know your SATs are coming up and I wanted to say I know you will do a terrific job and you don't have to let what is happening . . . right now . . . affect your future. You have to focus this year, Sadie, if you want to make sure you can go wherever you choose next year. I'm very proud of you and know you can do it." He kept talking for a while, and it almost felt normal to hear his voice inquiring about her studies, giving her his trademark pep talk.

She turned the phone off and poured boiling water into a mug. Every mug in the house was a heavy white square shape with a black interior. She sat down at the glass-covered table and laid her face down against its coolness.

"I always find pillows to be more comfortable," said Kevin, standing in the doorway between the living room and kitchen in his boxer shorts and an old ripped T-shirt that read *Vision Street Wear.*

Sadie shrugged in response. "Why can't you sleep?"

"I was writing," he said, and rubbed his face with his hands as though rubbing off a layer of skin. He always said "writing" in a way that made it sound to Sadie like *I was just curing some orphan children of blindness, no biggie.*

But despite his arrogance, and the way he walked around like he really, really wished he was still a teenager, Sadie didn't actually mind Kevin, or having him around. He was chill and nonjudgmental. His face and the way he looked at her hadn't changed at all since the arrest.

He walked over to the coffeepot, which was perpetually on and half full.

"So, darling, tell me your troubles."

"Did you know that the United States has the highest documented incarceration rate in the world: 743 adults incarcerated per 100,000 people?"

"I didn't know that so . . . precisely," said Kevin, running his hand through his unkempt hair and staring at her curiously. He didn't seem too concerned about her response. "Do you want to watch a classic movie instead of talking to this old fart interrupting your tea time?"

"Sure."

They walked into the living room. She sat on the couch, blowing into her mug of tea. He opened up the DVD drawer.

"This is a true classic," he said, holding up *St. Elmo's Fire.*

She took a sip. It tasted like twigs and was too sweet and she didn't want to drink it anymore, but it gave her something to do. She couldn't stop thinking about her father in his prison clothes.

Kevin curled up on the opposite end of the couch and turned to smile at her before he pressed Play. Though it would have seemed inconceivable just twenty minutes ago, she turned up her lips in an approximate symbol of joy, and she meant it. She liked the distraction of Kevin. They sat under separate blankets. Sadie stared straight ahead and watched the opening credits.

"I always watch this when I can't sleep and I can't write," he explained.

"I think this is one of my mom's favorite movies," Sadie said.

"Huh," he said. "I wouldn't have expected that."

"She's not so bad, my mom. She's actually a pretty strong person."

"No, no, I can see that. She certainly raised a strong daughter, if you don't mind me saying."

"I don't." This kept happening lately: Sadie went from hating someone to feeling happy and grateful to have them around in the same minute. She didn't feel strong, but she was happy to be faking it as well as she apparently was.

Kevin pulled out a joint from the Altoids tin he kept in the drawer of the coffee table. "Do you mind if I . . . ?"

"No."

He lit the joint, took a long drag, and handed it to her. She tried to pretend it was the most normal thing in the world, holding it between her thumb and forefinger, casually waiting a few seconds before inhaling. It was the first time she'd smoked with anyone besides Amanda or Jimmy. It was only the fifth time she'd ever tried it. She was usually the one who watched her friends smoke and then tried to laugh along, and mostly she just got bored and wanted to go read a book. Minutes passed, and the joint was finished. She just kept accepting it, and inhaling, and by the time it was a stub her entire body felt like an electrified stone. Kevin was not one of those smokers who laughed like an idiot. He just kept acting pretty normal. She opened her mouth and then couldn't close it. She felt her lips dry out, then her tongue, and she told herself to swallow. *Close your mouth, you idiot.* But her lips didn't get the message.

"Marijuana increases the heart rate by twenty to one hundred percent shortly after smoking," Sadie said, surprised that her lips could move to talk. "One is at increased risk of having a heart attack for one hour after smoking."

Kevin grinned. "Duly noted, nurse."

They watched the movie for about fifteen minutes. Not bad, a few too many saxophone solos. Eventually she could move her lips and her tongue, and finished her tea. She was starting to understand why people liked to get high when she felt Kevin's foot touching her leg.

She didn't know what to do. She kept staring at the screen. The feeling of Kevin's foot was making her feel so startlingly alive, his toes to her knee. Her bare knee, where the hoodie had crept up to her thigh.

Turn and look at him.

Just turn.

She contemplated putting her hand on his foot, in a gesture that said, I like that.

Oh my god, how dumb. That makes no sense. Wait, do I like that?

Her rational brain didn't know. But her body was warm, tingling. Rob Lowe's face on the screen, his strong arms.

Do I, even? Jimmy is upstairs. Kevin must be in his thirties, for Christ's sake. Gross. Just watch the movie. Why does the screen look so weird? Then she remembered that she was high, and she laughed. She expected him to laugh too, in response. He didn't. His foot felt heavier against her leg. Insistent. Instead of feeling horrified, she found the sensation not entirely unpleasant. In fact, she wanted to kiss him. She wanted to kiss *Kevin*? She'd never wanted to kiss anyone as badly as she did right then.

This is crazy. This is just because I'm high. People jump off buildings when they're high, or think they see god. This is nothing.

Finally she put the mug of tea down on the wooden arm of the sofa, trying to be casual. She turned her head to the right, just slightly.

Kevin had fallen asleep. His mouth slack on the square tartan couch pillow.

She understood immediately that his foot had simply moved in his sleep. His hands were curled around the blanket at his neck like a little boy. She felt *so* foolish. He snored gently. She tried to move away from his foot, but there was no more space on the couch. She pushed her hip against the arm of the couch anyway, and his foot just stayed in place. A white sweat sock with two thin blue lines around the ankle. The kind Elaine bought in bulk.

God, ego much, Sadie? The humiliation came fast and thick. *So fucking misguided.* She looked at his face, at how old he was, and was disgusted with herself. Why on earth would she ever want to kiss *him*?

Then the music on the TV got abruptly loud, and it startled him awake with a snort.

"Oh, Sadie," he said, moving his foot away as though her leg were covered in spiders. "Sorry, I'm not leaving you any, uh, room. I must've dozed off." He petted his foot, as if it were a dog, to brush something away.

"That's okay, Kevin. I'm just going to go back up . . . to bed."

He didn't answer because he'd already gone back to sleep. When she stood up, he stretched out his legs. He wasn't looking for action, he was looking for legroom.

She crept up the carpeted stairs, tiptoeing slowly past Elaine's room, and crawled back under the covers with Jimmy. He reached for her in his sleep. He kissed her forehead. "Where'd you go?"

"Downstairs to have some tea. I couldn't sleep."

"Huh."

"I smoked a joint with Kevin," she said, as though confessing something illicit. She expected Jimmy might get mad, or feel jealous. She felt guilt for what she had thought might be happening, even though it had clearly all been in her head.

"No fair, he never smokes me up anymore," he mumbled, and turned so that he was spooning her. He was hard against her lower back. This wasn't unusual. She reached back and grabbed him, the somewhat familiar but still kind of new feeling of him hot in her hand. He didn't move. He stopped talking. Sadie could tell he was wide awake with her touch but not saying anything. He probably didn't want to push his luck. His absolute stillness was arousing.

Normally, when they had sex, he initiated, and they did it the regular way, her legs in a V, hair splayed on one of his plaid flannel pillow cases, and the whole thing had yet to last more than about two minutes. This time she moved her hand up and down, the way she'd seen in porn, listening to his breath quicken. She turned around and pushed him on his back. She grabbed a condom from the stash in his bedside table and ripped it open. She fumbled a bit—this was something he usually did—but he lay there, eyes widened, perhaps afraid that if he moved or said anything she'd stop, or he'd realize it was a dream. She curled her hand around him, noting the chips in her manicure. She applied a little pressure and he got even harder, and moaned. She loved the sounds he made, involuntary, helpless. "Please," he mouthed. She let go and threw one leg over him, mimicking the position she'd seen in one of Kevin's magazines, riding him up and down. Jimmy seemed almost embarrassed, eyes fixed on her breasts under her open hoodie, his hands gripping her knees. She found herself imagining Kevin at the door, peering through a crack, watching. The image set her off. It was the first time she'd had an orgasm when someone else was in the room. Jimmy didn't know that. He had never asked.

"Wow," Jimmy said, "let's do it like that *all* the time. That was . . . wild."

He tipped his head back and fell asleep right away, and she lay awake, wishing she wasn't high but feeling a bit better, the same way she did after running, as though her muscles had finally relaxed, calming her.

IN THE MORNING, SHE woke up before everyone else. She saw the condom on the floor, stuck to the cover of a paperback copy of *Heart of Darkness*. She tiptoed to the bathroom and wrapped it in toilet paper and buried it at the bottom of the wastebasket. She wasn't sure what to do, settling in on the edge of the bed and watching Jimmy sleeping for a bit. She felt sore and a little ashamed, as though she had been taken over by some confident sex goddess overnight and in the light of day she felt like the same girl she'd always been. She briefly longed for the days of making out, when sex was still a mystery, a thing she'd *eventually* do. She didn't like being older in this moment, despite all the years she'd wished she could just get over the awkward, in-between feeling of being a teenaged girl, the feeling of being ugly in the body that is probably the most beautiful you will ever have.

Saturday and Sunday

17

JOAN HATED TO LEAVE HER DAUGHTER IN A HOUSE WITH a man she didn't even know, a man who wrote novels about Colombian drug cartels and another one about a homeless clairvoyant. Joan felt that he was really just some young sucker living off an older woman's hard-earned savings. Sadie brought home two of his books and Joan displayed them on the shelf in the living room, but she was definitely never going to read them. He had one of those author photos where his head was resting in his hands. No.

On Saturday afternoons, Joan usually did laundry and organized the week ahead. Andrew and Clara had returned, and Clara was organizing the dry goods pantry. Rows of dusty Mason jars were assembled on the kitchen table, beside a new roll of white masking tape and a felt-tip marker. Joan sat beside her, bereft.

"I want you to write *Bulgur, Couscous,* and *Kasha* on these labels," Clara said, handing her the labels and pen.

"I hate that she's at that house, with a man I don't even know," she said, writing out the first label in shaky cursive. The ink bled and feathered. She blurred the letters in *Bulgur* with the flat of her thumb, ripped off the label, balled it up, and started again.

"You need to wait for the ink to dry. And don't worry. Kevin is a has-been—someone who caught a break with his first novel fifteen years ago and never lived up to the subsequent five. We don't review him at the magazine anymore," Clara said, hoping that would make Joan feel better. "His career has gone to shit."

For once Joan appreciated how Clara spoke with authority, as though she had the right to make grand pronouncements about how everyone feels about culture, because she worked in the middle of where "it" all happened.

"Your anger at Elaine is misdirected," Clara said, amalgamating two separate jars of white rice into one. "Write *Basmati long-grain*."

"I don't care if it is," Joan said, complying. "I don't know quite how to explain it, but I'm just feeling whatever emotion occurs to me in the moment and going with it."

"You might be on to something," Clara said.

Joan took a card out of her handbag that a nurse from work had sent her. On the front were the words *If you're going through hell, keep going.* She handed it to Clara.

"Keep going where? Deeper into the hell? What a load of crap," she said.

"I think it's Buddhist or something," Joan said. "I found it comforting."

"What are you going to do about Sadie staying over there? It can't keep happening, right?"

Joan shrugged. "I certainly don't want it to."

LATER THAT NIGHT, JOAN encountered Kevin in the checkout aisle at the twenty-four-hour Safeway off the highway near Woodbridge. She was shopping fairly late, so that she could avoid most people she knew. He was standing in a shrug, cradling a six-pack with a bag of frozen french fries on top. He wore a sweatshirt with a skull on the back, and checkerboard-patterned Vans skateboard sneakers, like Andrew used to wear in high school. She didn't realize it was him in front of her in line, a lazy stubble mapping his jaw. She was staring off unfocused, and he turned to catch her eye.

"Heyyyy," he said, nodding his chin towards her.

He is too friendly, she thought. *He's going to pretend this whole mess hasn't happened, which is almost worse than the pointed, gossipy eye bulges.*

"Your daughter's great to have around the house," he volunteered.

She gripped the handle of her grocery cart. She looked down at the tub of low-fat margarine, the package of steel-cut oats, the loaves of whole grain bread. She could pretend to forget something, leave the checkout line, but an impatient guy holding giant handfuls of paper towels had hemmed her in. Joan resented every inch of Kevin existing in the world.

"Yes, she is," she said. "She is a wonderful girl," she

muttered, as though she were speaking about someone else's daughter.

"I helped her with her admissions essay yesterday," he said, placing his six-pack on the conveyor.

"Really," she said.

Kevin handed a crumpled twenty to the cashier, a young girl who smiled at him. "Thanks, man," he said to her, and turned again to Joan, whose skin was hot metal. "You have a good night, Joannie," he said, looking briefly concerned at her.

AFTER DEPOSITING HER GROCERIES in the trunk of the car, she sat in the driver's seat and turned to punch the passenger seat in rapid succession. It was what a therapist had told Andrew to do when he had anger troubles in junior high school. They bought him a punching bag and put it in the basement for him to pummel whenever he felt the urge.

It did nothing to calm her and made her feel ridiculous.

When she got home, she opened the door and almost tripped on Andrew's suitcase, which he'd placed by the pile of shoes on the mat. She regarded his shoes, well-crafted leather, as the shoes of a successful man. She remembered taking him to Harvey's Shoes in town every August before school, where he argued each time about the importance of having the *right* sneakers. Even though she had more money after she got married than she'd ever had growing up, she still thought it was silly to buy her kids all the newest shoes as the trends shifted.

Andrew was asleep on the couch with the TV on, an entertainment news program blaring. A famous model was dead, aerial footage of the body being carried out of a mansion on a stretcher. The light flickered against the wall, and Payton the cat was chasing it, making clicking sounds with his mouth the way he did when stalking birds. Joan was momentarily arrested by the image, the blanket covering the model's corpse, the medics walking her to the ambulance, the grating sound of the broadcaster's voice, the running type under the footage that looped twice before she turned it off. She shut his laptop that was open on the coffee table next to a box of Cheerios, top still popped open, alongside a bowl with several rejected floating Os. She sat in the easy chair, the one that still had the imprint of George's body in it. The headrest smelled of his hair product. Joan breathed it in and watched her son sleeping.

Moments later Andrew opened his eyes, stretched out his lanky body, and was startled by her still presence.

"Jesus, Mom, I didn't hear you come in," Andrew said, his feet poking out from under the sturdy plaid wool blanket. "I have a car coming to get me at 6:30 A.M. I'm going back for a day to get my stuff, see Jared, you know. But I'll be right back. I don't want you to be alone."

"I can drive you to the airport."

"I already called," he said, sitting up and taking his empty cereal bowl to the kitchen. Joan followed him.

"For god's sake, let me take care of *something*. You and your sister make me feel so goddamn useless!"

Andrew opened the dishwasher and set his bowl inside. "Mom, I think you should go talk to somebody. A psychologist. Someone in the city maybe, who doesn't know everyone here."

"Really? You think it's a good idea that *I* talk to someone? Remember how enthusiastic *you* were about that prospect?"

"I was a kid, Mom. Everyone has a therapist in New York."

Joan pulled open the dishwasher, took out the cereal bowl, and inspected it. "You have to rinse the dishes—this is an old machine," she said, rinsing it and scrubbing away a stubborn Cheerio. "Maybe you're right, Andrew."

He turned around and handed her a piece of paper. "This is the name of a support group. It's in Woodbridge. It's for female partners of . . . people in prison."

She looked at the paper. It said Sundays, 3 P.M., and there was an address. Tomorrow. "Thanks for this, Andrew. It's very kind of you."

"Good night, Mom. I'll be in touch. I mean, I'll be back in a few days, and you can call me anytime, right? You're not alone with this."

Joan was grateful for those words, but they seemed only to emphasize the opposite. She missed George. She heard his voice on the phone once a day, but never for long, and it didn't sound like him. He sounded like an imposter, and she felt as though she'd tripped and fallen into some alternate reality, the protagonist from some terribly implausible show on the Space Channel.

THE NEXT AFTERNOON, SHE drove thirty-six miles to the Woodbridge health clinic that hosted the support group for women with partners in prison. She arrived half an hour early, sat in the car, and watched women park their cars and go in through the side door. It was windy, and she put her hat in the glove compartment lest it blow away but then didn't get out of the car. More women arrived, some in minivans, others in compact cars; a few walked from the bus stop. She felt the same way she had felt when she was young and traveled to different countries: surprised that the world still looked familiar. The parks in Sweden and Morocco looked like regular parks she'd seen at home. The women who parked their cars and walked into the center looked like anyone. It's not as though she expected them to be wearing neon signs that said *Married to a Pervert,* but she had expected to see something that would give away their status, an indication however subtle, some sort of obvious physical sign of weakness. She looked at her phone, turned it to silent, and applied some Carmex to her lips. They were dry and flaking, no matter how much water she drank. The stress showed on her face. Every step felt heavy as she made her way inside.

Joan lingered outside in the basement hallway in front of a display of health pamphlets. She pretended to be interested in the details of diabetes treatment, as though she couldn't have written the entire pamphlet herself from memory. She waited so long to actually enter that she was a few minutes late, and walked in while a woman was speaking.

"The way I see it, he's sick. It's a sickness. You can't control what you're born with, right? My one kid's got the Down's syndrome. He can't help that neither. Now he's been found out, and he can get help, and he *wants* to get help. Who am I to leave now? I believe in second chances."

The woman who was talking resembled a pug dog; she had one of those smooshed-up faces. Joan took one of the two empty seats around the circle and couldn't stop herself from thinking that if the woman didn't hang on to this guy, she'd probably have a hard time finding some other man to replace him. Then she felt awful for thinking that.

The room was cold and the walls were mostly bare save for a few AIDS Awareness posters and one about getting your flu shot. The only man in the room was clearly the facilitator, wearing a sticker that read *Bob,* although she knew he was really Dr. Robert Forrestor, whose biography on the health clinic's website said he specialized in treating sexual compulsions and disorders, and had started this group after writing his last book, about the family life of sex offenders.

She had spent a lot of time staring at the photo on the website, concocting an entirely imaginary family life for him. She imagined his wife, perhaps an academic with graying brown hair and a soft middle, cutting up ripe plums for a fruit salad on Sunday afternoon.

He nodded at Joan warmly.

As the woman spoke, she pulled on the cuffs of her soft pink cable-knit sweater. There was a coffee urn, and stacks of Styrofoam cups beside it. Joan didn't know anyone actually used Styrofoam anymore. She looked around at the group, most of them in their thirties. They were all wives or mothers of prisoners, some of them *sex offenders.*

"Do you mean that if someone decides to rape someone, he's sick, he's not a criminal?" asked a woman with a purple streak in her hair.

A woman with a name tag reading *Mallory* scoffed. "Where would that rationalizing stop?"

"He's a criminal. Of course he did the crime. He's guilty. No one is saying it's right or excusing any behavior.

What we're saying—I mean"—and she looked at the doctor—"what *I* believe is that restorative justice is better than just sending everyone to jail so they can come out and reoffend, with more anger in their hearts, more hatred. If some men are able to face their demons and change, they should be allowed to, as long as they follow the rules."

It was a lot for Joan to take in all at once. She felt simultaneously grateful that these women existed and totally judgmental of them. For the next hour she listened carefully to their stories. A woman named Cindy who spoke in uncertain upspeak, every sentence going up at the end like a question, complained endlessly about how unfair her husband's PO officer was. "He won't let us live a normal life? And my husband is harassed so much, he's got no freedom?"

"What's a PO officer?" Joan whispered to the woman next to her, who was knitting a brown and red afghan in her lap.

"Parole officer," she hissed, annoyed.

Joan imagined what Clara would've said to Cindy. If you fuck with *children,* stop expecting anything but hatred from everyone. *Suck it up.* She just looked so pathetic, whining about how her husband kept taking shit out on her whenever he got frustrated.

"He should be thankful you didn't drive a stake through his heart for molesting your daughter!" Mallory practically shouted, unable to control herself.

Apparently this wasn't the right kind of thing to say. Joan took note.

"Our role is not to judge," said Dr. Forrestor calmly. "Our role is to listen."

But Joan swore that she saw Cindy smile to herself. Like *yeah, you're right.*

She hated the women in the group when they talked slowly, or mispronounced words, or cried, or expressed shame for staying with their husbands. She hated them because she could relate to them, and that meant she didn't really know who she was becoming, who she had been, who she was supposed to be.

WHEN JOAN WENT HOME, she ransacked George's office, looking for clues about where his money had gone, or evidence of something, anything concrete. She felt almost envious of the women in the group who knew things for sure. Facts. George's office was a room she'd never been much interested in, piled high with books and papers. She wasn't sure what she was looking for amongst the endless papers of theories and notes. The police had already been through it all, taking his hard drive and later returning everything banged up but apparently containing nothing of interest. "Not even one bit of porn," said Bennie at the time. "How many men can say that? Heck, how many women?" He looked pleased with himself, but to Joan it seemed to say that most normal men look at porn, and this was therefore just another way her husband was a freak of nature.

When she found nothing unusual at all, just the regular bits of detritus of his life, she curled up on the floor and wrapped herself in the old brown sweater he'd kept draped over his cozy oak office chair since the day they moved in, it seemed. It smelled like his aftershave still, and she inhaled deeply.

PART TWO

The Next Four Months

18

JOAN EMBARKED ON THE THREE-HOUR JOURNEY TO THE prison and back every Friday during the first month following George's arrest. She packed her brown leather cross-body satchel with magazines, granola bars, a hairbrush and compact, an extra sweater. She developed rituals. There was a truck stop where the same middle-aged woman with silver curls served her a medium with milk and half a sweetener every week. She often pulled the Volvo up on the side of the road to visit a particular farmer's cart, buying squash and root vegetables, beets, or kale with dirt still clinging to each leaf. She would rub a hearty apple on her shirt before taking a bite, standing on the gravel shoulder beside her car and looking out over the farmer's fields towards the mountains. In these moments she could pretend to herself she was visiting a great-aunt at a neighboring farm, or traveling to the outlet malls for bargains. She brought along easy-to-read entertainment magazines to glance at in line and discard at security. She even began to nod politely at people she recognized in the visitors' line. Some of the guards learned her first name. There was an unexpected humanity and sense of routine to visiting the prison now. Still, every time she pulled out of the parking lot and began the journey home, she cried. She'd pull over and buy a coffee only to sip it once and then hurl it with all the strength she had into the air behind the other parked cars in the Dunkin' Donuts parking lot. The anger was the most startling, and the most difficult to defuse.

Every week, George was allowed three adult visitors for ninety minutes in total. Sometimes Clara would accompany her in the car and then hit the outlet malls while Joan visited with George. She tried to convince the kids to come, but Sadie, after that first visit, stayed away. She spoke with her father on the phone a few times a week, but refused to go visit.

Andrew had basically moved back into his old room on the weekends and insisted on visiting with George by himself for half an hour whenever he went to the prison. Joan would leave at the halfway mark and wait for Andrew in the parking lot. She expected this was because he didn't want to be emotional in front of her. Improbable as it seemed, they settled into a new routine during this holding pattern—like when you've put gauze on a wound, and you're waiting it out, hoping no infections seep in. Joan went through the motions: waking and dressing, eating and driving, falling into bed exhausted, and numbing out with television and red wine. She was always planning to go back to work in a week or so; she needed the routine again.

On occasion, though, something would happen to shake her from the routine.

She stood in line at the Book Nook in Woodbridge, buying reading material to take to George. The cashier was a young woman, straight blond hair tied back with a purple cloth headband. When Joan smiled at her, the girl's face reddened, and she stumbled at the cash register, forgetting the decimal point and charging her $2,754.00.

"Sorry," she mumbled, trying to fix the error, which only seemed to anger the computer. The line behind Joan grew longer. The point-of-sale system made obvious beeping sounds of displeasure. Joan glanced at her name tag. *Tammy-Lynn*. Of course! Tammy-Lynn Harrison, one of George's brightest scholarship students. He'd spoken of her often and fondly.

"Hi, Tammy Lynn," said Joan, obliviously, "It's okay. I'm in no hurry."

The girl fumbled, muttered a hello, and called the manager over to fix the error. She bagged Joan's purchases and moved on to the next customer.

Joan lingered by the door afterwards, obsessed. Was Tammy-Lynn awkward because of the rumors? Joan felt she *had* to know. She went back into the store and pretended she had forgotten to purchase something. She lingered by a table of lavender candles and throw pillows. She grabbed a gaudy silver photo frame engraved with *Family is Love!* and brought it up to the cash. This time there was no lineup.

"Forgot this one," Joan said.

Tammy-Lynn scanned it. "Uh-huh, that's $7.57."

Joan handed her the credit card, staring at her a bit too long.

"What?" Tammy snapped. "Look, I know what I saw. I wasn't drunk. I know he's a nice man and everything, and he was so kind to me usually, but I know what I saw!" She was yelling then. Joan stumbled back, jostling a display of boxed chocolates.

Joan grabbed the frame.

"I wasn't drunk!" Tammy-Lynn yelled over the sound of soft eighties rock on the store speakers as Joan fled the scene. Joan stood outside on the sidewalk, momentarily forgetting where she'd parked the car. When she found it, she placed the frame behind the back wheel and listened for the crunching sound as she reversed over it.

EVERY SUNDAY, SHE WENT to the support group, even though she felt she didn't fit in. Regardless, it was a place to vent, with women who, whether she liked it or not, understood what it was like not to have access to your loved one, and to experience both anger and grief, love and rage, because of what he had done or might have done.

On Sunday mornings she'd get up and get dressed as though she were going to church like she usually did, but hadn't been since the arrest. She'd put on NPR and make breakfast for Andrew before he went back to the city, and then she'd sit on the back patio and cover her legs with a blanket and sip coffee, while church went on without her. Every week she'd make a list of household things to get done that day instead of going to the group, and then at the last minute she'd get in the car and drive to the group.

The facilitator was trying to encourage Joan to share more. She had four weeks of attendance before he gently prodded her to participate in the discussion. "Why don't you tell us about your visits to see your husband?"

"Well." Joan clasped her hands to keep them from flying away. "Sometimes he just talks, you know, about the book he's writing. I don't understand all the jargon, but I like to see that he's not just rotting away, that something still matters to him. I bring him books and magazines to read."

"Do you feel like he listens to you?" asked Shelley of the many cat sweaters.

"Yes. I mean, he always asks about the kids first, and then he asks how I'm holding up. Always. I feel like he is genuine in his concern for me—for us."

"Well, that's the least he can do . . ." Shelley muttered. Shelley was having a resentful week.

"He thinks I should go back to work, you know. He said, 'Joannie, you find so much meaning in it.' And it's true. I'm thinking about it. I do miss the routine."

"Do you speak about the charges against him?"

Dr. Forrestor never said *crimes,* which Joan appreciated, unless the husband in question had actually been found guilty or admitted to things.

"I always blurt it out right at the end of our time, when I know I have to leave soon. I always ask him to tell me the truth. George reacted badly to this at first, like I was the one who should be embarrassed for asking the question. I want to know, and I need to know, and I deserve to know, right?" Her voice squeaked at the end of the question.

The women sitting around the circle nodded in sympathy.

"Every time he says no, he says it so firmly and with resolve. But I've noticed that he looks different when he says it, like his eyes glaze over and he almost vacates his body, like his spirit has been lifted away. Does that sound crazy? Sometimes he just keeps saying it, no no no no, you know? As if repeating it makes it necessarily so. At first I believed him, the words were comforting, you know?"

"Do you believe him?" Shelley asked.

"I don't know. I change my mind all the time. My daughter says I'm in denial, and my son says he believes him. But last week when I asked him, he just exploded. He said, 'Don't you know how hard it is for me to hear you ask me that every damn visit? This is the one highlight of my treacherous, inhumane week.' He said that if I really loved him, I would believe him."

Several women sucked their teeth. "I've heard that one before," said Ann, a mousy woman who rarely spoke, whose husband had assaulted his younger employee.

"He has never spoken to me like that before," Joan said. "Despite the circumstances of why he is in jail, the encounters we had were always civil. I don't know, I was so shocked that I just apologized. I felt *guilty*." It sounded ridiculous as she admitted it to these women.

Joan wasn't sure why she had immediately assumed responsibility that wasn't hers. It seemed entirely out of character for her to do that. If you had to choose a Woodbury to be in a bar fight with, you'd want Joan. She didn't used to back down.

"Why should I fucking *apologize*? Was I that *easy* to manipulate? Who *am* I?" she said to the support group, who were rapt. How long had it been since she felt as though anyone was listening to her? Other than at work, it had been a very long time.

She proceeded to tell the women in the support group what she'd done after that. She pulled into the nearest mid-sized town, one that housed a university and a strip of hotels along a flat expanse of highway. She'd checked herself into the highest hotel on the horizon. She didn't even bother to bargain-hunt, she just chose the first one she came upon besides the Motel 6. It was a lavish five-star, and a valet took the keys from her shaking, cold hand and exchanged them for a small piece of numbered paper, which she quickly lost in her pocket. In the lobby she signed the credit card slip with an angular scrawl unlike her real signature and didn't really hear the concierge when he informed her of the checkout time and pointed her towards the elevators. She nodded at the bellhops, noted the entrance to a fancy steakhouse restaurant off the lobby as she walked, but she was not inside herself, truly. Her bones kept moving and she sank behind.

Her room was on the twenty-seventh floor. It overlooked a skateboarding and roller-skating park. She opened the brown curtains and stood barefoot on the carpet, even though she knew it was unwise to do so with so many diseases combed into each tiny thread, ready to attach to her skin. She pressed her nose against the glass as the electric heater warmed her ankles. She stared down onto the streets, pushing her toes into the fibers. Directly below the hotel she watched a lone roller skater, a very proficient one, skate around the perimeter. Her legs were so tiny from Joan's vantage point that they looked like little bird legs. Her movements and gentle rhythms mesmerized her. The sound of how George had spoken to her reverberated around the beige, tasteful decor.

"I ordered room service—I've never done that before! I opened the minibar and drank all the gin. It was kind of nice, actually. And I called my kids. I call them both at seven every night, usually."

She didn't tell the women that they only picked up about once or twice a week, and for those few times she was overwhelmingly grateful.

She was worried about Sadie.

For a few moments she'd felt regretful about her decision to get a hotel room. She was *fine* to drive. She just couldn't bear the thought of the long stretch of highway and all that time to think. She'd needed a rest. Her phone rang, and she saw the familiar work number appear on the screen, the chief of staff at the Avalon Hills trauma department. She answered hesitantly.

"Joan, hello. You know . . ." He cleared his throat, the way he always did. Acid reflux. She knew what was coming. *We think the stress of the position might be too much for you, all things considered.* Meaning the bad media reflected poorly on the hospital. *We have donors, you know.* Et cetera. She steeled herself against this possibility.

"I'm calling because I'm hoping that it's time for you to come back to work. You are missed. You run a tight ship, and your replacement is getting sloppy, you know. Confidentially . . ."

"Well, doctor . . ." Joan was so shocked she couldn't really respond. She kept staring out the window, at the cars that looked like toys driving down the busy street. The sight of partying youngsters, couples arm in arm. The skater kept on circling.

"I know this has been hard, and your coming back would be contingent on checking in with our psychiatrist, but I'm sure it won't be a problem. We all know how strong you are."

"Yes, well, this has been tested lately."

"Yes, I can imagine."

Joan sat down on the edge of the bed, adjusting the belt of her plush white hotel robe.

"I don't know if you've read the daily paper . . ."

"No, not yet."

"Well, the hospital issued a statement of support for you, and I hope that puts your mind at ease. We are here for you. You've given the hospital so many years, and you've done exemplary work, and we are aware that you were as shocked about the news as anyone could be."

"That is an understatement."

"Well, I will give you some time to think about it. But we're hopeful you can return within the week. Would you like to do that?"

"Yes," she agreed, hesitantly.

"Terrific," he said. "I'll set up that appointment with Dr. Chua and you'll be on your way back to work. Terrific."

"Terrific," she parroted, "thank you," before hanging up.

Joan had called Clara and told her she would be returning to work.

"Amazing idea! You need something else to do besides

support your husband," she said. Clara had been on her to stop being so generous with her caring ear, to access her anger.

"Clara, I'm in a hotel near the prison. I've stopped because I can't really deal with it. I think I might be going crazy." Going crazy felt like a low moan of white noise in her head; the light of the room looked so bright, her hands didn't seem to be her own.

"Good. You need to get fucking crazy. Some crazy shit has happened, and it's time you stopped trying to solve everything you know you can't solve."

"You know I'm a practical person, and if there is something to be done, I will do it."

"Yes, yes. I know. God. But what are you doing for yourself? Why don't you trot on down to the hotel bar and meet a man. Don't get his last name. Tell him you're a corporate saleswoman in town for one night only. And get it *on*."

"Clara! I could never. I'm *married*."

Clara cleared her throat. "My god, are you Amish? I think that when your husband's in prison and you're not allowed any conjugal break times, you gotta do what you gotta do." She laughed.

"Well, maybe you would, but I'm not like that."

"No, of course, you live for other people. It gives your life meaning. Do something selfish for once. He owes you one, right? For sticking it out. You should fuck any man you want and George should just say thank you, thank you, thank you for staying with me." She laughed again. Joan could tell she'd been drinking. She could hear people in the background. Clara was talking in the voice she took on when she was cognizant that others were overhearing. Her laugh was full and cackling. "I mean, it's not as if he was faithful."

"Fuck you, Clara. *Fuck you*." Joan hung up the phone and threw it on the ground. It didn't smash or make any sound against the plush beige carpet. She'd just alienated her only support system and she didn't even get the satisfaction of breaking something.

She'd dressed and gone down to the lobby of the hotel to check her email. She didn't like to answer email on her phone and had recently just disabled it entirely. But first she grabbed a newspaper and forced herself to read the article entitled simply WHAT WIVES DON'T KNOW. The article opened with details of George's case, and then chronicled several wives of famous sex offenders who had no idea, and quoted a researcher about how common this is. The words soothed Joan, that she wasn't the only fucking idiot.

The paragraph her boss had informed her about was towards the end. It read:

Woodbury, 52, is head of nursing at St. Joseph Medical Center in Avalon Hills. Following the arrest of her husband, she was described in a statement from her workplace as a "kind and compassionate individual" and a "long-serving, greatly admired and universally liked member of our team."

The statement had choked her up. She'd bit her lip, blown her nose into a scratchy hotel bar napkin.

Then Joan had checked her email. There was one from Andrew with a list of names and numbers of therapists in the city. One from Clara's iPhone saying sorry. She pictured her standing in the middle of the dinner party typing in the hurried response.

She called the first therapist on the list and set up an appointment.

Joan had then checked the home voice mail, and was relieved to hear that there were no threats or obscene messages. They'd tapered off over the last couple of weeks but still she anticipated them. Perhaps there was a new scandal the hordes were paying attention to now.

She had then sent Andrew and Sadie a joint email requesting they all have dinner. She wanted to see them. She needed to see them. "There are things we need to discuss," she wrote. It sounded official. But all she wanted to discuss was their lives, how they were getting along, how they were managing to cope. She had recently been experiencing an odd sort of nostalgia for when they were younger and required constant supervision. At the time she'd often felt as though she couldn't wait for Sadie to become independent, to have some time to herself, but now she longed for her seven-year-old daughter—watching her skate on the lake in the winter, her insistent voice calling out, "Are you watching, Mom?" or trying to get just a few more minutes' sleep before hearing "Mommy, Mommy, Mommy, Mommy" while a small hand tugged at the duvet.

As she'd clicked off the computer, she felt as though she'd accomplished a mountain of tasks and was now heading back to work. She was filled with purpose. For a short moment the pain and desperation that had become so commonplace lifted, and she remembered her real self again.

"Anyway, so I'm going back to work, and I'm thankful for that," she said now to the support group.

Dr. Forrestor looked at her, and she wondered if she'd been speaking for too long. He thanked her for sharing and moved on to the woman on her left, and Joan felt better, briefly, and less burdened.

19

KEVIN BRUSHED HIS TEETH IN THE EN SUITE BATH-room, watching Elaine in the medicine cabinet mirror. She sat up in bed reading *The Economist*. He tapped the side of his toothbrush twice on the side of the sink and put it away. The bathroom light was interrogative, its purpose to highlight the aging process. He couldn't put off telling her any longer. He'd been writing the book based on the Woodbury scandal in secret for a couple of months, and it was weighing on him. The news would hit the papers the next day that the pitch had gone to auction and a number of publishers had been fighting over it. He'd finally inked a deal. He didn't want to feel like a coward for one minute longer. He splashed his face with cold water, dried it on the hand towel.

"My new novel is based on a true story," he began, climbing into bed, "and tomorrow my agent is going to announce the advance I got to write it, and it's bigger than anything I've received before."

Elaine took off her reading glasses and looked at him, the magazine falling to the floor. "Oh my goodness! This is terrific news!" He hadn't seen her this excited about anything in so long, he felt sick at having to elaborate. She reached out and caressed his cheek. "Wait—did you change the whole book? What true story?"

"Well, it's about the Woodbury case, actually, set at Avalon prep. The narrator is, uh, his daughter. But it's fictionalized."

"Kevin . . ." She paused, and he could almost see the joy draining from her face. "That is tricky territory. You can't do that."

"Well, it's done. It's a novel. You can't penalize me for that. It's an incredible story, don't you think? It happened right in front of me. It wasn't possible to resist." He knew Elaine was too smart for that response, but it was all he had.

"It's not ethical," she said. "Sadie is not a character, she is a human being this family cares a great deal about. And I can penalize you for that. Why else would you have kept it a secret from me, if you didn't feel some kind of guilt about it?"

From there it took a turn to a deeper kind of conflict, with Elaine insisting it was a parasitic move because he was desperate to be relevant again, and that his masculinity was preventing him from learning from humility and truly working hard to improve, that he was too entitled and his early success had stilted him. That she was exhausted by him, and that this was the last straw, that he hadn't cleaned the bathtub even once in five years. They fought for hours, about his rights as a writer and Elaine's right to protect her kid. They never agreed. And she shut him out of her room, and he retreated to the couch, too angry to talk.

She was unsupportive and patronizing and didn't understand what it was to be a writer. That's what Kevin wrote in an email to the girl from Twitter he'd been flirting with, confiding in, for the last few months. That it was easy to be a moralist from your tenured tower. That she used her age in these moments to wield power. That she couldn't insist on being a control freak who wanted to make sure everything in the house was "done right" and then get upset when people were afraid to clean the bathroom wrong. For the first time he felt truly checked out of their relationship, as though he was getting ready to leave. A deep sadness enveloped him, and then more anger. The announcement in the paper the next day was supposed to be a highlight of his career, one he wanted to share with people he loved. How dare she be so selfish?

He curled up on the couch, and woke up several times. The final time, he found Sadie sitting on the coffee table, legs crossed, staring at him. She had the bong in her hands, and exhaled a long stream of smoke. He noticed she was wearing one of those linked rings like bruisers used to wear as weapons in his day, but her ring was made of tiny green flowers. He would write that detail down. She smelled of strawberry oil, and he noticed for the first time how her waist-to-hip proportions were perfect; the last time he'd really looked at her, she'd been straight and angular.

"I hope you don't mind." She smiled. Her nails matched the green flowers.

He did mind, as he didn't want to have to call his dealer

any more than he had to, and his advance check hadn't come in yet, so he was still broke. But he didn't say anything. At least he knew now that he wasn't losing his mind and forgetting how much pot he'd been smoking; this was where it had been going.

"How are things?" he asked, as though the situation was totally normal. He tried to memorize her face, the way it had lost its youthful sheen in the previous month, how her cheekbones seemed to actually be hardening, like a doll's.

"Same," she said, shrugging, giving him a weird smile.

He nodded back, wondering how to keep asking her questions without seeming to be interviewing her.

"Can't sleep?"

"Nope." She shrugged again.

She continued to stare, until he began to feel a bit uncomfortable. "I should go to bed," he said, as though he had fallen asleep on the couch by accident.

He wanted to tell her he was heading to see her dad in the morning. He wanted to see her reaction, but Elaine's voice in his head stopped him. He'd go see George and then he would head to the hospital to try to interview some nurses who worked with Joan. He was having a hard time nailing her character.

THE NEXT DAY KEVIN drove to the prison, stopping twice for large coffees along the way. The adrenaline and excitement he'd felt after he pitched the book had disappeared one morning as he stared at the blank page on his screen and felt a familiar thrum of potential failure behind his eyes. Now he really had to write the book. He watched Sadie and Jimmy sitting at breakfast, both on their phones, eating cereal, feet touching under the table, and thought, *How can I make this situation active?* George was in jail. His family was trying to keep on keeping on in his absence, dodging reporters and going to work and school. "To be clear, this is fiction," he wrote to his editor. His editor replied: "No alternate universes, no huge plot divestments though? Use all the usual storytelling elements, and make it as interesting as possible, but don't stray too far from the original."

He DIDN'T KNOW WHAT to expect when he saw George. He'd already written several chapters of conjecture based on his memory of who George was. But he had no idea how to reconcile the fact that people knew an entire other George, and he had never met the sinister side. Sure, he could be a Jekyll/Hyde character, but that wasn't going to be easy to portray. It wouldn't seem convincing. It did seem closest to the truth, though.

He'd met George before, at one of his backyard barbecues, and he'd seen him around town. George would lift his hand half off the steering wheel as he drove by Kevin when he was biking around the lake on weekends—the customary small-town thing to do. They'd exchange pleasantries at the Coffee Hut or drugstore, especially if their kids were in tow. George always struck Kevin as a bit of an intimidating figure, who was nonetheless approachable and jovial. He used to joke about him with Elaine, that he didn't seem real. He'd seemed too perfect, too good a husband, not enough darkness. When you don't seem real, there is generally something off about you, he thought. That's what he'd realized while examining character, figuring out the motivations of everyone he invented. He, of course, was the epitome of the other side of the story. Too real, all flaws. Kevin knew he would never win any charm contests. His propensity to stare off was disconcerting to some, but he didn't worry much about it. Elaine was similar, though in a muted way because she had to be so responsible all the time. But that was okay by him.

One of the only real conversations he'd had with George was at one of those barbecues, as Kevin was requesting another bourbon from the bar staff by the pool. The servers were wearing all white with ice-blue accents. It was like a scene from a 1970s movie come to life, and Kevin thought it was both pretentious and lovely.

"When are you going to start your own family, Kev? You can't stay twenty-five forever," he'd said. They turned to watch a group of kids running in circles around a patch of sunflowers. Even the toddlers wore designer clothes.

"I like the life I have," he'd said, thinking that would be the end of it. Usually it was. Most married men envied him, and the conversation that followed would be full of joking about the chains of monogamy.

"Sure, sure. You don't have to do much you don't want to do. But responsibility is what shapes a man," he'd said, draining the last bit of bourbon from a rock glass and swirling the remaining ice around. "There is a freedom in responsibility, you know, in confinement. Too much freedom can be dangerous."

It was only later that Kevin realized how richly ironic that comment was, as they were standing in the backyard of George's parents' estate, a house he hadn't had to scrimp and save for, buoyed by a trust fund.

Since he had decided to write the book he'd been watching and listening to the way Sadie spoke about her father. She mostly avoided speaking of him at all, even though she used to talk about him all the time. When she did mention him, she tried to do it in a way that made it seem as though she didn't resent him.

It had taken him a while to ask George for a meeting. First, Kevin wanted to write some sketches of the Woodburys' lives before the arrest, and then do some legal research. It took him a month to feel organized enough to approach George's lawyer, try to get an interview with George himself. He heard back less than forty-five minutes after he'd put in the request, which was unusual. George probably wanted to set the record straight.

When Kevin got in line at the prison, leather-bound notebook open and pen poised, he took notes of how the people were standing in line, resigned and weary. He tried to keep calm and focused on the task at hand. When George walked into the room where Kevin was sitting at a long table waiting for him, he looked like he had been physically deflated, as though someone had pumped the air out of his ample chest, and altered that handsome but nerdy face of his, so that he had the withered look of any man, sort of like Kevin's father actually, after thirty years at the mill, that whiskey face. The change in his appearance was startling.

"Hello, Kevin." George's hand felt smaller, weaker, but his handshake was the same. In charge.

"Hi, George. Thanks for helping me with the book."

"No problem, no problem. You know, I'm writing my

own book in here," he said, placing his hands behind his head in what Kevin remembered as a favorite position of teachers when they expect respect or compliments.

"Is that so?" Hearing non-writers talk about their books-in-progress was one of his pet peeves. It happened all the time, especially with people who then claimed to never *read* books. Although George had once been a promising intellectual, an avid reader. He could probably do it, Kevin reasoned.

"It's a memoir of sorts, about the penal system. It's a dreadfully mismanaged place—archaic systems of social order, everything is about race. It's very *Lord of the Flies* around here. Fascinating to observe and document—in moments, of course, when it's not a living hell."

Kevin wrote *writing his own book. Lord of the Flies.*

"How is Sadie? Is she still staying with you?"

"Yes, she is."

George grimaced slightly, looking down at his hands. *Repentant?*

"Is she healthy? Going to school?"

"Yes, very healthy. All things considered, anyhow."

"I broke her heart."

It seemed like the kind of comment that was looking for sympathy, not absolution or relief. It was obvious that both his wife and kids would be heartbroken. He wrote down, *sympathy seeking?*

He started to wonder if George was talking this way for his benefit, so he would take notes and write down *empathetic, concerned for his daughter.*

"This is awkward . . . I just need to know . . . if you're guilty."

"I am not," he said, so quickly that Kevin had to ask him to repeat himself to make sure he'd heard correctly. Kevin recognized he'd made a rookie mistake, going so hard and fast before establishing trust. They were then at an impasse. If he hadn't been in jail, George would surely have made an excuse and got up to leave.

"Tell me about the ski trip," Kevin said, doodling circles in his notebook.

"It was standard, the same trip I'd been on for dozens of years now. The school rents a charter bus, although some of the wealthier students come up in limousines. Those tend to be the kids who cause the most trouble. You know, they drink in the cars and their chauffeurs are well aware, and stay quiet, you know, for the sake of their jobs. Which is ridiculous, if you ask me, considering the liability, but I don't judge. Some of these kids have no guidance, parents always off all over the world, they're raised by nannies. I remember that. I was basically raised by my housekeeper, my beloved Andrea, may she rest in peace. Anyhow, the other five parents and I had quite a situation on our hands when the limos pulled up. Everyone from the buses got settled into their rooms, and we checked every student's bag for bottles. Fairly standard stuff. I don't know what went wrong, really. By the time it was evening and most of the good kids were assembled by the fire in the chalet or going for some night walks, a group of kids took off, I don't know where, really. But they returned around midnight and I had to deal with a few who were quite sick. I called their parents, but no one was reachable, so Dorothy and I gave them water and told them to sleep on their sides, that sort of thing, hoping for the best. That's the whole story. The rest of the weekend was fairly standard. Lots of skiing, one twisted ankle, two kids on hallucinogens who freaked out on the chairlift. That's about it. Standard stuff."

"Okay," said Kevin, taking careful notes. "Why do you think the girls are saying . . . what they're saying?"

"I have no idea."

"None?"

"None at all."

They were silent for a few moments. A woman visiting a man with a neck tattoo of a swan quietly wept.

"In my experience, most young women are still children—most of my students are. They might dress up like adults, and do provocative dances at the talent shows, and think they're twenty-one, but you can still see the child in them. And sometimes young women are simply beyond their years, you know? They have a wisdom that only comes with age, but they aren't yet physically grown. You can spot them in a classroom right away. Their minds are beyond their years . . ."

Kevin shifted in his seat, knowing a potential confession was to come, trying not to seem too keen, nodding passively. George seemed almost lost in his own monologue, didn't notice Kevin's anxiety.

"I know it's a cliché, the old soul. But some young people have that. And it may be confusing for some adults, sure. But I know what is right, and I believe in the law, and I know that no matter how old a young person may seem, any desire is simply left best to the imagination, or else it is a crime. An older person, and certainly an older teacher, has power and the young person does not."

Kevin's disappointment became evident across his face, and George smiled as though to say *gotcha you fucking con.*

"Well," Kevin said, "they have enough power to put you in jail."

George's face grew red, his fingers gripping the edge of the table. "I know right from wrong. If anyone even laid one finger on my daughter, I would lose my mind. Just lose it. Understand me, Kevin, there is a reason why someone is setting me up, but I don't know what the reason is. I have only done one thing I regret in this life, and it was a very long time ago."

"What was that?"

He looked down at the table between them and exhaled, beads of sweat dropping onto the Formica. "We can email," he said. "Or letters. Ask me questions that way. But I will never confess, young man. I haven't done anything wrong."

"You can trust me," Kevin said. He looked at George, trying to establish that trust, but he imagined George had been lied to for years by students, and could see the lie no matter how unfailingly he held his eye contact. "And please don't tell Sadie or your wife about the book. It would compromise things," he said.

George looked him up and down, considered it, then nodded.

20

SADIE KNOCKED ON THE SECRETARY'S DOOR. "DOROTHY?"
"Come on in!" she sang, looking up from her desk, an open Tupperware container of carrots and celery holding down the day's newspapers. A stack of *Support George Woodbury* signs were gathered in the corner, fading blue marker on white bristol board.

"I've been wondering how you are holding up. A bunch of us went to see your dad, to try to make sure he's keeping his spirits up and knows he's got our support," she said, sipping from a stainless steel travel coffee mug.

"I'm sure he's really happy to have you guys . . . in his corner," Sadie offered, adjusting her backpack on her shoulder and pulling both dangling straps.

Dorothy reached into her desk and pulled out a stack of stickers.

"Don't tell anyone I gave these to you, but my group made these." She handed them to Sadie as if she expected applause. The stickers said *Why Won't the Media Tell the*

Truth? and *Regret your behavior the next day?—Cry Rape and
Ruin a Man's Life* and *Free George Woodbury, The Age of
Consent is Misandry.*

Sadie grimaced and pocketed the stickers.

"Don't tell anyone where you got them. I could lose
my job. That's how ingrained institutionalized misandry is
in this country." She laughed somewhat hysterically before
focusing on Sadie. "What can I help you with today?"

"I need a note to explain my absences lately. You know,
some kids have been really mean, and I've felt really . . .
emotional."

"Of course, of course. I'll write you a note that allows
for some flexibility," she said. She pulled out a pad of attendance slips and started to write. Sadie played with the Zen
garden on her desk, read the text of her inspiring leadership posters on the wall.

"Did you grow up here in Avalon Hills?" Sadie asked,
making small talk.

"Yes, I did. I actually went to school with your father.
I mean, I went to the public school until the tenth grade
and then got a scholarship to come here. It was night and
day, the difference, you know. How much support you
kids get. Sometimes I think you need to be reminded of
that, just how good it is here."

"I'm sure parents remind their kids every time they
write a tuition check."

Dorothy didn't laugh, just handed her the note. "Anything else I can help you with?"

Sadie sat down in the chair and pulled at the sleeves of
her cardigan.

"How are you so certain that my father is innocent?"

"Oh, honey, I just know. I just know *him. Right?* I mean, you of all people, you know how good a person your father is?"

"Of course, of course I do, but . . ."

"You've never seen him do or say anything inappropriate in your life?"

"Never," she agreed.

"Well? There you have it. We all witnessed his instincts ten years ago when he jumped on a crazy man with a gun for the sake of the school. I mean, how much more clear an image can you have of someone with an upstanding character? You've spent more time with him than anyone else. We've all known him for decades. Guys with . . . guys who"—she paused, appearing to be choosing her words carefully—"take advantage or have any kind of sinister edge, you can sense these things. We'd have known years ago; we'd have a sense. This is what feminism has done, Sadie. They've blurred the line between the psychopaths and normal men who have a right to be men! They're taking over!"

Sadie pulled her knees up to her chest, crushing the note in a fist while Dorothy ranted. She was making a circle in the maroon carpeting and fiddling with the window blinds while she talked. Eventually she paused, as though noticing Sadie for the first time.

"Anyway, don't let the kids get to you, Sadie. They're just bullying and conspiring, and this will all be over soon. We've got his back," she said. "You should go back to class."

"Okay, sure. Thanks," she said, going out into the hall, trying to breathe deeply before heading back to physics.

She got to the door and peered in, saw Jonathan Moore hard at work on his laptop, Madeleine Stewart with her hand raised. She turned around.

Sadie had always felt at home at school. She had assumed she'd be a lifelong student, and then a professor or a politician. But walking out behind the field, wandering back towards Jimmy's house, it occurred to her that she didn't want to be there anymore, that she wasn't the same Sadie. What would it mean to let this change her? The things she no longer cared about were numerous, and she couldn't imagine that changing.

WHEN SADIE EMAILED THE info@rightsformen.com address listed on the sticker Dorothy had given her, she was informed that the next meeting was going to be held in a private room at the Applebee's by the highway. As soon as she got the email, while sitting alone in the make-out room reading *Sexual Personae* by Camille Paglia, she knew she was going to go. She didn't know why. She considered them slightly insane and possibly dangerous. But they had something she wanted: certainty about her father.

SHE LOCKED HER BIKE to a rusty street sign by the parking lot, watched as a group of townies hauled five children out of a minivan. She knew she shouldn't use the word *townies*. Once upon a time her mother was a townie, she supposed, though Joan would never describe her family that way. And that was a long time ago. She'd been to Applebee's after track meets, but it wasn't the kind of place her parents would take them for dinner. They'd go to the country club, or to one of the local organic food bistros in town.

The hostess, who stood at the little podium absorbed in her phone, pointed towards a door when she asked where the meeting was, and she realized that she shouldn't have worn her school uniform. It was too late to change now, so she just made her way into the room. It featured a long dining table with a group of mostly older men sitting around, and Dorothy McKnight standing at a giant paper flip board. On it was written *Fatherhood is a Right— Thanksgiving Potluck and Rally!* There were baskets of chicken wings and french fries, some spring rolls.

"Oh my," she said, noticing Sadie, still holding the opened door with one hand, a blush creeping across her face. "Gentlemen, we have a special guest. This is George Woodbury's darling daughter, coming to see how much we support her dad." The group turned to look at her, most giving a weird kind of avuncular smile in her direction.

"Come, sit by me," Dorothy said, bringing over a chair.

"I'm just here to see what you guys are, like, doing about my dad and stuff."

"We are behind him, one hundred percent!" Dorothy said.

The men nodded. When a man with a strange white handlebar mustache spoke up, Dorothy sat down.

"Your father is a symbol of all that feminism has done to cause hysteria in this world. Hysteria has become law! Feminists show specific signs of mental illness, and you can see, this is what happens when these women get too much power. Innocent men go to jail because girls aren't taught anything about being decent and responsible human beings. They are taught they can do anything, and deserve special treatment, and men have to pay for it." Everyone at the table nodded reverently.

"We should have more girls involved in this group," said Dorothy. "I think that's a great idea."

Sadie's whole body went cold, broke into a sweat, and her hands began to tingle. She nodded at them. They were people her father would call delusional nutbars. But some weird part of her wanted to believe them. Because if what they were saying was true, she could defend her father, she could take all the confusion she felt and turn it into something concrete. It was an answer.

Dorothy looked at her. "We need someone to help with our social media campaign. Would you be interested?"

"Uh, I'm not sure," she said. "Maybe I'll just hang out a bit first."

WHEN SHE ARRIVED BACK at Jimmy's, opening the door with the newest key on the golden chain around her wrist, Kevin's bong was sitting out on the dining room table. The bowl was already packed tight, and she heard the shower running. Clearly he'd prepared for a post-shower toke. When she sat on the couch, the objects in the room appeared to bounce slightly, moving around. The floor under her feet rocked as if she were on a boat. The unsettled feeling in her heart was beginning to colonize her body. She cupped her hand around the green glass of the bong and pressed her finger over the hole before lighting it. It made a pleasing bubbling sound as she inhaled, puffing out her cheeks. She exhaled, and the room shifted back to normal. She was so caught up in the moment, she didn't see Elaine standing in front of the TV.

"I don't know where you think you are, Sadie, but this is not a druggie den for teenagers," she said.

Sadie coughed, putting the bong back on the coffee table. Elaine picked it up. Sadie giggled.

"We'll talk about this later. Watch some cartoons or something. I'm calling your mom."

Sadie didn't care. All she knew was that she'd figured out a way to stop the spinning anxiety and to make everything a little bit funny at the same time.

21

S ADIE WAS BACK IN MS. ROCKBRAND'S OFFICE, MANY
years after the almost-shooting. It was no longer
above the stationery store, but in the basement suite
of her house, a stately wooden structure with a large front
lawn in the older part of town where Joan had grown up.

"It's been a long time," she said, ushering Sadie into a
big room with two stuffed recliners to choose from, a box
of plush toys in between the chairs. Sadie chose the one
closer to the window, and pulled off the oversized gray
sweatshirt belonging to Jimmy that she'd been wearing
nonstop since she left home.

Elaine had been very permissive in the tiny pink house.
She had turned a blind eye to Sadie sharing a bed with her
son, allowed her to stay home from school or come home
early if it got to be too much. She occasionally monitored
her assignments, but mostly it was as if the structure of
Sadie's life—the meetings, the sporting events, the

debates—all vanished. But Sadie understood that the incident with the bong had been too much for Elaine. She'd called Joan and they both insisted: the only way Sadie could remain at Jimmy's house was if she went back to Ms. Rockbrand to *express her feelings*.

"Everyone just accepted that it was okay for me to take a break. I've never taken a break from anything in my whole life. I have had after-school activities every day since as far back as I can remember. But I just can't give a shit about exams or how much bulk Saran wrap we can sell to finance the grad trip to Spain."

Eleanor nodded. "You've always been bright, and motivated. So how come this new interest in . . . marijuana?"

Sadie blushed, picked up one of the plush toys, and stroked its blue fur like it was a cat. "I'm not sure. It slows me down. I've been feeling like a hamster on a wheel, you know?"

"A hamster on a wheel?"

"Like I can't stop thinking and whatever, right? My brother Andrew smoked it all through high school. I don't know anyone who hasn't tried it. I mean, Elaine is a bit of a hypocrite making me come here. Her boyfriend smokes pot every night, it's how I get high, right?"

Eleanor wrote something down.

"That won't get him in trouble, will it? He doesn't give it to me—I steal it," she said.

Eleanor raised her eyebrows.

"I feel bad, don't worry. I'm not a criminal," Sadie said. "God, what if I am? What if I'm losing my sense of right and wrong?"

"Slow down, Sadie. You've experienced a huge trauma. It's normal to be feeling stress and anxiety and to seek out ways to cope. You're not a criminal."

Sadie exhaled, sat further back in the chair, wishing she could curl up and go to sleep.

"I have a boyfriend. We've been together a long time—almost eleven months now. But lately I have a new crush, and I feel like I can't stop it from happening."

"It's normal to have crushes," Eleanor started. "Sometimes relationships when you're young don't last all that long. It's okay. Your feelings are valid."

"Well . . ." Sadie debated telling her that it was Kevin, how much she thought about him during the day, tried to coordinate her schedule so that she'd run into him around the house. Didn't she have enough problems? "It's been a few months since I realized it, and I'm not going to do anything about it. I don't know why it feels so urgent these days," she said, though she knew the answer. Kevin had been unusually attentive to her, asking her questions about her life. She was almost sure the crush was mutual at this point.

"You're a teenager, you're going to keep having regular teenage problems, even while your life is inundated with adult realities," Ms. Rockbrand said.

WHEN SHE GOT HOME, Jimmy and Elaine were sitting around the table. Elaine was proofreading one of Jimmy's papers. They were arguing over semicolon usage.

"Semicolons aren't just intuitive, Mom," he said, frustrated. His paper was covered in Elaine's red pen markups.

Kevin was at the stove, tapping a wooden spoon on a soup pot. Sadie found it difficult to look at him. Her body felt magnetically drawn to him. Could everyone see that? It seemed impossible that they wouldn't. She tried to remember back to when she found him annoying, a kind of faceless adult who got in the way of their teenage freedom, but she couldn't. He had become an entirely new being. He'd bleached out his honey-brown hair so he actually looked a little like a surfer from a movie they'd watched about Californian surf culture.

She still loved Jimmy, of course. This was just some crazy thing her body was doing as a product of the stress of her life, she rationalized. "This is undoubtedly some Daddy-complex Freud bullshit," she'd written in her diary. Every other man even *half* his age was totally asexual and repellent to her. It didn't make sense. She was trying not to feed the insanity by indulging in it any more than she had to. She practiced her facial expressions in the bathroom mirror: betray nothing. The line of her lip perfectly straight.

Plus, when Kevin was writing, he was very easy to avoid.

Elaine seemed amused by Kevin's offer to cook. "Don't poison us, honey." Elaine and Kevin had been fighting lately. They were trying to hide it, but she and Jimmy had noticed. But they seemed to be acting okay again.

A half hour later, Kevin ushered them away from the kitchen table and into the never-used dining room, where they were greeted by a table set with fine china, plates of grilled salmon, roasted baby potatoes, and corn on the cob.

"With coriander, lime, and sea salt!" he said, grinning, passing out sprigs of green parsley-like herb.

"Wow, you're really trying, babe," Elaine said dryly. Sadie noticed the tension between them again. Nonetheless, she looked impressed. Kevin went to kiss her on the mouth, but she turned away and he caught her cheek instead.

"So, why are you in such a good mood?" asked Jimmy.

"I got accepted to go to a writers' retreat in Iowa. I was wait-listed, and they just called today to let me know I got a spot. For the whole month. I'm mentoring some young writers, and then I have half days to write. I get paid to be there, right? Awesome."

At 7 P.M., the phone rang. It was Joan. Sadie's father mostly called between 4 and 6 P.M. on Wednesdays, and her mother every night at seven unless she was at work. Her mother had also become less averse to texting and had recently started to use emojis. This meant a series of unicorns or smiley faces were always waiting for her when she looked at her screen.

Kevin made a big show of jumping up to check the call display, but he knew it was her. They left it up to Sadie whether or not to answer it.

Joan had been very angry that week. Sometimes it was about the hounding media or Bennie or how Andrew wasn't processing things emotionally or how Clara was heartless. She didn't want to answer, but she did. Sadie missed her.

"Hey, Mom," she said, sitting on the tall white kitchen stool cradling the cordless. Kevin looked up from the table and winked at her. *Winked.* Jimmy had corn in his front teeth when he smiled at her. He was being so nice to her that she could hardly look at him sometimes.

"Hello, Sadie," she said. "I miss you."

"I miss you too, Mom. You sound . . . less angry than yesterday."

"I am. I haven't been to see your father in a week, and I'm happy about that. I need some space!" She had that somewhat hysterical voice that actresses like Goldie Hawn got in movies when they find out their husbands are cheating on them. All her sentences went up at the end in a fierce soprano.

"Well, that's good, Mom. It's about time you started thinking about your needs." *How much space can she need? He's in a jail cell.* But she knew what she meant. Sadie wasn't one to talk. The more she didn't go visit her father, the worse she felt, and the more the guilt made her want to crawl in a hole.

Kevin was still staring at her, listening intently. She turned away, curling her toes under the lowest rung of the stool, and pressed her head against the refrigerator. *Maybe he also has a crush on me.* The thought made it hard to hear what her mother was saying. She fully checked out for a few seconds, and came back to the sound of her concluding, "And so I think it's time to sell the fucking house."

Joan did not say *fucking* as a rule. Not to her daughter. And she had never seemed to love any other house more than the Woodbury house.

Sadie felt as if she'd been hit.

"No, Mom. You can't."

"Sure I can. The house is legally mine now, entirely, until your father gets out of jail. I get a smaller, less show-offy house, and it saves us money and you have more money for college next year. You won't have to use the money your grandparents left for you."

Sadie burst into hot, involuntary tears. "I LOVE THAT HOUSE."

"Oh, Sadie, I'm sorry. I thought you would be all for this. You are, after all, choosing not to live here."

"Maybe I'll come back!" she said. Elaine and Jimmy turned to look at her.

"Of course I would love that. Even if I do decide to sell, it wouldn't sell for a while. Not a lot of people have this kind of money."

"Mom," Sadie said, standing up, "we need to talk about this in person."

"Okay, well, I'm working tens tomorrow."

"You're back at work?!"

"I'm not recovering from a stroke, Sadie. I can't spend my whole life managing your father's . . . incident."

"Great. I'll meet you in the doughnut shop in the hospital atrium at 9 A.M."

"Deal."

"Deal."

"YOU'RE NOT REALLY INTO me anymore, are you?" Jimmy asked after dinner, when he tried to pin her behind the couch when Elaine went up to refill the popcorn bowl. She concentrated on the ugly pink lilies on the wallpaper behind him, dug her feet into the plush white carpeting and cracked her toes.

"No, I'm just not into sex right now . . . given . . . everything."

She knew that she was lying as she said it. It was a convenient lie. She forced herself to believe it was true, though. She was fucked-up about her dad. She *was*. It made her question all of her intimate relationships. She just didn't know for certain it was actually the reason she was starting to find Jimmy a bit repulsive. What if you just had no control over how your body reacted to someone, and you woke up repelled by the person whom you used to find overwhelmingly attractive? This was something she hadn't considered possible. She felt as though something as random as the wind controlled her emotions.

"It's been months now, and we've only had sex that one time a few weeks ago. I thought we'd be all over each other when you moved in here." He pressed himself against her stomach, leaned down, and started to kiss her neck. The Jimmy she thought was so different from other boys was turning into a parody of the adolescent male. There was nothing more unsexy than someone asking for sex all the time. It was like someone had given Jimmy a handbook on all the best ways to turn somebody off.

He pressed one hand against the small of her back, continuing to kiss her neck and ear. He knew she usually responded well to this, but this time it made her stomach lurch. She contemplated just pulling him into the garage and blowing him to get it out of the way. But that was not in her character. Sex should be mutual, she believed, you should both want it. Jimmy generally believed this as well. Or at least he used to.

"I didn't move in here so you could have instant sex any time you want. I'm not a vag vending machine," she hissed, pushing him off her and rubbing the back of her hand against the wetness on her neck, grimacing.

He gave her a look of pure humiliation. She felt as though she'd kicked a puppy.

His mom padded downstairs with the popcorn and said, "It's time for *Criminal Minds!*" She tried to pretend she hadn't interrupted anything, as Jimmy ran up the stairs and slammed the door on the way outside. "What's with him?"

Sadie shrugged and got cozy on the couch, grabbing a handful of popcorn.

Elaine raised her eyebrows but said nothing.

SADIE DECIDED TO SLEEP in her own bed in the guest room that night.

"Maybe you should take some space for yourself," Eleanor Rockbrand had suggested during their last session.

It didn't solve her insomnia. When she couldn't sleep, and heard the sounds of Kevin's typing coming from his room, she snuck downstairs and watched TV, just to blur the sounds of her own worries. She worried about getting into college, about not getting into college. She worried about Jimmy and her not being together, about this nagging feeling she had that she wasn't in love anymore. That his incessant hovering was going to make her snap.

When Kevin came downstairs, he was startled to see her. "Oh, I saw the light and thought I'd left the tube on," he explained. Though clearly he'd come down to the basement to take a hit off his bong, which he had in his hand,

and she'd busted him. This was the second or third in-stance of accidental–not accidental running into each other between midnight and dawn.

"Can I have some?" she asked with a smile. She arched her back the way she'd seen girls do at school, and stepped closer, daring him. The feeling was thrilling.

"Well, you see, Sadie, when Elaine found out that we smoked that one time, she wasn't very pleased with me."

"Really?" she said, as though hearing it for the first time, as though she hadn't just been sent to therapy for this very reason. "Elaine is so chill."

Kevin laughed. "Yes, well, she is, yeah, I guess she is mostly," he said, as though considering it for the first time. "I guess she thought it was irresponsible of me, and crossed some adult–child boundaries and stuff. And that you are going through so much, and you don't need adults in your life to act like children." He sounded as though he was repeating word for word the lecture he'd probably received from Elaine. "You need, you know, role models."

"Well, that's very simplistic."

"Trouble is," he said conspiratorially, and clearly not actually hearing her, "I'm kind of a kid myself, still. Obvi-ously. Like I'm a goofy, harmless kid. No matter what I do, I'm still this way."

"You're a fun guy, Kev."

"Ha, see, for most adults, that wouldn't matter to them. But I like that you said that, that I'm a fun guy. I am, right? Plus, you're stealing it anyway, right?" He chuckled and lit the bong.

"No! Okay, yeah. Maybe sometimes," she said, coming closer to him.

He handed her the bong and said, "Fine, you little . . . pusher." He winked and walked towards the couch.

The wink hit her like one of those cartoon cupid's arrows. She took a hit, holding it deep in her lungs, trying not to cough. She exhaled a victorious stream of smoke, and passed it back to him slowly.

"I won't tell anyone," she teased.

"Good," he said. "So, how are things with your dad? Have you been for a visit?"

"Nope. Not since that first time. I don't like going there."

"That makes sense." He nodded. "Prison is not exactly pleasant. Are you angry because . . ." He looked to be choosing his words very carefully. "Are you mad because . . . your dad ever . . . you know?"

"Fuck no! No, no, no, never. GOD. I'm so tired of getting asked that question."

"Oh, sorry, I just wanted to know, you know, 'cause we're friends and all."

He said we're friends. I'm not just some guest in this guy's house! Her heart felt, as Amanda would say, all "melty."

Kevin is making me stupid. Making me use words that aren't real words.

"So . . . what are you writing right now?" She was trying to think of something to keep him there. "Still the teenagers? The canoers and the detective?"

"Yeah," he said absently. "Speaking of, I gotta go write! I'm on a roll."

She was sad that he wanted to leave her stoned all by herself in the basement watching a bad movie.

"Stay with me!" she said, putting on a fake pout.

"Ah, you sure are tempting, but really, I've got to keep the magic going."

He called me tempting.

Tempting.

This was an anecdote she would circle later in stupid hearts and stars in her diary.

AFTER A FEW MOMENTS, she decided to go upstairs and capitalize on the feeling of being in her body, and feeling weightless and calm. She crawled under the covers with Jimmy, and ran her hands along his chest, tracing his tattoo. He startled and then smiled. She ran her hands through his hair. He rolled on top of her and kissed her mouth, parting her legs with his knee. At first the kissing felt good, and the floating feel was pleasant enough, but as soon as he started fucking her, the revulsion returned. The streetlight through the window allowed her to see his face above her too clearly. She closed her eyes tight and wished he'd just hurry up.

After, he gathered her up in his arms and said, "I love you so much. That felt so good. I feel so connected to you. I feel like we're one body."

She briefly worried about how she should respond but realized his breaths had slowed and deepened and he was fast asleep. She pulled on one of his T-shirts and crept out of the room. Kevin was actually sleeping in Elaine's room, making it easy to smoke his bong in the basement, where she eventually fell asleep, knowing she'd have to move out as soon as she could. The haven Jimmy's house had provided had turned far too real.

22

THE HOSPITAL FOOD COURT WAS THE BOWEL OF A wayward ship, no natural light and few nutritious options. It was possible to look around and forget what season it was. Overtired health care workers hunched over fire-engine-red tables, spearing limp salad and texting their families. Visitors shared doughnuts, buttered terrible bagels, and drank coffee, best described as an adequate facsimile, heavily sugared to make it tolerable. Joan generally avoided the area, preferring to bring food from home.

She saw Sadie pushing through the crowd, arms crossed, heading towards her. As soon as Joan had tabled the possibility of selling the house on the phone the night before, she had felt regret. Why had she called up her daughter and told her she'd be taking away the site of her childhood—and all related stability—at such an unstable time? The guilt overwhelmed her.

She observed Sadie's walk, her demeanor, trying to assess for signs of ill health, a manic or depressive state. She'd been obsessed with George's health, combing through her recent memories for signs of a shift. Had he said or done anything out of character? What about his strange obsession with baking, with playing squash? She read research papers about men who suddenly acted differently, falling victim to brain tumors and resultant loss of impulse control. If he had a sickness of some sort, and wanted treatment or to become rehabilitated, then things could work out eventually. She'd begun to toy with the idea of reconciliation, even if he was in fact guilty, and to think about the role of second chances, the possibility of him going through enough therapy to truly change in a fundamental way. Then, after having that thought, she would get angry again. She would picture the earnest look on Tammy-Lynn Harrison's face. She felt as though she existed on a seesaw, swinging from one irrational thought to another.

She poured half a sweetener into her black tea as Sadie joined her. Joan pushed a waxy blueberry muffin her way and offered a fake cheerful hello.

"Hey, Mom, 'sup?" Sadie slouched into a chair, pulling the hood of her gray sweatshirt off her head, revealing a mess of knotted hair.

"I've been researching, about your father, about the possibility of a mental illness, undetected until now," she said.

"Mom, if he was sick, would that make him blameless?"

"Maybe. But it means he could try to get well, he could try to . . . atone. That is, if he's even guilty. We have to live with the uncertainty for now."

"I don't want to talk about him," she said curtly, picking a blueberry from the top of the muffin and popping it in her mouth. "I want to convince you not to sell the house."

"Move back in," Joan said boldly.

"Only if you don't put it on the market," she replied. Like mother, like daughter. "Ever. Like, even when I go to school. The house needs to be ours. Forever."

"Sadie, what about next year, when you're in college? The house is way too big . . . for just me—and your dad, if . . ." The reality of Sadie leaving and the future she had thought would be opening up, of living with just George again, without kids, of drinking red wine at night and doing whatever they pleased, being in their twenties again—that was never going to happen now.

Sadie appeared to contemplate the situation as Joan swallowed the lump in her throat.

"For now, then," Sadie said. "Don't do it now. I'll move back in."

Joan tried to mask her elation and speak calmly. "Okay, honey. I was thinking that we should spend Christmas with Andrew and Jared and Clara in the city. Would you like that?"

Thanksgiving has been a total bust. Clara had taken over the cooking, while Andrew and Joan went to visit George. The turkey hadn't turned out, but everyone tried too hard to pretend everything was fine. Joan kept going to the bathroom to cry. She was hoping she could make up for Thanksgiving by planning a better Christmas.

"Seriously?" She pushed her hair out of her eyes, lighting up.

"Sure. It's important for us to be together. But maybe we won't bring Jimmy to New York, if that's okay?" Joan prepared herself for protestations, but none came. Sadie just nodded.

"Yes, that would be best."

Joan tried not to register any surprise. She sipped at her tea. She didn't push her luck by asking about Sadie's college applications. She just enjoyed the moment of calm between them, and felt lucky to have such a good daughter. She had an intuitive feeling that Sadie would be okay. That she was a fighter, and she'd recover.

"I'll get my stuff and move back tomorrow, okay?"

"Great."

JOAN STARTED HER SHIFT, checked the flow chart, and noted who was on duty. The ER was pretty full—the start of flu and flu paranoia season. She was at her office door, pass card inserted, when Nancy tapped her on the shoulder. When Joan turned, Nancy's face broke out into a pink flush.

"Oh, Joan! I'm so happy to see you." Her expression was sincere and Joan was grateful for it, giving her a big hug, for which she felt a bit foolish afterwards. Looking over her shoulder as they hugged, Joan noticed a big bouquet of flowers on her desk, and a Welcome Back banner.

"Thanks for all this, Nancy. You didn't have to go to all this trouble."

"Oh, it was from all of us," she insisted. Though later Joan noted it was Nancy's handwriting on the card, and from the awkward chill she received from some of the staff she realized it had probably been all Nancy's initiative. Nevertheless, she was grateful.

Being at work, both managing the staff and seeing the occasional patient, filled Joan with the sense of purpose she'd been missing. She felt as if someone had thrown her a life buoy.

WHEN JOAN ARRIVED AT therapy that afternoon, she thought she was fine until she was asked, "And how are you feeling?"

She took a breath, momentarily annoyed that she was being asked about herself after a comforting day of looking after others. "Is it possible to be an intelligent human being—perceptive, intuitive—and also be married to someone who fools you so intensely, who is entirely a fraud, and you have no idea?"

"Do you feel like a fraud?"

"Is it possible to be smart and completely fooled?"

"Do you feel like a fraud, Joan?"

"Of course I do. Not only did I think I knew George, I was in love with him, and I thought I knew every single thing about someone I could possibly know. How does anyone ever get over that feeling?"

"You want to get over that feeling?"

"Why do you answer everything with a question? I am here for answers."

"You are here for answers."

"Now you're just repeating whatever I say."

The therapist folded her hands in her lap and fixed Joan with that professional non-stare Joan herself offered about three dozen times a day at work. She tried another tactic.

"I want to know if I am actually not a very smart person, if I've just assumed I was this whole time. If I'm actually a dimwit, an intolerable needy woman, blinded by love."

"I do not think you are dimwitted at all."

"Thank you. Finally you say something."

"You are frustrated with me."

"It isn't personal. I am frustrated with everyone. I can't stand Clara's impatience with me. I hate those women in the support group who have no other identity besides as a girlfriend or wife. I am *more* than that, right? I can be. I just loved that part of my life so much. I was happy."

"You were happy."

"I don't know if I can just let that go."

"Letting go is hard."

It went on like this until Joan wrote her a check at the end of the hour—an hour spent telling the therapist that life was shit and her asking Joan to repeat that her life was shit and in what way. Oddly, in the car afterwards, Joan did feel lighter.

Joan dialed Andrew's number when she got in the car, putting the phone on hands-free and pulling out of the parking lot. Joan could hear the noise of the city all around him in the background when he picked up the phone. She could picture him with one finger in his ear, blocking out Thirty-fifth Street on his way home from work.

"Have you seen your father?" she asked him.

Joan knew that he had. Bennie had told Joan as much, in one of his many unreturned voice mail messages.

"Yes, I have. He is so broken, Mom. I know I shouldn't feel bad for him, but I do."

"You feel bad?" Joan's heart broke.

"Okay, okay. Mom, I have to tell you. I don't know why, but I want him to be innocent. It's like a survival instinct, as if a bear is coming for him and I can only want to get him out of the way of that bear."

"I know it's hard," Joan said helplessly, pulling the car into the parking lot of the Krispy Kreme and going through the drive-through. The red light was on, the doughnuts were hot, and she ordered six with an iced coffee.

As she chewed through two warm doughnuts, stopping only to sip at the creamy iced coffee, Andrew talked through the whole case. How Bennie was no longer as confident, how he was reconsidering the not-guilty plea, how so much would depend on the judge, on who was on the jury, on so many variables.

"You know how much I hated Avalon Hills, how those kids tortured me. Some of those girls accusing Dad, they look just like the girls who spit in my face, who had their boyfriends kick out my car headlights and kick me into a corner and then piss on me as I huddled there. That's all I can see, when I see those girls—the evil suburban menace, you know? I know it's not fair to paint them with the same brush, when I don't know them. I know that even if people behave like assholes, they do not deserve to be treated badly. But my mind is reaching for excuses to take Dad's side. I want to believe him so badly."

Joan couldn't speak. She had no idea any of those things had happened to Andrew. She felt as though she were on a Tilt-A-Whirl, her son, her baby, being brutalized, and she never knew? He was crying now, she could hear his breathing through the phone, despite the cacophony around him of traffic and hollering. She wanted to protect him now, to make up for it somehow.

Instead, she listened as he took a breath and began speaking like normal Andrew again, composed and distant. "I've got to go meet Jared now. We have early evening tickets to a show. I'll call you tomorrow."

"I love you, Andrew. I'm so sorry. I didn't know."

"It's cool, Mom. Don't worry about it. It's okay."

Joan sat in the car, looking down at the crumbs in her lap, the grease stains on her purple cotton work pants. She felt sick from the sugar, dizzy from the caffeine. Why did she think she needed two doughnuts? She set the remaining doughnuts aside for Sadie.

When Joan got home that night, she was exhausted in a way that actually felt physical. So accustomed to emotional exhaustion, Joan welcomed the house, which was clean, and thankfully full of groceries now that she'd learned to use the online grocery service. Andrew called back to say that everything was set up for the following weekend. Jared had arranged to give Sadie a fancy spa treatment and haircut at his salon as a Christmas gift, and other than that, they were going low-key on presents. Just spending time together, maybe going to a movie.

Joan hadn't spoken to George since he blew up at her for questioning him. She didn't listen to his voice mails, either. Bennie told Joan he was very distraught over their lack of contact. "Good," she said to Bennie. "You make terrible choices, and you know they are wrong, then you should feel the impact of that loneliness."

She felt harsh as she said that.

She was still struggling with the feeling that she was

letting him down, that she was abandoning her husband at his lowest point. Compassion—it has its limits, she supposed. "You're allowed to be pissed off," said Clara, said Sadie. Even Andrew, in his way, had said it. "Don't be a doormat, Mom."

23

ANDREW WAS STANDING IN THE LOBBY OF THE VIVIAN Beaumont Theater, holding two glasses of wine, when Jared arrived a few minutes late. Jared regarded him with caution, and Andrew realized he was probably scowling. Jared cocked his head to the side in a gesture of concern, accepting the small plastic cup from Andrew's outstretched hand.

"I'm fine," Andrew said by way of a greeting.

"You don't look fine, you look exhausted."

"That's because I *am* exhausted," Andrew said. "Can I be tired without you acting like I have cancer?"

The crowd grew around them, necessitating that they stand closer. Jared put his hand on Andrew's arm and gave it a comforting squeeze that prompted Andrew to bristle just as an older woman with an oversized designer purse knocked into his arm, spilling his wine on the sleeve of his suit jacket, the Valentino he'd worn for an important meeting at work. He hissed at the woman.

"Well, don't stand in the doorway if you don't want to get pushed around," she said with a thick New York accent. Andrew grew livid, felt Jared moving him away towards the last-minute pre-show lineup at the bar.

"We don't have to be here, you know. We can just tell Evan we saw the play and he wouldn't know the difference. I sent flowers to the dressing room," Jared said, taking a sip of his wine and waving his Visa card at the server for two more.

"Why would we waste the money?" Andrew said, scanning his ticket, trying to understand where their seats were situated inside the auditorium.

"It's not a waste of money if we're supporting the theater. It's no use being here if you could use the time to rest, to catch up on some sleep. We could spend some time together at home, you know."

"Maybe you're the one who needs some rest."

Jared exhaled slowly. Andrew didn't want to be taken care of, and he didn't *want* to stop being stressed out. It filled him with a sense of active purpose, kept him from a restless sadness. He was tired of spending time with Jared that was fraught with tension.

Every meal Jared prepared, every solution to a problem he came up with, wasn't the right one. Andrew knew that Jared was becoming a punching bag for his own anger and helplessness about his father, and for the subsequent fallout of the stress on his career, his time, the things he enjoyed about life.

The lights flickered for the final call.

"My mom wants to spend Christmas with us here, in the city," Andrew said. "Would that be okay?"

"Of course, that would be amazing!"

Jared got really excited about Christmas every year, even though he was Jewish. Andrew always wished they could just order takeout and go to the movies, but he usually invited Jared to Avalon Hills, where Jared was the most excited about the rituals. They holed up at the Woodbury estate, seeing very little of the outside world. Jared had never even seen the town, or any of the local sites.

"I don't know if it will be *amazing*," he said, leading Jared into the darkened theater, "but at least we'll be together."

24

ONCE SADIE DECIDED TO MOVE HOME AGAIN, SOME-
thing she was preparing to tell Jimmy about later
that night, she felt a renewed sense of purpose.
Why was she suddenly an ineffective layabout? Why should
she let the haters win? She was the school's top student.
She had papers to write, a student council meeting to chair.

She drove back to Jimmy's during her free period,
straightened her hair, layered on some mascara, and threw
the gray sweatshirt in the hamper. She showed up last to
the weekly student council meeting. Cheryl was visibly
less than pleased to give up her seat at the head of the table.
The afternoon sun was sliding across the long oak table,
illuminating the dust on all the leather-bound books on
the floor-to-ceiling shelves. Sadie shut the door and the
din fell silent. Sadie smiled at Cheryl, a customer service–
style smile, brimming with teeth.

I dare you, said Sadie's smile. *Basic bitch, just try me.*

"Hello, Cheryl, nice barrettes," she said.

Cheryl touched the tiny golden birds in her thin, greasy shoulder-length hair and whispered a thanks, though she knew Sadie's comment was sarcastic. There was an uncomfortable pause before Cheryl realized Sadie was waiting for her to give up her seat; it was where the designated leadership sat. Sadie looked down at the fidgeting grade reps assembled, at Tony the aspiring CFO who wasn't great at eye contact at the best of times, furiously tapping on his tablet device, then at Jimmy, who was giving her an encouraging smile that said, *Get back on the horse!* Even though things at Jimmy's house had been strained, at school they put on a united front. And having sex with him had made him relax; he'd hovered less that day. Jimmy pushed back whenever anyone gave her cut-eye. It was the only thing that still ignited anything resembling passion in Sadie, and she appreciated it.

Cheryl handed out copies of the minutes from the last meeting, and the agenda for the hour ahead. Running meetings used to make her happy. They were so efficient. She got things done.

"First item," Sadie said, wanting the meeting to go well, scanning the list, "is . . . the Teacher of the Year award."

Some students snickered. Every year it went to her father.

"Well." She cleared her throat. "I'll need a volunteer to adjust the online survey from last year. Do we have a short list?"

"Uh . . ." Cheryl started, shifting in her seat. "I'm not sure you know this? But the site? Has been . . . hacked?"

"Oh yeah?" Sadie drew a lazy sunflower on her agenda.

Tony slid the tablet down towards her, set to the school's homepage, where a black-and-red screen with a YouTube video had replaced the usual content. She clicked on the video. A seventies disco song started up, and the video of her father accepting the award last year appeared, with images from Girls Gone Wild crudely edited on around it. Sadie's cheeks burned, but she took a deep breath, gripping the koala eraser in her pocket.

"Well, obviously this hacker is really . . . basic. I mean, if this is the best he could do. It's the most predictable hack in the world." She slid the tablet back to Tony and fixed him with a blasé stare. "So, uh, Tony," she said, drawing petals on the flower, "take the site down, obvi. I'm surprised the school hasn't done it already."

"It just went live," he said, shrugging and looking down again. Sadie knew at that moment that he was the lame hacker in question.

"Take it down. This school is just so . . . childish," Sadie said. "How is anyone going to survive next year at college with so few . . . social skills?" She looked at Tony again, forcing eye contact, until he physically squirmed. She moved on to the next item on the agenda.

She went through the list of student concerns, things that Sadie used to care about and that now seemed incredibly silly, but she kept up the facade of being interested in things like the job fair, the holiday bake sale fundraiser, fixing the espresso machine in the student lounge, and telling the animal rights group to stop flinging paint at their parents when they arrived for the talent show. Sadie concluded the meeting with an extra-hard slam of the gavel, which was largely decorative but nevertheless made a satisfying bang. She had completed this very normal thing, running the meeting, and she hadn't run out or gone home early.

"Going to the caf, want anything?" Jimmy asked, reaching out to grab her wrist as the group dispersed. She leaned in and kissed him, performing for the group a tableau of normalcy, the way things used to be.

"Chai tea?" she said.

He nodded, a smile breaking across his face. Her pretense wasn't just working on the group, it was working on him. Was he dumb or did he just wish the appearances were reality? Sadie wondered: if she kept faking it, would she start to feel normal again too? Could she trick herself with muscle memory and routine?

She was trying to hide the fact that she was elsewhere, in her head mostly. She was trying to keep up with reading and homework, keep her eye on the prize even if actually attending class was a problem. She had developed strategies—such as using the third-floor bathroom, which was the least populated and where she would likely see Amanda. She went there after the meeting to crack the window and lean outside, get some air. She texted Amanda a bunny emoji, their code for her to join her, and she arrived promptly, thankfully without a cigarette this time.

"Miranda Steele told your dad all about her parents' divorce, and she felt like he was her only confidant, FYI. Now she's so pissed. Like he betrayed her."

"Betrayed her how?" Sadie asked. "If he listened to her, how was that a betrayal?"

"You don't want to know the details," Amanda replied.

"C'mon, it can't be true. Just tell me. I've read everything in the papers," she said, trying to appear impenetrable.

"They would never be allowed to print these details in the paper," she said, like a threat.

Sadie paled. Yesterday Amanda had hugged her and told her things would be okay soon and that she loved her. Today she seemed like one of the catty girls from the hallway.

"And it *sounded* true to me," she said. "Plus, she's more of a social pariah than you now."

"No, she's not."

"Girl, you haven't been around. Someone set her dad's car on fire in their driveway, and Jonah Stewart was apparently *bragging* about it. The cops don't even care—they all remember your dad as some hero who took down that gunman. They think the girls are all liars, especially Miranda, because she's so pretty and because she's had sex with so many guys."

"How do you know how many guys she's had sex with?"

"Everybody does."

"I didn't realize she was getting harassed too."

"Some people might be giving your family side-eye and being assholes, but she's getting it worse, believe me. She convinced all the other girls to come forward, so now that their lives are being scrutinized, they're blaming her. And you know her parents—they're, like, always travelling."

"Wow, that's terrible."

"Anyway, gotta jet," she said, leaving Sadie in the bathroom alone.

Above the sink someone had written, *Sadie Woodbury sucks big dicks!*

Sadie returned to the lounge, where Jimmy was waiting with her tea. She'd booked the couch room for their study period. Since she'd stopped attending class regularly, the school administrators were letting her use the room to study, especially if she told them she was too emotionally fragile to be in a classroom with other students. She took her tests in the student government room while Mrs. Caribou watched.

Sadie had been reading Kevin's novels. She had decided to use one as an example of omniscient narration in an essay for her advanced English class. She described his second novel as "purposely tearing apart our expectations of narrative," but in truth she thought he likely balked under the pressure of his first realist novel and went surreal because it was easier. That's what Jimmy had hinted at, anyway.

Jimmy was hanging out with his friend Jason, who was so cute most girls couldn't even speak around him.

"Why don't you use Joyce instead? Or someone the teacher will be more impressed with?"

"Everyone will use Joyce. She seemed plenty impressed by the fact that I'm staying in the author's house."

He scoffed. "It's my mom's house. He's not as cool as you think he is. He's, like, a total slack-off. He doesn't even pay bills. Before you came, he like hardly ever hung out with me. He just wrote and then smoked joints all night and sometimes hung out with my mom."

"Well, maybe we strive too much, you and I? Like, how important is getting As, really?"

"You know I don't care about grades."

"That's because you get As without even giving a shit. You're just smart like that. But I bet if you started to get Bs, you would start to give a shit."

"Maybe." He shrugged. "Jason and I are going to skip the afternoon, go to the park. Wanna come?"

"Well, it sounds . . . *delightful,* but no."

"What is with you?"

"What do you mean?"

"You're just extra snotty today, like extra, extra superior."

"No, I'm not."

"I thought things were going to be okay again, because, you know, of last night. That was . . . beautiful."

Beautiful? Ugh. There was a long pause. Jason spun the wheels of his skateboard over and over, obviously feeling awkward.

"You going to Amanda's party tonight?" Jason asked. "Her folks are gone. Remember how fun it was last time?"

Sadie remembered watching the sunrise on the beach. It was when she and Jimmy had first got together. They'd kissed at the end of the night for the first time.

But she hadn't been invited to Amanda's party. No wonder Amanda had been weird with her in the bathroom.

"Nah, I don't really feel like it. Just a bunch of kids getting trashed, kinda boring."

Jimmy scoffed. "Uh, that last party was the best ever," he said.

Sadie shrugged, opened her book again. "I don't remember," she mumbled.

Jimmy glared at her. "Maybe it's not just that people are freaked out about your dad. Maybe it's 'cause you're acting like a total bitch."

Jason laughed, covering his mouth in shock.

She frowned. She tried not to let the insult throw her, looked down at her fingernails and picked at the skin around her thumb. Jimmy had never said an unkind word to her before.

"Sorry, Sadie. Fuck, I didn't mean that."

Sadie turned away, pretending to gaze out the small window of the couch room, which looked out onto a sliver of the school's roof. She was determined not to let him see her cry. She saw a fat squirrel with a full piece of bread in its mouth hopping along a drainpipe. She watched it until she heard him leave. When the door closed, the squirrel turned and locked eyes with her until it had swallowed the entire piece of bread.

SHE WENT TO JIMMY'S house after school to pack her things. Forget about breaking it to Jimmy. What would he care? She'd gathered everything together in the guest room when she heard his skateboard in the driveway. She decided to ice him out, hauling her bags downstairs as he was coming in, but he looked suitably contrite.

"Baby, I'm so sorry about earlier. Come to my room?" He grabbed her hand. His fingers were red and freezing. It was getting too cold out to skateboard.

She obliged, reluctantly, following him down the hall, knocking one of the sunflower frames off its hook with her shoulder by accident. She set it right. She sat on the edge

286 · ZOE WHITTALL

of his bed, which she noted he had actually made. He'd also picked up the strewn clothes and the room smelled less of decay and corporal pleasures and more like fresh air blowing in through the open window. He had prepared for her to be here. He wanted her to come back to his room.

"Nice cleanup job, babe," she said. She got up and ran her hand over a stack of magazines on his desk, all in order, fiddling with a pen stacked neatly amongst its peers in a Mason jar beside his computer.

"You're not my fucking sister," he said. "It was starting to seem like we're siblings instead of lovers. I *love* you, Sadie. I thought last night changed things back, but it doesn't seem like it."

He patted the space beside him. She sat down, but she didn't want to.

"I was super stoned last night. I don't even remember," she said.

Jimmy's eyes widened and then contracted, hurt. "I don't *care* if we don't fuck right now. I mean, I care, but more important is our love, right?" He spoke to the bookshelf, hands balled up.

"Yes, it's important. I'm just so . . . stressed."

She sat down on the carpet and grabbed his guitar. She played the C chord, the only one she knew. She heard herself being a jerk again but couldn't stop. This was important to him, maybe the most important moment of his day. And she couldn't bring herself to care.

"I know, but, like, being boyfriend-girlfriend is more than just doing it. You don't even look at me, not the way you used to. You bristle when I touch you, even just a hug."

She played the chord over and over again, feeling like a failure as a girlfriend.

"I'm going to move back home."

Jimmy just stared at her. That wasn't what he'd been expecting to hear.

"Maybe it would be better if we took a break from each other. Get some space, like, not break up but, like, spend less time together," she said, lifting the guitar back up and placing it on its metal stand in the corner of the room.

He looked as if he might start crying. "I guess so," he said.

She reached out to him, traced her hand along his jaw and tried to kiss his face.

He turned away, got up, and stormed out.

THERE WAS NOTHING LEFT to do but go back home. She decided to knock on Kevin's door before leaving, to say goodbye. She opened the door and found his laptop was gone, and his clothes were actually neatly ordered into piles. She ran downstairs.

"Where's Kev?" Sadie asked Elaine. "I wanted to say goodbye."

Elaine was folding towels on the kitchen table. "Oh, honey, he went to Iowa today, remember?"

"Okay," she said, pretending to be fine with that.

"I see you're leaving us," she said. "Are you sure?"

"Yeah, you've been so nice, but I should go back home."

"I'll give you a ride, then," she said.

Sadie shoved her backpack in the backseat of Elaine's

little Kia. Jimmy was skateboarding in the driveway, ignoring her. She pretended to look at her phone but kept him in her periphery.

When she got home, she curled up on the couch in the den and watched a marathon of home improvement shows. It was something she knew absolutely nothing about. If forced to build a house, she wouldn't know where to start. She appreciated that feeling.

She pressed Mute, and heard her mom on the phone with Aunt Clara.

"She's moody, she's stomping around with a sour look on her face. I'm so happy to have her back."

Every few hours she went out to the boathouse and used the one-hitter she'd stolen from Kevin to smoke what was left of the secret pot stash he'd hidden in the film canisters. She dropped the last bit between the boards of the floor and it fell into the water. Out on the dock she could see a bonfire on the beach at Amanda's house, the sound of Amanda's favorite song playing on repeat.

She was supposed to be writing in her feelings journal every day for Eleanor. So far she'd scrawled AAAAAAAAAAAAAAH across every page.

Fuck it, she decided. She got on her bike, not bothering with a helmet or a reflective jacket the way she normally did at night. She biked close to the edge of the ditch, her resolve strengthening the closer she got to Amanda's house, the music growing louder. She parked her bike against the oak tree and wandered around the house to the front, where a large crowd had gathered around a bonfire. A bunch of kids were drunk enough to be making out on the grass despite the cold weather. She felt a lurch in her stomach at the thought of coming across Jimmy making out with some other girl.

The kids sober enough to notice her gave her curious looks. Some said hello or nodded. She walked into the kitchen to get a drink and looked for Amanda. She'd been in this kitchen a hundred times before. She took a plastic cup and filled it with vodka from a bottle on the kitchen island. It was hard to believe, she thought, but she'd never really been all that drunk before. A little bit tipsy on wine once, but that was it. Never enough to forget anything, or do anything regrettable. She took a long swig and nearly threw up in the sink, but held it down. Her face burned hot, and she could feel the liquid going all the way down. When she regained her composure, and filled the rest of the cup with Coke, she noted a different group of kids in the room, all staring at her. They were young. Amanda's sister rose from the group.

"What are you doing here?"

"What do you mean? I'm here all the time," Sadie said, shrugging, her high quickly sharpening.

"I love that you're just pretending everything is normal. Not *everything* is normal. I don't want anyone from your disgusting family coming here ever again, do you hear me? Everything has been fucked up since that dumb trip!" She was screaming now, her friends gathering around her in a huddle.

Sadie stepped back, shocked. It stung, right in the middle of her chest, as though she'd had the wind knocked out of her entirely. "I'm sorry, but *I* didn't *do anything* to *you*."

The face she'd seen as a toddler, and on the annoying seven-year-old who followed them around, had become this girl's face, full of rage, with circles of black eyeliner around each eye.

A girl stood up behind Amanda's sister. "It's not Sadie's fault," she said. Sadie recognized her long wheat-blond hair. Miranda.

"Shut up, Miranda. You know what? Maybe it's *your* fault. We weren't going to say anything before you convinced us, and now my mom reads every text message, and no one will date me, and Mrs. Clarke suggested we all write essays about a time when we were dishonest and our lies ruined an innocent person's life, and she looked at me the *entire time*."

"We can't turn against each other," Miranda said weakly.

"Get out of my house, both of you," Amanda's sister said.

Sadie downed the cup of Coke, watching Miranda gather her oversized purse and leave, walking deliberately slowly with her head held high. No matter what she did, she seemed to have the grace of someone twice her age. Sadie gave her a head start before pushing through the dancers on the porch and stumbling down onto the grass. She watched Miranda peel out of the driveway in her mom's Lexus. She felt bad for her.

"Sadie," she heard a voice say before realizing it was Amanda, who put a hand on her arm. "Uh, listen, I'm sorry I didn't invite you, but you're not allowed here anymore, remember?"

Sadie nodded. She felt so foolish. Everyone was staring. One girl laughed, high-pitched and drunken.

She noticed Jimmy sitting by the fire, nursing a tall can

of PBR, looking her way but not getting up. He was sitting next to Brooke Neissen, who was poking at the fire with a long stick and looking casual and beautiful and calm in a way that made Sadie want to push her into the flames. Sadie stared at Jimmy for a few beats, waiting for him to get up and come to her. When she realized that wasn't going to happen, she ran around the house and got back on her bike. She peddled to the end of the driveway and paused, watching the darkness, hoping to see Jimmy, her ally, come into focus. The song switched, the crowd sang along with the chorus. She was already forgotten. She left, trying to stifle her sobs until she was surrounded only by forest. Then she began sobbing loudly, her cries echoing all around the lake.

Her phone beeped and she stopped on the side of the road, hoping it was Jimmy or Amanda. But it was an email from Kevin. "I've been thinking about you, a lot. I'm sorry I didn't get to say goodbye. How are you holding up?"

Instead of biking around Lakeside Drive, she turned left at the Coffee Hut, which was the exact midpoint between her and Amanda's houses. At first she rode just to feel herself go, and then picked a destination: the park close to the public high school. There was Billy's One-Stop Burgers at one end, a parking lot, and a circle of picnic tables near the edge of the woods that led into the state park. Teenagers hung out there at night. Everybody knew that. Sadie didn't, though. That area was for townie girls and the punk kids and people who did drugs. When she was thirteen, her father had bought them ice cream from Billy's after a piano recital. They'd walked by a group of teenagers, one with high blue hair that looked like cotton candy. As her father unlocked the car, he'd said, "I don't want to ever see you here hanging out with these kids, okay? This is what happens when teenagers don't have enough guidance."

Sometimes Amanda went there on Fridays with her friend from gymnastics club, but mostly Sadie thought it seemed dumb to just sit around and look cool, drinking beer out of soda cups and watching whoever inevitably started to fight. She'd been there with Jimmy before, but only to stop for food.

The area was pretty dead that night. Maybe she could just disappear. This was the kind of place where teen girls just faded into the trees, or wound up in Dumpsters, maybe not in Avalon Hills but certainly on TV. The cops must have come around. It seemed too quiet.

Inside Billy's One-Stop, the lights were so bright that her inebriation came roaring back. The restaurant hadn't been renovated in years, and still looked the same as it had when she was a kid. The radio played classic rock, and a girl was singing along, mopping the far corner and staring out at the parking lot. There was only one table occupied, by a woman who was feeding french fries to a chihuahua. Sadie stood near the counter and watched the dog eat a few fries. The woman smiled at her as though they knew each other somehow. Sadie thought that she had never seen anyone look so lonely. Although the woman didn't seem sad at all.

Sadie ordered a Diet Coke from an acne-scarred red-haired kid. She gripped the edge of the counter, watching the kid fill the cup and glancing towards the door, where she saw Dorothy enter with a teenaged girl. She looked down at the counter, staring only at the cup and removing the paper slip from the straw, hoping Dorothy wouldn't talk to her. She didn't want to be invited back to one of those fucked-up meetings. She was aware of them behind her, heard Dorothy say, "Buy whatever you want, Miranda, it's on me. Have a sundae! A burger—really, anything you want."

Miranda?

In her periphery, she noted that it was indeed Miranda, slumming at One-Stop Burgers. And with the school secretary? Was she in a David Lynch movie? Sadie bolted, knowing she had only a few seconds before she'd be noticed, and ran towards the picnic table closest to the restaurant door, where she sat as though waiting for a friend to come out. She could see Miranda and Dorothy hunched over trays of food. She noted Miranda's Lexus sparkling between the scattered offerings of Hondas and Toyotas.

The table was carved with missives, declarations, pejoratives, and dick drawings. She chewed at the straw, running her finger along *Jane Is So High* and *Missy Fucks Hard* and glancing back in the restaurant, both curious about and repulsed by Dorothy and why she would be at One-Stop Burgers with a student.

She pulled her hood over her head and looked down, scrolling through various apps on her phone, then reread Kevin's email. A group of kids showed up eventually, settling in at the next table, and looked over at her. She had her headphones on so they would think she was listening to music, but she was eavesdropping on bits of their conversation.

That's that girl.

Her dad, fucking pervert.
Rich kid.
Slutty private-school girls.
Best blow jobs, am I right?
Like you would know.
Shut up.
What is she staring at?
She looks sad. You like those emo girls, don't you?

Sadie was readying to leave when one of them lit up a joint, and she remembered what she had come for. She cocked a hip and performed the confidence she didn't feel. "Hey, are you holding? Or know anyone who is?" She'd heard that in a movie once.

When they stopped laughing at her, they pointed out an idling car at the edge of the lot. "He's a balding guy named Gary. He always wears a plaid shirt and smells like onions, but he's harmless."

"Thanks," she said.

The girl nodded and smiled warmly, before Sadie left and walked over to the car.

Gary was amicable enough. When she'd pocketed the two grams of pot, he said, "I also make my own organic yogurt and we're starting a line of pickled beets and radishes. Tell your parents! I mean, only about the pickles!"

She gave him an awkward thumbs-up and walked towards her bike. She was fiddling with the lock when Miranda came storming out of the restaurant, Dorothy behind her, dropping a large cup of soda that splashed all over her skirt but not bothering to pick it up.

"Miranda, it's okay. Let me at least give you a ride home, dear," she said.

Miranda stopped and turned around, glaring at her. "I have my own car, duh."

Miranda got into her car, music blaring as soon as she turned the ignition. Dorothy watched her peel out of the lot while trying to wring out her skirt. Sadie tried to stand still and not make any noise so she wouldn't get drawn into a conversation with her.

SADIE WAS PULLING OUT of One-Stop when her phone beeped five texts from Jimmy. All apologies. She typed *Fuck you*. Then erased it and decided not to reply.

When she got home, she packed the one-hitter and wrote Kevin a long email, about how she felt about her father in prison, Jimmy, her mom. It was pages long. In the morning she went to the track and ran and ran, and at each vibration of her phone she stopped, hoping it was a response from Kevin. Every minute felt slow, and looped.

She was lying on the grass by the track when his response finally came in.

"I've been wondering how you must be feeling. The complexity of it all."

Kevin was the perfect outlet, and he'd actually *asked her how she felt*. He wanted to know how it was *impacting her emotionally*. There was almost an entire page of questions. He wasn't being paid to ask, like Mrs. Caribou or Eleanor Rockbrand. He wasn't doing it in hopes she'd relax enough to be his normal into-sex girlfriend. He wasn't doing it because he was her parent and felt guilty or obligated. He was actually interested.

25

Andrew and Jared had resumed some moments of normalcy, but they were fleeting. It always felt as if the moment could break at any time. This morning, Jared placed a plate of crepes and caramelized peaches down on the table in front of Andrew, who appeared to be reading *The New York Times* on his phone but was really just skimming headlines. Andrew felt the weight of how hard Jared was trying, and how he just couldn't reciprocate, and he briefly longed for a boyfriend who was callous and self-involved.

It was a rare weekend, one when Andrew was home for its entirety. Jared had yet to accompany him back to Avalon Hills, which they both knew was straining their relationship. Andrew could tell that Jared's compassion was approaching its limits, but he was still behaving with care and patience.

"It's odd," Jared said, taking Andrew's phone out of his hand and turning it off dramatically. "My friends say so as well. Imagine a heterosexual couple, if your wife didn't come with you during a family crisis?"

Andrew spooned some Greek yogurt onto his crepes, inhaling.

"No one here is a wife, Jared," Andrew said wryly.

Not getting married, now that it was finally legal, was another sore spot. Jared wanted nothing more than an extravagant party, a celebration of hope and justice, as he called it. Andrew thought gay marriage was fine, but that the gay movement was obsessed with it as a way of begging the state to accept them, approve of them. He didn't want it. "We've been together for seven years. What would a party do? We both know we'll be together forever," he'd said, the standard line.

"Plus, my mom and sister are coming to us this weekend for Christmas. There'll be plenty of opportunity for you to showcase your wifely side."

Jared looked pained and pushed his plate aside.

"Are we a family, or what? Because if we're not, I am out. I'm tired of this. We're not in university anymore. I'm not someone to play house with when you come back from the baths."

Andrew was taken aback by Jared's sudden explosion.

"I want to go with you to see your father," he said.

"No."

"Why? What are you afraid of? Why won't you let me support you?"

"It just— It's too much. Why take that on?"

"Let me be there for you," Jared said. "You need support."

"No, what I need is for you to listen to me when I tell

you what I need, which is to not go with me to jail just so you can feel fucking needed. God, selfish much?"

"You're mad because I believe he's guilty."

"No, you're entitled to think what you want."

"Women don't lie about this stuff, Andrew. You need to accept the possibility, the probability, of his guilt."

"People, regardless of gender, lie all the time, about a million different things. You're being illogical!"

"You're being ideological," Jared said. "Just admit it's emotional, it's difficult to be objective, it's hard. Just say it: it's fucking hard."

Andrew got up, walked towards the sink, and threw his plate of crepes with such force that it broke in two as it collided with the stainless steel.

He grabbed his phone from the island and left the apartment.

26

AFTER SOME COAXING, JOAN CONVINCED SADIE TO come to her support group with her, for Family and Friends Day. Dr. Forrestor explained that it was important for their support systems to see the purpose the group served.

Joan woke up early and made strawberry pancakes to sweeten the deal. Sadie came in from her morning run and assessed the brunch offering. "I just think it's weird, the premise of the group. Is it so women can feel better about not divorcing their sorry husbands and getting on with their lives?"

"It's a place to vent our frustration or anger or sadness, with people who understand how difficult it is when a loved one is in jail and has done something terrible. It takes its toll on families, you know."

Sadie snorted. "Believe me, Mom, I know it does."

"Who do you talk to, besides Eleanor Rockbrand?"

"I dunno. Elaine, Jimmy. Sometimes Andrew and I talk on the phone."

"You do? That's wonderful." Joan took a sip of coffee.

"Andrew worries about you a lot. Sometimes I think he worries about you so that he doesn't have to feel what he feels about Dad." Sadie cut up a pancake into neat quarters, spiraled some syrup onto each portion, and took a bite.

"It's very difficult for me to share my feelings with you about what has happened. This is a safe space to share your feelings, if you want to, with people you'll never see in your regular life, and with the help of a counselor who has experience with people in our situation."

"What *is* a safe space? What does that even mean?"

Joan took a sip of coffee and stared out the back window. The trees needed pruning, the boathouse needed a new roof. She wanted to go back to bed.

Sadie finished her final bite of pancake.

"I guess it's only an hour."

"Afterwards we can do whatever you want—the movies, the mall, whatever!" Joan said.

"I just want to come home and keep studying," Sadie said, a little sourly, rinsing her plate in the sink and leaving it there.

"Okay, we'll go after I get back from church," Joan said. "Do you want to come?"

Sadie shook her head. She hadn't been to church all year. Joan's attendance hadn't been stellar since the arrest, but earlier in the week some of the ladies from the United Church women's group had called to see if she'd be coming back this week. She couldn't tell if this was out of pity or genuine concern. She didn't know whether or not to believe anyone anymore. If someone at work said, "I'm going to go get you a coffee," and then they returned ten minutes later with the coffee, Joan felt overwhelmingly grateful that they had stated the truth and then followed through. When she saw Mr. Henshaw out for a walk, she wondered if he was actually out meeting his mistress at the hotel by the highway—Mr. Henshaw with the pair of elderly basset hound rescue dogs, the cane, and a collection of miniature hound sculptures in his yard, the one who said, of his wife of forty-something years, "The old bat is still the love of my life, still beautiful."

"You just never know about anyone," she'd said to Nancy at work.

Nancy had nodded and rolled her eyes. "Don't I know it."

Nancy had been making sure no one was mean to Joan at work. She'd nip it in the bud when any of the gossipy young nurses whispered or threw a side-eye to each other. Joan was grateful, but was also growing a little miffed at the presumption that she and Nancy had some shared trauma.

One morning when Joan was waiting for an English muffin to pop in the toaster in the staff kitchen, Nancy hovered, selected an envelope of strawberry mint tea from the box beside her, and confessed to Joan what her late husband's secret was, the cause of his distress and suicide. After she said solemnly, "He was . . . gay," Joan had to stop herself from exclaiming, "That's it?" She knew that any kind of deception felt horrible, *but seriously,* she thought, *it's not like your husband was a serial killer or a . . . It's not the same.*

Instead, Joan had just nodded sympathetically. She needed to keep all the allies she still had.

JOAN WALKED INTO CHURCH during the second verse of "Morning Has Broken." The sanctuary was maybe only half full, and she knew everybody, even just by the backs of their heads from her spot in the last pew. Normally she sat close to the front to hear the sermon. Sharon McFarlane sat with her mother in the back as well. Her mother was aged, and she could easily lean her walker against the wall. Sharon turned and offered Joan a warm, genuine smile. She nodded in response. Whenever Joan smiled at people these days, she felt that if she really offered back her usual warm smile, it would somehow be deceptive or seem crazy. Like, what did she have to smile about? Everyone would know it was a lie.

In finding out about George's potential deceptions, she was starting to question her own ability to be honest as well.

She let her mind wander during the hymn, realizing she hadn't joined the choir this year, and that it was getting close to Christmas and the Woodbury family had received only two cards so far—one from Clara and one from Joan's great-aunt Judy in Florida. Normally there were a pile of them in a basket on the mantel that they would all read through on Christmas Eve. The Christies were having their annual drop-in at the end of Lakeside Drive, and Joan hadn't been invited. Some people she knew from church had taken pity on her, but that was just what it was: pity. They felt they were doing Christ's duty, and for the first time Joan could understand how humiliating it feels to be on the receiving end of dutiful kindness. She could now understand the women who received their carefully wrapped charity Christmas baskets, how they always said thank you with a pained sort of smile, some outright hostile. Joan used to drive around delivering the baskets after church on a Sunday every December. She used to think, *Oh, they are so stressed-out with the time of year, with not enough to go around.* But she now saw in these activities the glowing inauthenticity of the Church, reaching out to the disadvantaged for some ulterior motive, to *do God's work.* She understood that maybe the volunteers didn't even see the recipients' faces; they saw only points in God's good favor, and used their actions as proof that they were virtuous people despite their many repeated sins. Joan never would have thought this before; she had never doubted her own kindness or sense of duty. Why would you ever question people who were trying to do something good for the world? This new cynicism felt awful, but it came at her in moments that felt unavoidable. She didn't automatically trust anyone anymore. Trust was now something that required an extra beat, a moment of consideration.

Joan had been christened at Avalon Hills United Church, and so had her mother, her grandmother, and both children. She felt comforted by the woody smell, the art made by Sunday school students that lined the walls, made out of pipe cleaners, macaroni, and clumps of white glue. Even though George was pretty much an atheist in private, he was an active churchgoer and enjoyed chatting and debating with the minister over coffee about the finer points of the sermon. He helped to organize fundraisers and brought in theologians to talk on special nights, but Joan knew he had never really been a believer.

The minister spoke warmly, confidently, about the importance of community and connection. Tears streamed down Joan's face, and she dotted at them with a stiff Kleenex from her pocket, and then the sleeve of her blouse. No one noticed, but she felt as if a spotlight was shining on her, and that at any moment pitying eyes would all turn her way. The choir leader began the first verse of a song she didn't know, and Joan took the opportunity to dash out. She had thought maybe she'd stay for coffee and squares in the basement, a little catching up, but she was too frightened to face anyone.

Clara hadn't set foot in a church, apart from weddings and funerals, since she had mumbled her way through her confirmation ceremony in a hungover daze, something she had done to make their mom happy at the time. When Joan told Clara that she was attending church again to help with her loneliness, Clara had shrugged. "If that's what you're comfortable with, Joannie. But you know, church people are usually all fakey-fake nice and Jesusy on Sunday, but don't really give a damn when people are in real need."

"I don't believe that's true."

"When Dad died, they all brought casseroles over, but after two or three days no one stopped by to help with the sorting, or called to check in."

"We didn't ask for help, either."

"We shouldn't have to."

Clara believed that people rarely did the right thing on their own but, at the same time, that she shouldn't have to school everyone in decency.

"People cannot read minds, Clara."

Joan didn't want to be a spectacle, even though she'd known the entire congregation for most of her life. Why couldn't they return the care she'd given out over the years?

Joan sat in her car in the church parking lot, collecting herself, watching some of the Sunday school boys run around the lot, twirling their tiny ties like lassos. She missed being part of a team, walking into church with her arm linked in George's and hearing his off-key harmonizing on the hymns.

WHEN SHE GOT HOME, she kept the car warm and waited for Sadie to come out so they could drive to the support group. Joan warned her daughter while she adjusted the mirrors. "You may feel judgmental of people," she said, "which is understandable. I was that way at first. They might seem like stupid ladies, you know, the kind of women you might see on a talk show. But they have good hearts, Sadie. They have been through so much. And they keep coming back every week and they help each other out. It's very genuine." She was babbling, and Sadie nodded at her periodically. Joan was surprised by how she was describing the group; she hadn't really been all that aware of the shift in her feelings, that she'd begun to empathize with and appreciate the other women.

When they arrived at the health clinic, Joan put the car in park and turned to Sadie, who was texting.

"Honey, you okay? You'll be fine?"

"Mom, it's a bunch of ladies in a basement for an hour. I think I can hack it."

"Okay, because we can leave at any time if you aren't comfortable."

"Sure," Sadie said, opening the car door.

JOAN SAW THE BASEMENT the way she had the first time she attended the group; she imagined Sadie must find it strange and sterile. The room was already bustling with women and their awkward teenaged children, siblings, parents, and partners. There was a coffee urn, and a dispenser of watery hot chocolate. Joan filled a Styrofoam cup with cocoa for Sadie, who seemed grateful to have something to hold on to. Dr. Forrestor called everyone to sit in the wooden chairs assembled in a circle. A flip chart detailed a list of rules for respectful group dynamics.

"We're going to start with a go-around," Dr. Forrestor said slowly, scanning the circle and trying to look every-one in the eye.

Each woman spoke her name, introduced her family member, and said one thing she was grateful for. Joan tried to memorize their names as they went around. Barb, grate-ful for coffee, with her daughter Emma. Julia, grateful for her two sons' health, with her boyfriend. Amy, grateful for a lenient judge, with her mother. Shirley, grateful for the group's support now that her husband was back in jail for a parole violation, also with her mother. There were two new women. One, who spoke barely above a whisper, Trish, said she was grateful for her anger, because it kept her from feeling the full weight of her sorrow, and she'd brought her friend.

Then the second new woman introduced herself as Anna, and it was as if all at once everyone in the group, collectively, realized who she was: Anna Lansing, the wife of sexual predator and murderer Richard Lansing. She had cut her hair shorter, and it was fully gray, no longer auburn the way it had been in press photographs. Two years ago, the high commander in the U.S. Army had been tried and convicted for two murders and dozens more sexual assaults, as well as a string of break-ins and robberies of women's undergarments. Anna was said to have known nothing about it. Joan remembered reading the newspaper accounts at the time and thinking, *As if she didn't know!*

Well, now she understood.

Sadie had started off chewing her nails, looking bored, but when she realized who Anna was, she leaned forward, wide-eyed.

"I know you probably all know who I am: Anna Lansing, although now I'm Anna Taylor. That's my maiden name."

She spoke as though she had picked a point on the wall in front of her to address.

"This is my sister, Monica."

A chubby woman beside her with long blond hair held back in two gold combs smiled and waved.

"I've only attended this group once before, but I see Dr. Forrestor several times a week and he suggested I come to this session."

Dr. Forrestor interrupted. "I just want to, again, emphasize that there is a strict code of confidentiality in this room that we all must agree to. You may be tempted to gossip about the fact that Anna was here, but try to think about how you would feel in her position. It is a very brave thing that she is here today."

"I think that, well . . ." Anna's voice broke.

Her sister jumped in after twenty or so seconds of silence. "I think what has been so difficult for other people, myself included, to understand is that besides the horror of his crimes, besides everything he did, my sister is facing a terrible loss of her life partner, and everything that comes with that kind of loss. Even under normal circumstances those changes are incredibly difficult. And she has very few places that she can turn. She is judged very harshly by everyone."

Joan was so curious about Anna, wanting to know the details, and then she felt ashamed, knowing what it was like to be on the other end. Anyone she met who didn't shun her wanted to know the *dirt*.

She was so rapt, and so concerned with how Sadie was feeling, that she was almost surprised when her turn came around. While she had spoken openly at the group before, rambling on about every emotion, she was surprised by a feeling of shyness at the thought of Sadie hearing her voice. She faltered as she introduced herself.

"This is Sadie, my daughter."

Sadie blushed, gave everyone a half wave.

"My husband, Sadie's dad, is awaiting trial. We're kind of in a holding period right now."

Sadie picked at her fingers.

"One of the hardest things about this situation has been how to keep myself together enough to be a parent.

It hasn't been easy," she started. There were nods of reso-
nance from around the room. Sadie started to chew her
thumb. Joan quickly took stock of why she was bringing
this up. Was she looking for sympathy, trying to get Sadie
to understand? She decided to stop.

"My daughter is very smart, and very strong. I wanted
to bring her here today to see that we're not alone."

Sadie stopped chewing her thumb and half smiled at
Joan, nodding.

WHEN THEY ARRIVED HOME, Sadie paused before going upstairs, and pulled some things out of her coat pocket and
handed them to Joan.

"What do you think of these?"

Joan scanned them. "Where on earth did you get
them? Those nut jobs have nothing to do with your father."

"They're really convinced he's innocent. I thought you
might appreciate them, you know, their support," said
Sadie.

Joan snorted and looked at the stickers again.

"I think they are quite disturbed and don't understand
how the world works, really. And they're using your father's situation as a way to get attention for themselves and
their . . . ideas. Who gave them to you?"

"Dorothy. She's the leader of the group," Sadie said.

"Are you kidding me? Well, that explains a lot. Studies
do show that right-wing people have a lower IQ, which is
certainly the case for Dorothy," Joan said, reading the last
few stickers. " 'Just because she regrets it in the morn-

ing . . . ' Honey, I don't know exactly what happened between your father and those girls, and perhaps I'll never
know, but this kind of campaign is not something that
helps anyone, especially young women, or women in general. She should not be in a position of authority, that
dingbat. I can't believe her! Giving these to *you,* of all people. I'm furious. As if you need more things to wrestle
with."

Sadie paused, as though she was about to say something further, but she just gave her mom a hug and went
upstairs. Joan stood at the foot of the staircase feeling happy
for the hug, and uncertain what to do about Dorothy.

27

SADIE WAS RELIEVED BY THE PROSPECT OF THE IMPEND-ing Christmas trip to New York City. Even just knowing that she was getting out of town for a bit felt good. She pulled on her running gear, tugging at a frayed thread at the ankle seam. Her phone beeped with an email. Her pulse sped up, anticipating it might be from Kevin. She was trying to wait a few minutes before looking at any incoming mail. *Be cool. Just be cool.* But she couldn't help herself, and was disappointed to see it was an effusive email from Dorothy describing how the group loved her and she hoped she'd come to the next meeting, signing off with seven smiley-face emojis.

Sadie needed to get out of Avalon Hills and gain some perspective. She'd completed her exams, getting passable but not stunning grades, and she didn't care. She and Jimmy had resumed a sort of civil awkwardness. Elaine called or emailed every few days to check in. Sadie had been dreading Christmas, the first holiday of her life without her father, and going away meant she might not feel his absence as much. She wouldn't be waiting for him to make shortbread and thumbprint cookies. She wouldn't miss the way he wrapped presents so sloppily for her stocking, the presents themselves always perfect. Joan invariably gave her practical gifts, items that were useful. George always managed to choose things she actually wanted.

Sadie and Joan would spend the weekend with Andrew and Jared, and then Joan and Clara would go visit George on Christmas Day. Her father had wanted to see her, but Joan said no before Sadie even had to decide. She didn't want Sadie to have a holiday memory of prison.

Sadie pulled on her sweatshirt and was shoving her phone in her pocket when she heard it beep again. She took a resigned breath before turning it over to see if it was another one from Dorothy.

Kevin!

Be cool.

Dear Sadie, I hope you know how much I've adored getting to know you and really, you are such a sweet girl, and I want you to know how much you've impressed me with your strength. I hear you've moved back home; know you'll always have a home with us. I attached a song I've been listening to lately, and it makes me think of you. It's by Built to Spill. It's probably old-guy music, but I think you'll like it. The new book is going well here in Iowa. But don't tell anyone. I don't want to jinx it! Love, Kevin.

"Adored," "sweet girl," "impressed me," "always have a home with." No one had ever said things like this to her before. And he trusted her enough to talk about his new book. And he signed it with "Love, Kevin." She downloaded the song immediately: "Things Fall Apart" by Built to Spill, a band she'd never heard of.

She read the email three times, loosening her warm running clothes before finally venturing outside. She ran as though propelled by the email, composing a perfect response in her head. When she got to the end of the road, she paused at the gate to the Coffee Hut, where she saw Amanda putting a tray of coffees on top of her car and opening the driver's-side door. They looked at each other for a moment before Amanda motioned her over.

"You're a fucking jogging lunatic!"

The party—the way Amanda's sister had yelled at Sadie—sat between the two girls like a fence. Still, they pretended everything was fine, though they weren't acting the way they normally would.

"Why haven't you been coming to school?" Amanda put the tray in the car, taking one cup out and pulling back the tab.

"Well, I can't deal, really."

"Yeah, I get it. My sister hasn't been going either. And someone told me Miranda went to rehab or something."

"For what?"

"I have no idea," she said, tapping her nose.

"Right," Sadie said, stretching out her hamstring.

"Jimmy's got a new nickname."

"What?"

"Sulkboy."

"Huh."

"Seriously, the emo girls are lapping it up. You should be careful."

"We're on a break," she said.

"I heard, yeah. Everyone's talking about Avalon's number one couple's demise."

Sadie tried to adjust her posture into *who cares, who cares.*

"I kinda got a new crush anyway."

"Who?"

"He's an older guy, you wouldn't know him."

"How old?"

"Twenties . . ." she lied.

"Uh, that's kind of gross."

"No it's not. You'd get it if you met him."

"Don't ruin your life 'cause your dad's in jail. Remember our pact: no babies, no husbands until we live far away from here."

"I know. God!" *It was a mistake telling her,* Sadie thought. She definitely wouldn't get it.

"Anyway, I better get going. I wouldn't want any rumors getting back to my mom that we were seen canoodling."

"Ha."

"Actually," Amanda said, noting a few cars pulling into the lot, "maybe we should just make out and give them all heart attacks."

"I'll pass, as hot as you are."

"Yeah, yeah. I'm just not elderly enough for you." Amanda laughed at her own joke and got in the car.

Sadie turned the volume up high on her music and silenced her phone's other notification sounds. She ignored every human she saw, ignored the seven missed calls, and the texts from her mother asking her if she'd like lamb for dinner. She got lost in a reverie about her future life with Kevin. The famous author and his scandalously young girlfriend, doing her undergrad at Harvard, on his arm at fancy events in the evening. She would meet famous editors at dinner parties and write sassy first-person essays for their magazines. She ran until her face got hot and she felt like she might throw up, but the endorphin high was worth it.

When she stopped, she realized she was near Billy's One-Stop Burgers and went in to pee. Her hands were red and swollen from the cold, and she had trouble catching her breath. When she came back out, she saw the same group of teenagers she'd seen last time, sitting on the tables outside, and approached them.

"Hey," she said.

"You're very sweaty," said the girl with two green pigtails.

"It's kind of hot," said the blue-haired guy.

The girl poked him. "Don't be gross."

"I'm a runner. I ran from Woodbury Lake," she explained. Despite this being a very long way away, neither kid seemed impressed.

"Winter running, hard-core," said the girl. "I don't run unless, you know, someone is chasing me. So, how's celebrity life?"

Sadie couldn't tell if she was being mocked or if the girl was nice.

"Could be worse," she joked. "What's your name?"

The girl lit a cigarette and scanned her. "Lena. I can't believe you don't recognize me. This is Jay."

"Hey girl," said Jay. His voice was feminine though he looked really tough, like he could drop-kick you and then say something really witty.

"I know, we met here when I was looking to score some weed," Sadie said.

"No, man. Wow!" Lena rolled her eyes and looked at Jay. "You really don't remember?"

"From where?"

"I was in your class at Avalon. Like, from kindergarten."

"No you weren't. I'd remember a green-haired girl."

"It was brown before. I got kicked out for writing that story narrated by a school shooter. And I was, like, the only Asian in the school. So, you're basically racist."

"What? No, I'm not!"

"Just kidding, man. I was quiet. I get it."

Jay looked her up and down. Sadie wondered if the blue hair meant he was gay. Maybe they both were. Or a couple. He was shy maybe, not too cool for school. Jay lit a joint and passed it to her. They shared it, talking about a TV show, a YouTube celebrity, their parents, normal teenage minutiae. She was happy for it.

"There's going to be a party next week. You should come. Put your number in my phone." She handed it to Sadie, who added her name.

Sadie couldn't remember the last time she'd made a new friend.

. . .

IF HER DREAM OF running away with Kevin came to pass, her friends could all be new. A rebirth. "Went for a run, met a new friend," she wrote in her journal for Eleanor. "Thoughts about the future." That looked positive, she reckoned.

She got home and realized she had missed her father's call. Then she saw her mother sitting in the kitchen with Bennie and Andrew. There were papers between them.

"I'm sorry, I didn't realize what time it was," she said.

"You were jogging at nighttime? I don't like that. It's not safe. And it's cold out."

"The sun *just* went down," she said. She touched her eyes. She was sure they were red and that it was obvious she was high. But no one seemed to notice. "Dad called?"

"Yes, he did. You know he always calls at the same time."

"I'm sorry I missed it," she said.

"It's okay, you're still a kid. It happens."

Sadie pictured her father—lonely, in a cold cell—and her disregarding his happiness.

"I'm going to go to bed early. I think I'm coming down with something," she said. No one was listening.

She went upstairs, and read a text from Jimmy as she got into bed. *Come over when you're back from New York. We'll wear soft pants and play video games and Mom will make us eat all the cookies. It feels weird not to see you over the holidays. Please?*

Sure, she texted back. *That sounds sweet.*

28

JOAN AND SADIE SPENT THE MAJORITY OF THE DRIVE TO New York City listening to a radio program about human limits. The limits of the body, the mind, the spirit. Neither was in the mood for the Christmas carols on the other stations. Joan felt relief for the distraction, and was glad to see that Sadie was able to just sit still and listen, something Joan hadn't seen much evidence of lately. Her moods had been explosive after she'd moved home; one minute she'd be weeping with Payton on her lap, watching television—something she rarely used to do—and the next she was running outside, even though it was freezing, up and down the hill in the backyard. Joan was waking up an hour earlier than usual to prepare healthy meals, line up fish oil capsules and a multivitamin beside scraps of paper that read "I love you! Bean salad and quinoa in the fridge for your lunch! Back at 7—chicken pot pie for dinner!" Joan used to hate that her mother would channel her concern for her as a child into food, but it was the only thing she could think to do for Sadie. Joan could spend only so many hours on the edge of her bed, asking her how she was feeling, waiting for the inevitable "Just leave me alone." Joan didn't blame her. It was a stupid question. How was anyone supposed to feel under the circumstances?

Andrew and Jared lived in the West Village in an apartment above a bookshop. Jared had inherited the lease from his ex-boyfriend, who'd been renting it since the 1970s. It was very small, but inexpensive for the area. Jared's salon was right around the corner on West Tenth Street. The New York City of Joan's youth, the one she had visited a few times a year for most of her young adult life until she had children, had disappeared. The Village was quiet and clean, full of designer dress shops, hair salons, juice bars, and coffee shops. Sadie and Joan gripped their matching purple canvas rolling suitcases and carried them up the narrow staircase to the second floor. The hall way smelled like a sweet insecticide that seemed to stick to Joan's tongue. Sadie bounded up the stairs ahead of her, while Joan paused on the landing to catch her breath, gripping the glossy black railing. She hadn't been exercising enough. Sadie knocked emphatically on the door.

Jared smelled like a forest when he hugged Joan. She stood back, took in his clean-shaven face, the angle of his jaw. He was almost blindingly handsome, which was matched by the natural kindness that emanated from everything he said and did. "Joan," he said, squeezing her upper arm warmly, "I'm so glad to see you again."

She believed him. She could trust him, she realized. She'd developed a new awareness about people and their intentions, something she never used to think about consciously. Her son was lucky to have Jared. She squeezed his sizable bicep and pulled him into another hug, which made him laugh. She hugged Andrew next, whose hugs often felt like handshakes, and she wondered if Andrew even deserved Jared, in some ways. She was unable to stop being critical of her son sometimes, because she saw her worst qualities reflected in his behavior: his short fuse, his fussiness, the way he worked too hard.

Joan looked around at their home, a cramped space decorated to make it appear bigger. The furniture was mostly black, white, or gray, and in shapes that appeared uncomfortable, at odds with the human body. They had a fake silver Christmas tree, set up on a speaker. Everything was rectangular, there wasn't a curved angle in sight, only clean lines and lack of color. Joan thought it was cold and probably impractical to heat. Sadie walked over to a long-haired gray-and-white cat perched on a diamond-shaped pillow in the large window that overlooked the street.

Jared took Joan's suitcase and rolled it towards the guest room. "Joan, I am just so pleased to have you in our home. Hotels are so impersonal, and we got this great new Murphy bed behind the bookshelf for guests." Joan tried to wrap her head around the fact that he was her son's boyfriend. It was surprising almost every time she met him. It was one thing to know it and to understand it, but to see it and deal with it was quite another thing.

He led her to the guest-room space behind a floor-to-ceiling bookshelf. Jared had already pulled the bed down. There was a lilac duvet with bright green throw pillows and a stack of turquoise towels in descending order of size on the edge of the bed. Otherwise the space was completely bare. Jared showed Joan how to open and close the wooden screen that would allow her some privacy. Joan wanted to slip into the bed and just lie there, stop time from moving forward.

Instead, she leaned her overnight suitcase against a side of the bookcase and followed Jared back out into the open area, the kitchen and living room combo. *Fake it till you make it*, she thought, which is exactly what one of the women she disliked in the support group kept saying. She thought it was ridiculous and reductive, until it proved very useful almost every day.

Andrew busied himself around the island in the kitchen area, making a pot of green tea and setting out a basket of Christmas cookies. Sadie sat at the table texting, beside her mother and Jared. Andrew kept putzing around as they small-talked.

"Andrew," Jared scolded him, "you can actually sit down with us. You don't have to do the dishes *now*. He's so obsessed with cleaning, honestly."

Sadie giggled. Joan didn't think either of them had ever seen Andrew be put in his place.

"That's funny. Andrew never lifted a finger at home," Joan said. She picked up a star-shaped cookie. It was still warm. She wanted to be hungry. She took a bite and made an approving noise.

"Andrew is so into baking lately."

Sadie broke out in laughter, then paused. "Oh, you're serious?"

"No, no, he doesn't have a lot of free time, but baking is very meditative, right?"

"Jared. Enough," Andrew said, but he was still smiling, filling up a bulbous glass pitcher of water, throwing in some lemon slices from the fridge. "It's soothing my nerves. I've had a lot of trouble sleeping."

"Me too," said Joan and Sadie at the same time. Jared scanned them with a sympathetic look.

"I've been teaching Andrew about some basic self-care principles my naturopath is keen on, with some vitamins and supplements for stress, and some mindfulness techniques."

Jared trailed off as Sadie texted and Joan looked around at the life her son had built. Her once lonely, too-smart, and cynical son who never seemed to have time to visit had created his own home here, in this city she'd always considered cold and uninviting, prohibitively expensive, individualistic, and devoid of comfort. The apartment was filled with plants and other signs of vibrancy. He had been doing well, she realized, before this all happened.

LATER, THEY TOOK A walk around Lower Manhattan, bundled up in their winter coats, hands clutching phones locked on the camera setting. Shoppers bustled around them with arms full of gift bags, irritated at their slow touristic pace.

In the evening, in lieu of a Christmas Eve feast, they ordered three kinds of mac 'n' cheese from a specialty restaurant and played Scrabble, approximating a normal family visit. Clara came over for some eggnog and they watched *How the Grinch Stole Christmas!* while Joan finished knitting the last pair of mittens she was making for gifts: a black pair for Andrew, ice-blue and green stripes for

Jared, red for Sadie. They'd decided not to exchange purchased gifts, just homemade things, and not to do any of
their usual traditions. "The advantage of New York is you
can avoid all those expectations," Andrew said when Joan
asked him if he was sad to miss Christmas in Avalon Hills.

ON CHRISTMAS DAY, JARED opened up the salon just for
Sadie; his gift to her was some fun spa treatments. Joan, Andrew, and Clara were going to the movies.

Joan watched Sadie get settled into her chair in the
back of the spa space, after they'd received the grand tour
and Joan had turned down Jared's offer of a relaxing lavender oil massage and manicure. The idea of being touched
with such care was inviting. How long had it been since
she'd actually been touched by another human being for
more than two or three seconds? But she felt as though her
arms were wooden and splintery, and that she didn't deserve such luxury. She was afraid that if someone touched
the base of her neck, or the swollen muscles in her shoulders, they would unleash some of the emotions she wasn't
even aware were present, loosen the netting of repression
that held her body together. So she accepted Jared's jars of
homemade plum jams and red pepper jellies instead.

They waited for Clara outside the salon. Andrew's
phone chirped an electronic sparrow song. He pulled it
from his pocket and walked a distance away. Joan took her
own phone out and snapped a candid photo of him.

"Hey, Bennie," he said. "Uh-huh. Uh-huh. What?
Where is he now?"

He hung up the phone and turned to his mother. She saw that he was crying. It was the first time she'd seen Andrew cry since he was in grade school. He blinked both eyes, then shut them tightly.

"Dad's in the hospital. Someone tried to kill him."

29

A FINE COATING OF SOFT CHOCOLATY LIQUID COVERED Sadie's arms and torso, and instead of feeling like a human dipped doughnut, as she had anticipated, the smell dissolved all the tension she was holding in her muscles, and every inhale seemed to bring her closer to herself. "I understand now why rich ladies do this," she said to her masseuse, a thin brunette with a racing stripe of pink blush across her whitened cheeks. But why did she say that? She was obviously a rich lady's kid.

Jared poked his head through a long velvet curtain. "How are you, little sis? Did I tell you or what?"

"Jared, I feel amazing." She felt a swell of affection for him as he smiled wide back at her. Maybe she could move to New York, stay with them. Maybe the problem was the town, the circles she was surrounded by, the excess and wealth.

"Andrew was supposed to come back after he helped

your mom with the bags, and now he isn't answering his phone. Has he texted you?"

"I don't think so," she said.

The masseuse was massaging her face before applying the final bits of a body wrap to her cheekbones when Sadie's phone vibrated inside her handbag, slumped under the spa table.

"Maybe that's him," she said.

The massage therapist seemed almost hostile when Sadie reached an arm into her purse. "You're not relaxing!" she commanded. Sadie sat up mid-rub to check her phone.

"No, it's an email," she said. Reading Kevin's name, her face erupted in a grin. Sadie felt that her whole body was probably noticeably throbbing through all the chocolaty product.

"He probably just went back up to the apartment," he said.

Sadie couldn't hear him, could only read and reread the email.

Sadie lady, how are you? Merry Christmas! Jimmy says you two broke up. Don't worry, you'll work it out. He's lucky to have a cool chick like you. Or you'll find someone else who sees how smart and beautiful you are. Just thinking about you today. I'm sitting by the fire in a cabin with my parents, enjoying the fact that I just came up with the perfect ending for my book. My agent loves it! I'll be back in Avalon Hills tomorrow. I'm looking forward to seeing you.

The masseuse pressed a warm face cloth on her skin, washing away the product with a gentle hose and massaging her head, arms, and legs. Then she washed Sadie's hair with a shampoo that smelled of fresh fruit and painted her nails a bright pink called New Revelations. "Very grown-up," said the esthetician. Sadie didn't tell her that several chemicals in nail polish have been linked to diabetes, and that spa workers have astronomical rates of asthma and respiratory illness. Sadie realized she'd stopped her incessant fact quoting. Tidbits weren't coming to her the way they used to. She was getting used to silence, to speaking when spoken to.

Sadie floated around, feeling soft-skinned and smelling like expensive vanilla extract. After the spa, Jared showed her around the neighborhood, bought her a vanilla bean cupcake, and they walked back to the apartment.

"Do you know why Andrew doesn't want me to come home, to help out more with the case?" he asked, his voice squeaking out, as he unwrapped a chocolate cupcake and took a messy bite.

She shrugged. "I dunno. I just assumed you were too busy," she said.

"No, I keep offering to come. He doesn't want me to."

"He's always been a bit of a lone wolf, and he hates Avalon Hills, so I'm not entirely surprised."

"Why does he hate it so much?"

"I'm not sure. Because it's boring?"

"That can't be the only reason."

Her phone beeped again, and she couldn't help but check. She'd responded to Kevin's email—that she couldn't wait to read his book and was happy to know that he was coming back because she missed him. "I miss you." She just wrote it like that, straight ahead. Why not be bold? She didn't mention anything about Jimmy, and signed it with three *xxx*'s. Later she thought maybe that was immature-sounding. She kept rereading the line "smart and beautiful." *He thinks I'm smart and beautiful! My whole life I've been told I'm smart, but never beautiful.* Pretty, her dad used to say. Cute. Hot, Jimmy used to mumble while trying, always semi-successfully, to unhook her bra. *Beautiful* was a grown-up word. Her mom always associated being pretty or too interested in fashion with weakness. But this compliment felt good.

WHEN THEY GOT BACK to Jared and Andrew's building, a forty-something woman was standing in the entranceway. She had blunt-cut bangs and a white fur coat cut at the waist. She stared at them in a way that made it seem as if she was trying to place them.

"Excuse me," she said. "I'm trying to find Andrew Woodbury. Do you know him?"

Jared looked at her curiously. "I do," he said.

"I'm his sister," offered Sadie, in her small-town way.

"Oh. OH," she said awkwardly. "Do you mind giving him this?"

The card said *Sarah Myers, Starling Crafts—ethical repurposed handbags* with an email address and phone number.

"What is this about?" Jared asked.

"It's a little bit complicated," she said, "but we used to know each other, a very long time ago."

She turned and ran back out onto the street, walking with purpose.

"That was weird," Sadie said.

"Totally," Jared said, opening the front door and climbing the stairs.

When he handed the card to Andrew, he seemed confused and shoved it in his pocket.

"I have to talk to you alone," said Andrew, giving Jared a serious look.

"What's up?" asked Sadie.

"Adult stuff," he said, pulling Jared into the bedroom and closing the door.

"Where's Mom?" she called, but they didn't answer.

IN ANDREW AND JARED's bathroom, the room started to spin again, and Sadie crouched down on the floor. She'd run out of weed. She opened the medicine cabinet and saw a bottle of clonazepam prescribed to Andrew. She googled the name on her phone and thought, well, that will do. She took two and went back to the kitchen, where Jared had made her a cup of hot chocolate.

She smiled at him, feeling the absence of any bad feeling, feeling safe. She knew she must be high, but this was definitely better than any high she'd felt before in her life.

30

Joan and Clara drove away from New York City, hitting nonstop holiday traffic, and quickly realized they weren't going to make it to see George in time for visiting hours. Clara pulled Joan's car over to gas up and Joan leaned against the ice machine outside the station, begging the charge nurse on his floor to make an exception, but she wouldn't. Joan was able to get more specific information about his condition, though.

"He's conscious now, though barely," she told Clara as they stood in line at the cash register. "He has serious bruising on his neck. Apparently the guard intervened and saved him."

"He'll be okay?"

"He can't talk due to the laryngeal fracture. They were able to insert a stent, and things should heal up. But right now he is in a lot of pain and will require monitoring for several days. He's handcuffed, and mostly sedated."

Clara booked a double room in a hotel near the hospital while Joan paced the parking lot, letting Andrew know what was happening.

When they pulled out of the service station, Joan's phone buzzed from its spot in the console between the front seats. Joan read the text from Bennie out loud for Clara. "'Book a room and get some sleep. He'll be fine. He's out of the woods. Meet me first thing in the morning.'"

"I made us a reservation at a hotel. It's going to be okay."

"Waiting feels like I might lose it completely. I have no patience left to draw on," Joan said as Clara skirted around a slow car.

"You have no choice. And you have to tell Sadie," Clara said, muting the annoying robot voice of the GPS.

"No, I'm hoping she won't see it. I've asked Andrew to try to keep her away from the news until she gets home tomorrow and I can deal with it. I'll call her first thing. I just wanted her to have a fun holiday without worry. I couldn't even do that."

"Well, sometimes bad things happen and there's never a good time for it. Get some sleep and I'll drive you to the hospital early in the morning," Clara said.

WHEN JOAN WOKE UP the next morning, she was confused about where she was until Clara came bustling through the door of their shared hotel room with a tray of coffees and a newspaper.

"It's hit the local papers, but luckily some dimwit shot his wife and kids yesterday, so it's below the fold." She held up the paper. Indeed, the article was smaller than the large-printed MAN SHOOTS FAMILY THEN SELF. It read simply, AL-LEGED SEX OFFENDER ATTACKED ON CHRISTMAS DAY WHILE INCARCERATED.

31

KEVIN HAD A SKYPE MEETING WITH HIS AGENT EARLY
in the morning on the day after Christmas. He
propped the laptop on a side table in the guest bedroom of his sister's cabin. His niece and nephews were
running around outside the door screaming, playing with
the boxes their toys came in. Kevin was hungover from
drinking too much Scotch with his brother-in-law the
night before. He took a sip of the warm beer he'd apparently fallen asleep drinking, and pressed the Call button.

His agent's face appeared a bit fuzzy in the half screen.
He shuffled papers for a few moments before he cut to the
chase.

"This isn't the draft, Kev. It's good in parts, you know,
but George is too clean. He's not a villain. I need the abuse
in detail."

"Well, I don't have any details. The girls involved in
the case aren't allowed to talk to me."

"Well, you're a writer—imagine it. We can't have a

book where the monster is actually a sweet old guy everyone defends. There needs to be more conflict. Don't be
afraid to be imaginative. Use your fictional storytelling
devices. It's going to be *based on* the true story, right? You
can take some liberties."

"Really? Did James Frey teach us nothing?"

"He's too empathetic so far, and it's too confusing.
This is a novel, but we need some black-and-white facts
here. Write the rape scenes. Go wild!"

Kevin nodded. The screen froze. He got up and drained
his beer.

KEVIN LAID THE VICTIM impact statements out on the bed,
beside the three sexual assault memoirs he'd taken out of the
library and skimmed. He had to nail the voice of the girls.

Write the rape scenes.

He pictured private-school girls, how they would dress
and talk, writing a list of the possible sensory details, what
a ski lodge looked and smelled like. He remembered his
private-school crush on Karen Ridgley, the way she'd
stand at the end of her driveway waiting for the school bus
across from his house. She always pulled her skirt up higher
right before the bus arrived. One day, when he was home
sick from school, he watched her sneak home in the middle
of the day with a boy, and he stood in the window of his
bedroom with the binoculars, trying to see what they were
doing, even though he was feverish. He caught a glimpse
of them making out on the couch, and returned to bed,
imagining what they were going to do.

He lay back on the bed and tried to picture Karen,

getting turned on the way he had as a young man. He imagined her shirt unbuttoned, her skirt tossed aside, and then her being prey to someone like George Woodbury. As soon as the imagining got too real, he lost his hard-on. He stared at the blank screen of his laptop, the hangover overwhelming him. He used to always be ready to go, but now it seemed, the closer he got to forty, that was no longer the default. Then he got an email response to the group query he'd sent to all the girls involved in the case whom he'd been able to find on Facebook. Miranda was the only one who had replied. But she was the main girl. He pumped his fist in the air, took a deep breath, and opened her message. He took notes in his flip book as he read.

— *Parents not supportive of her going to cops.*
— *Former party girl, sober since ski trip.*
— *Lonely?*

By the end of the email, he knew she wasn't lying. Too many details, all of them convincing. She had all the money in the world, but she'd lost a lot by coming forward. He googled her name. An old Twitter feed with cleavage selfies, white girls throwing gang signs, silent since the arrest of George Woodbury, and several Facebook groups and Tumblr pages that, politely put, disparaged her credibility, with comments more cruel than anything any critic had ever said about Kevin's books.

He got in his car and drove back to Avalon Hills, to the room at the Hilton that was getting expensive but was starting to feel like a home of sorts, to finish the draft.

32

ANDREW INSISTED ON WAKING SADIE UP SO EARLY ON the day after Christmas that he was able to drop her off at Jimmy's house by ten. She slept most of the drive from New York, thanks to the second pill she'd stolen from the bathroom when she woke up sweating and alarmed at 3 A.M. Andrew was moody and drove too fast, but she barely noticed.

She realized that Jimmy was one of the only friends she had left in Avalon Hills. The sympathy any of her other friends had displayed after her father's arrest had faded away, and mostly she was a social pariah at school.

She used the key Elaine had made for her, and found them in the kitchen making pancakes. It looked like a scene from a commercial where a company is trying to convince you to spend more quality time with your family by using their products.

"Hey honey!" Elaine exclaimed, coming over to offer

Sadie a powdery hug. Jimmy was more reserved, just nodding, but he couldn't contain his smile. His relaxed demeanor and lack of immediate jumping on Sadie made her like him again for a moment. It was as if he had heard the universe telling him to calm down.

"How was New York City?" Elaine asked.

"It was great," she said. "Relaxing."

Elaine began pouring the batter into a cast iron skillet. Sadie worked up the nerve to ask what she wanted to know.

"How's Kevin? When is he coming home again?" She tried to make it sound casual, like small talk.

"He's already back in town," said Jimmy, eyes rolling.

"Where is he?"

Elaine paused and ran some warm water over the top of the maple syrup bottle in the sink.

"Kevin and I are having some problems."

Jimmy snorted. Sadie was ashamed to admit that her heartbeat sped up a little. Maybe he'd confessed he had feelings for someone else?

"Right now he's staying at the Hilton while we're talking through some . . . grown-up issues."

Elaine rarely used terms like that; she was usually more straight-up.

Jimmy put down his mug. "Mom, what the hell do you mean? Did he cheat on you or something?"

"No, of course not, nothing like that."

"He's supposed to be doing so well. He apparently sold his new book for, like, a million dollars or something. I read it online."

"That's true, Jimmy. We should all be happy for him in that way. Now help me with these pancakes," she said, motioning towards the plates.

"What, now that he doesn't need you to depend on, he's not going to stay anymore?" Jimmy was visibly upset, taking a plate of pancakes over to Sadie. "Doesn't he want to stay here anymore? Now he has money, he doesn't need you?"

"You're acting like he was a kept man, Jimmy, and that is ridiculous and not at all true."

"So what is it then?"

"Jimmy, for the last time, it's private, between Kevin and me, and you do not get to know every detail."

She sat down at the table with her own plate but didn't touch her pancakes. She watched as Sadie and Jimmy took a few bites while she sipped her coffee.

"Look, I'm sorry if this is upsetting, but you're going to have to live with the uncertainty for a few days until things get sorted. It's not my intention to have Kevin leave, and it's not what I want. But there are some things you cannot control, as we have all learned—especially you, Sadie— these past few months."

Sadie's head was racing with possibilities. Maybe he was brushing Elaine off, and wasn't telling her why. Or maybe he'd even told her—but then why would Elaine be so nice to her right now? *Maybe she knows he has feelings for someone but doesn't know it's me.* Kevin was a smart guy; he'd know to keep his mouth shut on this.

Sadie got up and went to the bathroom so she could text Kevin. *I hear you might not be home as planned. What's up? Xo*

He responded immediately. *Oh, it's a long story and it has to do with my book. Elaine can fill you in.*

Kind of a cold response, she thought. She went back out to the kitchen. The room was empty. She could hear Jimmy in the living room playing video games. The dirty plates sat on the table, the leftover food congealing. Sadie gathered them up and started rinsing them in the sink and putting them in the dishwasher.

"I should go home and feed Payton," she said to Jimmy, calling through the divide into the living room. He pressed Pause and stood up.

"Okay, sure." He followed her to the door. "So, like, I didn't want to say anything, but how's your dad recovering?"

"What do you mean?"

"You know, after what happened . . ."

"What happened?!"

Jimmy's eyes widened. "It was on the front page this morning . . ." He fished in the recycling box by his feet. TEACHER CHARGED WITH ATTEMPTED SEX ASSAULTS INJURED IN CHRISTMAS PRISON ATTACK.

"How could you not know? Didn't your mom tell you? I mean, we were trying not to bring it up, you know, to let you do the talking, and that's why I figured you looked so distracted."

She scanned the article to make sure he was alive. He was. In hospital.

"Obviously, my mother would rather I find out this way," she said. No wonder she'd left. Why would she lie? Why would Andrew and Jared both lie to her?

She looked at her phone. Seventeen missed calls from

her mother. "Well, she *has* been calling and I haven't called her back." She thought about calling Andrew. After he'd dropped her off he probably went to see her dad in the hospital. Why didn't they tell her? Take her along? She was sleepy and still high in the car, so maybe he didn't think she could handle it.

"Come back inside. You should come in and relax and let me take care of you."

"I'm so sick of feeling like I'm in need of care or comfort. I'm pissed off. I need to go home."

She ran outside, not even sure how she'd get home. Then she remembered she'd left her old bike strewn beside their house. It was cold, but she didn't feel it. Her hands went numb on the handlebars all the way to the outskirts of town near the highway turnoff where the hotels and conference centers had their own little universe. It started to snow, and then rain. She knew she was cold but didn't feel anything. Cars beeped at her, not expecting to see a bike on the side of the boulevard in this kind of weather. When she finally arrived, lungs hurting, hands burning from the cold, she stashed her bike behind the Hilton Dumpster, took off her winter coat, and undid two buttons on her blouse in the reflection of a car window.

33

JOAN AND CLARA MADE IT TO THE HOSPITAL FIFTEEN minutes before the start of visiting hours. They met Bennie in the ICU waiting room. Joan, forgetting this wasn't *her* hospital, pushed through the double doors of the ICU. Clara and Bennie stayed in the hallway. A security guard sat in a hard-backed chair at the end of the bed looking less than thrilled. He was startled by her arrival, but quickly caught on to who Joan was. It was likely the first time he'd seen a woman age years before his very eyes, in the span of a few seconds.

George was handcuffed to the gurney. The room, like much of the hospital, was in serious need of funding, seemed filthy and obviously understaffed compared with the trauma center. George looked as if he'd survived a bombing.

"George," Joan said in a whisper, leaning over him, investigating the bruising on his neck, doing a quick vitals check. She did these things instinctively, without quite realizing it. He opened his eyes briefly, tried to speak but couldn't. She put her lips to his forehead and kissed him gently. When she pulled back, he gripped her hand in what felt like terror.

"It's going to be okay, George. It will all be okay, don't worry. You're going to recover and you're going to get out of jail and all will be normal and fine again," she said. She sat beside him, murmuring words of comfort, while tears fell down his swollen, disfigured face. Joan had witnessed hundreds of injuries in her career, but to see her husband this way made her sick and angry in a way she'd never experienced.

She watched as he fell back asleep, until she heard a stirring at the entrance. It was Andrew.

"Andrew, it's okay. He's going to be okay. What are you doing here? I needed you to stay with Sadie at home. But come sit by your father. He needs our support."

"Sadie's at Jimmy's. We left before dawn. I couldn't handle waiting any longer," he said. He continued to stand near the door, not looking at his father. Joan stood up, offering him the seat next to the bed, but Andrew shook his head. "I need to talk to you."

"Andrew, *come see your father.*"

He didn't move from the doorway, just leaned forward a bit, took a look at the machines monitoring his father's vitals, and stepped back into the hall.

Joan gave George's hand a squeeze and he opened his eyes. "Andrew is here. He hasn't been sleeping lately. I'm going to go talk to him, but I'll be right back."

Andrew was pacing the hall, hands balled in fists.

"Andrew, he should know we're here supporting him. For god's sake, he was almost *murdered.* He's your father."

Andrew shook his head. "Mom, Bennie needs to discuss something."

"What could possibly be more important right now?"

Andrew didn't answer, just led her back to the family room, where Bennie was sitting in one of the scuffed pink plastic couches, leaning over his laptop.

"Joan," he said, shutting his computer, "things aren't looking good. We've come up against a significant roadblock and it could sink the case. My research team will need to speak to you at length about this. Andrew as well, but he already knows about it."

"What does he know?"

"You should sit down," he said, motioning to the couch across from him. She remained standing. An orderly mopped the floor, figure eights of bleach.

"Actually, Andrew already knows about it because he brought it to our attention, this morning."

"What does he know, Bennie?"

He sighed heavily. "Do you know the name Sarah Myers?"

Joan racked her brain. Nothing. "No."

"Think back to when you lived in Boston, in that apartment building, when you started going back to nursing school."

She resented hearing her life trajectory parroted back to her. Clara got on her phone, texting away distractedly.

"Is this conversation entirely necessary right now? George needs me," she said.

It clicked into focus then: Sarah Myers, the skinny girl with the gap between her front teeth, who always wore an oversized Black Sabbath baseball shirt. She put up an advertisement in the laundry room that read "Responsible babysitter in Apartment 3A. Available after school until midnight" in red and purple Magic Marker scrawl. Joan had pulled off one of the fluttering tags with her number when she was preparing to return to nursing school in the evenings. After that, George picked Andrew up from day care and Sarah would sit with him at their place while George went to do office hours at school.

"Why on earth would you be asking about our old babysitter?"

"Mrs. Woodbury . . ." Bennie's pause indicated what Joan already knew, what was slowly bruising down each arm, until every fingernail felt like it had been slammed in a door, and her inhalations came fast and shallow.

Clara looked up, tuning in. "What? What's going on?"

"Mom, I need you to stay calm," Andrew said, leading her to the couch and gently encouraging her to sit down. "She Facebooked me a few days before Christmas. A weird note. I wasn't sure what to make of it. She said she used to babysit me when I was little. Then she showed up at our apartment yesterday, and left her card with Jared. So I called her after you left. I was so curious. She saw something about the case on the news. She wanted to find me, talk to me, about something that happened before we left Boston."

"Mrs. Woodbury, what happened when she stopped looking after Andrew?" Bennie asked.

"She only stopped because George's father was sick and we decided to move. I think I brought Andrew over to say goodbye—probably, anyway. That poor girl's mother was such an alcoholic. So what happened? Why is she calling?" Joan said.

Andrew looked at the floor. His fists clenched in his lap.

Bennie referred to some papers in front of him. "George apparently gave her mother a large sum of money in return for her agreeing to keep quiet, after . . . after an incident between him and the girl."

"Sarah," said Andrew.

"Holy shit," said Clara.

Sweat drenched the backs of Joan's legs, sticking to the plastic couch.

Bennie said, "George and my father arranged everything, in secret, before he retired. I was able to look into the files. George paid for Sarah to go to college. She has suffered for years from emotional difficulties, she claims, as a result of what happened, and completing college using his money—it just never felt right to her. She spent most of the money, she traveled. She developed a considerable addiction problem that she has since recovered from. Her mother died more than ten years ago, and she feels like she needs some closure on the subject. So, when she heard the news on television, she called the police. She said that before her mother died, she apologized for taking the money instead of calling the police. She said that they were poor, and her mother was an alcoholic, and she thought it was the most positive choice for her daughter. Apparently, because of their particularly low station in life, it was likely she wouldn't have been believed anyway, and sadly, I tend to think that is accurate, especially for the times. Proving rape is never easy, even today."

Rape. The word landed hard between them. No one had used that word before without the *attempted* preceding it.

"So this entire time, for our entire *lives*, he has been supporting this young woman? Out of guilt?"

"Out of fear of getting caught, more likely," Clara snorted.

Andrew rubbed his nose with his hand and squinted as though lost in thought. His face paled, anger grew along his jaw as it tensed. "It means he's definitely fucking guilty, Mom."

"How could I not have *known*?" Joan's voice reverberated around the room.

Bennie spoke more quietly. "The majority of sex offenders are very adept at living completely double lives. Most partners would never know, would never even suspect. Though I must emphasize that this is just an accusation—it hasn't been proven."

"Of course, of all the people in the world, he was just too smart, too, too charming. Who didn't love George, right?" At this point she was standing up, pacing around them. Andrew shook his head back and forth.

"All this time I've been sticking by him, I've been *believing* him. What a fool! What a fucking fool! She was a child."

Andrew spoke up. "Mom, it's okay. Sit down. Let's just finish this and process our emotions later."

"Don't talk down to your mother, honey," said Clara. "She's allowed to express her feelings."

"Why didn't Sarah press charges?" Andrew asked in a quieter voice. "Is it possible that the attraction was mutual? She was a teenager, right?"

Bennie actually chuckled at this. "The law is the law, Andrew. You can't reconfigure this with your sexual liberation theory of law, or whatever. She was thirteen years old."

"You're right, you're right," Andrew said. "I didn't really mean that. I'm just . . . grasping at straws."

"It is also possible that more victims will come forward, and you need to be prepared for this potentiality."

Joan quickly marched back into George's hospital room. He was asleep. The window blinds clicked against the glass, moved by the breeze from a heating vent. If Joan could've got away with it at that moment, she would have pressed one of the pillows to his face and held it still, in one swift silencing rage.

Instead, she fluffed up the pillows around his head, and underneath the wet, hardening thrum of rage she felt an immeasurable depth of sorrow at being abandoned. The only sign that love still resided within her and between them, fighting like a gasping bird to stay alive for one more second, lay in the fact that even now, she couldn't do him physical harm, even though it was the closest she'd ever come to understanding the act of violence. This felt like the end of love.

She watched him breathe, knew his body would recover. But her George was dead.

IN THE FAMILY ROOM, she waited with Bennie, trying to fill out legal forms and talking to the prison warden, who had a way of addressing her as though she were in cahoots with her husband, or an imbecile. The suffering, stupid wife. She wanted to rip at his mottled face with her hands.

She called Sadie again, but it went straight to voice mail.

She tried to call Elaine, but she didn't answer. Andrew tried as well, eventually giving up and driving back to Avalon Hills.

INSTEAD OF BEING GENTLE with Joan, Clara was insistent that she be decisive. "What do you want me to do?" Joan asked her on the highway, cups of coffee between them. "You seem so clear. What should I do now? With this knowledge?"

"I want you to let go. I want you to just let him go for a while. It will be months until the trial. Show him the kind of consideration that he has shown you, which is exactly none."

"You act as though I can just stop being married."

"Uh, you can. You're not Amish. But that's not what I mean. I want you to accept the fact that none of this is in your control, and you cannot change what happened, and you have to start taking some steps towards ending your marriage."

"I have accepted it. I have started to move on, by going back to work and going to a therapist, but the rest will be a slower process, and you are the one that is going to have to accept that."

Clara lifted her coffee to her lips and the car hit a pothole, causing it to spill all over her sweater. She swore a string of curse words and then whipped the coffee cup out the window.

34

SADIE SAT IN AN OVERSIZED ARMCHAIR IN THE LOBBY OF
the Avalon Hills Hilton. She watched a long line of
guests pulling suitcases in and out. Two kids played
tag, one bumping into her legs as he ran by. Her jacket was
soaked from the rain that was almost snow, so much so that
her shirt was stuck to her back. She combed through her
hair with her fingers. Kevin wasn't answering her texts.
Eventually she walked up to the desk clerk.

"I'm here to see Kevin Lamott. I can't remember his
room number," she told the young attendant, pretending
to pat down her jeans pockets for a piece of paper with a
number on it.

The desk clerk smiled at Sadie with all her teeth and
looked at her computer. "Sure, honey, who shall I say is
here to meet him? Are you his daughter?"

"No, no. Just tell him it's Sadie."

"Sadie, okay." She dialed, kept scrolling through her
computer. "There doesn't seem to be a response. Perhaps

he's in the dining area? Would you like to leave a message?"

"No, that's okay. I'll go look in the restaurant."

"Sure, it's right across the reception area, those darkened doors."

Sadie turned and walked towards the restaurant, wishing she were wearing a dress, or anything dry, really. Instead, she was in wet jeans and a T-shirt she'd bought with
Jared, which had seemed so up-fashion and city-like, but
which now just looked clinging and drenched. She was
fairly certain she came off as a lost and neglected child.

The restaurant host stood at a podium by the entrance.
He wore a navy blue blazer emblazoned with a gold crest,
much like the Avalon school uniforms. He greeted her sus-
piciously. "Early lunch? Breakfast? How many?" he asked.

"One, just me. I'm just looking for someone," she said,
walking past him and into the crowd.

Sadie spotted Kevin sitting at a booth by the bar across
from a guy in a suit with bright white hair. "Kevin!" Sadie
said, and approached the table with a smile, as though she
had just bumped into him on the street.

He looked startled. "Wow, Sadie, what the heck are
you doing here?" He was tanned, nothing like when he
hermitted in the house all winter. He was wearing the
plaid shirt he always used to wear, but it looked better
without the jogging shorts and flip-flops.

"I was looking for you," she started. It occurred to her
that she should have rehearsed something, thought of
something concise to say.

"You were, huh?" He looked at his friend oddly, a little

bit uncomfortable. He didn't invite Sadie to sit down. "Well, did you have a good Christmas? You look like you need a raincoat. Such weird weather out there, global warming and all. Not exactly festive, huh?"

"Yeah, I was just biking by and knew you were here and stuff, and thought I would come say hello." Everything she said was coming out wrong, garbled-sounding. As if anyone just biked by the highway in the middle of winter.

His friend regarded Sadie closely and extended his hand. "I'm Gerald, Kevin's agent. We were just talking about how he's going to get very rich on this book." He smiled in a way that didn't look like it was meant to betray the feelings that smiles usually indicate.

"Yes, Elaine told me!" Sadie said.

"I'm sure she didn't really say that," Kevin grumbled. "She's not exactly thrilled about the book."

"Oh, she'll be thrilled soon enough when you can fly her around the world," said Gerald with a smarmy smile.

"You've never met Elaine, have you?" Sadie asked, feeling suddenly protective of her.

Kevin looked pained. Sadie took this as a sign that he knew he would rather be sitting next to *Sadie* in first class, not Elaine. They just hadn't figured it out, the small details. *It's not as though he could just come right out and say it.*

"So, your dad. Is he okay? I saw in the paper."

Sadie shrugged. "He's going to recover." She felt like she was talking about someone else. That her father had already died.

"Your dad? Kevin, this isn't . . . ?"

"Yes, Gerald, this is Sadie."

"Oh my gosh! It's so great to meet the inspiration for our heroine, the lovely Lori Fine!"

Gerald stood up to reach for her hand. She offered it limply while he shook it, as though Sadie was someone worth shaking hands with. She took a step back. "What do you mean?"

"Gerald, she hasn't read it yet. It's something I—"

"I'm the heroine in your book?" She smiled, tried to play it cool, but her heart would not stop pounding in her ears. A blush blossomed across her clammy, mascara-streamed face. She couldn't believe it. He was being so obvious.

"Sort of," said Kevin. "I've been meaning to tell you about it in person, I just wasn't ready yet."

"You know," said Gerald, dipping a piece of toast into a sloppy egg yolk, "I've met your father, so I know who the real Mr. Fine is, but to meet you—it's simply extraordinary. You are like the moral center of his narrative."

Sadie sat down next to Kevin in the booth, forcing him to move over, but their legs still touched. "What do you mean, my dad? My dad is in jail," she whispered.

Gerald's eyes widened. "Kevin, my god, you haven't told her anything?"

Kevin took a long sip from his glass of beer. Gerald handed Sadie his phone, linked to a newspaper article. Under the headline KEVIN LAMOTT SIGNS 6-FIGURE DEAL TO WRITE BOOK BASED ON WOODBURY SEX SCANDAL, the article read: "Lamott, best known for his literary debut novel *Hands On,* which won the National Book Award ten years ago, had personal access to the family, and Poplar Press is claiming this will be his breakout book, having already sold rights in advance to over 23 territories."

"You wrote a book about my dad's case?"

"It's fiction, really, and Elaine told me that it wasn't right to do this, but you see, I have to write when I'm inspired to, and this was just too much, happened in my own house. And really, you will love Lori, Sadie, you will. There's a lot to love about her—just like you."

Sadie didn't know whether to feel angry or flattered. She felt a bit of both. Mostly, she felt startled. And cold. The dampness of her clothes started to burn through her.

"Has Elaine read it?"

"Yes."

"And she's mad?"

"Yes."

"Why?"

"Because ultimately she doesn't understand the process of writing fiction, Sadie."

"No, it's because I don't understand exploiting a girl living in your own house to feed your overdeveloped ego and desperation to succeed."

Elaine was suddenly hovering over them as if in the clouds.

"Elaine! I'm so glad you could meet us for lunch," Kevin's agent said, grimace-smiling at her.

Sadie began to feel weak.

"I wasn't exploited! My feelings are real! You just can't handle it, and you"—she stood up, pointing at Kevin— "knew it. Don't pretend you didn't."

"Knew *what*? Sadie, my god, what are you talking about?"

"About you and me . . . our . . . connection."

She heard Elaine say, "See? See, Kevin? She is not some plot point for you to use. She is a troubled young girl, her family has gone to shit, and you don't actually care about her feelings. You are a fucking narcissist, and unless you change your book and keep her name out of the publicity machine, I will never speak to you again, do you hear me?"

Gerald spoke up. "Elaine, let's just all take a breath, okay? Have a seat. Waiter, get this lady a mimosa over here. We're celebrating, after all." He patted the booth beside him.

Elaine remained standing.

Gerald continued. "Tying the book to the story of what really happened here is what we're gunning for publicity-wise. It's the best hook in the world. We're going to release it the week of the trial. He lived with her, he knows her. Consumers *love* a real-life connection. It's not exploitative, it's passionate, it's real life, it's raw, and it's what will ultimately be redemptive. It's fucking *Oprah*-worthy, let me tell you. You could all be very rich!"

"Oprah doesn't even have a show anymore," mumbled Sadie.

"You smarmy piece of trash, don't you ever address me again, you understand?" Elaine's normally cool tone of voice had vanished. Kevin and Gerald paused in what looked like fright. She turned and grabbed Sadie's hand.

"No," Sadie said meekly.

"Sadie, trust me. Kevin is not your ally here."

"But—"

"Now, come with me. I'm taking you home."

"I have my bike," she mumbled like a six-year-old.

"We'll put it in the trunk. Let's go," she insisted, as if they were running from some sort of bomb about to explode.

Sadie followed her out into the lobby, past an army of valets, and into the parking lot. She grabbed her bike and placed it awkwardly in the trunk of Elaine's minivan.

Before she started the car, Elaine turned to Sadie.

"Did Kevin come on to you?"

"No. I don't know. I think I misunderstood some things." She started to cry, pulling at her wet shirt.

"What did you mean in there?"

"I just thought . . . I just thought that he liked me." She sounded like a schoolgirl. "He was so interested in talking to me, but I guess it was . . ." She couldn't finish the sentence because she just didn't want to admit it.

"For the book?"

"Yes," she admitted weakly. "Yes, I suppose it was."

"This is why you dumped Jimmy?"

"I guess. Jimmy and I spent so much time together, I just started to get bored. Every time I turned around, he was just *there*. He was like a dog or like a brother."

"That happens sometimes," Elaine said gently. "Although he really loves you. He's been a mess since you left."

This made her heart hurt a little, thinking of Jimmy hurt. She didn't want that.

"Are you sure Kevin never said or did anything inappropriate?"

Sadie considered it. "Not really," she admitted. "Is it bad that I kind of wanted him to? Not because I wanted to hurt you, of course. I'm so grateful for you. God, I wasn't even *thinking* of you, if I'm being totally honest. I separated you from the whole thing. I just got so wrapped up in this idea of running away with him forever."

Elaine sighed. "He *is* a charmer. But have you thought that maybe it had to do with the running-away part? Maybe you ran away to us, but we really aren't far enough away from everything."

"Yeah."

Elaine turned the key in the ignition, silencing the blaring talk radio station.

"I'm sorry I tried to steal your boyfriend," Sadie said, sobbing.

"It wasn't your fault," Elaine said in her matter-of-fact way. "And this whole experience has been rather instructive—for me, anyway. Sometimes being an adult doesn't prevent you from making terrible choices." She honked at the car in front of her and pulled out onto the highway. "Do you want to come over, or would you like to go home?"

Sadie couldn't believe that Elaine would welcome her back into her home after what had happened, that she wasn't kicking her out of the car onto the side of the highway.

"Home," she said. She turned on her phone. Twenty-three missed calls from her mother.

35

WHEN JOAN GOT HOME, SADIE WAS ALREADY IN BED under the covers, a slow electronic moan emanating from her iPod dock. Payton was pacing around her, kneading his paws into the pillow. Joan moved a pile of her clothes from the edge of the bed and sat down. "I'm sorry I didn't tell you about your dad . . ."

Joan couldn't say it. She didn't want her to conjure any gruesome images.

"It's fine, Mom. I don't need protecting," Sadie mumbled, sitting up.

Joan reached over and ran her fingers through her daughter's hair, pushing some strands behind her ear. "He's okay. He's going to be okay."

"I'm so glad, so glad," she said. "I miss him." Sadie closed her eyes, refusing to engage any further. "I'm just so tired."

Joan kissed her on the forehead and said they'd talk about it in the morning.

· · ·

JOAN'S THERAPIST'S OFFICE WAS in a three-story professional building above a Starbucks in a suburb thirty minutes away. Joan had rarely been to this particular town, and she felt good walking around and feeling a bit lost. It gave her a task: find where you are and where you're going. Before this all happened, it would have frazzled Joan, not knowing where she was. She would have been sweaty and annoyed, refolding the map book that fit awkwardly in her purse, pressing fingertips in the smudged-out edging; every moment she spent lost would have felt like a waste of her time. Now it gave her direction, in that literal way she appreciated.

Joan told her quickly about how George had been hurt in jail, and about Sarah Myers. That George would remain in hospital for another day or two before being transferred back. The therapist's eyes widened, even though Joan could tell she was trying to keep a neutral expression.

"That's a lot for you to deal with," she said, keeping eye contact with Joan, who sank back into the comfortable chair, unsure what to say after reporting the facts of her insane holiday. Dr. Taylor allowed for some silence. Joan pressed her thumbs to the bridge of her nose, trying to quell a sinus headache.

"I have dreams lately," Joan said after a few moments, "that take place before this happened. Nothing really big happens in the dreams. I get up and take a shower and get dressed for work. Sometimes I make breakfast for Sadie, and George and I go for our walk around the lake that we used to do every morning. We stop and get coffee at the Coffee Hut. Sometimes there is mist as the sun comes up, sometimes it's bright and sunny. I wake up from those dreams feeling worse than I do when I have nightmares. Realizing I will never have that normal morning again. It's crushing."

Dr. Taylor nodded.

"Routines can be so unremarkable, even boring, you never think about them, until they change," Joan said.

Dr. Taylor and Joan were wearing the exact same cardigan sweater, a lilac cotton blend with tiny pearl oval buttons. They also had remarkably similar haircuts. From the year on her degree posted above her desk, they were presumably about the same age.

This had put Joan off during their initial session. Doctors are supposed to be older somehow, if not in years then in levels of experience. Joan knew this was shifting, and many professionals were now younger than her by many years, but trusting someone with her psychological well-being, well . . . she had been hoping for someone with clear memories of the Kennedy assassination, who could look down on her by at least a decade and offer some worldly, aged wisdom.

When she'd arrived today, she wasn't sure what she wanted to say to Dr. Taylor. But once she got started, she found she couldn't stop. When she left, she expected to feel unburdened, lighter, the way she had after her previous appointments. But she didn't. She kept seeing her therapist's detached face nodding, taking notes, in that same sweater. Joan wanted her to tell her what to do, to explain Joan to Joan. But of course, she couldn't do that.

Joan stopped at a coffee shop on the way home. She ordered a scone and a mug of tea and sat down at a table.

She was trying to practice being alone in public, being alone in the world and relaxed. It felt awkward. She picked up a paper, forced herself to read through the local news. George's beating had actually stalled debate about the merits of the accusations. One headline did catch her eye, in the arts briefs section: KEVIN LAMOTT TO PUBLISH NOVEL BASED ON WOODBURY SEX SCANDAL. "The celebrated local author has written the book from the perspective of one young female victim, and her friendship with the daughter of the teacher, a character based on the popular science teacher from Avalon Hills preparatory school, known widely for its rigorous and high-achieving academic standing."

Joan left her hot tea and scone and got in the car.

ELAINE LOOKED AS IF she had been expecting Joan. She was sitting at her kitchen table, hair pulled back in a wide elastic headband.

"I want to see Kevin," Joan demanded in lieu of a hello, pushing her way through the glossy white door of the ugly pink brick house.

"Kevin isn't living here right now," Elaine said.

This Joan wasn't expecting. She had come up with a monologue that she'd rehearsed on the drive over, a rage-fueled diatribe with several moments of cutting wit and savvy social commentary, as well as some personal jabs at his paucity of integrity and surfeit of balls.

Elaine offered Joan some tea from a pot that had been steeping far too long; her first sip was bitter and soupy. Joan stopped drinking it after one swallow, instead just warming her hands on the mug. She looked around the house, the mess inside Elaine's head made manifest in the disarray.

"Listen, Joan, I know you must be justified in wanting to injure Kevin in some way. Believe me, truly believe that I am sincere when I tell you that I am angry at his sense of entitlement over your family's story, and it is in fact the very reason why we are currently separated."

Joan took in that information, stirring the tea she was never planning to drink.

"But I can't control what he does," Elaine said, wrapping her hands around the teapot. "I can only react in a way that I think is right. And I don't think it's right to condone it, and I feel betrayed that he didn't tell me what he was writing about, that he went away and got swept up in the industry bullshit, and didn't consider your family, or his own. I mean, he wrote a scene about Jimmy and Sadie having sex, for god's sake. He didn't even bother to change the physical details of what they look like. Jimmy is just devastated."

Joan wasn't sure what Elaine was expecting her to say or feel. To sympathize with the disintegration of trust, the loss of her family? They were playing in different leagues on that front.

"Well, at least Kevin is still out walking around in the world. At least his mistakes weren't catastrophic."

"I wasn't trying to compare at all, Joan. I wasn't. I guess I was trying to defend myself. I know that the whole town has ganged up on you and your family, and that hasn't been fair at all, and you lack support in so many ways. I honestly cannot believe how you manage to get up every morning. I feel like what Kevin did is in the same vein as those vigilante hysterics who call your voice mail or throw eggs at your front door, and worse . . ."

"I suppose . . . Thanks for saying those things. It is nice to hear that someone recognizes how hard it's been." She looked at Elaine and for the first time she didn't distrust her, or dislike her, anyway. Her face seemed to change. She looked humble and worried, and Joan realized she really wasn't her enemy, or an obstacle, after all.

"Also, I think that your daughter may have developed a crush on Kevin. I assure you that her feelings were not returned, and Kevin did not behave inappropriately in that way. I think that she misinterpreted his interest in her for the book. I feel terrible that she likely felt used in this way."

"What the fuck are you talking about?" Jimmy stood in the kitchen doorway. "That is not true at all. As if she would like him! She just liked that he let her smoke pot and stuff."

"Jimmy, it was more of a misunderstanding. Kevin is not a parent and does not have an accurate understanding of what being an adult around children means, really."

Joan stood up when she experienced what could only be called a moment of clarity, in that she recognized she was not willing to engage in another family's drama when she had enough of her own to deal with. Elaine and Jimmy continued to bicker and Joan was halfway to the door when Elaine reached out and touched her arm.

"You know, Kevin's been interviewing George in prison. He's known about the book for months."

Joan, pulling on her boots, barely reacted. She was so used to hearing humiliating things in front of strangers. She was mechanical, just walking to her car, getting in, and driving away, tears streaming down her face, without really feeling anything.

JOAN STOOD IN THE entrance of George's hospital room, clutching the door frame, peering inside. She glanced at the guard sitting in his hard-backed chair in the corner; he looked up briefly before returning to the game on his phone.

George was to be transferred back to the prison medical ward later that morning; she had only a few minutes at most. She wasn't even supposed to be here. It was almost New Year's Eve, the first she'd be spending alone since childhood. The nurse at the desk, whom she'd met at an urgent care conference years earlier, had called to tip her off. Still, she wasted minutes just standing there, looking at him while he slept, moving the chalky remnants of an antacid tablet around in her mouth.

When she finally walked in, putting her purse down on the side table and opening the blinds to allow in some sunlight, his eyes fluttered open and he tried to speak her name. It came out in a low rasp.

"Don't try to talk. You might scar your throat forever," she said.

He reached for her hand. The guard cleared his throat. Joan glanced his way, and then back at George. She didn't say anything. She held his hand, and from that contact she felt the love she'd always felt and she let it flood her senses. She basked in the memory of it. It was only when the guard made a noise again, this time a hearty fake cough, that she was shaken from her reverie. Then George's hand was hot, and she dropped it because it felt like a fabric she couldn't touch without feeling profoundly uncomfortable, a jolt of neural discomfort.

They sat there as though at any moment Godot would come sweeping in. Since his arrest, certain moments felt endless, others went by in a heartbeat. His waiting meant that she was waiting. Her life, which had once been active, was now defined by waiting. She could do small things, such as go to work, buy the groceries, call Clara and discuss what she should or shouldn't be doing or deciding. But she couldn't mourn what she'd lost because what she'd lost wasn't really lost yet, in any concrete way that could be talked about.

She stared at him, stood up.

"Sarah Myers," she said.

George's eyes popped from the shock, and if he hadn't been restrained, Joan felt he would have bucked like an animal. Then he closed his eyes tight, the way a child might when he thinks closing his eyes makes things disappear. He brought his hands up to his face, the IV line straining.

She knew this was as close to an admission or apology as she was going to get.

She turned and left the room.

WALKING OUT TO HER car in the hospital parking lot, she had to decide either to drive home and rest before her night shift began or to go to a support group meeting. Both seemed like terrible ideas. She sat in her car, key in the ignition, with the radio on so she could hear the traffic, which was supposed to come on every ten minutes. At 9:11, she heard the announcer say, "And now for the latest traffic . . ." and then stopped listening, waking again when he shifted to the weather. "Dammit," she said out loud, startling herself, looking around to see if anyone had seen her talking to herself. She waited until 9:21, but it happened again. Finally she just turned the radio off and started the car, creeping out of the parking lot, making her way towards the interstate.

She made the decision about what to do with her day both passively and impulsively, by watching the exit to Avalon Hills go by from where she drove in the left highway lane. It's not that she didn't want to veer over, she just didn't do it. Maybe it wasn't lack of desire but lack of ability to make a choice. She looked ahead, wondering if she'd also miss the exit for Woodbridge and just keep driving until she reached the next horizon, then the next horizon, until she ran out of gas or reached the sea.

As she drove, she tried to remember Sarah Myers, but could see only the gap in her front teeth, and remember the pink stretch pants she'd outgrown but still continued to wear all the time with the yellow jelly shoes. These were children's clothes. She remembered how scared she was to be a mother, how unprepared. That her own mother told her it would get easier, and it did. But it was still hard to leave Andrew with a babysitter to go to school at night. Not as hard as being a housewife, though. She remembered how angry she felt when George would come back from school. She resented that he didn't have to be tethered to a crying baby all day long. Then, when she hired Sarah, she almost turned around on her way to class, because the longing was too much.

Sarah would be in her late thirties or early forties now.

Joan was in her fifties and hadn't really believed in any birthday since she was thirty-five or so. She was still shocked whenever she looked in a mirror. This is a life? This is what happens?

She pictured George when Andrew was a baby and he was in his late twenties, the green and gray plaid shirt he used to wear over a Marlboro T-shirt, brown tattered cowboy boots, the way he used to dress to disguise his class status. After Andrew was born, he went through a phase of acting like a teenager again, not wanting to be home with the baby, drinking too much, as if he was rebelling against getting older. She'd forgotten about that period. When she eventually had to yell at him, something she'd never done before, telling him to get it together and accept that their lives weren't about themselves anymore, he pouted but then acquiesced. It was a trying time in their young marriage. How could she have forgotten those details? She'd revised their history in her mind to be seamless, as though they'd never hit any marital bumps before this one. Was what happened with Sarah part of the time when he was acting like a spoiled, entitled child?

The trial was still a few months away. For the first time, she wasn't desperate for it to happen. She had the certainty about his guilt that she'd been looking for, and it felt more like confirmation than shock, if she was really thinking about it honestly.

EVENTUALLY SHE SWITCHED TO the right lane, and took the exit for Woodbridge, passing by the Target and the retirement home and the stretch of suburban homes now so familiar she could autopilot her way to the health center. When she parked the car and gathered her things, she decided just to keep quiet at this session, be a witness to others' pain.

But it was a smaller group than usual, and the plan was thwarted when Dr. Forrestor turned to her first and instead of a generic greeting she could easily respond to with a "pass," he said, "Last time you met with us, you had stopped visiting your husband every Friday. Is that still the case?"

"No," Joan said. "I took a break from the regular visit, yes, but I actually just came from seeing him this morning."

She briefly considered leaving it at that and letting the focus shift to Melissa, who was biting her cuticles and staring bug-eyed at the floor. But what was the point of not sleeping all day? Perhaps it would help to talk about how his eyes popped when she said the word *Sarah*.

"I found out some things I just can't overlook."

The women nodded.

"He was beaten up pretty badly in prison," she started. She'd told other people this, and they'd all reacted with concern and shock. The faces of the women looking back at her in this group hardly changed at all. They nodded. They'd probably held bruised hands, looked at fresh shiners through panes of glass.

"I found out something, from our past. When we were young, and my son was just a toddler, we lived in Boston when George was almost done with his PhD. He had his defense schedule and everything, but he changed his mind. He came home one day and said he'd decided we should move back home to Avalon Hills. I was so happy—I hated the city, it was hard being alone with the baby all the time. He said it was to care for his father, who had just gotten sick, but I found out this week that it was because he had . . . assaulted our son's babysitter, and he paid her off and moved us home. I had no idea."

Some of the women looked down uncomfortably, shifting.

"I have to leave him," she said.

It was only after Joan said it out loud that she knew it was right.

"I've learned to live without him. I'm sad, angry. I miss who I thought he was, but I have to do this."

She didn't expect applause, but she felt something close to it inside. The relief of having made a decision and the certainty she was right.

Dr. Forrestor repeated back to her what she had said, in that calming active-listening way, and hearing it cemented it further.

When Joan got home, she walked upstairs and got into bed, still in her coat, dropping her purse and boots on the floor. Clara knocked softly on the door, holding a cup of coffee. Opening her eyes felt impossible. The muscles in her face wouldn't allow it. She felt Clara sit down on the edge of the bed, and tuck in the duvet tight around her.

"I know I have to leave him. I've decided to. I just can't go much beyond that right now, okay? I *know*."

Clara looked surprised. "I heard about that bullshit Kevin Lamott novel. I've blackballed him in an editorial meeting, but the managing editor might go over my head about it. Apparently he's an 'it' interview for the spring season."

"Good for him," she said.

"You're not serious. Joan, you are a character in his book. So is Sadie."

"It's not as though I have control over the story that gets played out in the media either," Joan said. "I have to just give up and let the sharks eat me—the cops, the lawyers, the media, the opportunistic, exploitative writers who decide to prey on my daughter. I have no control, Clara. And that is the entirety of the life lesson I have learned from this experience. No one has control. At all."

The sigh Clara emitted was loud, and turned into a grumbling groan that startled Payton, who was asleep on George's old pillow. Joan didn't want to tell her that George had been interviewed for the book, that he hadn't even told her. It would only fuel more reaction from Clara, and she was too exhausted.

"I need to sleep. I have a night shift tonight," Joan said. It was the first in a string of five night shifts, and the first one was always the most difficult in the best of circumstances.

36

SADIE HEARD THE HARSH WHINE OF THE GARAGE DOOR struggling to rise around seven in the morning, signaling the safe arrival home of her mother. When she was little, she would feel comforted by this sound, and sink into a deeper sleep. It was Joan's third night shift in a row, and Sadie sat up, nudging Jimmy awake. He moaned, cracked his knuckles, and tried to pull her back into a cuddle.

"We forgot to set the alarm, babe," she whispered. He was supposed to have woken up an hour earlier and gone home.

"Shit," he mumbled into the pillow, before sitting up and scrambling to pull on a T-shirt. They heard Joan open the dishwasher downstairs, the click of the morning news coming on.

Sadie and her father used to use Joan's five night shifts a month as an excuse for a a bit of hedonism. Supermarket

cakes containing novel-length ingredient lists of preservatives, iced thick with frosting the color of nothing found in
nature, which left a chemical aftertaste. They'd drive to the
corner store instead of walking or biking, so that George
could buy a full-flavor beer, a ginger beer for Sadie. After
dinner, usually pizza or Chinese takeout, he'd smoke a cigar
on the back porch and Sadie would bring out her homework
and they'd talk through some of the assignments, both feeling a little sick.

THESE WERE THE FIRST night shifts Joan had worked since
Sadie had moved back home. Sadie was nervous about being
alone in the house, and on the first night she'd called Jimmy
in a panic when she'd heard a noise outside around midnight. He'd come over, and they'd slept wrapped around
each other.

"What should I do?" Jimmy asked now, sitting up and
pulling on his T-shirt.

"You could try to sneak out the side way, or you can
just lie here. She may not come check on me. We could
just leave together once she's asleep."

"I'll chance it," he said, getting back under the covers,
lying flat.

Sure enough, a few minutes later, she heard Joan on
the attic ladder. Sadie rolled on her side, hoping to block
Jimmy, but she'd be busted if Joan actually pulled herself
up into the room. Luckily, Joan remained eye-level with
the floor, hands around the last rung of the ladder, looking
up at Sadie lying there pretending to be texting.

When Sadie finally made eye contact with her mother, Joan smiled at her warmly. "I'm going to sleep now. Just wanted to make sure you were okay. I left you some muffins on the table," she said.

"Okay, Mom. Good night," Sadie replied, not looking up from her phone. Joan went back downstairs, and Jimmy started to giggle under the duvet. Sadie hit him with her hand and shushed him. He went back to sleep, while Sadie scrolled through Kevin's Twitter feed and Facebook page for updates. He'd been quiet in the social media sphere ever since their encounter at the hotel. Jimmy said he'd backed up a U-Haul truck and loaded his whole office into it.

Jimmy woke up to Sadie staring at him.

"What?"

"I want to go back to the way things were."

Jimmy put his hands over his face to hide his grin.

"Yes, yes, me too, I want that," he said, reaching over to kiss her. She responded and then pulled back, compelled to ask him something first.

"Are you dating anyone else?" She leaned over to apply the coconut lip balm she kept on her bedside table. He shook his head. The relief she felt overwhelmed her so much that she had to look away and nervously reapply the lip balm.

"Well, I did have a girl ask me out, though."

She clicked the tube shut and tried on an unconcerned facial expression.

"Oh yeah, who?"

"Cheryl."

"Seriously?" Cheryl wasn't someone known for dating. At all. Sadie assumed she had an intact hymen, spent her

Friday nights watching musicals with her mom. "What did you say?"

"I said that I still loved you."

"And?"

He shrugged, shifting around under the duvet nervously. "To be honest, she told me you weren't worth my time. That she'd make a better girlfriend. I told her I wasn't interested."

"That bitch!" Sadie said, smiling, trying to prove she wasn't bothered. She climbed on top of him, taking off her shirt.

"Then she offered to blow me anyway," he said, grinning.

"No fucking way," Sadie said. She pulled the pillow out from under his head and hit him with it, got up, cocking her hip faux casual. She pulled a bra from the back of her desk chair and clipped it around her waist. "Was she any good?"

"It didn't happen."

"Are you serious? You turned down a blow job even though *I* dumped *you*?" She pulled her bra up, running a finger under the elastic to adjust it, before pulling on a uniform shirt.

He winced visibly at the cruelty of her tone, the mention of her dumping him.

"Not really . . . Mrs. Collier walked in just as she was about to—"

"Oh."

"I don't like her. I'm not even attracted to her . . ."

"Well, if you were willing to let her do that, then you have to find her attractive somehow."

"Not really."

"Whatever, it's fine. Let's split . . . We should actually get to school on time today."

"You're jealous," he said, smiling.

"I'm not jealous of Cheryl!"

"Well, she's not four hundred years old like Kevin," Jimmy said.

"I didn't have a crush on Kevin. I was confused," she said.

Jimmy started down the attic ladder, ignoring her comment. "Come on, I can't be late again."

When Sadie reached the landing, he put his mouth on hers, but she pulled away. It wasn't his fault, and she had no leg to stand on, but she felt angry about Cheryl anyhow.

37

WHEN JOAN WOKE UP IN THE LATE AFTERNOON AFTER her last night shift, she found Jimmy and Sadie in the kitchen, making open-faced tomato and pickle sandwiches. Sadie's legs were pulled up against her chest where she perched on a high stool, and Jimmy was at the toaster, slathering slices with mayo when they popped up.

"This is the perfect amount," he explained, "for three slices of pickle and two tomato. I've tested it."

"I like it with a bit of Dijon," Sadie said.

"The horror!"

Jimmy turned the music up, and they both started rapping along perfectly with a song emanating from one of their phones as she entered the kitchen. They looked up at her but kept singing as she prepped the coffee maker.

"Are you guys stoned?"

"No," Sadie said. Jimmy laughed.

"Because we are being scrutinized. I wouldn't want

reporters to snap a photo of the deranged daughter. Are you two back together?" Joan crossed her arms. Why was she chastising them for looking happy and relaxed for the first time in ages? Why couldn't she just let the moment happen? She pulled at the sleeves of her housecoat and tried not to be so grumpy.

Jimmy looked at Sadie's face for an answer. She took a bite of her sandwich and shrugged while she chewed. Kids could break up and get back together so easily. The way they looked at each other, it was as though nothing had happened. Joan wanted to take a photo of that moment.

"Mom, stare much?" Sadie offered up a look that was part smile, part scowl, just like she used to. Joan wanted to tell her to savor these moments, but she just fumbled with the coffee tin and looked out the window at the lake.

She pocketed her phone and decided to leave them alone. She looked at the to-do list she'd written on the back of an envelope and put up on the fridge. The first item was *George's Office*. Now was as good a time as any, she reasoned, to box it up.

It existed like a dusty tomb; the housekeeper ignored it and so did everyone else, generally. When she opened the door, she was overwhelmed by the stale smells, the ones she still associated with him: cigar smoke, the spice candle layered in dust, his aftershave.

She moved around the room faster than she had moved in months, as though her muscles had lost years overnight, springs uncoiled and fluid. She flattened out crumpled papers, threw away notes she was pretty sure George would have thought essential, looked for clues, and when she found none, she recycled everything else. The landline phone rang three times in a row, Bennie's number on the call display, but she didn't pick up.

Her cell rang next. She went to her office and retrieved her paper shredder, put Andrew on speaker while she fed pages of George's work into its teeth.

"Mom, you can't abandon Dad completely before the trial," Andrew said. "What is that noise?"

"You visit. You call. I need space! I'm shredding his thesis!" Joan yelled. There was a pause on the other end of the line. "I'm sorry, Andrew, I shouldn't yell at you like that."

"It's okay, Mom. I get it," he said. "I'll call you later."

She gathered up the refuse in clear plastic bags and put them into the recycling bin outside. She hauled the tallest kitchen stool upstairs and sprayed down the curtain rods and polished the window panes. His large wooden desk, normally covered with papers, mail, books, mugs filled with pens, and knickknacks, was completely empty by the end of the evening, everything in a file box and placed in the hall closet. Joan set the vacuum robot to On, left the room, and closed the door. George had never allowed the housekeeper into his office, and it was a dusty, disorganized space, and she bet that the rug hadn't been vacuumed in years.

WHEN CLARA'S TEXTS WENT unanswered, she showed up at the house. When Joan got down on the floor to whiten the baseboards, Clara put on giant plastic gloves, tied her hair up, and joined her. Every room looked as if a bright white highlighter was embracing it.

"Have you told Sadie about Sarah Myers?" Clara started, whitening what was already white as Joan rubbed uselessly at a scuff mark.

"I think Sadie has had her heart broken enough for one year," she said.

"You're probably right," Clara said, standing up and going into the kitchen. "Is she visiting him yet?"

"No, she's still refusing to go. But they speak on the phone regularly," Joan said. "I just want her to finish school, solidify her plans for next year, stay on track. I don't want this year to ruin her life."

"I don't want that for you either, Joan," said Clara. "You should call the divorce lawyer."

"It's not like I have a lot of great years ahead of me either way," said Joan.

"Uh, way to be upbeat. I'm going to make you watch that Molly Shannon 'I'm Fifty' skit from *SNL* again."

"I'm not like you, Clara. I'm not independent. I don't love being alone."

"Well, sometimes you just have to accept a shitty situation, Joan. Accept it, and maybe your feelings will change."

PART THREE

The Week Before the Trial

38

ANDREW REALIZED HE WAS SEEING ANOTHER SEASON change in Avalon Hills. His father's trial was now only one week away, and it was warm enough to wear a T-shirt and sit in a strip of sun on the dock. He no longer felt strange to be back in this landscape as an adult. He was looking out at the horizon across the water and it soothed the jagged edges of his psyche. He was building new associations with the town, with the house. When people recognized him at the drugstore, he was no longer the gay kid who came home for Christmas. Now, he was the eldest Woodbury, who was sticking around to help out. The more he was seen, the more people got used to him. He'd even seen Alan, the cop who used to bully him, and been awarded the nod, that small-town ac-knowledgment that was like being part of a club of some sort. Still, he missed the city every day and couldn't wait to leave.

He dipped his toes in the water and leaned back. The

phone buzzed again, and he picked it up to see an endless scroll of calls from various people. A co-worker, Clara, and Jared over and over. Emails came in, all with similar subject lines, like "Have you seen this yet?" They all linked to a Gawker article. The headline read AVALON HILLS GYM TEACHER RUMORED TO HAVE RELATIONSHIP WITH WOODBURY SON WHILE HE WAS STILL IN HIGH SCHOOL.

He clicked to Facebook, where his entire page was filled with outraged speculation. He deleted his account, leaned his body all the way back against the dock, and called Jared.

"Okay. I need you this time, honey. I mean it."

"THIS IS ANDREW WOODBURY and I want to say on the record that the rumor about myself and the coach at school is not only patently ridiculous, and obviously fueled by small-town homophobic attitudes, it's libelous. If you don't retract immediately, I will be serving you with a lawsuit." Andrew hung up the phone.

Joan was running in circles around him, mopping the kitchen floor. "Your coach? Really, Andrew? Is this true?" This news would have gutted her a year ago, but he supposed that now it probably didn't seem so bad, by comparison. He felt a bit of relief at her finding out, knowing. But he didn't want to add to her grief, either.

"Yes, it's true. It's not a big deal. He was in his early twenties, I was seventeen—hardly a difference at all."

Andrew felt a strange, protective feeling for Stuart. This was the kind of thing that would just devastate him.

"I'm going to take a shower," he said, the only excuse he could think of to leave the room. "Jared will be here any minute."

THAT EVENING, WHEN JARED pulled the car into the Woodbury estate driveway, Andrew met him outside and convinced him to go to Icons!

"Let me take my bags in and get settled, don't you think?"

Andrew nodded impatiently, helping him with his suitcase. Jared hugged Joan while Andrew took his things upstairs. Then he told his mother they were going out and wouldn't be long. Jared drank a glass of water and shrugged his shoulders at Joan and Sadie as he followed Andrew out the door. Andrew headed to the car as Jared called after him, trying to keep up.

"Is this about Stuart? How are you feeling now that the secret is out?" Jared asked, getting into the passenger seat. "What made you change your mind about inviting me here?"

"No one else would get it. I need your support." Andrew adjusted the mirrors and plugged his phone into the stereo, turned his music on and then up. Jared turned the volume down as Andrew backed out towards the gate.

"I can support you about everything, Andrew. You don't need to be alone. This is a heavy secret to come out."

"It's not a secret, Jared. It's just my life. It's not uncommon and I'm not ashamed of anything. I'm just worried about Stuart, what it's going to do to him." He turned to point the remote control gate opener through the gap between their seats and then clipped it back onto the sun visor.

"You're worried about Stuart? That's interesting."

"Interesting? He doesn't have much, Jared. Just his job, just this small-town life. Being gay around here isn't easy."

"I know, honey, I know. But he's an adult. He was *always* an adult. And this is one of the wealthiest, whitest areas in the country. Forgive me if I don't play a tiny violin for him."

"Gay men of his era are constantly told they're privileged, but do you know what they went through? Most of them had terrible isolated childhoods, then lost half their friends to AIDS. Can you imagine if twenty of our friends just up and died?"

"Stuart's not *that* much older than us, Andrew. He decided to stay closeted, and live with the associated misery. I just don't feel bad for him. I feel bad for you, in this situation."

"Oh Christ, not you too."

"I'm not trying to pathologize you or use the *abuse* word, but don't you ever think about it? That it was wrong?"

"No, it wasn't wrong at all."

"Okay," he said, pausing for a moment. "Okay. I believe you."

"No, you don't. You're placating me because you don't want conflict," Andrew said. "That's not very New York of you."

"No, I understand it's not always black and white in these situations, and seventeen is old enough to know what you want and with whom. I get it. I do. I'm just protective of you, babe. I just want you to be okay."

"I'm totally okay," Andrew said, turning the music back up and gunning the engine. The Beastie Boys prevented any further conversation.

Andrew could have driven this route in his sleep, and had driven it drunk so many times in his youth, pretending to be coming home from a late theater rehearsal or from watching movies at his best friend's house. He'd bet he could close his eyes and still get there in one piece.

Jared laughed when he saw the parking lot outside Icons! "Is this where icons are murdered? It's an unmarked cement block. It's like the fucking 1950s. It's kind of . . . romantic. How does anyone know what it is?"

"That's the point. Someone has to tell you," Andrew said, turning off the car.

Jared pointed towards the only other building in sight, a brick block painted purple that stood a few feet away from Icons! "What's that building?"

"That's Sappho's Muse," he said.

"You are JOKING."

"I'm not, babe."

"It's so rough trade," he said.

"Woodbridge is an industrial town, serious poverty. This is the only gay bar for three counties," Andrew said, gritting his teeth, feeling a bit embarrassed that Jared was seeing him here.

"Were you scared of this place when you were a teenager? I mean, your childhood photos look like they're taken from 1990s J.Crew catalogues," Jared said.

Andrew knew then why he'd resisted showing Jared

this side of his past. Jared grew up in Brooklyn, the son of leftist artists. Small-town gay life was fascinating to him— the secrecy, the danger, the customs. Andrew knew the bar would end up being an interesting anecdote he told at parties back in the city, weaving it into the narrative he understood to be Andrew's life before New York. The truth was, Andrew didn't share much about his childhood, preferring to refer to it in general terms such as *typical suburbia, nothing special.*

"This is bananas," said Jared as they walked towards the entrance. "They don't even have a sign! It looks like a biker clubhouse!"

INSIDE THE BAR, A group of ragtag queens were giving a show, all of the performers sitting at a table up front and taking turns getting up at the mic. The place was fairly packed. Jared was, as expected, thrilled to be watching the performers rotate through the seventies classics. He found a stool by the bar and took it all in, pumped.

Stuart was at his usual table, just as he was the night Andrew went dancing with Clara. "Don't look right away, but that's Stuart," Andrew whispered to Jared, who looked right away. Andrew swatted his leg.

"Wow, he's . . . a jock. He looks like Tim Allen. Introduce us," Jared said.

"No!"

"Come on."

"Let's get a drink first."

They ordered pints, and as they sipped their beer, he

told Jared stories about his time as a regular fixture at Icons!, with an ID that read *James Patterson*. Every once in a while he stole a glance at Stuart, who was now sitting beside the same young companion from the last visit. Stuart didn't look happy to see Andrew.

"I feel like I'm in an Andrew Holleran novel!" Jared said.

Andrew frowned and wished he'd come by himself. It was disorienting to be both his regular self and his old self at the same time.

They were almost done with their pints when Stuart approached Andrew at the bar.

"Reporters have been calling me nonstop," he said. "They came to the school. It's all over the Internet."

Jared shimmied closer to them, proffering his hand for a shake. "Stuart, I've heard so much about you. I'm Jared."

Stuart turned to Jared, confused. "Who?"

"Jared—Andrew's partner."

Stuart shook his hand, gave him a quick scan, and turned back to Andrew.

"The principal told me I have to get a lawyer," he said. "I can't afford that."

"I have no idea where they got this information. I called the original reporter and denied it. I threatened libel."

"Oh honey, don't do that. You know that if you did sue, they'd find someone who knew us. Someone would talk. It would just be worse," Stuart said, sloshing some beer around, which landed on Andrew's leg. Andrew dabbed at his jeans uselessly with a cocktail napkin, listen-

388 · ZOE WHITTALL

ing to Stuart slur his words and repeat himself. Jared gave Stuart the sympathetic look he reserved for old people or the homeless.

"Okay, okay. I thought I was doing the right thing, denying it."

Stuart nodded. "Let's just not speak to anyone at all. It will die down. We shouldn't be seen together." He looked around, scanning the crowd, none of whom were paying the slightest bit of attention to them.

"It will be okay. The media is mostly obsessed with my father. I'm sure you'll be forgotten."

"Except everyone thinks I'm gay now, you know, at work and stuff."

"Well, who cares? It's not a crime. Take a positive from this and use it to be more open about it. There are other gay teachers at the school, I'm sure."

"I don't know, I don't know. Everyone thinks gays are pedophiles, and fuck, this is, like, their proof."

"You should be more careful about your, uh, date over there," Andrew said.

"Oh, that's Jay. He's twenty-three," Stuart said. "Don't worry about Jay."

Andrew nodded and regarded the young man at the table again. He looked even younger than Andrew remembered. Stuart wasn't being careful at all.

"Did he used to go to Avalon?"

"Why does that matter now?" Stuart yelled, drunkenly. People turned to look at him.

"Okay, well," Andrew said, "I should get going, then, unless you have something to say to me."

Andrew considered asking him what the fuck he'd

been thinking, dating a student before hate crime legislation and gay-straight alliances were a thing, when people didn't think twice about chasing you down an alleyway with a baseball bat for having the wrong walk. Just being gay was risky, but dating a student was crazy. He remembered the time they were making out by the ridge, and two guys had pelted them with bottles and rocks until they ran to their car and sped away, bottles smashing against the back window of Stuart's secondhand Toyota hatchback. Was Andrew really worth the risk? Was it really love, the way it had felt for him at seventeen, when the thought of Stuart made him feel more alive than he'd ever felt before? Was that what love was?

Stuart said, "No, I don't."

"Okay, good then. Good."

Stuart paused for a few moments. He didn't offer a hug, or a look of affection. The feeling emanating off him was *please leave me alone forever, don't remind me of who I am.*

Andrew wondered if Stuart had always been this sad, this un-self-aware. Then again, who would Andrew be if he had to live here again? Likely a hermit, a pothead, sitting on the dock and growing more odd by the year. Andrew was antsy to leave, kicking his feet under the stool like a child. Stuart went back to the table, and Jared ordered another two pints.

"Wow, that was intense, babe," he said, squeezing his leg.

"Yeah. Sad, really," Andrew said.

Another drag act came on the stage, and the crowd hollered. Before the next act, Andrew could tell Jared was catching a buzz.

"Let's go make out in the alley! Or do they have some sort of cellar/back room situation? Is there some secret bathhouse around the block the cops might bust up?" Jared asked.

"The basement has an area . . ." Andrew admitted. "But I don't want to go there."

Jared looked at him as though he'd suggested they not visit the unicorn cage at the zoo.

Andrew turned on his stool and surveyed the room. The pulse of an old house song from the 1990s vibrated everything. The kid beside Stuart stared at Andrew, winked, and kept staring. He stood up slowly and nodded his head towards the back room. Jared squealed under his breath.

"I want to go home," Andrew snapped. He stood and pulled on his jacket. Jared downed his drink and shrugged.

"Looks like we still got it, old guy."

"No fucking way," Andrew snapped.

"I was kidding. I was just trying to lighten the mood. We can go. It's okay." Jared reached out to put his arm around Andrew to comfort him, but he was rebuffed.

Andrew swore under his breath. If they were in the city, he'd have grabbed a cab home alone. They got in the car without speaking. Andrew squealed the tires as he pulled out of the parking lot, merging recklessly onto the freeway. *Who gives a fuck. I'm so tired of this!* Foot on the gas, heavy, heavier than it needed to be. Jared in his periphery, and everything Jared said making it worse. He felt the wetness on his cheeks before he realized he must be crying, which didn't match the rage he was feeling. In the distance he heard Jared's voice, at first soft and kind, and then rising in a panicked crescendo. "Pull over. You shouldn't be driving. You need to calm down. You're driving like a maniac. Pull over now. Now!"

"You found it *so* cute, all those pathetic fags in their sad little town," ranted Andrew, "wanting to go make out with some kid!"

"That's not fair. I did not want that. I was happy to know he thought we were hot, Andrew."

"You just want a story to tell our friends back in the city about this backwoods town!" He heard himself yelling but didn't feel he could speak any other way. It started to rain and he flipped on the wipers, still gunning it above the speed limit, playing Ping-Pong between the cars now. A semi truck slammed on his horn. Andrew knew he wasn't actually mad about Jared being amused by that kid's attention. That wasn't it at all. Still, he kept drilling his point.

"Andrew, I understand you're angry, but it's not fair to take it out on me. Are you trying to kill us?" Jared slapped his hand down on the dashboard, and Andrew finally registered what was happening. *"Slow the fuck down!"*

Andrew pressed his foot gently on the brake, breathing hard. He saw the upcoming exit for a service center, and he pulled off, parking in a spot near the edge. He got out and slammed the door, walked towards the grassy area beside the gas station. He tried to calm his breathing, uncurl his fists. He went into the gas station and bought a bottle of water and a Snickers bar. When he got back to the car, Jared was in the driver's seat.

Andrew handed Jared the chocolate bar. "I'm sorry," he said.

"You really scared me," Jared said, turning the key in the ignition and adjusting the seat.

"I'm sorry," he said.

"Why are you so angry with me? What have I done, except try to support you this whole time? Do you think I've been having a good time of it?"

"I don't. I don't know why I've been so angry at you. I guess I'm projecting."

"That's for fucking sure," said Jared, as he checked his mirrors and pulled out onto the expressway.

Andrew put his cheek against the cold of the passenger-seat window and stared out at the night passing by, quietly weeping.

39

S ADIE BARELY WENT TO SCHOOL IN HER LAST SEMESTER. She got several early acceptance offers to colleges, picked Columbia almost at random so she could be closer to Clara and Andrew, figured out how to write her exams and papers independently, and kept mostly to herself. When she wasn't hanging out with Jimmy, she was spending time with Lena, who'd been texting her their encounters at One-Stop Burgers. Lena didn't demand much of her, and it felt easy to be around her. She liked to get high, listen to music, and watch weird movies. Going to her house was like going to another town or reality.

Jimmy and Lena were not fans of each other, so she'd been doing some dancing around, trying to make sure they didn't overlap much. It was mostly Jimmy who didn't like Lena, but when pressed, he could never really explain why, beyond slipping into a tirade about how he didn't like that everything had changed so much. "I wish you'd come back to school, hang out like we used to." But Amanda had basically dropped her for good, and no one else really wanted her around. She talked to her father once a week on the phone, and it was awkward but she still missed him and felt conflicted all the time. The trial was a week away now, and she felt it like a looming cloud of anxiety.

The only thing she couldn't get exempted from was a final speech in her social sciences class. Mrs. Rae didn't give a shit about her problems, and wouldn't accept a position paper as a replacement. She snuck into the back of the class so she could do her thing and then leave quickly. She generally sat at the front of every class, next to Cheryl and the other keeners, maximizing that percentage of each grade given for enthusiastic participation. Every time she had to be at school, she felt that Cheryl was everywhere.

She chose the desk farthest back and closest to the door, just before a girl with hand-drawn fake tattoos on her knuckles reading *Hate Slut* approached her with a sneer. "That's my seat."

Sadie sat down and returned the sneer. "Forever? This is your seat until the end of time? I don't think so." Sadie didn't break the gaze until the girl huffed and turned away, sitting at the desk beside her. Sadie pressed the eraser in her pocket, pushing her thumb into it so hard she felt a part of it give way and break off.

Cheryl got up and cleared her throat. She managed to look holier-than-thou but also like a little kid, shaking hands on three-by-five index cards. "My talk today is on how to give enthusiastic affirmative consent, and also how to recognize it. You can tell a lot about how someone feels through their body language. Let's start by defining *con-*

sent," she said, continuing in what sounded to Sadie like blurs and beeps.

"The definition of *consensual* is 'affirmative, conscious, and voluntary agreement to engage in sexual activity.' If someone doesn't say no or resist, it doesn't mean consent. You have to hear them say it. Being drunk or high can mean a person isn't legally able to give consent."

Sadie felt a sudden wave of exhaustion. The room was warm, and the girl beside her was carving *Sick Of It All* in the wooden armrest with a protractor.

"Now, let's talk about the importance of self-respect," she said, pulling out a PowerPoint screen and darkening the room.

Miranda was sitting next to a girl with shiny brown hair. Amy? Emily? Sadie couldn't remember her name. Miranda always looked at Sadie with a pained sort of expression, and Sadie had generally avoided all interactions with her since the arrest. She turned now and stared at Sadie, as if she wouldn't stop until she got a reaction. With the shades down and the lights off, the girl beside Sadie pulled her gum out of her mouth and balled it up, still staring hard.

"Hey," the girl whispered.

Sadie didn't respond, pretended to be absorbed by Cheryl's inane presentation.

"Hey, I'm talking to you, Sadie. Are you deaf?" The girl threw her gum at her. It landed square in the middle of her chest and bounced to the ground. Sadie swallowed hard and kept looking ahead, unwilling to crack.

Mrs. Rae shushed them and the girl gave a mock look of shock.

"Personally, I prefer older men," she said.

Sadie gripped the edge of her seat, overwhelmed by an urge to punch the sneer off her face.

"I like it when they get a little rapey," she whispered, laughing. "Miranda is the worst. She just went to rehab."

Miranda turned. "Drop it." But she didn't.

"Heard your dad got some karmic payback in prison."

Sadie stood up and stumbled to collect her things, Cheryl stopped talking, and everyone turned. Mrs. Rae said no one was allowed to leave, but Sadie didn't stop. Laughter echoed in her brain all the way to the parking lot.

She sat in her car, head on the steering wheel, and texted Jimmy, asking him to come out. She watched him emerge from the side door, pulling his blazer over his head and running in the rain.

"What happened?" he said, getting into the passenger seat.

"I hate everyone here," she said, turning to embrace him.

They drove around and pulled into one of the public boat launch areas around Woodbury Lake. She lit up a joint and passed it to him. They sat in silence for a while, listening to the rain on the top of the car.

"Only a week left, and then this whole year is over, really. I just want to know what will happen. I feel so itchy all the time, like I can't imagine waiting to know."

"Come here, babe. It's okay." He urged her onto his lap, where she cried for a few minutes into his collar, fingers laced around his neck. The sound of the rain reminded Sadie of camping, or rain on the boathouse roof, before this terrible year began. She reached under his shirt and traced her name on his chest, then she kissed him, felt him grow hard underneath her. She pulled back and looked at him. He was blushing and looked away, then pulled her closer and kissed her hard, hand on the back of her neck.

He reached his hand under her skirt, but she pulled it away. She whispered, "Bleeding," as an explanation, a lie.

She thought about Cheryl, her brazen offer. She'd only ever gone down on him once, early on, before they'd actually had sex for real. He once asked to go down on her, but she'd been too embarrassed. His hands were on her breasts now, she could feel them moving, but she didn't experience anything except annoyance. She looked at his face, his half-lidded eyes, heavy. His breath quickened, and he grinded against her. It was raining so hard outside that she was pretty sure no one could see in the windows.

Sadie reached down and unzipped Jimmy's jeans. He bit his lip, surprised.

"What are you doing?"

"Shut up," Sadie said, taking him in her hand, and then her mouth. She was completely divorced from what she was doing, mimicking the girls in Kevin's magazines, and he came so quick it took her by surprise, and she had to stop herself from throwing up.

"Oh my god, Sadie, thank you. That was amazing," he said. She sat back in the driver's seat, popped one of the orange Tic Tacs from the console. Her phone vibrated. She felt like garbage.

"Calculus," she said, "starts soon. You shouldn't miss it."

He looked at her, confused. "Nah, I'll skip. Let's go to your house. Let's, you know, hang out some more." He put his hand on her leg. She wanted to rip it from his shoulder.

"I'm supposed to meet Lena," she said, looking out at the lake, starting up the car.

"Right," he said. "Are you okay?"

"Yup," she said. She could tell he didn't know what to do, so he kissed her gently on the mouth. She reversed out of the boat launch road and turned the radio on.

"I'll come by before dinner?" he said.

"Sure," she said.

She packed her one-hitter and texted her dealer. He said to meet him at One-Stop Burgers, then she answered Lena's text.

LENA SEEMED GRATEFUL TO have a reason to skip the final period at the public school. They shared a plate of fries, Lena drawing obscene shapes with the ketchup, as they played Have You Ever?

"Have you ever given a blow job?" Sadie asked.

Lena took a sip, and blushed.

"How many times?"

"A few times, with my last boyfriend. We had great sex."

"How do you qualify that? What makes it great?"

Lena grabbed a bunch of fries, shrugged. "We had great chemistry, I guess. We would sit next to each other in class and I felt like, if he touched my shoulder or my leg, even for a second, my whole body would feel like it was on fire. Kissing was the best. The *best*. I'd kissed a few boys before, but it was like this wasn't even the same activity at all."

"Wow," Sadie said. "And you didn't think blow jobs were gross?"

"No, just kind of weird at first. But really, what he liked best was going down on me."

"No way. Boys always say they'll never do that."

"He was super into it. It was awesome."

"Why did you guys break up?"

"He moved to Vancouver. We still email and text, but it's kind of doomed."

"Huh. I got back together with my boyfriend. I just gave him a blow job, like, two hours ago."

"Whoa! Hard-core lady. Was it good?"

"I don't know. I don't know how to answer that, I guess."

"Sounds like it wasn't awesome," Lena said.

"I guess not."

"That's a bummer," Lena said. "Maybe you should stop hanging with those Avalon prep kids, they're garbage. Except you, of course."

A year ago Sadie would've punched someone in the nose for saying that, but today she just nodded at her new friend. She realized it was getting late, and Jimmy would be at her house soon.

"Come meet me here tonight and we'll get so faded and you can forget about your bad BJ day. There's supposed to be a good party at my friend Mike's place."

"Will everyone recognize me?"

"Nah, no one gives a shit at my school. Everyone knows the shop teacher fucks a bunch of twelfth-grade girls all the time. You can be free to be whoever you want," she said, grabbing the final fry.

"That sounds perfect," Sadie said, stealing the fry from her hand and popping it in her mouth.

40

Andrew didn't realize Sadie was gone until Jimmy knocked on their bedroom door at three in the morning. Jimmy didn't wait to hear a response before he rushed in and stood over them like the specter of death. Jared, startled, let out a yelp before Jimmy clicked on the bedside lamp.

"Sorry to wake you dudes, but your sister never came back and I'm worried. She was hanging out with Lena after dinner and her parents say she's not there. She's not answering her phone, my friend-finder app says her phone is off or dead, and I texted and called everyone we know. I posted about it online and no one knows where she is. She's nowhere. I don't have a car, so can I use yours?"

Andrew had sat up, confused. "She's probably at Amanda's house."

"No, I biked over there, she's not."

Andrew sat up and reached for his robe. "It's okay,

we'll find her. Just give me a minute and we'll get the car and go look for her."

They went back to Amanda's, to the burger joint by the highway where the "bad" kids hung out, and to all the twenty-four-hour corner stores, looking for her bike or signs of her. They even went to Kevin's new condo. Andrew watched Jimmy pound on the door until the gold *6A* swung loose, revealing Kevin, confused and holding a baseball bat, while Jimmy yelled at him with a kind of anger Andrew didn't realize a laid-back kid like him could possess.

"If anything happened to her, it's your fault," Jimmy yelled.

Andrew eventually had to go grab his arm and urge him back into the car. They drove back to the Woodbury house, woke up Joan and Clara, and called the police.

41

IN A DREAM, SADIE WAS LYING ON WARM SAND, MAKING out with Jimmy. He ran a finger under the waist of her bikini bottoms. "Yeah, you want that?" she heard a voice say, but it wasn't Jimmy's voice. She woke up to the feeling of something moving between her legs, and just as she realized she wasn't in her bed, and wasn't alone, she felt a sharpness, someone's finger inside her. Her eyes popped open, and she reached down to grab the hand by the wrist. "Hey," she mumbled, bottom lip drooling, rested against a patch of thick carpet. "Sorry," said the voice. She pulled a strand of fiber from her lip and examined it. Orange. What the hell was it? She coughed. Someone was spooning her, and the voice came from a boy with messy red hair who was now pretending to sleep. Who? She pushed his shoulder. "Who the fuck are you?" He continued to pretend to be asleep.

Sadie looked up, blinking into focus a flat-screen TV on an unfamiliar wall playing a Nicki Minaj video on mute.

She remembered texting Lena from outside the Coffee Hut, after her second post-dinner rotation around the lake on her bike, asking her for directions to the party. A deer had been standing beside the Dumpster, flirting with the heavy padlock, eyes shining in her direction. She had begun to feel what was either a panic attack or an out-of-body experience as she stared the deer in the eyes.

When she got to One-Stop she sat at the picnic tables and met up with Lena, who'd already befriended half a bottle of Maker's Mark. There was a newspaper open on the table, and an ad for Kevin's book.

"I hate that everyone knows everything, that they'll read this book and think it's my life."

Lena took a swig and said, "I dunno. It's not great when everything is a secret. My grandfather molested me and my sister. My mom didn't want him to go to jail 'cause he's so old, right, but it was up to us to decide if we wanted him to. It was so weird. Obviously no one wanted him in jail, he's so old now. So now we have to have supervised visits only," she admitted. She said it all so casually.

Sadie tried to just nod and not act horrified the way everyone looked horrified at her when she talked about her dad.

"I guess that's partly why I like hanging out here all the time with my best gaylord friend. 'Cause I kind of wish an adult had been, like, uh, you're only ten and so maybe you shouldn't be the one to decide if an old perv goes to jail. My family are bonkers. I mean, not like I believe in the prison system."

"You don't believe in prison?"

"No. I believe in restorative justice. Plus, the system is

rigged. If it was full of white people and CEOs, I'd be a little less hard on it."

"But people who do bad shit, what should we do with them? You don't think people should be held accountable?"

"Of course they should be held accountable."

"How then? And what about serial killers?"

"Fuck, I don't know the answer to everything. I just think we should be a little more critical of a fucked-up, racist system."

She was carving SADIE AND LENA BEST FRIENDS FOREVER into the wood with her pocket knife. Sadie ran her fingers over the cuts and laughed.

Lena looked up and blushed. "Hey, so let's go to that party!"

Lena insisted Sadie double her on Sadie's bike. Sadie had laughed really hard, trying not to fall, as they rode along Maple Street, sipping the whiskey from an empty pop bottle and yelling out the words to "Add It Up" by the Violent Femmes.

That was her last memory, before time stopped making sense.

SHE COULD SEE SHE was in a basement, the dim morning light starting to shine through a high window, the related warm glow abrasive against her skin. She was under a blanket. One kid was snoring loudly. She lay still again. There were at least a dozen kids asleep on the floor. She was trapped between the other bodies. While contemplating the situation, still holding on to the guy's wrist, she pressed her nails into his skin.

"Ow! Sorry," he said. She'd never seen him before.

"You were *not* asleep just now."

He sat up, stretching. He took a swig of warm beer, and offered it to her. She grimaced, holding back from throwing up. She heard a girl's voice across the room, some giggling. It was Lena. "Oh man, that was a night to remember. What I can remember of it, anyway."

"I thought, because of last night and everything," he said, "that you would be game. You were moving around like you were awake."

"What happened last night?"

He blushed. "You don't remember?"

"No."

"You guys were making out on the couch!" Lena yelled from across the room. "Man, you were *sooo* faded." She laughed.

Sadie turned her head, spurring a swirl of nausea, to see Lena roll from a somersault into a handstand, the shirt Sadie remembered leaving the house in falling to cover her face, revealing a gray sports bra. Sadie looked down and realized she was wearing a Thrasher T-shirt, the one Lena had been wearing earlier in the night.

"We traded shirts," Lena explained. "You really wanted mine! You said it was perfect for your new life as a vagabond."

"I did?"

Lena laughed as if her blackout was the funniest thing she'd ever witnessed, breaking her handstand and curling into a ball on the floor. Sadie pressed her hands to the carpet, stood up, lost her balance, and steadied herself against the arm of a chair. She found her shoes in a pile by the door, almost all the same brand of sneakers in different colors. Had there ever been water inside her body? Her mouth was a pile of crackers, her skin drying cement. Was there oxygen outside? Would temperature ever make sense again?

"Let's all go have breakfast!" Lena said.

"Yeah," said the boy.

Sadie shook her head. "My mom is going to be worried." She fished her phone out of her skirt pocket. It was dead. "I didn't mean to stay out all night."

"Last night you said you were disowning your whole family!"

She headed towards the stairs. Why did anyone ever drink alcohol when it led directly to this feeling?

"You okay? We're still besties, right?" Lena sounded worried, jumping up and giving her a hug on the bottom step. Sadie nodded *of course*. The boy who was drinking the beer followed her.

"Sadie, right?"

"Yup."

He paused on the landing. "It's all cool, right? It's all good."

"What is?"

"You know, what happened last night?"

"What?"

"You said you had a boyfriend, so I get it. I won't say anything. I just, you know, you were crying and stuff, and I wanted to make sure it was okay."

"Why was I crying?"

"I don't know. You wouldn't stop. It was a bummer.

You walked up and, like, grabbed me and kissed me and then you, like, cried and threw up."

"Alcohol is a depressant, dude," Lena said.

Sadie was looking at him, trying to steady his face, but the room spun. She bolted for the door at the top of the stairs and threw up all over a tulip garden. A mom with a stroller watched her from the sidewalk. The boy ran up behind her.

"Are you okay? I'm so sorry. I'm sorry, okay?" He gave her a big hug. She came up to his armpit, and he smelled awful. "You put your number in my phone, so I'll text you. You're so much fun!"

She pulled away, repulsed, pulling a bit more carpeting off her tongue and hoping she wouldn't throw up again.

"Totally, text me or whatever," she said, backing away. She got to the sidewalk and tried to orient herself. She reached into her pocket for the koala eraser and it wasn't there. Exhaustion turned into a loud sound, an alarm.

She ran back into the house and pushed the boy out of the way to get downstairs. She rolled over the remaining sleeping bodies, looking for the eraser. She ran her hands over every inch of the basement carpet. She crawled around on the filthy bathroom floor. At this point she was crying uncontrollably.

"It's an *eraser*?" Lena asked, giving her a look that said, *So what the fuck?* from the doorway of the bathroom.

"It's sentimental!" Sadie yelled, but what she wanted to say was that it was the only thing keeping her safe. She realized it was stupid, but she believed in it. She had believed in it for years.

"It means something to me!" she yelled again. Everyone who was still lying on the floor woke up. They looked at her as if she were a crazy person.

"You're losing it, dude. Stop screaming, we're all a little rough here," said the beer guy.

"Go die in a fire," Sadie said, wishing she could punch him in the face. She needed that eraser. She slumped down against the wall and closed her eyes. She felt her father's arms around her, the way he smelled as he carried her out of the school on the day of the shooting.

She heard the boy laughing. "Who the fuck *is* this chick? She's hot, but she's fucking nuts."

Sadie snapped out of it, ran upstairs, grabbed her bike from where it was inexplicably splayed on the front lawn. She tried to bike away, but her chain had fallen off. She dropped the bike and kicked it like a toddler.

"It's okay, Sadie, I'll fix it," Lena said, appearing like an apparition. Sadie curled up on the ground.

"Who the fuck is that guy?"

"Mike, remember? You were super into him last night. He's harmless."

"I don't remember anything," she said, "after we got on our bikes."

Lena furrowed her brow, giving the chain one final yank and running the pedals around to test it. "Shit, girl, that sucks. You feeling bad because of Jimmy?"

"I feel bad because I messed around with someone and I don't remember it at all!"

"Oh, you never blacked out before?"

"No."

"Well, you'll know for next time, I guess," Lena said, handing her the bike, "not to mix booze and pot."

"Yeah," she said, getting on, trying to focus on the horizon. She was almost too sore to sit on the bike seat, and she stopped several times on the side of the road to throw up. Her knees were stuck with clumps of gravel, some cutting her skin. She heaved and sobbed. This was his fault, she thought, lying down on her back as if she were making a snow angel. She wouldn't be here, wouldn't be feeling so terrible, if George wasn't in jail, if he hadn't done the things he was accused of. Maybe people are often terrible, she thought, feeling the wind of passing cars and sitting up, pulling at strands of long grasses, trying to hold back another round. *Fuck my dad. Fuck him,* she thought.

SHE FOUND THE FRONT gate ajar and a police car denying her the gratifying downward roll towards the garage. "Mom!" She dropped her bike, double-jumped the front step, running straight into Joan, quite alive and furious, flanked by Jimmy, Clara, Jared, and Andrew, and a silver-haired cop who regarded Sadie with a grunted "This must be her?"

Joan hugged her in a way that was meant to be painful. Sadie, still fogged by the hangover, was slow to realize that she was the emergency, that the *something terrible* which had occurred was that she didn't tell anyone where she was going.

"Oh my god, you smell like garbage," Joan said, drawing back to scrutinize her appearance then hugging her tightly again, "literal garbage."

"Why are you freaking out?"

"Uh, you went for a bike ride and never came home!"

"None of our friends knew where you were. No one! Everyone online is, like, posting about you being a missing person," Jimmy said. "Where were you? We thought a crazy person who was mad at your dad had kidnapped you!"

"Well, obviously I'm fine. I just went to my friend Lena's friend's house to watch a movie and we fell asleep by accident."

The cop sighed, and took his leave.

"Who the heck is Lena? I've never heard of her," Joan said.

"She used to go to Avalon," Sadie said.

"That makes no sense," said Jimmy. "Is that a *hickey* on your neck?"

She grabbed her neck. "No, of course it isn't."

"Why didn't you text? We must have sent you fifty messages," said Andrew.

"My phone died. I'm so sorry, guys, I didn't think you'd notice."

Joan's face paled. "You didn't think I'd notice that you'd disappeared?"

"No, I dunno. I wasn't thinking," she said, wishing she could make them all go away, before sprinting to the downstairs powder room and heaving, though there was nothing left to come up.

42

CLARA AND JOAN LINGERED AT THE BOOK NOOK, waiting for the real estate agent to arrive, running their hands along the New & Noteworthy display table. Joan picked up a copy of *Father Father* by Kevin Lamott. The ending was made up, since the verdict hadn't happened yet, but the book still had a "Based on a True Story" tag line. Joan held the book open so hard that she accidentally tore a page. She knew she wouldn't recognize herself in its pages, but she wasn't recognizing herself in her own life right now either.

"I read the advanced copy we got at the magazine. The father character gets ten years in jail. The daughter becomes a drug addict with a lesbian lover. The mother moves into a trailer just like Julie Cooper on *The O.C.*"

"Who?"

"Never mind. The son stays a lawyer but starts visiting a dominatrix to deal with his guilt, because the 'Andrew' character is straight. It's ridiculously terrible," said Clara. "The masses will fucking love it."

"Should we buy all the copies, so no one can read them in Avalon Hills?" Joan asked Clara, half hysterical-sounding.

"No, just let it die, and feel comforted that hardly anyone reads anymore," she said.

"You're a journalist," Joan said.

"I'm an illogical sadist," Clara said. She picked up a copy of Joan Didion's *The Year of Magical Thinking* and handed it to Joan. "This is a book that will speak to you," she said, bringing it up to the cash register.

AN HOUR LATER, JOAN was following the real estate agent around a condo. The agent was perky, with red highlights in her shiny brown bob, and Joan hadn't listened to a thing she'd said as she monologued her way through the two-bedroom space. The walls were a bright kind of white. Absent. Anywhere. As they stood together on the expansive balcony, surrounded by tasteful potted rubber plants, Joan could see the lake in the distance, and the hospital only a few blocks away. She wanted to buy all the furniture in the condo too, she wanted all new things, and she didn't want to think about it and what it meant. She didn't want to use the salad spinner they'd had since the 1980s, the thick cutting board they'd received as a wedding gift.

"Sign them," Clara said when the real estate agent handed over the papers.

Joan put them in her purse.

"Joannie, come on."

"You know I'm giving up the last installment in my trust if I do this."

"Only if you get divorced," Clara said, "and would that be so bad? It's just money."

"If only Dad were alive to hear you say that."

"You know what I mean."

"I worked hard for that house, the kids were raised there, and it's not fair that I should be the one to move."

"He may not fight you on it. What has he said so far?"

"He has no idea," Joan admitted.

"No matter what happens at the trial, he won't be in jail forever. You're going to have to face this, and make some concrete, practical decisions. This is a good one. If he stays in jail, you have an investment property. You can afford it."

"For now," she said. "I guess."

They thanked the realtor and left, opening a bottle of wine when they got back to the house and sitting on the dock.

SHE HADN'T GONE TO visit him since he'd been transferred from the hospital at the end of December. They'd spoken on the phone. He'd written her letters, occasionally beautiful and always apologetic, full of regret and remorse of unknown veracity.

She couldn't stop dreaming about Sarah Myers. She began to have trouble going to sleep, staying up watching movies, doing anything to avoid it. She started asking him questions every time they spoke on the phone. The last time they spoke, he lost his temper. "Joan, why are you bringing this up again? Every bloody time we talk."

"Don't evade the question. You owe this to me, to everyone. I'm hanging up unless you tell me what happened."

"Okay, okay," he said, inhaling. She'd curled the duvet around her, trying to calm her heart so she could hear every word. "I was young, and it was a confusing moment, and I misread some things."

"Not excuses, the truth."

"The truth is, I think I was emotionally stunted. I think I was still feeling like a child, and we'd just had one, and I just wanted to be a kid. I think I acted like a kid, and related to her as a kid would. I've been reading about this, about how some adults regress from trauma, and act out this way. Some offenders are just sociopaths, and some are acting out of an innocent misfiring in their brain."

"You're talking to me like I'm one of your students, George. I'm not going to believe every half-baked theory you concoct to make yourself look naive. You did a terrible thing. An unforgivable thing that requires intense self-reflection and accountability and work. Hard work. Do you understand that?" Her eyes were shut tight, and she didn't realize she was shouting, loudly. Payton jumped up from where he'd been sleeping on the pillow and ran to hide under the lounge chair in the corner.

"I'm sorry," George whispered, and then there were gulps of sobbing. She hung up the phone. He didn't sound sorry; he sounded sorry to have to have this conversation, upset that he was caught.

JOAN STARED AT THE papers all night, as Clara tried to distract her with wine, by playing old records they'd loved as kids. By evening's end, Joan had penned her name on the line for the condo that made it all official and finite and certain, and Clara applauded, and literally patted her on the back.

The following day, she would gather the family together for the first time in months. It was important to Joan that they be united in the courtroom, supporting George. She thought it was the right thing to do, not just for appearances but to honor whatever shred of their history was real.

But inside, she was seething. Her anger felt infinite. Whatever happened, though, whatever she had to do to keep her family together in the meantime, Joan now had a place to land.

PART FOUR

The Trial

43

JOAN OPENED THE BACK DOOR OF THE TOWN CAR AND lowered her head in to nod at the driver. Then she stood with her back to the open door, waiting for everyone to come out of the house. "We have to show up together, stand together as a family," she'd said while filling everyone's coffee cups at the breakfast table. She fiddled with the brooch she was wearing on her lapel, an amber pin that used to belong to her late mother-in-law. George gave it to her on their first anniversary. She must have worn it the last time she wore this blazer, which was at George's arraignment hearing. She hadn't purchased any new clothes since then. She unhooked it, pricking her thumb in the process. She watched a bead of blood rise, detached from the pain, as Andrew and Jared came down the front steps. She pitched the brooch off into the rock garden that lined the driveway. Her phone rang. Bennie's face. Accept or decline. Her thumb was too sweaty to work the screen.

. . .

ANDREW HAD BEEN TO court dozens of times, but only when he could influence the outcome with his tenacity and ability to over-prepare for every possible scenario. This time he had no control, and the result was that his father would either go to jail or be set free. He wanted George to be found not guilty—of course he did. But he didn't want him to be absolved in a general sense; he wanted to see his father atone somehow. The prospect of him being free, of having to deal with that, was also daunting. He felt ashamed to admit that to anyone.

"Do I look okay?" Joan asked him nervously.

"Yes, you're channelling your best Julianna Margulies," he said, getting into the car and smoothing out his trousers. Jared held his hand but there was a distance between them that was undeniable. That they were breaking up felt inevitable.

Clara got in next. Andrew knew she was the only one who was sincerely hoping George wouldn't get out.

"Your father wants to talk to you," said Joan, handing the phone to Andrew.

"I just want you to know that whatever happens, I love you and Sadie and your mother more than anything. I'm doing everything I can to be exonerated and to have this whole mess put behind us," he said.

"We're on our way and we're here for you, Dad," Andrew said, robot-like. Though he didn't quite believe the words he said, he knew he had an obligation to say them.

He passed the phone back to Joan as Sadie emerged from the house, followed by her new friend Lena. Sadie

wore a modest green dress with the shoes Joan had polished the night before, but both of the girls' hair had the
same shock of turquoise in their bangs.

"How very 1998," Andrew said dryly when they got in
the car. He could tell they were both stoned but didn't say
anything about it. He knew that Sadie was conflicted about
her father. She still didn't know about Sarah Myers, and he
felt some guilt that she didn't have all the information. At
the same time, he wanted her to be a kid who could still
get excited about dyeing her hair.

Joan was the last one in the car. She stood outside, the
phone on speaker.

"Is it looking good? Are you hopeful?" she asked Bennie.

"Joan, I have no way of knowing for sure. So much
depends on the judge's leanings, and what Miranda is like
on the stand. I'm prepared and confident, but I can't know
the future."

"Okay," Joan said. "See you there."

Andrew watched his mother settle into the front seat.
He wondered if she felt as unsure as he did.

THE FIRST THING SADIE noticed when she was ushered into
the courtroom was the heat. She looked around, trying to see
if she was imagining it. No one looked at all sweaty. How
could she be the only hot person? She knew her face was red-
dening; the high collar of her dress irritated her neck. Her
mother gripped her left hand as she walked ahead of her; Lena
held on to the strap of Sadie's purse as she followed.

"Jesus, your dad is popular," Lena whispered.

Sadie wished she wasn't stoned. Indeed, many of the powers that be in town were there to support George's innocence, prominent businessmen who sat on several boards with him. Even the mayor sat in the front row, and then a swell of teachers from Avalon Hills prep. The girls and their parents seemed outnumbered. It wasn't as though anyone was advertising their position on George's guilt, but Sadie could tell where they stood by looking at them. Her legs stuck to the wooden bench almost as soon as she sat down. She heard high-heeled sandals clicking down the aisle as people took their seats. A group of men with stern and weathered alcoholic faces, wearing T-shirts that said *Men's Rights Are Human Rights*, packed two rows at the back. Dorothy stood against the back wall. Elaine and Jimmy were there too. When Sadie caught his eye, he waved, then jumped up and ran over to her, leaning awkwardly over the bench to kiss her cheek but catching her earlobe instead. He whispered, "I love you."

Kevin walked in wearing a ridiculous hat and sunglasses, as though he were some kind of celebrity. He was with a younger woman with long shiny hair, sunglasses that eclipsed her face, and very tall boots. Sadie could tell Elaine was trying not to look at him, but she kept failing. Jimmy shook his head and put his arm around his mother. Kevin stared at Sadie, gave her a half shrug and a little-boy smile, and she gave him her best side-eye in response, pretending to apply lipstick with her middle finger.

WHEN GEORGE WAS LED into the room, the crowd gasped in unison. He had lost weight, and appeared to have aged twenty years in the time since his arrest. Dorothy let out a sob, which prompted Joan to turn and look at her with such derision that she quieted down. Joan wished she could have banned Dorothy and all the wing nuts who had attached themselves to the case.

George was seated right in front of her, and his proximity was both familiar and enraging. He was trying to project calm, but she could tell he was terrified, the same way he'd been when they'd seen a bear on a camping trip once—fear so intense he couldn't mask it entirely.

Joan was relieved when the judge arrived and took his seat at the bench. He seemed tired, as if the crowd were going to lunge at him. "If you are here to support the accused," he said, "please stand."

Joan wasn't expecting him to say that, and grabbed on to Andrew's arm as she stood. When she turned to the crowd, she gripped him even tighter, whispering, "Oh my stars," an expression her grandmother used to use. Almost the entire courtroom was on their feet. Jared, Sadie, and Lena also looked amazed as they stood. Clara remained seated, arms crossed, scowling at George. Joan kicked at her and she stood, sighing.

Sue Whalen, notorious local journalist, watched with her notebook in her lap. She'd published a front-page newspaper article that morning suggesting the girls had lost their minds in some sort of childish female conspiracy or form of mass hysteria. She'd written that George Woodbury was a valued member of their town, having saved a generation of children from a madman—or had everyone forgotten that?

Joan was the composed, cherished wife. She felt stuck

in her skin. She tried to look grateful. She could barely admit it to herself, but she almost wanted Sarah Myers to waltz in the back door and tell her story, even though she knew she wouldn't. She didn't actually want that pain for her family. She didn't want more attention either, or the pity. A few women from the support group came and sat behind Joan, giving her nods of support. Bennie turned and gave Joan a reassuring look.

The judge spoke again.

"There have been some new developments in this case," he said. "Our key witness has recanted her story after being presented with evidence of several inconsistencies. We also have a new witness, the concierge from the Forrest Ridge Ski Lodge, who saw Mr. Woodbury enter the hotel room of the Avalon Hills administrator Dorothy McKnight at 10 P.M., which corroborates the alibi provided by Mrs. McKnight. As such, and as the testimony from all other complainants relied on the initial testimony of the original girl, there is not enough evidence to continue with the trial. The charges against George Woodbury are hereby dismissed."

The room let out another collective gasp. Dorothy whooped, and the men's rights folks clapped, patting each other on the back. George put his head down on the desk and started to cry, then leaned over to Bennie and hugged him. Sadie looked back at the crowd as they murmured in excitement. Kevin looked shocked. Jimmy mouthed, "Are you okay?" She didn't respond. She noticed Miranda, standing with Dorothy, wearing a baseball cap. Everyone was looking at her, and she paled, pulled the hat down further, and ducked out.

"Oh my god," she whispered to Lena.

"What?"

"Miranda, the main chick," she said, "who recanted. The men's rights people must have gotten to her."

"Or maybe her story wasn't straight. Maybe she lied?" The way Lena said it, Sadie knew she didn't believe it. Sadie looked at her father. He was going to come home. She felt relief, and so grateful, but mostly overwhelmed. What would their life look like now?

The judge cleared his throat and banged the gavel.

What followed was a mass of confusion and chaos. The photographers captured Joan in an embrace with her husband, tears in her eyes, but her feelings were far more complicated. When he was arrested, she'd felt as though he'd been ripped from her arms by a bear. She'd been inconsolable, irate, and desperate for his return. She didn't know what to believe now, or what she should want. One of the women from the support group touched her shoulder, startling her. The woman pulled her into a hug. "It was god's will! You should be so grateful. You're so lucky."

But that wasn't what she was feeling at all.

EPILOGUE

GEORGE SETTLED BACK INTO LIFE AT WOODBURY Lake and published the book he'd written in jail, a memoir of his childhood, his feelings about prison and the prison system, how he felt as a failed scientist. It was dedicated to Joan, his "only love."

George insisted Joan stay in the house, but she moved into the condo instead, lonely and angry and totally unsure about what to do. She got cable TV and watched it every night and made lists about taking art classes and going to yoga in the mornings, but she rarely did.

George begged her to come home and resume their normal life. Every time they talked, she seemed closer and closer to taking him back. All the labor she'd put into the house, how she'd pictured growing old there, how happy the garden made her. What she wouldn't give for afternoons on the dock, mornings in the canoe. Over time, her rage was softening. Every time he talked to her about working with his therapist, righting the wrongs he had made in this life, she was moved to consider the possibility.

She'd yet to experience the surge of independence one hears about in pop songs about men who have done women wrong. "I Will Survive" playing in the drugstore made her weep with rage. She was not strutting around. She was circling, falling. She stalled signing the divorce papers, aware that when she turned sixty she'd be entitled to half of the trust fund set up when they got married. It was a huge amount of money, which she'd been planning to use for travel since she was in her thirties. If she moved back, she would book tickets for France, for Italy—by herself, she reasoned. Maybe she'd take Sadie along. She'd have more financial security. Maybe she and George could be friends, resume a sort of platonic normalcy, if he committed to therapy and rehabilitation.

Every time she had that thought, though, she'd remember the girls in the courtroom and Sarah Myers sunbathing on the pavement of their apartment building, and the rage would return. Clara created a dating profile for her online, and she went on some dates, but she found it too hard to trust people. She missed having a partner, a best friend, so much. Weekends felt unbearably long, and she often took extra shifts at work.

She'd watched Andrew grow colder, more caustic, visiting Avalon Hills less than he had before, and rarely speaking to his father. Jared moved out because Andrew's moods were out of control, something she only learned from Jared. She'd been posting things on his Facebook, inviting him to come for dinner, and he finally had to let her know.

She called Sadie every Sunday, and she heard the revelry of dorm life in the background. Sadie sent her an email telling her how she was trying to forget the last year of high school and move on. "I'm working so hard, Mom, but there was an ease with which I used to learn and it is not so easy anymore, to concentrate and to have perspective, to think critically, and engage. My professors have all said the same thing, that my anxiety seems to be a barrier. I've gone to the counseling center here, but haven't found a good fit." The one good thing that had come out of everything was that Joan felt closer to Sadie than ever before, and watching her grow into an adult felt like a blessing. She'd changed her major to Gender Studies. She'd cut her hair short and started lecturing Joan on the phone about all sorts of things. Joan remembered that age, feeling like you know everything. Every time it felt annoying, Joan reminded herself that she was happy to hear Sadie engaged with life again, finding meaning and purpose.

George called Joan relentlessly, trying to reconcile, and sometimes she answered but mostly she did not. When Sadie and Andrew did come home, they would all meet and go out for lunch and it would feel like torture, like getting to visit the life you wanted and had expected to have. George spoke and acted the same way he always had, but Joan's perception of him had shifted so radically she felt as though she'd experienced some sort of brain injury.

The town seemed to have collective amnesia. It was only on rare occasions that women were even slightly cold towards George, and he usually won them over with his relentless charm. His friendships seemed unaltered. The only real difference was that he was no longer employed at Avalon Hills prep; but he was almost at retirement age anyway, so it didn't seem all that unusual to outsiders. He even kept in touch with his former fellow inmates, some of whom he continued to tutor in jail.

Everyone in the family had changed significantly, except George, who often *told* them how he felt he had changed. He seemed confident that his family would come back to him, and that Joan would return. And one particularly lonely week the following November, when the skies darkened early and the cold was damp and endless, she did.

ACKNOWLEDGMENTS

Thank you to Andra Miller and Ballantine Bantam Dell, my agent Samantha Haywood, Gillian Fizet and House of Anansi Press, Janice Zawerbny, the Ontario Arts Council, the Toronto Arts Council, the Canada Council for the Arts, and the Writers' Trust of Canada.

I am grateful for the early editorial guidance of Michael Shellenberg, Heather Cromarty, Andrea Ridgley, Marcilyn Cianfarani, Chase Joynt, Tom Leger, Jake Pyne, Will Scott, Ange Holmes, and Lisa Foad.

Special thanks to the generous anonymous folks who answered my questions about what it's like to have family members in prison and/or be related to a sex offender.

ABOUT THE AUTHOR

ZOE WHITTALL is a national bestselling novelist in Canada, a finalist for the 2016 Giller Prize for *The Best Kind of People,* and winner of a Lambda Literary Award for her second novel, *Holding Still for as Long as Possible,* which was also an American Library Association Stonewall Honor Book. Her debut novel, *Bottle Rocket Hearts,* was named one of the top ten essential novels of the decade by CBC Radio's Canada Reads and Best Book of the Year by *The Globe and Mail.* She's published three volumes of poetry, most recently *Precordial Thump.* Her novels have been translated into Korean, Swedish, and French, and adapted for feature film. Originally from Quebec, she has an MFA from the University of Guelph and lives in Toronto, where she works as a TV writer.

zoewhittall.com
Twitter: @zoewhittall
Find Zoe Whittall on Facebook.